Praise for

"I adore all of Amy Spalding's books and *On Her Terms* is no exception. This book is about coming out and coming into your own later in life, finding the courage to do what you want, instead of what's expected of you, and, of course, falling deeply and gloriously in love."
—Jasmine Guillory, *New York Times* bestselling author

"*On Her Terms* is a delightfully funny and tender ode to second chances, all the romantic feels, and finding—and loving— yourself at every stage in life. A bright jewel of a romance."
—Ashley Herring Blake, bestselling author
of *Delilah Green Doesn't Care*

"Nobody look at me while I'm reading an Amy Spalding book because I'm worried I have the cheesiest grin on my face the whole time! *On Her Terms* is so funny but also disconcertingly relatable if you happen to be a queer person still figuring out your own queerness later in life."
—Alicia Thompson, *USA Today* bestselling
author of *With Love, from Cold World*

"*On Her Terms* is a big-hearted time machine to those tender days of early queerdom. This book is a love letter to latebloomers, and to everyone who believes it's never too late to get everything you've always wanted."
—Kate Stayman-London, bestselling author of *One to Watch*

"Nothing makes me happier than diving into Amy Spalding's vivid and hilarious LA, and *On Her Terms* is no exception! A tender, sizzling romance wrapped around a beautiful story of first queer love, friendship, and the cutest pets around. A knockout!"
—Carlyn Greenwald, author of *Sizzle Reel* and *Director's Cut*

Turn the page for more praise!

On Her Terms

Also by Amy Spalding

At Her Service

For Her Consideration

On Her Terms

Amy Spalding

KENSINGTON
PUBLISHING CORP.

kensingtonbooks.com

KENSINGTON BOOKS are published by
Kensington Publishing Corp.
900 Third Avenue
New York, NY 10022

ISBN: 978-1-4967-5116-4 (ebook)

ISBN: 978-1-4967-5115-7

First Kensington Trade Paperback Printing: March 2025

10 9 8 7 6 5 4 3 2 1

Printed in the United States of America

To anyone who's ever worried it's too late to come out—
whenever you want is the perfect time

Chapter 1
The Truth Is Out There

I *think I can, I think I can.*

I hated it as soon as I thought it. What was I, a little engine who could? No, I was a fully grown adult, and I could make it up any hill I wanted, thank you. All I needed was to keep walking, two more blocks, right up to the door of the bar and step inside. People did things like this every day.

Well, people walked into buildings. Did women in their mid-thirties frantically google "places to be gay in los angeles" at 3:00 a.m. after waking up and realizing the bed was half-empty because they'd broken up with the best shot they'd had at *forever* and then the very next evening walk directly from their office to the bar that was high up in the search results?

Maybe not.

A couple of guys fell into step behind me, and I didn't worry any more than I usually did as a woman out in public alone, which was more than *never* but not *lots*. I didn't even necessarily think anything when I heard the word *ass* because, after all, there were plenty of asses in the world; mine was only one of them.

But the talk between the men became pointed, and I felt that sinking realization that it was exactly my ass and my body they were discussing. Their voices grew louder, like they were eager for my reaction, and even though this section of Sunset Boulevard was far too busy for me to worry about safety—much—I hated that I had no good solution. In my dreams I'd whirl around and give them a lecture about bodily autonomy and the male gaze, but somehow I didn't think they were in a learning mood.

I also hated the thought of marching away from them into the queer bar, even though I knew they were unlikely to follow. The decision to head over to the first location in my newer and queerer life had been born of sleep deprivation and the panic of dying alone; a mild case of street harassment hardly seemed a good omen to begin this quest tonight.

There were a few fast food or fast food-ish restaurants nearby, so I figured I could step into one and wait for the men to continue on to wherever they were heading, some nightmare bro convention at the heterosexual hipster bar down the block, perhaps, to discuss crypto or X or Snyder cuts, and compete for who could casually cross their arms the hardest and stand with their legs furthest apart.

"Hey, assholes," a voice called out, bright like a bell. "Maybe this is cool behavior under whatever rock y'all normally live under, but this is a society and you're disgusting."

I turned in the direction of the shouter to see a short woman around my age, dressed in a brightly patterned jumpsuit with color-coordinated Crocs. I could feel that the group of men had turned in her direction too, and from the muttered apologies and dashes across Sunset and away from her, they had not been prepared for such a confrontation.

"Fucking babies," the woman muttered. She was Asian American with a short haircut that was more boy band than chic pixie, and for some reason she seemed vaguely familiar. "You OK?"

I nodded. "Yeah, what's being a woman in the world without bros talking about your ass sometime? It's fine."

"It's categorically *not fine*," she said, shaking her head. "But I'm glad you're OK."

"Thanks to you," I said.

"Eh," she said, waving her hand dismissively, like she yelled off street harassers every day. There seemed a possibility that she *did*.

"I should . . ." I gestured feebly behind me, toward my office and the safe little lot where my car was waiting for me.

She raised a perfectly arched eyebrow. Sometimes I became furiously jealous that other women hadn't overplucked in the early aughts and weren't now dependent on biannual microblading appointments.

"Weren't you going to Johnny's?" she asked. Her tone was casual, as if I walked up to queer bars every night. I supposed that she probably did. For this perfectly browed and stylish and badass woman, going to Johnny's was a normal thing to do. It certainly wasn't the first domino poised to knock over a loop of heteronormative life stages tiles.

"Yeah, but—"

"Trust me, those guys aren't following us in," she said. Her hands were on her hips, but somehow still I felt that her hand was stretched out to mine, tugging me in her direction. My feet stepped closer to her, practically of their own accord.

"No, I just—"

"Come *on*," she said, and this time I didn't just take timid steps in my Converse, I hurried down the sidewalk toward her, and we fell into stride together. I was only five-foot-two, but somehow she was even shorter. For once I felt well-paced with someone.

"If I canceled my plans every time some asshole yelled something at me," the woman said, holding open the door for me, "I'd be a hermit. No offense to hermits. It's just not for me."

I tried my best not to gape around the bar, to act neutrally and not like when Dorothy Gale ended up in full Technicolor in Oz or when Jenny Schecter stepped into the Planet for the first time. But my middle-of-the-night googling had included an image search, so I'd actually already known that the interior looked simply like a nice Silver Lake bar. Yes, it was my first time in a queer bar, but it wasn't the land of the unknown; it was a well-researched search result.

"Are you meeting someone?" the woman asked.

"No," I said, remembering my late-night fantasies. Me at the bar, looking beautiful and alluring. Cute and mildly intriguing, at least. An unknown woman on the next stool, looking interested and open and ready to lead me into this new world. Now that I was here, wearing my work clothes, and everyone was just a regular person who didn't care about the nervous and awkward woman who'd just arrived, the fantasy seemed especially . . . fantastical.

"Is that weird?" I asked the woman, as I scanned the crowd for proof that it was OK that I was here, that I wasn't the oldest or least cool person in the building. That I didn't look the least queer, whatever that meant. Still, I had an idea of what *queer* looked like, and I wasn't sure it was head-to-toe ModCloth, medium-brown hair in a grown-out bob I wasn't sure I wanted to maintain, and a pair of pink cat-eye glasses I'd splurged on from Society of the Spectacle.

The woman burst into laughter. "Why would that be weird? Come on, there's two seats at the end."

"Oh," I said, "you don't have to babysit me, I'm sure you have people you're—"

"Weird or not, Clementine, I also was headed here alone," she said, as a jolt rattled me.

"How do you know my name?"

"What do you mean?" she asked, leading me through the lightly crowded room to two empty barstools at the right end of the bar. "We know each other."

"Wait, we do?" I eyed the tall barstools and schemed the least awkward approach.

"No," the woman said, "they've got a little ledge around the bar."

She demonstrated by stepping up first and then sitting down easily at the tall bar. I did the same and, for maybe the first time in my adult life, sat down almost effortlessly at a bar top.

"This place is short-person heaven," I said. "So how exactly do you know me? Is it rude I feel kind of bonkers?"

"The owner's girlfriend is like my height," the woman told me. "So nothing here is awkward. What do you want to drink?"

"That doesn't seem fair," I said. "First you rescue me, now you have to buy me a drink?"

"You're right," she said. "I'll take whatever non-hard seltzer's on tap, thank you."

I made eye contact with one of the bartenders and put in the order for my usual drink and the woman's seltzer. I knew it didn't really count as buying a woman a drink, except then I wondered if it did. The fantasy had not unfolded like I'd imagined it, but there was no getting around the fact that, despite that, I *was* sitting at a bar with an attractive woman who was making conversation with me. Was this actually as easy as I'd hoped it would be?

"We met at your office party," the woman said as the bartender deposited the drinks in front of us. "Multiple office parties. Every holiday season. A few other random ones that felt only tangentially work-related. And that summer party to celebrate some milestone."

"Five years in business," I said, and vaguely remembered chatting with her about hors d'oeuvres while feeling guilty that I'd left Will on his own. "Are you with one of our clients?"

"Nah, just a friend of the company," she said. "Also not one to turn down a party invite with free snacks and an open bar. Even after I stopped drinking. Keep those free La Croix coming, man."

"Oh," I said, my Diet-Coke-and-Maker's paused at my lips. "Is it OK that I—"

"Yes, of course," she said. "If it was hard for me to watch people drink, I wouldn't hang out in a bar, would I?"

"I guess not. Still—"

"Still, nothing. I agreed to do a Dry January with a friend for moral support the other year, and then I noticed I felt better and was making better life choices, so it seemed like maybe something I should continue. Dry forever."

"Makes sense. And I'm sorry I didn't recognize you. Work events are always a lot." It wasn't a lie. I liked to keep my professional and personal lives separate, everything in its neat spot like a bento box. Work parties always felt like a Tupperware container that fell on the floor in the back seat of your car, just knocking everything together. "Will you remind me your name?"

"Chloe," she said. "Chloe Lee. How's your boyfriend?"

"Oh." How had I managed to forget her? Now, I could picture her clearly, wearing a similarly bright outfit and laughing with me about bacon-wrapped dates or whatever while Will stood alone in a corner of the outdoor space. *I'm not good at parties*, he always said, which was fine except for the times I needed him to at least fake it for a little while. Still, I remember feeling guilty when I finally joined him again, even though it was only now that I realized it had been because I'd had a better time talking to Chloe than camping out in that quiet corner with him. "He's not my boyfriend anymore."

She took a swig of her seltzer and set it down as a smirk settled across her face, practically stretched out to her jawline. I remembered how a jawline had done it, once upon a time, me staring at an actress's face, up on a movie theatre screen like it was the only thing in the world. *I wish I could put my thumb right there*, I'd thought, imagining what it would feel like if we'd kissed. By the time the lights came up, I knew I wasn't straight. A few weeks later, I met Will.

"I figured," Chloe said, still smirking, still in possession of that strong jawline, still looking right at me. "A girl doesn't tend to go to Johnny's alone if she's got some boring guy at home waiting for her."

"He isn't boring," I said. It would have been so much easier if he was! Or inconsiderate! All those stereotypes about guys not being able to find the clitoris? Will could have led expeditions!

"Ah, so it was just that he's a man?" Chloe asked with a grin.

"No, that was fine, I'm bisexual so whatever." I said it like it was nothing, but it wasn't nothing. It wasn't something I'd said many times aloud. It wasn't old and well-trod information to most people in my life. "It was just that . . ."

"Just what?" Chloe asked, leaning in a little.

"You're really—"

"Nosy? Yeah, tell me about it. No, literally, tell me what your non-boring boyfriend—"

"*Ex*-boyfriend."

"—what your ex-boyfriend was, if not boring, that ended it."

I took another sip of my drink as I tried to think how to phrase it. No one had heard it from me, not really. The problem was that it was tough to talk about without saying the whole truth, and I wasn't sure the whole truth was for everyone.

"We wanted different futures," I said.

"Like one of you wanted to go to Mars with a robot and one of you wanted a self-driving car on earth," she said with a laugh.

"Yep, that was it," I said, hoping that was enough. Her stare didn't falter, though. Her stare told me that nothing but the truth would get me out of this.

"We met in college, and—seriously, he was a really good guy. The best in a lot of ways. Almost everything was easy. Like in our twenties, it was *the easiest*. I wanted to move back to LA after college, and he wanted to move here too. And we found a place together and both got good jobs and had friends and all the stuff you want to happen."

I couldn't believe how fast it had poured out of my mouth. Weeks without one real truth aloud and now all of it to a—well, not a *stranger*, but not far off. Still, I felt like I wanted to keep going, and not only because Chloe was still watching me intently.

"Anyway, then—you know. You turn thirty, and all of your friends start getting engaged and then married and suddenly people are *pregnant* and you go home from like the millionth baby shower of some acquaintance, to your boyfriend, like, so happy for everyone but also so relieved you have a different kind of life, except—"

"Except he wanted all the weddings and babies too?" Chloe asked.

"Yeah, exactly, it turns out. But I kept thinking—I don't know. I felt like even though I'd never seen myself as like a bride or whatever, we could get married in a courthouse as a compromise or something, and then hopefully the kids thing would just kind of . . ." I laughed now at my former self's naivety. "I thought it might wear off! And he'd also genuinely want exactly the life we already had."

I downed the rest of my drink. "Anyway, it didn't. It felt like more and more he'd say things about our future *adult* life together, when we're married, when we have kids, all of that, and it was like—"

"You're an adult already!" Chloe said, waving her hands wildly.

"Literally exactly," I said, feeling warmed from her words as well as the intensity with which she said them. "I'm thirty-six!"

"That's practically middle-aged," Chloe said, and we both cracked up.

"Thanks, that's comforting." I shrugged. "I tried to talk to him about it but even though before it was like we always just kind of *got* each other, it was different. I could never get out the right words or—I don't know. I actually started getting terrified every time he'd say something like *Hey, can I ask you something?* or *Hey, I've got a question for you*, or even just *hey* because it felt like a proposal was lurking around any given corner, and then I'd have to say no and break his heart or, like . . . kind of accidentally get married."

Chloe's eyes widened. "Oh my god, Clementine, did you accidentally get married?"

I laughed and shook my head, while Chloe flagged down a different bartender, who she seemed to know.

"Can you get my friend a drink on the house because she just went through some weird bullshit with a man?"

"I don't need—" I stopped because Chloe and the hot bartender dressed in a vintage Amoeba Records shirt and faded Levi's seemed to be in cahoots and also this was what I'd wanted when I'd told my friends that Will and I had broken up. Instead they'd acted like I'd unrolled a funeral right in front of them on our group chat.

"Let me know how this is, and also I'm sorry about your man bullshit," the bartender said, kindly, before setting a pink cocktail in front of me and heading off to serve another customer.

"You didn't have to do this," I told Chloe.

"I like using my connections," she said. "So, if you didn't get accidentally married, what happened?"

I sighed, and it didn't feel like enough, somehow, so I sighed again. "Last month we went to the wedding of one of his colleagues, and afterwards he looked . . . I don't know. All misty-eyed."

Chloe made a face. "Gross."

"Stop," I said, though I laughed. "Then he stared at me in this really serious way that wasn't normal for us and said he was going to drive up soon to talk to my father about *my hand in—*"

"No," Chloe said, shaking her head. "What year is it? The days of yore or some shit?"

"I mean, I know some people like tradition and everything but that had never been us before." And I'd reminded him of that, but sometimes in the middle of talking to someone you saw the distance in their eyes and how for them the real conversation had already happened in their head and you weren't really part of it.

"Anyway," I continued, "I woke him up at like three a.m. that night and told him we didn't want the same things, and even if I got married someday it wouldn't be in some kind of white-dress-and-traditional-ceremony kind of way that involved *my father's permission*, and even though I think kids are great and hilarious and the future and blah blah blah, I'd never seen myself as a mother and that wasn't going to change. And I didn't want him trying to give up what he wanted, so it made sense to end things."

It also hadn't made sense at all. Will had been my life for literally half of my life. Will and I were an *our* more than I was a *me*. Will made the morning coffee while I did yoga and then I did the morning dishes. Will checked the locks before coming to bed because he knew it made me feel safer.

But the early morning hours after the breakup had been the best I'd slept in months, like my body knew something my heart hadn't fully accepted yet.

"Good for you," Chloe said. "Also, he does sound boring."

I laughed and tried a sip of my cocktail, which lacked the comfort of my usual but was a little tart and a lot of refreshing all at once. Maybe it was time to give up all my old usuals. "He wasn't. I still feel like a jerk for breaking his heart."

"Nah, you did the right thing," she said. "If it makes you feel better, I get it completely. It feels like all of my friends are getting married or having babies and it's like they're all adults and I'm the child. I didn't think I'd have to deal with so much of it, being queer and all, but it turns out this shit comes for all of us."

"Love is love," I said, and we both burst into laughter.

"So what's your story?" Chloe asked.

"I thought I just told you," I said. "I thought I just told you in, like, *great detail.*"

"That was your backstory," Chloe said. "Sorry, is it weird to say *backstory* after those jerks just harassed you about your ass?"

"Chloe," I said, and burst into even louder laughter, as she joined in.

"Why are you, Clementine I-don't-know-your-white-girl-last-name, walking into Johnny's alone post-boring-guy breakup?"

"It's Hayes. And you're really . . ." I tried to think of a nicer word than *nosy.* "Are you a journalist or something? A podcast interviewer?"

She shrieked with laughter. "I'm a dog groomer! I told you, I'm just nosy."

"I bet you ask dogs questions all day," I said. It sounded like flirting out of my mouth, but that was because it was. I hadn't flirted with anyone for real in—oh my god, nearly twenty years? But it didn't feel effortful with Chloe. It just felt like talking.

"I don't have to ask dogs questions," she said. "They're eager, you know?"

"I'm not . . . *not* eager," I said, but even my tone dripped with hesitancy. "And I'm not really sure why I'm here. Do people even meet in bars? Everyone's just on apps, I guess."

"'Do people even meet in bars?' Clementine, please. Of course people still meet in bars. I meet women in bars—in this very bar—all of the time."

I gulped at the thought of it, the reality of me and a woman and this bar and where it could lead. Was I actually ready for it—every single thing that *it* entailed? I felt seventeen again, in all of the worst ways.

"So you broke up with your boring boyfriend before he could ambush-propose you," Chloe said, "and since you're a little bit gay, you thought it was time you dated a woman instead."

I wanted to protest her easy summation, but what was there to protest? "Something like that."

Chloe grinned at me, but whatever heat I'd hoped had been building between us was gone—if it had even been there in the first place. My inexperience felt tangible, taking up space at the bar between us. "Tale as old as time."

Yes, by the time someone was quoting a Disney song lyric at you, it didn't seem very likely they hoped to take off your clothes later.

"I can always spot 'em," Chloe said. "Baby gays and the big new world of queerness."

"Queerness isn't new to me," I said, feeling a frown pull my mouth downward. At work I often worked hard to keep my face neutral; it wasn't good for business to let your clients see how terrible you sometimes thought their ideas were. "I've known I was bi since—"

"Sure, of course," Chloe said. "You saw a hot girl like Kristen Stewart or your gym teacher, whatever, now you're single and you're making up for lost time."

"It was Gillian Anderson," I said, which made Chloe snort.

"Well, good luck out here," she said, hopping to her feet. "I should run. My dog's been home alone for a while and if we don't get in our walk soon there'll be hell to pay later."

"OK," I said, wondering if I should stand and leave as well? No, I would wait a respectable amount of time, and when I was certain she'd walked away, I could head back to my car and then back to my home and my cat and all the other things that didn't make me feel like I was a clueless teenager again.

"Here," Chloe said, shoving her phone into my hands. "Put in your information."

I gave her a look, but wordlessly tapped to her contacts and typed in my name and number. She snatched the phone back from me and typed furiously. By the time she'd headed out of the bar, my phone dinged with a new message from an unknown 323 number. When I opened the text, a photo of Gillian Anderson as Dana Scully gazed right at me.

I had no idea how to respond and so instead I flagged down the hot bartender—to be fair, they were all hot, but the one who knew Chloe and had given me a free drink just happened to be the hottest—to close my tab.

"How'd that drink work out for you?" she asked, running my credit card. "I'm thinking of adding it to the menu. Did it help your man trouble?"

"Yeah, my man trouble has been handled," I said, wishing I could signify that I wasn't a straight woman with *current* man trouble, I was a queer woman with *previous* man trouble and I was ready for whatever was next. "You should add it to the menu so that whenever I have girl trouble, it can handle it as well."

I literally grimaced as I said it, the clunkiest way a person had probably ever attempted to come out.

The bartender, though, just laughed and shoved her hair back from her face. "If you're hanging out with Chloe, yeah, I should probably put a rush order getting it added to the menu."

A startled laugh popped out of me, and I added a giant tip to my credit card receipt before walking outside. Had it all actually gone OK? I'd come out to a stranger, exchanged numbers with an extremely attractive woman, and all before 7:30 p.m. on a Tuesday. The next phase of my life had truly begun.

Chapter 2
It Should Be Surprising

By the time I sat down at my desk at my office the next morning, my phone was lit up with texts. Before my breakup, I'd been an early riser. Up with the sun, yoga on the patio, side-hustle tasks from my home office, half my to-do list crossed off by the time I arrived, early, at work.

I never would have guessed that Will had been some kind of glue holding the responsible bits of my life together, but in the weeks since he'd moved out, my nights stretched later and my mornings became more acquainted with my snooze button. Yoga and sunrises seemed like friends I hadn't talked to since college; the other morning I'd leaned over to pet my cat and yoinked something in my lower back as if all of my flexibility had packed up and left with Will. My ADHD had been well managed with medication and careful scheduling since my diagnosis a few years back, but it felt like all it took was this one life change for everything to fall offtrack.

My inbox chimed with three new messages in the span of a couple seconds, so I turned my phone face down on my desk and set all my attention on my work computer. The truth was that I'd worked in the entertainment industry since I'd arrived right out of college, and I'd learned at my first assistant gig that the workday rarely actually started at nine, and even more rarely beforehand. I might have missed my old self, with her crossed-off tasks and ability to pet cats without bodily harm, but it was doubtful anyone at my office had even noticed. Getting here at nine sharp instead of ten-'til still meant that I was usually the first executive in the door, and my routines here were still, blessedly, intact.

Anyway, it seemed unlikely that the texts I'd already received would contain the one I not-so-secretly hoped for. Chloe Lee didn't seem like someone who'd text a girl before business hours. She also didn't seem like someone who'd text a girl like me at all, but I'd stared at Gillian Anderson's face on my phone several times last night to accept that it had indeed happened.

I had no idea what to make of her, and that, in and of itself, contradicted something I'd very much wanted to be true. When the idea had been new, just a little germ of something growing in my subconscious, ending things with Will and starting over, there'd been this one hopeful light that glowed stronger and brighter as it all took shape.

It wasn't only that I felt like I'd missed out on something, realizing that I wasn't only attracted to men only figurative moments before meeting a guy I'd date for nearly twenty years. It was that—well, I knew women! My best friends—Will excepted, if Will counted—were women! *I* was a woman, with three-and-a-half decades of experience being one. There was no way, I'd thought, that dating women would be more difficult than dating men.

And now I was only a few hours into my first attempt at my new queer life, and I'd honestly never felt so confused by a person and their intentions before.

"Good morning!" Tamarah, the department assistant, leaned into my office. She was dressed in a bold yellow fit-and-flare dress that was striking against her dark brown skin. Her dark brown braids were tossed casually over one shoulder. I'd absolutely never looked so put-together in my early twenties. Her hands were even wrapped around a steaming ceramic mug of green tea; Gen Z seemed to make such healthier morning choices than I ever had as a youth.

"I saw all of those vendor proposals come in," she said, nodding at my inbox. "Should I drop them into the presentation? Just so you know, Aubrey asked me to put together a deck, so . . ."

"No, I haven't even reviewed everything yet, help Aubrey and then check back in with me," I said. "Please and thank you, sorry, tell me if I ever sound like a taskmaster."

"You could *never*," she said. "I'll check in with you in a while."

"Sounds good," I said, turning back to my inbox. Eventually, I made my way through my morning emails, popped into the office kitchen for a cup of coffee, and returned to my office to flip over my phone and see if my hopes were to be dashed or not.

Family meeting tonight, urgent, 7pm sharp!! Attendance is MANDATORY!!

Five minutes later, my brother Greg had sent a follow-up message: **Dinner will not be served!**

Three minutes after that, another message from Greg: **Red alert! Don't park in the driveway!! It's being repaved!!!**

I sighed deeply and, instead of dwelling on the annoying evening I was bound to have, tapped back to last night's text from Chloe. If a photo of a fictional FBI agent counted as a text. Did I actually hope she'd text me, or did it just fulfill the fantasy of the woman at the bar and my number in her phone? Honestly, at the moment I couldn't sort out the difference. It had been so long since I'd wondered if someone was interested in me, and everything had changed since. It had nothing to do with the fact that Chloe was a woman; when Will asked me out, iPhones didn't exist. There wasn't really any social media to speak of. I did have a cell phone when I met Will, a tiny flip phone my parents had insisted on buying for me before sending me off to college, but I don't remember going around exchanging cell phone numbers on campus. You always just found people. And one day later after chatting in the campus bookstore, Will cut me off on my way into my Marketing 101 class, and that was that. Twenty years ago it seemed like people met each other that way all of the time. Now it might as well be the story about my grandparents on my mom's side meeting in the line to vote for Dwight D. Eisenhower.

Are you getting these messages?? Please confirm!!

I sighed and texted back to my brother that I'd try to make it by seven. He and his wife lived up in the suburbs, where we'd grown up, so rush hour traffic made it tough to guarantee an on-time arrival. I actually had no idea why I'd agreed to these demands so quickly; I had better things to do with my evening than jump when my brother said how high, but at least whatever this was would then be over with. Maybe other people would be alarmed at an urgent and mandatory last-minute family meeting, but the last time Greg issued a red alert, it was to inform me that I needed to chip in a few hundred dollars to buy some fruit trees and other plants for Mom and Dad's backyard, a gift we had never before discussed. Tonight, I was sure, would be similarly low-stakes.

I knew that I should have just established some firmer boundaries with Greg long ago, but I was sure I'd missed that opportunity when it had presented itself. This was just how things had settled, now that the two of us were adults. And so now I did things like fight traffic for a family meeting that could have been an email.

Tamarah popped back into my office. "Aubrey might need me for a while, but if you need my help, tell me it's urgent and I'll avoid her instead."

I laughed and shook my head. "No, please don't hide from anyone. We'll get everything done before deadline."

"The audience research stuff is really interesting," she said, dropping the volume of her voice a few notches. "But I really like all the media stuff with you. Do you think that could ever just be its own job? It seems like you're really busy, and I'd never complain about having a lot to do, of course, but—"

"No, understood," I said. "I think there's a lot to consider— and most of it wouldn't be up to me. But it's been on my mind, too, so I'm glad you brought it up."

When I'd started at Big Marketing Energy, I'd been thrilled at the prospect of building a department from nothing. The owner and president of our boutique marketing agency encouraged me to do things the way I'd always wanted to back in the days when I reported to other people. And I *had*, and slowly over the last five years, media planning and buying had earned BME a bigger and bigger percentage of their yearly profits. But I was still a one-person team with a shared assistant, and the more business that came my way, the more I wondered how sustainable the current setup would be. If Tamarah was feeling it too, things were definitely shifting.

My day continued like most of my workdays did; unremarkable but full of enough small tasks that I felt mildly satisfied when I was wrapping things up at the close of it. Google Maps said I could still get to Greg's in time to ring the doorbell at seven sharp, but as I slipped on my cardigan and grabbed my bag, my boss, Phoebe Reyes, leaned into my office.

"Hey, great work on that digital proposal," she said, her tone bright. "You know how I feel about a well-designed slide."

"I do, but I have to give Tamarah credit there; she's very good in PowerPoint."

Phoebe had started this company completely on her own after running marketing at a couple of major studios, but none of those viciously competitive and potentially toxic vibes seemed to have worn off on her. She worked as hard—if not harder—than anyone who reported to her, and yet the entire team tended to put in reasonable hours and the idea of a work-life balance was all but taken for granted. Considering she had a beautiful family and an incredibly cool and aspirational friend group, she was absolutely leading by example there.

"I was actually thinking..." I shook my head quickly. "Sorry, I'm sure you have somewhere to be. I won't derail your PowerPoint slide, love."

Phoebe laughed and stepped into my office. I knew she was only a few years older than me, but she projected authority in a way I'd never possessed—and felt comfortable stating I never would. Today she was in a blue patterned button-down over gray slacks, with casual blue boots completing the look. Her short, nearly black hair had started graying over the last few years, but the effect only made her seem wiser and, somehow, cooler.

"What's up?" she asked, casually leaning against my desk. I'd give anything to be a person who could casually lean.

"I've just been thinking how much busier I've been on a pretty consistent basis," I said, doing my best to make hand gestures that showed that I in no way thought this was a serious matter. "It isn't just the proposals; we seem to be booking a higher percentage of the work we're proposing, and we're just such a small team."

"Sure," Phoebe said with a nod. "It's like one and a third people."

"Yeah, exactly. Which has been fine, but, lately, I wonder..."

"If the media team should be expanded into a full department? I can't say I haven't thought about it, too. Tell you what, why don't you put together a presentation for the board, and we'll see how it goes."

I nodded quickly before her words actually sank in. "Wait, we don't have a board. Isn't that just you?"

Phoebe grinned and made her way back to my doorway. "Yes. It's just me."

"When?" I asked. "Did you have something in mind?"

"No, take some time to think about it. Maybe within the next couple months?"

"Sounds good," I said, and while it sounded a great many things—stressful, unexpected, terrifying—that much was true, too.

"Oh, and I think we've got another project from Celebration Pictures coming in next week," she said. "I don't have all the info yet, but sounds like Jeremy's calling because it's got a queer subplot and he always trusts us in that category. Don't worry—I know straight people are very capable of doing the media planning for gay movies."

"Uh-huh, of course," I said, looking down at my hands and then at the doorframe near Phoebe and not making eye contact whatsoever. Coming out had always sounded like a big and serious thing I might have to manage someday; I'd already semi-rehearsed the kinds of things I might say if I fell in love with someone and was eager to tell the world. But I didn't have a queer girlfriend and a great love story! I just had queer thoughts! I wasn't having queer sex; I was watching queer porn. This particular speech I hadn't rehearsed at all.

"I should get home to my wife and kid," Phoebe said, fortunately apparently completely unaware of the maelstrom of identity weirdness swirling around in my brain. Would coming out feel different if I had a straight boss? I genuinely had no idea.

Phoebe headed out of my doorway and down the hallway. "Have a good night, Clem."

"You too," I said, and waited a polite few moments before heading out to our parking lot. By now I was going to be at least five minutes late, and while that would have been no cause for alarm for anyone else in the greater Los Angeles area who understood how both offices and rush hour traffic functioned, I spent the drive north on the 5 Freeway steeling myself for the reception that was likely awaiting me.

I parked right in front of Greg and Marisol's place. It was a sweet little suburban home, stucco and siding and shiny tile. If it were plunked down in the middle of the Eastside of LA, I'd love it, but I'd never entertained moving back to the suburbs for even a split second. Home reminded me of growing up, the clichéd path of never quite fitting in, in ways I couldn't fully pinpoint, to the escape route of college in another state. Even if it was only a couple dozen miles up the freeway, it was the world I left behind.

Despite Greg's earlier text, the driveway looked the same as always, so I walked right up it to the front door and rang the bell.

"Hi, Clementine," Marisol said, swinging open the door. It didn't make a whole lot of sense to me that someone-not-awful willingly married my younger brother, but Marisol was nothing less than wonderful. "How was the drive?"

"Not terrible, so I'll take it." I gave her a light hug before stepping inside. "Your hair looks great. I saw your Instagram story about growing out your bangs—"

"You're late." Greg walked into the room and glared at me. Actually, he was already glaring at me when he entered the room. "Some of us have to get up early for work and can't make plans late at night."

I glanced at my phone. "It's seven-oh-six."

"Greg actually has something exciting to talk to you about,"

Marisol said with a smile. "And thank you. I don't think I'm ready to grow out my bangs yet."

"You made the right call. I did it like six years ago— remember? I looked like a disaster for like a solid four months."

"No," Marisol said, shaking her head. Her wavy dark hair rippled like a princess's out of a fairy tale. "You never look like a disaster."

Greg cleared his throat. "Mom and Dad's fortieth anniversary is coming up in a few months, and I've decided we should throw them a party."

I frowned because it was actually a pretty good idea and I should have had it before him. I supposed that ending my long-term relationship gave me some leeway, but I still hated the idea of being less thoughtful than my younger brother.

Also, the truth was that even though a great deal of my adolescent identity had been tied up in being the good kid, the kid who easily made my parents proud, the kid with a bright and hopeful future, now that I was down in LA proper while Greg was five minutes across town with a beautiful wife and two adorable children, I'd definitely been demoted to lesser child. Of course he'd come up with a thoughtful party and I had done absolutely nothing.

A medium-sized crash sounded from down the hallway, and Marisol darted off like this happened all of the time. I supposed when you had kids, life was probably just one medium-sized crash after another.

"Do you need to go—" I started, but Greg cut me off with a quick shake of his head.

"Marisol's handling everything. If you had kids you'd get it. It's not all some big emergency."

"I didn't say that it—sure." Greg seemed constantly set on framing everything through the lens of how much harder and more serious his life was than mine, except when it was actually less hard and less serious, which was also something he could somehow hold against me. It was easiest to just let it go. "Anyway, yes, I agree that we should throw a party. What do you need from me? I'm happy to do whatever."

Marisol walked back in, hand in hand with Lulu and Julian, who were four and five, respectively. Both of them looked more like my sister-in-law than my brother—or, well, me— with their dark hair and tan complexions. I was glad that my family's future generations didn't have mouse-colored hair or pasty complexions; it felt like an improvement for the Hayes descendants.

"Your aunt Clementine is here," Marisol said. "Don't you want to say hi to her?"

While they had inherited their looks from their mother, the kids had clearly inherited their dad's feelings toward me, because this question was met with a mild shrug from each of them.

"Hey, guys, I like your sweatpants," I said, because I did— child-sized versions of regular track pants were objectively adorable—and also because I never knew what to say to children. I'd assumed once I had my own niece and nephew that it would be different, but it didn't matter that we were related. I was still making desperate and awkward small talk while their small eyes judged me.

"Aunt Clementine, is it true you fell off a seesaw?" Lulu asked.

"No," I said, confused at the accusation. "Wait, I did, but it was a really long time ago. I was your age."

"It's really easy to stay on a seesaw," Julian said—well, barely said, through his laughter. "There's handles!"

"You must be bad at seesaws!" Lulu said, as Greg joined in their laughter. Nice to know he wasn't entirely humorless these days. I was torn between wanting to save the good name of my teeter-tottering self and letting go of something that happened over thirty years ago.

"It should be a surprise," Greg said, as Lulu shrieked and Julian threw a Squishmallows squirrel at my head.

"That was all very surprising," I said, unsure if I was allowed to throw stuffed squirrels back at small children. Probably not, despite that it was tempting.

"He means the party," Marisol said with a laugh. "Don't you think your parents would love a big surprise party?"

"Oh, um, maybe," I said, trying to imagine it, all of us popping out and screaming *Surprise!* at my parents. Mom and Dad weren't exactly popping-out-and-screaming sorts, but they did always thank us earnestly whenever we did something for them. "Surprise parties are hard, though. You have to do all of this weird lying to keep the secret. I did one for Will's thirtieth, and by the time the day of the party rolled around I was ready to just tell him."

"You know, some of us have real jobs," Greg said, because a while back he'd misunderstood one of my Instagram posts and decided that I did relatively little for a living. "So we're used to hard work. I think we should make it a surprise party and not take the easy way out."

"Fine," I said, resisting the dig about my job because doing otherwise—up to and including "accidentally" once sharing my LinkedIn profile to our family group chat—had never made a difference. "So, again, what do you need from me? Tell me and I'm on it."

"I have a list," Marisol said, handing me her planner, heavy with color-coded tabs. "Maybe figure out what tasks you can handle and we'll work on the rest?"

"Sure," I said, as the squirrel flew over my head, "that makes sense."

"Does Will's friend still work at that brewery?" Marisol asked. "I remember he got us that great deal on those kegs for my work party the other year."

"Oh," I said, taking a step back from everyone. "Will and I . . . aren't together anymore."

Greg and Marisol exchanged a look, as I wondered how many more times I had to share this information. It made me want to wear a hat with *I broke up with Will* beautifully hand-stitched on the front.

I knew that lots of people had an ongoing group chat with their family. Will, for example, was in constant contact with his parents and two younger sisters via text. I was certain that group chat was overly active the day of our breakup. My family, though, had just never pulled toward communication that way. Our group chat very rarely activated.

"Anyway, yeah, I can still probably talk to Mateo," I said, though I wasn't firm on the politics of breakups yet. Will had kind of been my first and only, as far as relationships went. Could you text your ex's best friend to get a discount on beer? What had Will told Mateo about me? I'd always liked Mateo, with his dad-joke sense of humor and the way he treated brewing beer like creating great art. Maybe I'd just never get to talk to Mateo again.

"Great, I'm going to put your name by that task," Marisol said, clearly unaware of the beer-related panic roiling through me. Was it good or bad that no one seemed to notice all of the crises unfolding in my brain? "Do you want to take a photo of the list and then text me what sounds good to you?"

It was a better idea than anything I'd come up with, so I took out my phone from my purse to snap a photo. My home screen announced *Chloe Lee New Message* but I calmly unlocked my phone, navigated to my camera app, and took only four blurry photos before I managed a good one.

I knew that people with kids tended to eat earlier than I did, but I still thought that Greg and Marisol might ask me to stay for drinks or a snack or something, but it became clear our interaction was over. So even though it had been less than a half hour since I'd arrived, and I couldn't imagine that anyone else in the world would think this was a conversation we needed to have in person, I kept all those thoughts to myself.

"Why are you leaving?" Greg asked, as I slipped my purse's strap over my shoulder and stepped to the door. "You're supposed to take that envelope."

"What envelope?" I asked, calmly, instead of screeching *What the hell are you talking about*, a move for which I felt I practically deserved an award for restraint.

"Here you go." Marisol rushed over smoothly, a big padded mailing envelope in her outstretched hand. "We remembered how nicely you had everything framed for our wedding present, and thought you could take some photos of your parents and a copy of their wedding program to have done the same way."

It was such a thoughtful idea I couldn't be annoyed. And also maybe I'd misread the situation, maybe snacks and a drink were next up. I glanced hopefully in the direction of the kitchen.

Greg caught my eyeline. "I said *no food*."

Oh my god. "You said *no dinner*, actually."

"We already ate. Anyway, now you can go," Greg said, his voice awash in finality. OK then!

All I wanted to do, really, was to swing through a drive-thru—the suburbs were so great for drive-thrus, compared to my neighborhood—and get back on the 5 for what I hoped would be a traffic-free drive home. But that text message was too hard not to think about, so I was still parked right outside of Greg and Marisol's when I tapped on the bright red *1* notification.

What are you doing tomorrow night? Meet for drinks at Johnny's?

The text took over my thoughts the entire time I sat in the In-N-Out drive-thru and the entire time I sped fifteen miles above the speed limit down the 5 so that the French fries were still vaguely warm when I arrived home.

"I'm back," I called, even though in our two weeks of living together I'd learned that my new kitten roommate did not run to greet me. After all, I'd never run to greet Will, and yet I'd still appreciated when he called out a hello to me. Though I hoped that the cat and I would have a different—and more hopeful—future together.

Will was allergic, so I'd written off cat ownership as a goal that would remain unfulfilled. And I'd accepted that, rabidly following Instagram cats in lieu of loving any of my own, making cat toys at first for acquaintances but now on a regular basis for Etsy customers. But after my night of frantic gay-googling, I realized that women were not the only thing I could add to my post-Will existence. During downtime during the next workday, I downloaded a pet adoption app and then spent that evening swiping right on tabbies and tuxedos. By morning I had seven follow-up emails, and more adorable kitten details than I thought possible. Eggnog loved to groom your hair while you watched TV! Mr. Buttons played fetch with crumpled up bits of newspapers! Kevin gave kisses on your forehead! I made an appointment with the first rescue organization that had responded, and found myself driving to Pasadena that evening to meet a tiny Siamese mix named, concernedly, Jesse Pinkman.

"Gus, Walter, and Lydia are all already gone," the rescuer had told me. "Only Jesse is left."

"Just like on the show," I'd said, and she'd given me a funny look while I'd waved a feather on a wand for Small Jesse Pinkman to bat at. *You're the one who gave these kittens weirdly not-topical meth kingpin names*, I'd thought, *so why am I the weird one for remembering who lived and died?* I hadn't really known how to end the interaction, but then Small Jesse Pinkman had climbed up on my shoulder and purred when I'd petted him, so that was that.

I stared at Chloe's message awhile longer while I wolfed down my burger and fries. Small Jesse Pinkman dashed out from under the sofa and hopped up next to me, where he bit a fry directly out of the tray. I probably was supposed to discipline him, but a kitten with a French fry in his mouth was too adorable to yell about. Plus I admired his moxie; he saw what he wanted and he went right for it.

Feeling inspired, I replied to Chloe. **Sounds good. 7?**

Chapter 3

A Non-Pomeranian Predicament

I finished at work earlier than expected on Friday, so I headed over early to the bar. Tonight's walk was, luckily, free from ass-oglers, and I'd just downloaded a new queer romance novel to my Kindle app, and so even though I might have spent a large part of the night before—and all of my work downtime—wondering if I had an actual date with an actual woman, I decided to take the signs from the universe and relax. My hair had behaved during blow-drying this morning and fell perfectly into its wavy bob. I was wearing one of my favorite dresses, a blue-and-white checkered fit-and-flare dress that made me look, I hoped, a little sweet and a little sexy and a lot curvy. Other plus-sized women, I knew, complained about what a large percentage of available clothing was darling and twee, and while I supported the criticism, I didn't mind it. Give me your sweetest checked pattern, your most darling woodland creatures print, your softest lavenders and pinks and lemons and limes. I loved the idea of taking up space, but adorably.

"Hey there," the hot bartender greeted me. "The new drink? An old drink?"

"The new one's good, thanks," I said, flustered already at the idea that, two visits in, I was now some kind of regular at a queer bar, and maybe I was less than an hour away from an actual date with an actual lesbian. Though maybe I wasn't. What did I want as the answer to the riddle of Chloe Lee anyway? Those good omens that told me to stop overthinking had somehow vanished, and here was everything turning around in my brain again like stones in a rock polisher.

Once my drink was deposited in front of me, I took a sip and told myself to chill the hell out. The good signs were all still present. I'd lived long enough on the Eastside to have picked up at least a little witchiness, recreationally, and I let myself be calmed by the vibes inherent in the easy end to my workweek, this bar, my cocktail.

I read a couple of chapters of the book, and pried myself away after the meet-cute to check my email. Work was quiet—for the most part, the entertainment industry liked its weekends to start by Friday afternoon whenever possible—but I had a forward from Greg in my personal inbox that made me frown before I'd even opened it.

It had been like this as long as I could remember. Greg thought I was ridiculous, I got mad, neither one of us took the other one seriously about anything, rinse and lather and repeat. I kept waiting for something to shift our dynamic, but here we were, hurtling toward our late thirties—Greg had a wife and children, for god's sake!—and nothing had fundamentally changed between us.

Luckily, the email from Greg was just a forward from Marisol about the list she'd put together and her ideas for who should handle what tasks after receiving the text with my ideas. Because it was the work of my incredibly reasonable and realistic sister-in-law, the division of labor made sense to me and I hit *reply-all* to fire off an enthusiastic assent. Actually, I *nearly* hit reply-all, because I caught my name in a paragraph below the list, and I saw that Marisol had included a note to Greg in her original email. It was more than a small miracle that Greg and Marisol had met, that I had someone in my corner when it came to Greg, or at least who knew how bad things could be between us and did her very best to keep the peace. I skimmed her message to see if there was any additional information I'd need to start my share of party-planning, and actually drew back from my phone when I saw it.

Greg had obviously not been meant to forward this, but he did anyway. Was he thoughtless on purpose, I wondered, or accidentally? Which was worse?

It's so sad for Clementine that Will dumped her. Though maybe it's for the best since he obviously never wanted to marry her! I'd die if I were over 30 and single in LA but she's been posting cat pics all over Instagram so I guess she's made her peace with it. Just make sure she's not overwhelmed with wedding anniversary tasks that make her think too much about being single. Poor Clem.

I wanted to type a response, but what even was there to say? Greg had already made it clear he didn't have any respect for me, even when Will and I were still together, so there was hardly anything I could say *now* that would help. Marisol, though, I'd thought was on my side, or at least as much on my side as a person could be who was married to the enemy. Well, not *the enemy*, that couldn't have been a healthy way of looking at one's own brother. Still. Just because Marisol and Greg had gotten married in their twenties, like a lot of people I knew who lived up in the suburbs, I hardly thought she'd been viewing me as some sad single lady who'd been waiting around for Will to propose. Even though there could be a general small-town vibe in the so-called proper timing to do things, I hadn't picked that vibe up in my own family. But it turned out that even when I'd had someone and had *not* been posting cat photos to Instagram, Marisol had been judging me. It turned out she was decidedly not in my corner after all.

"You're early." Chloe hopped on the barstool next to me. I'd hoped her outfit would give me some clue if this was a date or not, but her colorful striped sweater and jeans were both perfectly stylish and fairly casual and I felt no more enlightened to what this evening might hold.

"So are you," I pointed out.

"And you look pissed."

I waved it off. "Just family stuff. And I got off work early."

"Same," she said, flagging down the bartender. "A Pomeranian with a flaky owner canceled on me, which shouldn't have surprised me."

"Why, is that a stereotype of Pomeranian owners?" I asked, and she laughed. I loved how bold it was, a loud *ha!* that made me feel, at least briefly, like the funniest girl in the world.

"No, I don't think so, I meant people in LA in general. I'll have to ponder that, though." She ordered a soft seltzer and hopped up as soon as it was in front of her at the bar. "Let's go grab a booth."

I tucked my phone into my pocket—I only believed in dresses with pockets—and grabbed my drink before following Chloe across the bar to a booth along the back wall. In the short walk I hadn't thought about how different it would feel to be sitting across from her instead of shoulder to shoulder, but despite that we were now sitting further away from each other, the direct eye contact felt like a move forward in intimacy.

"So I've been thinking about your little predicament," Chloe said, raising her eyebrows.

"I have a predicament?" I asked. "And it's . . . little?"

"Your whole being a baby queer with no real-life experience except thinking about how Gillian Anderson tastes, ready to nail down some IRL babe."

"Oh," I said, looking down at my diminishing cocktail. The eye contact was definitely a lot, at least when I was being confronted by such harsh truths, including the unspoken fact that this was most definitely not a date. "That predicament."

I had hoped, of course, that it wasn't a predicament at all. As overwhelming as the idea of queer dating seemed, after a lifetime that looked pretty straight on the surface, I really had thought that perhaps I'd walked into one queer bar, talked to one attractive woman, and would end up in something that—if not a *relationship*—would function as the training wheels to my new overtly queer life. Chloe's words made this idea scramble out of my brain, though, as if the desire was embarrassed of itself and would not be sticking around to assess the reality of the situation.

Though I wasn't sure, either, if I had actually wished it *was* an actual date with an actual prospect, and not—well, whatever this situation was. I'd thought about dating women, *in general.* Somehow, though, I hadn't thought about *specific* women. It was a real paradox how I'd somehow overthought everything while simultaneously missing so much.

Also, it hit me that I'd never been on an actual date in my life. Since Will and I had met in college, we'd gotten to know each other at campus events and parties, and by the time we'd wandered off-campus to dinners and movies and concerts, we were already together. I couldn't believe how unprepared I was for single life—dating someone of *any* gender. Showing up at a bar. Taking it to some other location, dinner or a movie or wherever people went to get to know each other when it was new. First kiss since Will, first hookup since Will, first person seeing me naked since Will.

"The thing is," Chloe said, and then took a long, slow sip of her seltzer. I tried not to watch her lips on the rim of the glass. Maybe I did kinda-sorta wish it was an actual date. "I have a bit of a predicament too."

"Is it related to Pomeranians?" I asked, feeling rewarded by another laugh.

"I guess I have two predicaments, only one being Pomeranian-related," she said. "A couple of my friends are getting married. Soon. There are all these events, as you might guess."

I nodded. "Let me guess. Engagement party, bridal shower, bachelorette party, rehearsal dinner—wait, is it a destination wedding?"

"Ooh, you're good," she said. "It *is*. So, yeah, there are all these extra dinners planned since everyone will be out of town together. And do you know what I love, Clementine? I love dinner plans! I love going out of town with all my friends! But now that I am literally the only member of my little friend group who's not coupled-up, I feel like I've somehow gotten demoted to, like, the group's child. Or *pet*."

Marisol's email flashed in my head.

"Why are you grimacing?" Chloe asked.

"Just believe me that I fully understand where you're coming from," I said.

"Good, perfect. Because I was thinking that what I need to get through this and rise back from *pet* to my previous position of *peer* is a girlfriend."

It felt like my turn to take a long, slow sip of my beverage, while I wondered what the hell Chloe was getting at. If we were inside of a romance novel, there was nothing else she could have been suggesting besides *fake dating*, a trope I abhorred. Give me enemies-to-lovers any day, or the mild taboo-breaking of a workplace romance. That fake setup always seemed so bound for disaster that my anxiety would never allow me to relax enough to root for the characters.

But this was real life. So I knew that couldn't possibly be what Chloe was getting at.

"You," Chloe said, pointing to me with a little finger-gun gesture I somehow found wildly adorable, "also need a girlfriend. An ex you can reference when you're out there for real. Someone who can teach you the ropes—so to speak, I'm not running some kind of kink workshop here. So what do you say?"

I took another sip. And another. And kept going until my tumbler was drained.

"I can tell you're really mulling this over," Chloe said, jumping to her feet. She was wearing Crocs again, and I was fuzzy enough from chugging my drink to get hung up on the fact that I'd never expected to be attracted to anyone wearing Crocs. "Let me get you another drink. What about food? Do you want some chips and queso?"

"Well, *yes*, but—Chloe. Are you seriously proposing some kind of fake-dating situation?"

"Exactly," she said. "Glad we're on the same page. Are you a vegetarian?"

"No," I said, and she grinned and practically skipped away from me, back to the counter. When she returned a few minutes later with our drinks and a number card so our food could get dropped off, I was still sitting there with my phone in my pocket, too—*stunned?* Too something to do anything but sit there in silence.

"You look like someone died," Chloe said, which made me laugh.

"No, it's just—we can't really do this. It's absurd."

"Clementine, that's been my whole life," she said. "*Oh, Chloe, don't do that, it's absurd!* Look at me, though. I'm doing great, absurd for three and a half decades now."

"In books, whenever people try some kind of fake-dating shenanigan, it always eventually goes sideways," I pointed out.

"Yeah," Chloe said with a scoff, "in books! In real life it probably happens all the time successfully, but why would they put that in books? It's too boring."

"Wait," I said, and took a sip of my drink. A long sip. "So

you think, in real life, people are fake-dating each other all of the time, and most of the time nothing goes wrong and whatever end-goal was set is achieved?"

"Nailed it," she said, holding her glass in the air. "That is *exactly* what I think."

"Since I'm not sure how I would fact-check that . . . let me ask how this even works? People know us, if by tomorrow we say, oh, I have a girlfriend you didn't know about—"

"Please!" Chloe gestured wildly. "We're queer women. People expect us to U-Haul after a couple dates. Call someone your partner after a month. No one's going to bat an eye, I promise."

"I . . . people . . . it's . . ."

Chloe looked lit up from within. "Oh my god, did I break you?"

"I'm glad you're enjoying this so much."

"No, no, of course," she said, back to making big gestures again, her hands waving around wildly. "No one's going to bat an eye *at Chloe*, you're thinking. You were practically secret-married to some boring man and people are still expecting you to mourn the death of your heterosexual happily-ever-after and not emerge smiling with a woman. Everyone's eyes will be batting at *you*."

"That's very accurate, actually," I said. "While somehow also being wildly inaccurate."

"Story of my life." She leaned forward and grinned widely. "I'll make it easy on you, though. Look at how bossy I am! People will believe I cajoled you into something."

I found myself laughing. "I don't know. I have pretty firm boundaries. People won't think I let someone steamroll me into queerness."

"Well, yeah," Chloe said with a shrug. "It sounds like you're going to have to come out to people. But that's all rolled up in your predicament already, right? This lets you come out to people without the pressure of also maintaining a new relationship. You know I'm your fake girlfriend no matter what. I'm not going anywhere, at least until my friends are married and on their honeymoon."

I thought about that, saying the words aloud, *I'm bisexual*, for real, the way I'd rehearsed them. It wasn't that I'd never; Will knew from early on, and I'd casually said it here and there, often only in Instagram DMs or other slightly anonymized places. *Oh yeah, I'm bisexual but I'm with Will so it doesn't come up much*, or *of course I mainlined all of the new* League of Their Own, *I'm bisexual after all*, or *yeah, I heard the new Fightmaster single, I am a bisexual with a premium Spotify account*. It had always been a kind of throwaway comment, even though I'd taste the lie in that as I threw it away. My identity was bigger than gay storylines and not hidden away by a relationship with a man, but I'd never treated it that way. If I started dating women, I'd have to start saying those words for real, full of all the meaning they actually held, and in more situations than the ones I'd already listed in my head. It probably wasn't the best move, on a deep and symbolic level, to start openly and sincerely discussing my identity via a fake girlfriend and fake relationship.

Though, of course, it was flattering. When I'd headed to Johnny's the other night, I hadn't only worried that I wouldn't look queer enough. It was all the other stuff too, that I was in my mid-thirties and sometimes looked tired even when I wasn't. And even though I liked my curvy body and how it looked both in adorable dresses and without any clothes on, it wasn't as if fat girls had ever had an easy time of things. Now that I was ready for whatever was to come, would anyone even want me? So, no matter what a bad idea this was, to be wanted, even on a completely fake level, felt *not terrible*.

"I don't think it's a good idea," I said, and Chloe frowned. "Not to sound too self-help-y, but I'm entering this new phase of my life, and I should probably do it with as much honesty as possible."

"That's incredibly mature," Chloe said. "Which is not the descriptor people tend to use for me."

"Well, *me either*," I said, and we both laughed, right as a waiter dropped off a tray of tacos and chips with queso. "Ooh, I forgot food was coming."

"This is what kind of fake girlfriend you just turned down," Chloe said, leaning forward to unwrap a taco from the tray. I loved people who ate enthusiastically, who all-but-literally dove into delicious food. In LA I saw so much of the opposite.

"No, I get it, you'd keep me ensconced in queso, all I'd have to do is lie to everyone I cared about, and, truly, when I put it that way, it doesn't sound like a bad bargain."

"I'm telling you," she said, dipping a chip into the thick queso. It was homey, Tex-Mex style, not some watered-down hipster version with real cheese instead of the perfection of Velveeta. "Oh my god! The Pomeranian's calling."

"How does he dial with his little paws?" I asked, and Chloe made no attempt to hide her laughter as she answered the call.

"Sunset Junction Pet Spa, Chloe speaking. Uh-huh. Yes, I do understand, but the shop closes at six, so once you were . . ."

I pulled out my phone as Chloe patiently explained why she wasn't waiting around Sunset Junction Pet Spa, and refreshed my email. Nothing, not even a desperate-sounding sale email from Unique Vintage, had come in, and so Greg's forward of Marisol's email still sat right at the top of my inbox.

"Sorry," Chloe said, stowing her phone. "He tried the set-my-alarm-for-a.m.-instead-of-p.m. excuse on me, like I've never heard that before. I practically invented the a.m.-instead-of-p.m. excuse."

"I've done it before," I said, "for real. And you can't tell anyone, because it sounds like such a lie, even when it's true."

"See, now I'm wondering something," she said, and finished

off a taco before reaching for another. "Maybe you being afraid to be my fake girlfriend has nothing to do with your morals and ethics. Maybe you're just a bad liar."

I opened my mouth to protest but—"You're not *not* right. I *am* a bad liar. But I still think it's bad karma."

"Fine, fine," she said, though she grinned. I doubted much kept Chloe Lee down for long.

Chapter 4

Awkward Feats of Magic

"Small Jesse Pinkman, it's Saturday," I muttered the next morning, faintly hungover from the previous evening's cocktails, though even stone-cold sober I did not react well to toy mice being dropped upon my face before seven a.m. I tossed the mice out of my bed and waited for him to scamper away. First, though, he pounced at my hair and lightly batted my nose with his soft paws. How did anyone get mad at kittens? Even at this hour, his shenanigans were too adorable for anger.

Since I now woke up with a collection of cat toys in my bed, I grabbed a couple of bouncy yarn-wrapped balls and tossed them through my doorway. Dual purposes were served; yes, the kitten was now flying through the air en route to the yarn balls and literally therefore out of my hair, but I practically couldn't even believe how cute he was when he leapt boldly. Having a kitten was like watching adorable reels on Instagram all day.

After carefully measuring out Small Jesse Pinkman's breakfast and brewing my coffee, I headed into my home office-slash-spare bedroom-slash-arts and crafts station. The year before I'd started my job at Big Marketing Energy, I had been working at an ad agency that had taken on a giant entertainment client. My workdays went from manageable to overpacked. I wasn't someone who hated work; I loved the creativity of putting together digital media campaigns that satisfied client goals and came in at or under budget. I also loved finishing up my day sometime between six and seven, and leaving work to watch TV or have drinks with Hailey and Fiona or eat dinner with Will. This client, though, expected us to be on call with the urgency of ER doctors, and so even my free time felt drenched with the anxiety sweat that had become my new normal.

In the future, if a job necessitated an upgrade in deodorants, I'd know right away that it was time to get out.

I hung in there, though, and since I had been so mentally drained, even when I had free nights it felt too exhausting to go out or pay attention to award-winning premium cable dramas. On a whim, I'd unearthed the sewing machine I'd inherited when my grandmother died a few years before, and sewed together a few scraps just to get my sewing mojo back. It had been late October, so I'd sewn up a little scorpion and posted it to my Instagram with the requisite *Scorpio season is coming.* The next day, six of my followers had commented to ask if it was a cat toy and where I'd bought it, and before long I was spending my downtime from work sewing together astrology-shaped pieces of felt to stuff with high-grade catnip and silvervine for friends, and then my own Etsy shop. There was something about an evening spent fussing over stuffed fish and crabs and twins that calmed the swirling swamp of work anxiety.

Now that I had a job where I was allowed to set actual work-life boundaries, I didn't crave evenings locked away with my sewing machine the way I used to, but I still set aside time at least once a week to stay current on orders and maintain back stock of the most popular signs. (Scorpio-themed toys sold out constantly, no matter whose season it was.) It wasn't the kind of small business that was going to make me rich—or even ever fully support me—but considering how much of my life was spent in front of screens, I loved the respite from them, loved the buzzing of my grandma's machine, loved seeing my little piles of inventory restock.

By the time I'd gotten all my orders ready and the back stock replenished, it was past lunchtime. Pre-breakup, Will would have wandered into this room with food and a reminder that even freelance cat toy work needed lunch breaks. I thought of Chloe ordering queso and tacos for us last night, and then snapped out of that pretty quickly. Last night had not been a date; Chloe Lee did not think of me that way. She was not going to make sure I ate lunch or remembered to get fresh air. Chloe Lee only needed me for a disastrous-sounding situation based on lies and make-believe.

But all women wouldn't feel that way, would they? Or was Chloe's warning about baby gays out in the world something to take seriously? I couldn't be doomed with all women right out of the gate; that felt statistically improbable.

Instead of sitting home with brand-new fears—the old ones had been enough already!—I jumped into the shower so I'd look a little more human running errands. Up where I'd grown up, Saturday afternoon grocery shopping and such were not occasions to worry about one's general aesthetic, but my corner of Los Angeles could feel like such a small town. It was rare to dash into the Silver Lake Trader Joe's without seeing someone I knew—and that was before I had an ex who had managed to find an apartment less than a mile away. When Will had offered to let me buy him out of the condo and move out, I assumed he'd be moving more than point-eight miles away, but it wasn't as if I'd wanted to leave Silver Lake either.

And of course it wasn't that Will hadn't seen me look my worst; we were together over a decade, years in which we'd each—separately and, over one terrible weekend, together, had food poisoning and other frankly disgusting maladies. And also, I'd been the one to end it. Will was the heartbroken one. I was the one checking out women and thinking about buying new underwear.

I still didn't want to risk him seeing me looking less than— well, I was buying groceries and considering a Target run for cleaning supplies. It wasn't about looking great. I just didn't want Will to see me anything less than average. Average would be fine. I wanted his broken heart to heal, but I still wanted him to picture me looking sexy and adorable, *say you'll remember me/buying Fabuloso/wearing my best leggings* and all. But it wasn't Will I accidentally rammed my cart into in front of the Trader Joe's cheese section; it was my boss. And, no, not my boss's cart. More like my boss's rear end.

Also I felt strange that I recognized my boss's ass so I pretended that I hadn't.

"I'm so sorry," I said in my nicest and most professional tone, aiming my cart away and preparing to make a run for it.

"Clementine?" Phoebe asked over her shoulder.

"Oh my god, Phoebe," I said, pretending I wasn't trying to run away from the scene of the crime. "This is embarrassing."

"Is it?" she asked good-naturedly. She was dressed in jeans and a hoodie I was fairly sure cost more than my entire outfit combined. Phoebe did *casual* like a Roy sibling. "I don't mind if you know I buy cheese on the weekends."

"Ha," I said in far from the jovial tone I attempted. While Phoebe was absolutely my favorite boss I'd ever reported to, and someone I respected highly and thought of as a mentor, I loved the hard-and-fast boundary between work and the rest of my life. Obviously I'd been the kind of kid who hated glimpsing one of her teachers buying cough medication at CVS; I once ran into my statistics professor carrying a Victoria's Secret shopping bag in a mall elevator and dropped the course as soon as I got back to campus.

"How's your weekend so far?" Phoebe asked casually.

"Oh, you know, the standard usual," I said. "Yes, I'm aware that *standard* and *usual* mean the same thing."

"That's just how standard and usual things are," Phoebe said with a grin. "I understand."

"I'll let you go," I said, upping my not-at-all-jovial tone to almost-cheerful, and making a beeline to the cash registers. I hadn't gotten any frozen flatbreads or Fancy Cheese Crunchies but I knew when to abandon a mission and escape quickly to safety. I also knew that most people wouldn't have been thrown by chance interactions with their very nice bosses, but my boundaries seemed to have permanent settings.

I was not at all in denial that my brain didn't always function like other people's. I even asked my therapist once if she thought my ADHD explained why I hated surprise interactions that bled my worlds together. She'd paused for a moment and said, kindly, "Maybe, though, I don't know, sometimes people can just be particular about things." Annoying to think sometimes my weirdnesses defied professional explanation.

Back at home I got through my chore list, got in some quality playtime with Small Jesse Pinkman, and read a big chunk of the romance novel I'd started the night before—even if that only stood to remind me of Chloe and our exceedingly strange evening together.

It wouldn't always be like that, I reminded myself as I got ready for a long-delayed night out with my friends. I'd meet someone, and when she got my number she would use it for more than to text me gifs of Dana Scully. And when she asked me out, it wouldn't be as her fake girlfriend. It'd be for something real.

I had to believe that or I'd cancel plans (again) to have a breakdown (not again—well, not exactly). My friends and I had been scheduled for a night out nearly two months ago, but then Hailey's daughter had come down with an ear infection and so we rescheduled for last month, and then I'd been the one to cancel because instead of meeting my friends for small plates I'd ended my relationship. Hailey and Fiona had—both separately and on our never-ending group chat—offered to take me out, but I'd resisted. It wasn't that I didn't love my best friends— what kind of asshole would I be if I didn't?—but I didn't know how to explain any of it to them. The kind of life I'd fled from was exactly the life my friends had. There was probably a way to describe the situation to them that wasn't judgmental and patronizing, but every version I'd rehearsed came out terrible.

I had no idea how long they'd let me avoid them, but it turned out that the answer was three and a half weeks.

"Clem!" Fiona tackled me into a hug, which was her normal violently affectionate greeting. Fiona was tall like a model so she had something like eight inches on me, and she had a Tae-kwondo black belt as well as more than a passing familiarity with Krav Maga techniques. In probably every other version of the universe, we wouldn't know each other—much less be best friends—but early on in our careers we'd met at an enter-tainment industry networking mixer, rolling our eyes at the same just-playing-devil's-advocate bro, and the connection had stuck.

"You look great," I said. "A pointless thing to say, I know, as you always do."

Fiona did a tiny curtsy, her sharp blond bob swinging per-fectly back into place. Even though it was the weekend, she looked like a boss in her cap-sleeve top and wide-leg jeans. I'd tried on a similar pair of pants recently but on me they looked less C-Suite Casual and more Clown Couture.

"Enough about me," she said, taking out her phone and checking the screen. Fiona was a finance bigwig at Pantheon, the entertainment company behind almost every comic book movie, and even though my film-related job mostly took week-ends off, I understood that hers wasn't the same.

"Everything OK?" I asked.

"Uh, that's for me to ask you," she said, dropping her phone back into her pocket. "And, yes, it wasn't work, just Hailey running late. Let's see if they'll seat us without her."

I checked my phone and found it empty of texts except one from Greg. **Did you find out about beer yet???** Ugh.

"Oh, we were already texting about something," Fiona said, heading to the host stand. "It was easier for her to just tell me."

"Maybe we should have offered to meet her up there," I said, instead of dwelling on my friends leaving me out of the group chat.

Fiona grimaced. "And end up at some chain restaurant? I don't think so."

"Look, I might have run from the suburbs, but don't knock all chain restaurants," I said. "A chain restaurant gave us Cheddar Bay Biscuits, after all."

We were seated right away at a table on Greekman's patio. The restaurant had been a cozy Jewish deli, but the owners had transformed it into a hipster Greek restaurant, complete with this luxe patio in the middle of the strip mall parking lot. There were actual wood floors, greenery climbing the walls that hid the literal parking lot, and classic blue and white décor. It was the kind of place I wanted to hate for being kind of ridiculous, but it was also delicious and beautiful, two of my favorite descriptors. In some ways, that was LA in a nutshell.

"So I know we should wait for Hay to arrive," Fiona said, "but how *are* you?"

"I'm good," I said, upping my tone at odds with the note of sympathy in her voice. Fiona wasn't one to be overly sentimental, so my hackles were already up. "How about you?"

"Well, I'm fine, but . . ." Fiona tipped her head at an angle I assumed she'd practiced for moments in corporate meetings where she had to look particularly kind. "Oh, Hay's here."

I waved frantically to get her attention, while Fiona looked on with an eyebrow raised.

"I think she'll recognize us."

"Oh, fuck you," I said, and we were both laughing as Hailey made her way through the patio to us. Once we'd hopped up to hug her, and Fiona's head was no longer at that manufactured sympathetic level, I felt something calm wash over me. Why had I avoided my friends for this long? No, I wasn't sure they'd understand why my breakup had felt so necessary. But they'd seen me through everything in my adult life so far—Hailey had seen me through even more! We'd met in grade school and were best friends by middle school. I was the one who'd brought the three of us together in the first place, once my new friendship with Fiona had been solidified.

"So how *are* you?" Hailey asked, once we were settled in at the table and browsing the menu. I glanced up from my phone and saw that Hailey was making a face in my direction, sympathetic but sad, warm but already prepared for the worst.

"Yes," Fiona said firmly, setting her phone down on the table with a small *thud*. Her face pulled into, somehow, the exact same expression. It was the face that actress Laura Linney always seemed to be making. I swear, I could feel her patronizing gaze through the screen. "How *are* you, Clem?"

"I'm fine," I said, maybe too quickly, because their expressions didn't change. "Really."

Adding a *really* never convinced anyone, but it was so irresistible.

"I have to say that I was *shocked* when I heard," Hailey said.

"Absolutely floored," Fiona agreed. "If I were a betting man, it would have been me and Alex before you and Will."

"That's *terrible*," Hailey said. "Let's not joke around about any of us getting divorced. Or—"

"But it's surprising," Fiona said, an insistent note in her voice. "I assumed by the end of the year you two would be engaged. Though I guess to be fair I thought that last year. And the year before."

"*Fiona*," Hailey said in sort of a stage whisper, and a little surge of panic zipped through me knowing this was absolutely a discussion they'd had with each other, more than once.

"Oh, come on, we're friends here," Fiona said with a casual flick of her wrist. I'd always loved that Fiona said what she felt, no bullshit, but I guess I loved it less when it was about me.

"That's not really what I . . ." I trailed off because even though I'd had the conversation with myself a million times, I still didn't know how to broach it with my friends. Fiona might be the type to say exactly what she felt, but I had no idea how to say this big thing without potentially looking like a giant judgmental ass. Sharing feelings had always been something for other people, someone like Hailey, who was flowing over with them and couldn't help sharing, or someone like Fiona, who was in firm control of everything and could let out the exact right amount.

"I can't believe him," Hailey said with a shake of her head. Her face still held that sad-for-you expression. When I glanced at Fiona, I saw that she was making the exact same face too. Two Laura Linneys facing me.

"It wasn't—"

"Are you ready to get some drink orders in?" A waiter popped up seemingly out of nowhere like an awkward feat of magic.

"Yes, please," I said, trying not to sound too desperate for both the alcohol and the distraction. "I'll have the White Negroni, please."

"Oh, no," Fiona said with a curt shake of her head. "Water is fine for me."

"Oh, that sounds good," Hailey said. "Just water for me as well."

The waiter headed off, and Hailey beamed at Fiona. "Are you—"

"No," she said quickly, "but there's about a three-month window coming up where I can get pregnant and not ruin the next fiscal year, so I'm preparing."

"Oh, so it's for sure?" I asked, because even though of course Fiona had a five-year-plan, the baby part had always felt like a question mark scribbled beside the list, not its own bullet point. Secretly I'd hoped that meant that neither of us were having kids, and we could give Hailey's daughter lots of our cool aunt energy (I was determined that *someone* would think I was a cool aunt someday) and still go out on the nights when Hailey couldn't make it because of parental duties.

I wanted everyone I cared about to get everything they wanted, but maybe Fiona didn't really want kids that much, it was tough to tell. And it was one thing to have *one* best friend with a baby, one best friend with a whole new set of responsibilities and mom friends and a suburban home with a literal picket fence. If Fiona joined the ranks, I could practically see our group chat quieting while the two of them talked to each other and their other mom friends and I was just . . . alone. In meme terms, I contained two wolves, and while one said that the center would hold even as friendships shifted, the other snarled as she was overtaken by a desperate clutch to keep at least this part as it had been.

"Nothing's for sure, Clem," Fiona said with a laugh. "Maybe my womb's dusty and barren. No way to truly know until I take the system out for a spin with the training wheels off."

"So in this situation, your IUD's the training wheels?" I asked, and the three of us burst into laughter. And it felt like the three of us again, the friends who'd gone through all major life events together since we were in our early twenties and had no plans of stopping. In a flash I felt silly for holding back; these weren't random married women who wouldn't understand my choices. Being moms or moms-to-be didn't disqualify our friendship. These were my people.

"I was the one who—"

"Made any decisions yet?" Our waiter had magically appeared again, this time with my cocktail and water for all of us. Fiona took control and ordered what felt like most of the small plates and sides, which was great as far as I was concerned. Finally, our order was in, and the table was just the three of us again.

"I was actually the one who ended things," I said, and took a sip of my drink. By the time I'd set my glass back on the table, Hailey and Fiona were staring at me with wide-eyed and pained expressions.

"Every face you've made tonight has been terrible," I said.

"What?" Fiona shook her head, as if to clear my nonsense out of her ears. I assumed she did this in meetings with high-ranking executives all of the time. "Why would you do that?"

Hailey still looked horrified. "Will's so . . ."

"We wanted different things," I said in my calmest and least panicky voice. "And you two are my best friends, so maybe you could try sounding less like you just found out I have a terminal illness or something."

"Well," Fiona said, gesturing to nothing with an outstretched hand. "It *is* a bit like that, isn't it? You don't want to die alone, right? You've said it a thousand times."

"I'm not sure I said it like that. . . ."

"How different could you want things to be?" Hailey asked with a frown. "You two were the only two people I know who actually like the French fries at In-N-Out."

"They're fine if you order them extra-crispy and eat them while they're still hot!" I said, and realized I was defending the wrong thing. "You can't possibly think that's the basis for everlasting love, Hay."

"No, of course not, that's ridiculous," Fiona said, her brow furrowed. "The French fry example is just one of many ways that the two of you always seemed to synch up. And obviously we love you and respect your choices—"

"Obviously!" Hailey piped in.

"But it's hard for me to understand why you'd end it."

I tried to look meaningfully at my friends. Their expressions didn't change. It didn't make sense to me that they could know me for so long and not inherently feel how differences had crept up on Will and me like a Venn diagram pulling off into two completely separate circles.

"He told me he was going to drive up and ask for my father's permission for my hand in marriage." I let out the last words so ploddingly slowly because I expected one of them would cut me off before I could even finish the sentence. Instead, they both stared at me like the good part of the story hadn't happened yet. Fiona even gestured, like, *keep going.*

"Guys," I said. "You know that sounds bonkers, right?"

I watched as they looked to each other and then back at me. It was as if there was a window or glass door between us where we could see each other just fine but were definitely in two different rooms.

"It's a little patriarchal," Fiona said. "I'll give you that."

"It's *romantic*," Hailey said. "I still remember how nervous Michael was, so stressed out, and I had no idea what was up. And then he got back from my parents' and knelt down with the ring and everything made sense to me."

Her voice rang out with a warmth like it had just happened, like it was still just as special as the day it had. It probably was. And I knew there wasn't much more I could say about my own situation, because why would I want to take that away from her? Why would I want to denigrate any part of the life that she loved?

"It just didn't seem like he knew me very well," I said gently. "If he thought that was something I wanted."

I watched my friends' faces to see if I'd successfully made my case.

"Remember that report they did?" Hailey asked. "Women are more likely to get struck by lightning than get married after forty!"

I guess that I had not, successfully or otherwise, made my case after all.

"That article was proven statistically incorrect," I said,

though even inaccurate and sexist information could be hard to shake out of your brain. "And, also, I'm only thirty-six!"

And, also, why did any of that matter if I didn't want it anyway?

"But—"

"Even though Will and I both think In-N-Out has *amazing* fries, thank you, he's someone who wants to get married and . . . even though, yes, I want to grow old with someone, I guess I just don't—" I cut myself off because the life Will had wanted was the life Hailey already had, and the life that Fiona was on track to conquer. When we were younger, all of our dreams made so much sense to each other. It was like we carried them together. There was nothing I couldn't have told them. "Anyway. Even if a lightning strike's more probable, I guess I'm OK with that."

"Besides getting electrified," Fiona said with a tiny smile.

"Besides that. Do I have to do a whole 'not that there's anything wrong with getting married' so I don't look like an asshole to the two of you? I'm more than happy to, if you need it."

Since Hailey was still frowning, I said it, and then said it again for good measure.

"I just hate to think of you as alone," Hailey said, reaching out to take my hand. "You're such an amazing person, Clem."

"I'm not alone," I said. "I have you two."

Their sad faces had somehow returned at that. At *that*! The power of friendship! If that wasn't enough to wipe those looks off their faces, what was?

"And Small Jesse Pinkman," I reminded them, even though I knew that for some reason cats only made women seem lonelier.

"Plus a fulfilling job I really love, remember." Why did it feel like I was making excuses? All of this was true. Why did my dearest friends still look as if they just saw a dog get hit by a car?

Hailey leaned in, her expression matching her voice in sad softness. "What if you slip and fall and there's no one there to help you?"

"You could choke," Fiona said. "A piece of steak takes you down, and before they can find you, that little cat starts eating your body."

"Well, also," I said, talking faster than, perhaps, I was thinking, and no longer interested, maybe, with the truth, "I'm already dating someone."

The panic of my lie hit me precisely as their faces went from *poor-Clem* to *tell-me-more*. The lie, I felt, had more power than anything real I'd said tonight.

"Is that why you ended things with Will?" Fiona asked, the promise of intrigue coloring her tone.

"No," I said. "Of course not. It's much newer than that."

"Ooh, new," Hailey said with a dreamy sigh, resting her chin in her hands. "Not that Michael isn't practically perfect, but *new*. I can hardly remember it."

"Seriously," Fiona said. "I barely remember when it was still exciting to see Alex's dick. Now it's just there."

"*Fiona*," Hailey said, somehow still shocked by our friend who had been exactly herself for as long as we'd known her.

"You know it's true," Fiona said, and the fast way Hailey's visible shock wore off told me that she absolutely agreed.

"Well," I said, "I should say."

I ended the sentence there, not exactly on purpose, but because—I mean, what was I doing? I'd refused to do this. I assumed I'd never hear from Chloe again. In fact, for all I knew, she was already hashing out fake relationship details with some other woman.

"You should say what?" Fiona asked.

I knew that it was my last chance to get out of this. Make a joke about how I was dating my cat, my job, my brand-new vibrator. I should have done anything but dig myself in further.

"I'm dating a woman," I said, watching their eyebrows travel sky-high. "I mean, not to be cisnormative about it, the whole new-dicks thing. Anyone can have a dick. Or big dick energy, like Fiona."

Fiona's shock must have worn off quickly because she seemed so pleased to be recognized for her BDE. Hailey, on the other hand, was still making an expression so surprised that her eyebrows had disappeared under her shaggy brown bangs.

"You both know I'm bisexual," I said quickly. "I've mentioned it before."

"You've mentioned that you think Tessa Thompson is hot," Fiona said. "Which, big deal. Who doesn't. I didn't know you meant it like this."

"*Like this*," I repeated.

"Don't take it some bad way," she said. "You know what I mean. I'm an ally!"

"Love is love," Hailey said, nodding earnestly.

Fiona held out her arms. "I went to Smith!"

"So . . ." Gentleness drenched Hailey's tone. "Is *this* why you ended things with Will?"

I shook my head, and felt that wasn't forceful enough so I shook it some more. Our waiter arrived with our hummus and panzanella, and the three of us made quick work of divvying up the dishes.

"Okay," Hailey said, dipping a tomato into hummus. "How did you meet her?"

"At a bar," I said. "Well, not really. Walking to the bar. Some creeps were street-harassing me, and she scared them off."

"What does she do?" Fiona asked. "This rescuer of yours."

"She's a dog groomer," I said, and Fiona frowned. "Don't make that face."

"What face?"

"The if-a-job-doesn't-require-an-MBA-from-Wharton-it-barely-counts face," I said.

"Oh, please, I've never made such a specific face," Fiona said, and Hailey and I burst out laughing. Already it felt safe again, and again I felt like a jerk for underestimating my friends.

In fact, if I forgot about the fact that I was lying, everything felt great.

"How's the sex?" Fiona asked, and Hailey's eyes darted over to stare at Fiona yet again. We were, after all, not *And Just Like That* friends. It was already a lot thinking about Alex's figuratively old dick.

"It's," I said, and then paused. There was the lie of it all, of course, but I felt the urge to still get it right. Chloe's bright eyes flashed into my mind. Her ease moving through the world. Her maddeningly mixed signals. The way her top lip was a little fuller than her lower lip. The way I couldn't stop thinking about her lips, especially right now.

"Oh my god, your face," Hailey said, in a hushed whisper.

My heart pounded in my ears. "What?"

"You're red," she said.

"It must," Fiona declared, "be mind-blowing. Fuck it, my womb's empty right now. I want a drink. And more details."

As Fiona yelled over our waiter, it hit me that I couldn't remember the last time my friends had found me this interesting. Ending my nearly decades-long relationship had brought on sympathy, not curiosity.

Now, though, it was like I was brand-new.

I ended up leaving my car parked on a side street near the restaurant and Lyfting home. Fiona could keep up with finance bros, so whenever I drank with her, my cocktail consumption ticked upward. I, after all, had a BA in advertising from a liberal arts college, where we were more likely to get a little stoned and watch low-budget arthouse films.

By the time I let myself in and scooped up Small Jesse Pinkman, though, I was more sober than not, and a wave of *what did I do* crashed over me. But petting a purring kitten and thinking about an attractive woman were both stress-killing activities, and before long I was curled up on the sofa in my pajamas and a detoxifying face mask and my cat and my phone.

We would have to have parameters.

Three dots appeared almost immediately. **Clementine, I'd expect nothing less.**

Chapter 5
European Sodas

In the bright light of the morning, the night before seemed more like a hijinks-filled dream and in no way something that had actually happened. Quickly, though, the facts flashed back, not in the ephemeral haze of something my subconscious cooked up overnight, but in the stark details. I was due at Loupiotte for brunch with Chloe and her friends at ten, and finding the whole thing poorly thought-out did not make this fact any less true.

Last night had been panicky, desperate, stupid. Now I was supposed to meet a bunch of strangers while pretending Chloe was my girlfriend, even though I not only barely knew Chloe, I'd never even had one single date with a woman? No, no, no.

We've rethought this by now, right? A rush of relief settled upon me once I'd texted. Chloe, sure, emanated more chaos than your average individual, but it was hard to imagine she hadn't awoken with the same regret. Meeting the friends was something you built up to, right? You didn't just dive into a group of complete strangers.

Her response came back fast. **I've rethought nothing. Ex-**

cept that I should pick you up. It'll look weird if we arrive separately.

I had to admit that she was right about that much, and texted her my address before reviewing myself in my full-length mirror for approximately the hundredth time that morning. I'd never *really* done one of those meet-the-friends brunches before, considering that Will and I met in college when we were too broke for brunch and usually slept too late anyway. I hadn't had to think much about whether or not I was good girlfriend material, or whatever your significant other's friends were supposed to evaluate. Will and I just *were*. And now that we *weren't*, I was up for judgment. I had both no idea what Chloe's friends would think of me, and no idea when the I-never-had-to-think-about-this-before-I-broke-up-with-Will milestones would end.

For a split second I wondered if having the life you didn't want was worth having far fewer awkward interactions. It probably wasn't, but I definitely hadn't weighed this aspect in my breakup decision-making, that was for sure.

I ended up wearing a midi-length dress in a bold geometric print that I'd paid too much for because ads for it haunted me on Instagram until I gave in. Still, it hung well and, I thought, hit the sweet spot between generic and insufferably twee, where my needle usually landed. Not that I minded looking twee, but I was determined to make a decent impression on these strangers and so my best—or at least most expensive—dress it was. I had no idea if I looked queer enough, or queer *at all*, or even how to evaluate those standards, but since I *was* queer, I decided whatever I wore became inherently queer in the process.

Hopefully.

Anyway, if this whole thing was a disaster, which seemed likelier than not, I'd bail. Chloe and I hadn't actually worked out any parameters yet, and it wasn't as if I'd signed a contract. I'd do this brunch and if it was clear that this was as terrible an idea as I assumed, I'd get out of this. I'd probably have to stop going to the queer bar, but there had to be other ways to meet women. I'd be fine.

Hopefully.

My doorbell rang, which was so unexpected I looked at my phone as if maybe I'd misheard my text notification sound and not that Chloe Lee was at my front door. But when I looked out the peephole, there she was.

"Hi," I said, opening the door. Chloe wore cutoff coveralls in a shade of bright pink that was somehow a bit punk rock and not at all sweet. A broken-in pair of black motorcycle boots completed her outfit, and I hoped mine looked halfway as good. I'd kill for effortless style; suddenly I worried I was more like *effortful*.

"I didn't know you were coming in," I said. "Sorry if it's messy or if there's cat fur everywhere."

Her brown eyes practically literally lit up. "You have a cat? Like a stereotypical cat who's hiding from me, or one of those dog-personality cats who'll meet me and let me pet them. If you couldn't tell, I'm hoping for the second."

"I'm . . . actually not sure, we're still new to each other," I said. "Me and the cat, that is. Will was allergic, so—"

"Of *course* he was," Chloe said, looking around my front room. It was, a lot, I knew. So many people shied away from bright pinks and vibrant greens and oranges that were *just shy* of neon, but I never felt so much like myself than when surrounded by color. Will had never dissuaded me, the guy whose dorm room never had more on the walls than a faux vintage *Die Hard* poster, but still. I didn't need to ask him to know there was a limit, and so I stayed on the safe side of the invisible line.

Will gone, though, meant my browser windows were replete with open Target and Etsy tabs, my walls were rapidly filled with framed prints, and a huge pink and red rug was unrolled in the middle of my living room. I couldn't justify a new sofa (yet), but a couch full of Opalhouse by Jungalow throw pillows? Easy breezy.

"Your condo's cute. I've been, like, halfway looking, and it turns out that a lot of them are terrible."

"*Terrible*," I agree. "Like paying all the money in the world for what amounts to a sad apartment that's now yours forever. It took me a while to find this place, so hang in there."

"Oh, *shit*," Chloe said in an awestruck tone, and I realized that it was because Small Jesse Pinkman had darted into the room. "Will he let me pick him up? Never mind, you don't know, this baby's new, your boring ex was, amongst the lengthy list of flaws, allergic."

"He seems up for it," I said, and watched as Chloe leaned over to scoop him up.

"I want to bail on brunch and spend the rest of the day holding this kitten instead," she said, rubbing her cheek against Small Jesse Pinkman's fur. "What's his name?"

"Before I tell you—"

She burst into laughter. "I love names that require disclaimers. Remember, I work with pets for my job. I've seen everything you can imagine, and then some."

I held my hands out to my sides. "I don't know much about cats. When I got him, he already had a name, and I didn't know if it was confusing for him or bad karma to change it. So, with that, I introduce you to Small Jesse Pinkman."

Chloe laughed even harder. "You know what? Perfect. Let's help him start a little catnip empire."

"See, it's cute when it's catnip."

She kissed the top of his head and set him down on the third level of his cat tree. "I guess we should go, even if this would be more fun. Can you drive? My car's full of dog hair."

"When you put it like that, sure," I said, and grabbed my key ring from the hook. "Do I need to know anything about your friends in advance?"

Chloe turned to me, her lips curling up in a smirk. "Queer Brunches 101? The Care and Feeding of Millennial Lesbians?"

I rolled my eyes with deliberate casualness, even though a ping of worry bounced through me that there were indeed things I needed to know that I hadn't even thought to ask. My dress being queer enough was only the tip of the gay iceberg.

"That isn't what I meant," I said. "Like, 'Fiona's a great person even though she's such a capitalist so just don't bring up all billionaires being unethical because that's her life goal.'"

"A completely hypothetical example, I'm sure," Chloe said with a snort.

"Don't worry, you won't have to meet my friends," I said, and then pictured their ravenous faces desperate for even morsels of details I could offer them. "Probably."

Chloe followed me out and then down to the parking garage. "I don't think I have too much to prepare you for that you don't already know. I kind of hate my friends' dog, but maybe that's more of a warning about me than them."

"Or the dog?" I asked, which earned me another snort as we got into my Prius.

"Don't laugh," Chloe said, "but my dog is my best friend. I have to pretend dog mortality doesn't exist just to get through each day. He's a snarly asshole, and I love him to fucking death. Then my friends get this perfect dog—in fact, I *helped* them get this perfect dog, since I knew they were looking and because of my job I'm always hearing about dogs who need homes. But I didn't know she was some poster child of perfect dog behavior, and now it feels like no one has patience for Fernando anymore. Like they all learned well-behaved dogs exist so it must be something I'm doing wrong that mine's not."

I was quiet for a few moments. "*Are* you doing something wrong?"

"Oh my god, fuck you," she said, and we both cracked up. "And, probably! Hard to look at the evidence and not think I'm at least partially to blame. He's a good dog, though. Just annoying sometimes."

"I mean, aren't we all."

She grinned at me and it felt like a ray of sunshine zapping right into my chest, warming something deeper than whatever fake thing we were up to. I reminded myself sternly that we were indeed up to something fake and also not to dwell too much on how her thighs looked disappearing into those cut-offs.

"Are your friends suspicious?" I asked.

"Probably," she said, and I shot her a look so quickly I nearly ran a red light. "Calm down, Clementine. Not that this is an arranged situation. How would that even come up? *Are you two only pretending to be together so that people stop treating you like you're sad and lonely childish losers?* If anyone asks that, I'll obviously say no."

"You know what I mean," I said. "I don't make a habit of pulling shenanigans on people. And you're the one who said your friends would probably be suspicious."

"I only meant that I never bring girls to brunch," Chloe said in an infuriatingly chill tone, "so it'll, at the least, pique their interests."

"Is brunch a big deal?"

"For *these* queers? It's the biggest."

My heart rate skyrocketed, and my car's Bluetooth chose that moment to connect, blasting "Do You Hear the People Sing?" from the musical *Les Misérables*, which I hadn't even been listening to.

"Sorry," I said, hitting the power button as quickly as it was possible to hit a power button.

"For what? I love singing the songs of angry men," she said, and we both laughed. "Clementine, if you think I'm *not* some musical theatre–loving person, we should get that cleared up now. I totally *am*."

"Me too," I said, "though my phone does randomly decide

I want to listen to things from my music library without consulting me and it's always exactly as jarring as that."

"Yeah, one night I was hooking up with a girl and I had my music on shuffle—"

"Such a risky move!" I said. "My heart started pounding the second you said the word *shuffle*."

"Correct, because it turns out that Abba's 'Super Trouper' is not an inherently sexy song, though not the worst, unless your shuffle algorithm's gone rogue and follows it up with *nine* more Abba songs."

I laughed so hard that tears dotted in the corners of my eyes. "Did you *count*?"

"Clementine, I did." She gestured out the window. "I doubt we'll find a better parking spot than that one."

I swerved to get to it, and Chloe cracked up.

"Is that how you park?"

"Parallel parking's hard! I'm from the suburbs. The outer suburbs." I backed up and pulled out and kept going until my car was comfortably mostly parallel with the curb.

"I know that queer people are objectively worse at parking, but this is really something," Chloe said as we got out and headed across Kingswell toward Vermont Avenue.

"Should we hold hands or something?" I asked, realizing this was all about to happen. We were steps away from Loupiotte Kitchen.

"Nah, no one would expect that from me," Chloe said. "Though who knows what they're saying in the group chat they definitely started without me the second I said I'm bringing someone."

"Oh yeah," I said, "my friends definitely have one of those too. I think it used to be about babies and pregnancy, but now I assume it's devoted to my relationship status."

"Outside-the-group-chat solidarity," Chloe said. "Anyway. I'm not really squishy with people I'm seeing, so we're fine."

"By 'squishy,' do you mean does-a-lot-of-PDA?" I asked.

"Yeah, why?"

I fought back a grin that felt . . . well, like something this definitely wasn't. "I don't know. It's cute."

Chloe elbowed me sharply. "I'm many things, but not cute."

"Sorry, charming. Is charming one of the things you are?"

She shot me a smile I would have categorized as both cute *and* charming, but before I could sort out what it meant to see the shape of my fake date's mouth as either of those qualities, I spotted something far more distracting.

Phoebe, my boss, was standing in front of the restaurant next to her wife, Bianca. Phoebe didn't step out of the way as we approached, as I would have done, and anyone watching could probably see exactly what was happening. But, no, I was like the idiot in a horror movie who kept going further down into the basement while everyone watching the movie screamed at her not to.

"Oh," Phoebe said, an undefinable emotion—confusion? suspicion?—coloring her gaze as we made eye contact. "Clementine—"

"Clementine!" someone called, and I turned around to see my former coworker Nina walking toward us as well. She was trailed by her fiancée Ari, who was holding the leash of a very cute Border collie. "It's so good to see you."

"You too," I said, briskly, waiting for her to step aside as well, despite the mounting evidence that my solid boundaries between my work life and my everything else were liquifying at record speed. I remembered, in a white-hot flash, meeting Chloe at that company party years ago. *I'm friends with the boss,* she'd said dismissively before steering conversation back to the hors d'oeuvres, so dismissively that I hadn't thought to log that comment until this very moment. *I don't think I have too much to prepare you for that you don't already know,* she'd said, minutes ago in her car.

"I'll check in for our table," Phoebe said, as it lodged in my gut that when she said *our table* that really meant *our table*. I was our!

"I thought they didn't take reservations for brunch," I said, because most Angelenos had a running list of restaurants in their head with pertinent details about hours and reservations and parking, and for some reason my brain had decided to focus on that instead of the horror unfolding here.

"Oh, god," Bianca said, smiling widely at me. I hadn't been surprised when I'd met her that Phoebe's wife was gorgeous—dark, wavy hair like she'd always just left Drybar, eyes that were more gold than brown, a gleamingly bright smile; after all, I was pretty sure Phoebe could land anyone she wanted. But Bianca was also always extremely friendly, in our limited interactions, and even though she was about a hundred times more glamorous than I was, I loved that she was plus-size like me. After working this long in a size-obsessed industry, I did feel something comforting about knowing that my boss had married someone who took up as much space as I did.

"Don't get us started," Bianca continued, rolling her eyes in Phoebe's direction, and I snapped back to the reality in which my entire world was dissolving into a fizzing liquid of panic. "She's befriended multiple members of the waitstaff so they hold a table for her whenever she wants."

"You should be *happy* about this," Phoebe said to Bianca, though her gaze dragged over me and then abruptly away. "Who wants to wait in line for brunch?"

"It's because you're *too happy* about it," Bianca said, but she shot Phoebe a smile I recognized, the exhaustedly delighted feeling when your significant other did something both annoying and thoroughly *them*. "But, sure. Go check in."

Everyone—everyone but me, obviously—laughed as Phoebe walked into the restaurant. Another obviously queer couple walked up to us, and I wondered just how large this friend group was. And was it all couples? Suddenly I had a lot more sympathy for Chloe, navigating this on her own. I'd only been single for a very short amount of time, and it had taken no time for Fiona and Hailey to demote me to a sadder human, but at least our hangouts were just us, not me and multiple happy couples. We had occasionally hung out in couples, all six of us, but it had hardly been the regular.

"It's so good to see you, Clementine," Nina said. She looked the same, glossy brown hair like a brunette Disney princess, a flowy floral maxidress, and no-nonsense Birkenstocks.

"You too," I said, genuinely. I'd been suspicious the other year when Phoebe had let me know she'd hired a friend as a marketing coordinator when a position on the creative team opened up, but Nina had been so friendly and funny whenever we ran into each other around the office—plus we had similar taste in style, which was sometimes the quickest way two plus-sized women bonded. BME was also a small company, so word spread quickly regarding just about anything. This meant that, not long after she'd started, I also found out that she was exceedingly good at her job. Somehow, though, it wasn't until that season's Oscars when Nina took a bunch of time off work and then showed up in the televised audience *kissing the best supporting actress winner* that office gossip caught up on the fact that she was in a relationship with an indie film darling. It surprised none of us when, not too long after, she left BME for a TV-writing gig. The news of her engagement reached me—not on social media, of course, I valued my work/life boundaries way too much for that!—via entertainment news reporting Oscar winner Ari Fox's engagement.

"You've met Ari, right?" Nina continued.

"Holiday party, yeah," Ari said, stepping around Nina and passing off the dog's leash to her so she could shake my hand. "Good to see you."

Ari Fox, it should be said, was extremely attractive. Movie star attractive. Cheekbones that could cut diamonds, sleek asymmetrical haircut, skin without visible pores, a smile that felt like a secret just for you. It was overwhelming. *She* was overwhelming. And also just, apparently, a regular member of Chloe's friend group. The group that also included my boss and a former coworker. This ridiculous fake-dating scenario was nothing, as I'd obviously hoped, like the queer training wheels I needed to ride a gay bike or however I should finish that metaphor. This was like the LGBTour de France.

"And this of course is Cristina," Nina said, gesturing to the dog. "Cristina, meet Clementine."

The dog—Cristina?!—held up a paw to shake.

"Oh my god," I said, shaking her fluffy paw, "so cute. It's nice to meet you, Cristina."

"Traitor," Chloe mumbled, and I barely swallowed a laugh.

"I think we've met, too," said one of the people who'd just arrived. "I'm CJ, they/them pronouns."

I shook their hand, vaguely remembering their expensive-looking buzz cut—how did a buzz cut look expensive?—and the way their button-down-over-jeans look was somehow a little preppy, a little rumpled, and very queer all at the same time. I worried I should have remembered everyone better. And I worried—for the eighth or ninth time today—that I didn't look queer enough to be taken seriously here, but among this group I didn't really stick out, at least visually. Everyone absolutely had their own look going on.

"I'm not sure we've met," said the person who'd arrived with CJ. "I'm Sofia, she/her pronouns."

"Clementine, she/her as well," I said, shaking Sofia's hand. Her black hair was curly on top and faded to a buzz on the sides, probably by the same expensive and queer barber who'd done CJ's hair, and her striped T-shirt, faded jeans, and perfectly-creased-at-the-toe Doc Martens were both an impeccable 90s look and a perfect complement to CJ's outfit. I wondered if Chloe and I made sense together aesthetically. And then I wondered if that mattered. I never minded that Will had a perpetual jeans-tee-hoodie situation, never thought I needed to complement or contrast. Was it different? Was this something I could also frantically google?

And also why was I worrying about something literally surface-level like clothes when *my boss was here*?

Phoebe returned with a server who led us to a table for eight, magically held as promised. I ended up between Chloe and CJ, and directly across from Phoebe.

"Should I order some wine for the table?" Ari asked.

"As long as Chloe has something to drink," I said, almost automatically, and then felt strange for bringing up a small and specific and potentially sensitive detail.

"I'll be fine," Chloe said with a hand wave, and I saw the couples exchange little smiles. As a former-but-recent member of a long-term couple, I knew the look well. I knew, mind-blowingly, that all the real couples thought that this fake one was adorable.

"They have those European orange sodas I think," I said, which made Chloe laugh.

"I figure out what to drink all the time, you know," she said with a well-placed elbow to my side.

"Sorry, I made it weird. I actually really like those sodas."

"Well, me too," she said, rolling her eyes, though I could see a smile sparkling behind the expression. "European sodas are all better than American."

"That's true," Nina said. "Diet Coke is so good over in the UK."

"I can't believe you spent your European vacation *drinking Diet Coke*," Phoebe said.

"Not exclusively Diet Coke," Nina said. "Most countries have Coke Zero."

"Yeah, picture it, Sicily, last year, my beautiful and sophisticated fiancée bypassing a local red for a can of European's finest Coke Zero," Ari said with a heavy sigh, and the whole table cracked up. Even the dog seemed amused.

"I *also* drank the red," Nina said, which just made us laugh even harder.

And then the waiter came and we ended up with two bottles of wine for the table, and orange soda for everyone, and as everyone laughed at Nina listing the beverages she'd consumed in England, France, and Italy, I felt something relax in me. Seated across from my boss or not, it was a hard group to hang out with and manage to stay too much in one's own head.

"How's business, Chloe?" Phoebe asked, once we'd all put in our orders. From the way everyone looked her way, I could tell she was basically the president and CEO of this group as well.

"It's been good," Chloe said with a shrug. "It's always steady."

"Have you thought about ways you could grow it?" Phoebe asked, and even though others were turning and leaning to start other side conversations—and even though I was eager to be part of something here that didn't have to do with Phoebe—I couldn't pull my attention away to focus on anyone else.

"I'm just one person, remember," Chloe said. "I'm good."

"As long as Pomeranians don't flake," I said, and then worried I shouldn't have butted in. Not just to *any* conversation here, but one with Phoebe, specifically.

But Chloe laughed. "As long as that, yeah."

Phoebe still looked serious. I'd seen this narrowed gaze countless times in meetings when clients were eager to bring up nonsense and she needed to keep the room on task. "You wouldn't have to just be one person, though. You slowly expand your workforce, you add people who groom cats, you up your advertising budget—I'm sure Clementine has already suggested ads on Meta, Nextdoor, even—"

"No, Phoebe, believe it or not," Chloe said with a patient smile, "that hasn't yet come up between us."

By now everyone's focus had shifted to us, and, this was it, and so quickly! An opportunity was here already: the friends would see through this charade, Phoebe in particular would finally voice the strangeness that was the two of us in this social situation together, and not only would this be a temporarily humiliating situation, I'd probably have to quit my job and then move to some remote village where no one had ever heard about fake dating and my participation in it.

But the entire table sans Phoebe burst into laughter, and it was obvious from the direction that laughter was facing that it was at Phoebe's expense and not Chloe's and mine.

"I remember early on in our relationship," Nina said, her eyes darting between Ari and Phoebe, "all those romantic texts we sent each other about digital marketing."

"Constantly," Ari said, completely deadpan, and even Phoebe joined in the laughter this time. Chloe and I were off the hook!

"Wait, I have a question," CJ said, their tone serious, and my heart sped up yet again. Was this it? CJ seemed so quiet and contemplative; was this what was going on in their head this whole time? "Is flaking a Pomeranian thing?"

"Oh my god, I asked the same thing the other day!" I said, relief flooding my system and amping up my tone more enthusiastically than the situation called for. CJ, though, high-fived me, and then the rest of the crew was making up fake dog stereotypes. ("Nothing bad about Border collies, though, right?" Ari asked in a tone that seemed earnest.) Our food arrived and almost before I knew it, we were back on the sidewalk in front of the restaurant, and it was all but over.

"We should relieve our sitter," Phoebe said, as Nina and Ari were asking their dog to shake hands goodbye with everyone. This time, I nudged Chloe and she shot me a tiny but clear side-eye, and we managed not to allude to any more than that until we had said goodbye to all the humans as well and had gotten back into my car.

"See?"

"The dog is . . . a lot," I agreed. "But . . ."

"But she's cute and who *doesn't* like to shake hands with a dog so I should just get over it?"

"Well—" I started, and we both laughed. "No, Chloe. Did you not think it was important to warn me that one of your friends *is my boss*?"

She raised her eyebrows as I swung the car out of its spot. "That's how we met."

"Sure, a work party is how we met. That doesn't automatically translate to *have brunch with me and your boss and her wife and also your former coworker and her Oscar-winning fiancée.*"

"Who else's wedding situation would I need a plus-one to?" she asked in the most *this is so obvious* tone, and something jolted in my chest.

"And that was also information you didn't think was important?"

"No, that was information I assumed you already knew," she said, casually.

"So this whole arrangement is so I'll travel with you *and my boss* to some destination wedding where a celebrity is marrying someone I used to work with."

"You've summed it up well, Clementine," Chloe said.

I opened my mouth to speak, but I couldn't think of what to say that would make it more obvious than it already was. Part of me was convinced that Chloe had withheld all of this because *who would agree to it otherwise*? But her manner was seemingly so blasé and also unrehearsed that it was hard to believe she'd trapped me here on purpose.

I knew that I didn't want to believe she'd trapped me here on purpose. Because what kind of person did that make her? And what kind of person did that make *me*, because maybe I'd let myself get trapped anyway.

"Thanks for driving," Chloe said as I pulled up to my condo. "Next week you can meet me at my place and meet Fernando and then I'll drive."

"What do you mean, next week?"

"Brunch is weekly," she said with a shrug before hopping out of the car. "Good first one, though!"

She slammed the door before I could respond, which for all I knew was the traditional ending for a fake date! And that was probably for the best, because what could I have said anyway? *I can't wait to meet your dog, I do not care that he doesn't shake hands like a tiny businessman.*

The thought made me laugh, so I texted it to Chloe as soon as I pulled into my parking space. She tapped the *haha* reaction on my text almost immediately, and—despite every single reason I shouldn't have smiled at anything to do with this situation—I grinned at the thought of making Chloe Lee laugh yet again. Somehow I'd managed to finish the LGBTour de France after all.

Though normally when people made it across that finish line, they weren't less than twenty-four hours out from rehashing the details with *their boss*—not that this metaphor was holding very well. All I knew for sure was that I didn't feel anything like a winner.

Chapter 6

A Flattering Turning Radius

Early at work the next morning—so early that I was still sipping my iced espresso I picked up every day on the way in—Phoebe leaned into my office.

I'd worked several jobs before landing this one at BME. It had been a fluke that the first one had landed me in media planning, as an assistant to a studio executive at Disney. Yes, I'd studied marketing in college, but I'd spent my undergrad years working on creative strategies, designing ads and writing copy and building pitch decks. I showed up to the informational interview my friend's mom had snagged me with my creative portfolio in hand, only to be asked in increasing detail about my Microsoft Excel skills. Before I knew it, I'd been offered a temp gig in the media planning department, covering assistant duties while the team interviewed to find a long-term assistant.

For all of those dreams of being some modern Peggy Olson, I really *was* skilled at Microsoft Excel. And all of those brilliant ideas dreamed up by the other Peggys and Dons of the world had to go *somewhere*, and the *somewhere* was what media planners handled. We were the ones to figure out what TV show to run the ad in, or where the beautifully designed billboard should be located, or how much to spend buying sponsored posts across social media platforms.

It had never been the side of advertising I was interested in, but even straight out of college I was savvy enough to know that, even in Los Angeles, studio jobs didn't necessarily come along every day. It was close enough to the work I actually wanted to do, so I threw myself into the work. I was offered the long-term job, and before I knew it, I was years into a career in media planning. Sometimes Will told me he was sorry my creative dreams had died—which was rich coming from someone going over lines of code every day—but I really didn't see it that way anyway. There were still ways to be creative within my role, it just looked a little different than I'd planned.

And, truly, what about life didn't?

Before BME, the work had been stressful. Clients who couldn't make decisions and then blamed me when media opportunities were no longer available. Bosses who asked for fifteen different versions of the same report and then sent over emails to clients taking none of that info into account. A cost-effective and brilliant plan basically laid to ruin because the creative shop couldn't get client approval on the ads in time and yet somehow blamed my team. When I landed the interview at this new female-led boutique entertainment marketing agency, I was excited but knew realistically that it would likely be more of the same. Yeah, film and TV were a lot more interesting than that six-month stretch when I got placed on an agency's consumer-packaged-goods team and did research on potential mouthwash consumers, but the pressure was *a lot more*, too. There was only one season premiere, there was only one opening box office weekend, and execs were always eager to blame any failure on the marketing team. It often created a culture of fear, and I wondered if it was worth it, just because it was more interesting to market the latest season of my favorite premium cable prestige drama than Listerine.

Then I'd interviewed with Phoebe and felt the vibe shift almost immediately. She'd come from the same sorts of roles I had—only more creative and much further up the chain of command—and didn't want to keep living in that world of fear and blame, either. She built her own company so she could do the work she loved but in a world that rewarded not just hard work but collaboration and cooperation. It was, by far, the most functional place I'd ever worked, and I admired Phoebe beyond how I'd ever thought of a boss before.

Which is why it was most assuredly *not great* that I was pulling some sort of shenanigan on her, no matter how chill Chloe was about the whole thing.

"May I?" Phoebe asked, gesturing to my door. *Oh, god.* But I nodded, since she was the boss, and she stepped in and closed the door behind her. *Oh, god times two.*

"I should say—"

"I'm so sorry, Clementine," Phoebe said, running a hand back through her short hair. "I feel terrible."

I didn't know how to respond or what she could have to feel terrible about and I also didn't know why I'd blurted out *I should say* because what should I even say? So I took another sip of my iced espresso instead of trying to finish my sentence.

"I know that sometimes the queer community—especially, I know, lesbians—have had a history of excluding bi and pan folks, or denying their queerness. But I want you to know that I don't feel that way at all," she said in a heartfelt tone. "I'm well aware that bi-erasure and such is rampant in the queer community, but I do my best to push back on that whenever I can. I married a bisexual person, after all! I'm friends with plenty of people who identify as bi or pan."

I noted her slightly higher-pitched tone, the quicker cadence of her speech, and I realized for maybe the first time that I'd ever witnessed, Phoebe Reyes was *nervous.*

"All of that talk the other evening about straight people being capable," she said, shaking her head. "I apologize."

"Oh," I said. "I'd practically forgotten about that."

"No, I know better than to assume someone's sexuality and then put them into the position of having to nod and agree with an untruth or out themselves on someone else's schedule. I just thought—no, it doesn't matter what I thought. And I'm also sorry for all of that *some of my best friends are bi*-ing I did just now!"

"I was with Will for a long time," I said. "You didn't know. And it sounds like some of your best friends *are* bi."

Phoebe laughed, but her expression softened. I'd always liked that she could be tough as the industry required when need be but it never seemed to compromise who she was the rest of the time. "I also hadn't realized that you and Will had broken up. Not that you're required to report that to your boss, of course."

"I just don't like talking about personal things at work," I said, in as nice a tone as I could muster. Because now it felt like this was all personal. Since brunch yesterday, the personal was extremely unavoidable.

"Of course," Phoebe said with a nod. "But—"

"But Chloe didn't tell me brunch involved you, so, here I am," I said, still trying to sound nice.

"No, of course she didn't," Phoebe said with a laugh. "But— sorry, how awkward is this?"

"Oh, god, *very*," I said, thrilled we could just acknowledge that, and we laughed together.

"I know we both are cautious of not overstepping any boundaries of professionalism, but I'll still say that I hope this present awkwardness doesn't negatively affect your relationship with Chloe."

"Oh, no," I said, shaking my head as if the notion was ridiculous. After all, for reasons entirely unknown to Phoebe, every related notion was ridiculous.

"Chloe's one of my favorite people in my entire life," Phoebe continued. "She's family to me. I wouldn't stand in the way of her happiness merely because of some light office awkwardness."

"OK," I said, and Phoebe chuckled.

"I'd say that you're off the hook and we never have to discuss this again, but unless you broke up with Chloe yesterday for throwing you to the wolves and by *the wolves* I mean *me*, it seems that we'll be seeing plenty of each other now."

"I didn't, so, yeah. I guess so."

"We'll navigate it," Phoebe said, sounding a lot more like her usual confident self. "And I'll follow your lead—no one here needs to know the details of your personal life, and no one in your personal life has to know any details about your job."

"Besides you," I said, and we both laughed again.

"Besides me, exactly." She gestured to my door. "I have a thousand or so emails to get through, and I'm sure you do too, so I won't keep you any longer. But, truly, I'm sorry for any assumptions I might have made, and I'll do better moving forward."

"It's really—" I caught myself because what even was it? It didn't feel right granting someone forgiveness when you were the one caught up in some fake scenario that might look a lot to an outside party like lying. I guess to an inside party, too.

Luckily Phoebe was already on her phone and headed out, so it didn't seem to matter that I never finished my sentence.

Chloe texted toward the end of the workday, a vague **What are you doing tonight? Errands I should have run yesterday,** I typed. Two glasses of wine and a large French brunch had not been conducive to the productivity I'd imagined for the rest of my Sunday. **Why?**

Why the air of suspicion? Was just going to ask you to grab drinks if you were interested, but sounds like you've got boring things to worry about instead.

Excuse me, nothing is LESS boring than making sure Small Jesse Pinkman has enough food and treats to survive in the manner to which he's now accustomed.

I went back to the post-campaign report I was analyzing, but my phone buzzed again. And then it buzzed several more times in succession.

You're right, that isn't boring. If you're going to some fancy hipster pet store, let me tag along. Fernando is dangerously low on several items vital to his comfort level as well. Also this is your warning that you just got added to the group text chain.

I scrolled back on my phone and saw that, already, the conversation was about eleven messages deep from unknown numbers about brunch options for next Sunday.

FYI a warning tends to come BEFORE and not after something's already happened.

Chloe responded with a gif of Dana Scully with a caption that read **If this is monkey pee, you're on your own** that made me burst into surprised laughter.

Wait, what does this have to do with anything? Honestly I'm a little afraid to ask.

Ask for forgiveness, not permission. And distract them with hot fictional FBI agents. Are we going out for organic pet food or what, Clementine?

I couldn't remember the last time I'd run boring errands with anyone other than Will. Were errands a couple thing? Was

Chloe somehow planning for us to run into her friends, caught in the act of the mundane intimacy of pet-food shopping? Had I overthought this? No one, of course, had taught me the right level of thought I was supposed to put into a real-life fake-dating scenario. In fact, nothing beyond romance novels had prepared me for such a situation at all.

Chloe texted me her address, and I swung over and parked on her block. Her apartment was a second-story walk-up in a nondescript building off of Commonwealth Avenue. Once she let me in, though, I grinned at the bright décor filling the space; it was less twee and maximalist than my décor, but overall not a dissimilar vibe.

I stepped in to check out a framed geometric print, but I'd barely managed to move when a small blur of brown frizzly fur barreled at me.

"Hey, buddy, this is my friend Clementine," Chloe said, dropping down low so she was at the same level as the dog, who had ears like if a teddy bear was . . . pointy. And stressed out. "Clementine, Fernando."

"Is he named after the Abba song?" I asked, and she cracked up while the small terrier gave me what I could only read as a suspicious and questioning look and then barked about seven times in high-pitched succession.

"Not entirely," she said, scratching between his ears. "I found him wandering traffic on San Fernando. But, yes, the Abba song sealed the deal."

"Your place is *cute*," I said, gesturing at the walls, filled with artwork in bright shades. I was still figuring out mine, now that I wasn't compromising Will's minimalist style with my own, which was . . . decidedly less so. "Your apartment's big enough to have a front room!"

"I know, I pay next to nothing and it's enormous. My land-lady's super old, though, and I know her kids will wait about five minutes after she dies to jack up my rent."

"Fingers crossed she lives forever," I said. "I mean, not just because of your rent."

"LA's a seller's market," she says. "It's OK if it's just because of my rent."

We both laughed, and Fernando sniffed my legs and shoes with the energy of an anteater on cocaine. I found myself hoping I was making a good impression on him, Chloe's actual best friend. His tail wagged as he continued sniffing and the sharp barks had decreased both in volume and quantity, so I glanced at Chloe, my eyebrows raised.

"Wow, you are *desperate* for his approval," she said, and I wondered if I was that obvious or if she could just read me that well. "Let's go."

I followed her out the door and then she led us behind the building to a parking lot where she unlocked the doors to an old light-blue Bronco. Up until that moment I hadn't thought much about what Chloe drove, but this vehicle did seem right.

"Pet food and then human food?" she asked.

"Does *human food* mean the grocery store or does it mean dinner?" I asked.

"Great question. I guess it could mean either, but I meant dinner where I paid someone to make food for me."

"Dinner where someone else makes food for me sounds great to me, too," I said, even though—what even *was* this? For some reason my only instinct at the moment was to go with the flow. "So does every brunch option of the thirteen or so that's been floated in the group chat for next week. Is it always like this?"

"*Always*," she said, shifting the manual gearshift as she took off down Sunset.

"Fernando's really cute," I said. "He doesn't seem like a demon at all."

Chloe let out what I could only describe as *a guffaw*. "I didn't say he was a demon! Only a snarly asshole."

"He didn't seem like that either," I said. "Well, *too much* like that."

"Yeah, well," she said, shooting me a look, "he liked you. But don't let that go to your head."

"Too late," I said, and we both laughed. Chloe drove to the pet store in Los Feliz that had a mural of strangely proportioned animals on its front windows, including a dog that looked like ALF. Inside, I grabbed everything Small Jesse Pinkman needed while Chloe lugged around a giant bag of dog food.

"You must be strong," I said, and immediately regretted it because complimenting someone's strength always carried at least a whiff of flirtation. As of now, I couldn't even tell if Chloe was someone I'd flirt with for real, if the situation was different. It was hardly that she wasn't hot—because of course she was. And of course I could feel that she knew that, the way I felt certain anyone who could be described as *a real live wire* walked around with a few extra helpings of confidence. When I'd imagined my hypothetical queer future, it had hardly been with a real live wire though; whoever I fell for, I was sure, would feel safe and comfortable, just the way Will had from almost the very first moment.

"I do OK," Chloe said seemingly effortlessly despite the giant bag in her arms. "It's important in my line of work."

"Do you have to groom giant dogs?" I asked as we walked up to the checkout.

"Sometimes I do, yeah. Me and a Great Dane, it's weird how equally matched we are."

The cashier glanced between us. "I'm ringing these up together?"

"Absolutely," Chloe said before I could even wrap my head around being read as a couple by a complete stranger. It was more, it hit me, than mildly flattering.

"I can Venmo you for that," I said as we carried our purchases out to her Bronco. Her purchases, really.

"Nah, let me do at least one nice thing for Small Jesse Pinkman," she said. "Do you have any other errands to run or should we figure out our human food situation now?"

"That was mainly it. And he really has plenty of food! I'm just nervous about running out. I've never had someone solely dependent on me before, and it's mildly stressful."

"Yeah, I felt the same way when I got Fernando. I didn't stockpile food or anything but I did maintain an impressive arsenal of low-level anxiety."

"Really? You don't seem like someone who gets anxious."

She exhaled loudly as she backed out of the parking space. "Why is everyone always like this about me? Chloe, you seem like you never cry or feel nervous or have feelings!"

"Shit," I said, because while of course I didn't literally say that, that was absolutely at the heart of what I had. "I'm sorry."

"Whatever," she said, her eyebrows drawn together and creased as she pulled out onto Hillhurst. "I'm used to it."

"Yeah, well, you shouldn't have to be and I—" I laughed as I decided to just say what I thought. "I don't know. People who can drive a stick always seem so tough and no-nonsense."

Chloe's scowl lifted as she burst into laughter. "Clementine! I am *full* of nonsense, what are you talking about?"

"You *are* tough, though," I said, secure about that much even though, really, Chloe and I barely knew each other. "I mean, you lifted that giant bag of dog food. You lift Great Danes all the time."

"I'm *strong*," she said. "And I only lift Great Danes occasionally."

"I promise I'll start treating you like the nonsense-filled strong person you are," I said. "Until whenever that wedding is. I should have checked in on that already, actually."

"It's in two months," Chloe said, sounding unconcerned about my availability. Maybe that much was fair. "The last week in September."

"I can make that work," I said, instead of dwelling on my very empty calendar, though that did remind me—"Actually then, a couple more weeks than that? I can't show up single to my parents' anniversary party."

I had no idea how showing up *visibly queer* at my parents' anniversary party would go, but it was at least honest. Well, as honest as a fake girlfriend could be. Which I suppose wasn't very. How was this so confusing and convoluted already? There was a reason I hated this trope.

"Great, then it's two months plus two weeks," Chloe said, sounding very casual for someone enacting a whole set of lies.

Though, to be fair, that described me as well. To *also* be fair, though, I didn't feel very casual about it! I was going to introduce my fake girlfriend to my family metaphorical moments before we ended it, just to make one measly party less painful?

Then Greg and Marisol's email flashed through my mind again—*Poor Clem*—and I knew I only wanted to walk into that party next to a significant other. Fake or not.

"Where am I driving?" Chloe asked. "What do you want for dinner?"

"Make a U-turn and see if we can get a table at All Time?" I asked.

"Oh, god, they have the best salad," Chloe said. "Wait, don't judge me for that. A salad is so boring to get excited about."

"No, I love that salad. Make a U-turn!"

Chloe laughed, turning right down the next side street. "Clementine, I'm extremely flattered you think this vehicle has the turning radius for U-turns."

Chapter 7
Queer Sins

We only waited a few minutes for a table at All Time, which felt like a miracle, even on a weeknight. Every even semi-decent restaurant on the Eastside seemed an impossible mission without a reservation, but to me it was part of the fun. I loved snagging a table, I loved a shorter wait than usual, I loved choosing a restaurant just because we could get a table without waiting and discovering how delicious the food was. Sure, the group chat I'd been added to was *perhaps* a bit ridiculous in their attention to a brunch restaurant selection, but there was also a tiny voice whispering that these were my people.

All Time looked like a lot of other restaurants around here—a big, airy dining room and an outdoor patio, where Chloe and I were seated, packed with plant life and wooden tables and chairs, tucked away just enough it was easy to forget you were on a busy street in a busy neighborhood. I knew that people back home, my parents and brother included, hated the idea of the hustle and noise of LA proper. But once you lived here, you knew how to find patches of calm.

If this were a real date, it would be pretty perfect. As things stood, though, now that I had time to sit and the conversation had paused, I wondered again what exactly we were doing. Pet food in the car, a fairly romantic ambiance, and witnesses to our sham of a coupledom nowhere to be found.

"What are we doing?" I asked, right as Chloe said, "This feels like right after college."

"What?" I asked her, and I realized I was relieved to have an excuse to not dive into whatever talk I was about to launch.

"You know, you and your roommates, running errands and getting food together after work," she said, looking up from her menu. "Though back then it was more like a Big Gulp and a 7-Eleven hot dog. Before I blew half my weekly budget on drinks at the Good Luck Bar or wherever."

"Oh, I miss that place," I said. "I feel like being in your thirties is just this constant stream of RIPs to places you loved."

"People you loved, too," Chloe said, propping up her chin with her fist. "Wow, sorry, that was immediately darker than I meant to take us."

"Accidentally dark also feels like just another side effect of being in your thirties," I said, and Chloe laughed. The level at which I liked making Chloe laugh may have been far too high, but at least I was on to that fact. "I'm kind of jealous of that post-college experience. I moved back here with Will, so we were just . . ."

"Domesticating?"

"Yeah, something like that. Pretending to be upstanding grown-ups. Before we bought the condo just a few years ago, we loved going to open houses for expensive places we could never afford, just to see what they were like inside, acting like we belonged there with all the real grownups. I don't know if I regret it, exactly—we had so much fun then, sometimes I think that was like the most in love we ever were." It was actually something I realized as I said it, and it hit me like a rush of heartbreak and nostalgia, the way things were. "I went out with my friends, of course, happy hours were the biggest deal in the world to us back then. But errands and hot dogs and too much money spent on whatever I was drinking in my twenties—whiskey sours?—sounds really fun too."

"Whiskey sours here too," Chloe said, her grin stretching out even wider. If this were a real date, I was pretty sure I'd think it was going well. As things stood—actually, that reminded me. Even if I wasn't sure I should tempt messing with the vibe right now.

"So—"

The waiter popped up to take our order, and I decided to ignore that it felt like the universe was telling me to let go of the question and the unsettled footing lurking beneath the entire evening.

"So," I said again, after our order was in and yet before Chloe had a chance to say anything else distracting. "Can I ask what exactly we're doing here?"

She shot me one of her ridiculously charming grins. "Having dinner, Clementine."

"Don't," I said, though not smiling was truly impossible. "You know what I mean."

Chloe shrugged. "I needed dog food. You needed cat food. And we both needed human food, as we've reviewed."

"Well, sure, but—"

"Are you accusing me of something?" she asked.

"No," I said quickly. "*No.* But—"

Another server stopped by with my cocktail and Chloe's mocktail, and I laughed and held up my glass so she'd clink it.

"I genuinely feel like the universe is like, please stop talking, Clementine, and yet I'm ignoring it."

"I respect that," Chloe said. "Shut up, universe. Clementine is speaking."

"Anyway, yes, I am your fake date until the wedding is over and my parents' fortieth has been celebrated," I said. "But tonight?"

"I don't think I'm guilty of any subterfuge," Chloe said.

"No, but—actually, can I say something?"

She didn't smile, but her dark eyes flashed with—well, with *something*. "Always."

"So maybe this isn't something I made explicitly clear, but my work/life boundaries are really important to me. Like I'm not friends with any of my coworkers on Instagram or whatever. And I get that you couldn't have known all of that, but I really can't believe you let me show up to brunch *with my boss* with no warning." I took a deep breath, hoping my tone wasn't harsh. I didn't feel harsh, after all, just unmoored. "And like now. It feels like you have some whole plan you're enacting, and I'm just at your mercy.

"And if this was just it, the brunch and it's all over, the wedding this weekend, fine. But we're in for more than two months of this, and I feel like—honestly, I don't know what I feel like." I didn't want to say *unmoored* aloud; no one even semi-normal threw around *unmoored*. "We joked around about parameters, but maybe we need actual ones."

"If you feel like there's some big plan I'm enacting, I can promise you I am definitely *not*," she said, casual as always despite we were having a conversation in which I almost said *unmoored* in a shriekish tone. "I barely plan anything. Which, sure, is its own problem. But maybe not the one you think is happening. Clementine, I *wish* I was some grand mastermind."

I laughed, and thanked a server as he dropped off the aforementioned salad for us to split.

"Also," I continued, "you only mentioned that it was a wedding."

Chloe shrugged. "What other information did you require?"

"No, seriously, come on," I said. "It is a *celebrity's* wedding. It involves *my boss*. And I have to assume, mastermind or no, you knew that if I knew all of this going in, I would never have agreed to do this in the first place—don't shrug casually again."

"Clementine," she said, leaning in to dish the salad onto our small plates. "I don't know how else to shrug."

"Seriously, though."

"I *am* serious!" She laughed, though, which hurt her case. "Come on. I need a date. You need someone to refer to as your ex-girlfriend so you don't scare all your prospects off with your baby-gay status. This is a win-win."

I decided to focus on eating instead of weighing whether or not this situation was actually win-win. Or my apparently terrifying baby-gay status.

"And tonight was really as simple as errands and food," Chloe continued. "I don't really miss my twenties, but I do miss that. Now everyone's basically married with kids or pets and it's harder to grab someone for a couple hours to do anything. Not that my friends aren't all incredible people, but I guess sometimes I miss when they weren't also so *mature*."

"I know you probably think I'm full of shit, but I do know what you mean," I said. "I know I was with Will for, like, my entire youth, but, yeah. When my best friends got married and one had a kid, it felt different. Not that I don't want people to prioritize their partners and children, but . . . I don't know. Even when things were great with Will, I could feel how my friends seemed to be getting less willing to put aside other things to meet up or whatever. Sometimes I worry I just refuse to grow up."

"You're very adult!" Chloe said. "You have a job I don't even understand, you own a condo, you have a car from this century, you provide for Small Jesse Pinkman."

"Oh, right, that adult checklist I forgot about, nailed it." I ate a few bites of salad. "I do like that you and your friends seem to prioritize each other so much. Weekly brunches. An exhaustingly active group chat."

"No, they're good. There's my disclaimer about my friends. They are wonderful people and I should probably feel worse about lying to them than I do."

A server dropped off our strip steak and sauteed greens we'd decided to split, and Chloe got to work right away dividing everything.

"So I really understand why you don't want to do the whole friends' wedding thing dateless," I said, and speared a piece of steak with my fork. "Oh my god, this is so good."

"*So good*," Chloe said, closing her eyes. "I know it's practically a queer LA sin not to be a vegetarian, but, *fuck*, I love red meat."

"Where are you from?" I asked, thinking about all the time we were about to spend together and the fact that I barely knew her at all. "Sorry, not in a racist way. Just, where did you grow up? Sorry, is that worse?"

Chloe laughed so hard she choked on her mocktail. "I'm from the Bay Area. And it didn't sound racist until you started piling on all those disclaimers. My family is from Korea, by the way."

"Not that I asked!"

She was still laughing. "Not that you asked. What about you?"

"The suburbs here. Valencia is what I tell people, since it sounds better than Saugus. My parents are still there, so are my brother and his wife and his kids."

"Agreed, Saugus is a gross word," she said. "Nina used to live up there, but you knew that already."

"I didn't," I said. "Remember? Work/life boundaries."

Chloe wrinkled her nose. "There's not wanting to see pictures of your coworkers in their swimsuits or whatever, but it seems weird you didn't know Nina had basically just moved from the same place you grew up. Do you not talk to people?"

"Well, not about personal things, no."

She gave me a look like I'd just announced I'd actually been born on Mars, so I went back to my steak which didn't judge me at all.

"You should talk to people," she said. "It's weird if you don't."

"I don't think it is," I said. "I think there are just different ways of being a person, and I'm not the kind who . . ."

"The kind who *talks to people*?" Chloe cracked up, and I had to admit that it didn't sound great. "Maybe you should try to be, then."

"Hmmm," I said, which only made her laugh harder, even though I had not set out to be funny. "Anyway. I do understand why you're doing this."

"Encouraging you to act like a semi-normal person?" That charming smile was back, as if she was fully in charge of how it was deployed. I suspected that she was.

"Pretending to date me to get through your friends' wedding," I said. "Through the queer celebrity wedding of the fall or whatever. But . . . this isn't like a weird movie from the eighties where you have to show up with a particular date to a particular event in order to get your weird aunt's inheritance or whatever. So why don't you just get a real date and take her?"

Chloe wrinkled her nose. "I don't want a real date."

"Oh," I said. "Do you not—actually, I don't know if this is any of my business. I'm not trying to overstep any boundaries and barge into your identity."

"Oh, no, I'm not aromantic or anything, if that's what you're getting at," she said. "You're nice to check. I just am not great with relationships. I like my space, and I like not having to ask someone else what we're doing that weekend, and I like coming home and having nothing but complete silence and Fernando greet me. And it sucks that people—including people I love dearly—act as if that's not a valid adult life."

"I know what you mean," I said, even though it was only some of that, the white picket fence and two-point-five kids life, that I didn't want, no big white dress or old-fashioned traditions. Finding a person to spend forever with was still highest on my list of life goals. Now that Will was out of the picture, it sounded with a new urgency.

That said, coming home to silence plus Small Jesse Pinkman had been nicer than I would have guessed.

"So, no, I don't want to make some poor girl deal with me," Chloe said. "Whereas you know exactly what you're getting into."

I laughed. "Besides my boss and the Oscar winner."

"Exactly, besides that!" Chloe cracked up again. "Don't bail on me now, Clementine. We need each other way too much for that."

I hadn't even thought about bailing, though, because the only thing more awkward than showing up to that brunch with Phoebe would be if I were to never show up again. I knew that if I quit this whole stupid shenanigan, my boss would clearly find out I'd been lying to her face and I'd then obviously have to also quit my job and start a new life with a new identity, somewhere no one had ever heard of me or Chloe Lee.

And I was fairly certain that awkward fake-dating scenarios did not actually qualify for the Witness Protection Program. Which meant there was no getting out of this.

The texts started the next morning, before I'd even left for the office.

Clementine, we've been discussing, and it is CRAZY that you have A GIRLFRIEND and WE HAVEN'T EVEN MET HER YET!

While I am, as always, startled by Hailey's commitment to all-caps, I'm in firm agreement with her sentiment. Let's plan drinks soon. Dinner?

What kind of food does she like? Should we pick somewhere FANCY? Do we need to impress her??

I assume she lives on the Eastside near you; I've never met a lesbian who doesn't.

FIONA! I told you that you can't just assume she's a lesbian. She might be bi like Clementine! Or pansexual, a lot of people are pansexual these days.

"Oh my god," I muttered aloud. Small Jesse Pinkman scrambled over because he assumed that if I was talking, I was talking to him. I admired how much he centered himself, honestly.

"This is going to sound very obvious," I told him, scritching between his little ears, "but it turns out that this fake-dating situation with Chloe may create more stress than it solves."

Small Jesse Pinkman purred, his eyes closed in bliss. It must have been nice.

"OK, little buddy, since you seem out of actionable advice, I should go to work."

My phone dinged as I let myself out.

Trust me, the pansexuals all live on the Eastside too.

Chapter 8
Like Normal Humans

Obviously, in retrospect, I should have been even more nervous to roll up to brunch last Sunday. Hindsight, etc. Still, my anxiety had not been at a particularly low level. Tonight, though, on the way to dinner with Hailey, Fiona, *and Chloe*, my nerves had found new heights to soar. They had self-actualized!

"You're making a weird face," Chloe said, as I parked the car a block down Hyperion Avenue from Casita Del Campo. "And you're comfortable being so terrible at parallel parking, so I know it's not that."

"Wait, is it that bad?" I shrugged and turned off the car, already giving up straightening out the car any more. "I just need this to go OK. There are at least a million ways it could go sideways."

"You're overthinking this," she said, hopping out to the curb.

I sighed and took my time grabbing my bag and joining her on the sidewalk. "I'm not. If anything, you're underthinking it. What we're doing is *ridiculous* and if we get found out—"

"How would we get *found out*?" A laugh bubbled out of

Chloe. "Do you think your friends are going to be all *are you two only pretending to be together so that you can avoid awkward social scenarios?* No one will think that."

"No, but we don't know each other very well."

"That's *normal* early on," Chloe said. "Do you expect them to quiz us like some old nineteen sixties game show?"

"Not with those handwritten cards or anything, no," I said. "Fiona can just be—I don't know. Very focused."

"She's the one who loves capitalism," Chloe said, nodding. "The other one's the mom."

"No, don't say she's *the mom*, she's a whole person besides that," I said, even if I apparently hadn't made that clear enough for Chloe to realize it. I tried to think of a quick fact about Hailey to offer Chloe, but someone walked up quickly behind me and I did my best to step out of the way right as I saw that it was Fiona.

Chloe's eyes narrowed at the apparent stranger getting up in my space, so I shook my head lightly and smiled. "This is Fiona."

Fiona shot her hand out like an important businessperson eager to close an important deal. "Fiona Stockton."

Chloe shot me the tiniest of bemused looks, but Fiona saw everything.

"You're Chloe Lee?" Fiona asked, still finishing the handshake. How long did business handshakes go on in her field? The marketing side of the entertainment industry ran more on emotion-free hugs. "I googled your business. It seems you've had a lot of success. Have you thought about expanding or franchising?"

"Hey, let's all act like normal humans and go see if Hailey's at the restaurant," I said, backing down the sidewalk and hoping they'd follow.

"She's running a few minutes behind," Fiona said, walking over to me and then, of course, taking the lead. I tried to let it go, again, that there was apparently a full ongoing conversation between my best friends that didn't include me at all. There was so much about my life—especially these days—that didn't include my two best friends, after all. Still, it was tough keeping it from getting under my skin. Just another sign that they were headed off in a separate direction, and maybe eventually there'd be even less use for me.

"But let's get the table," Fiona continued. "Chloe, I saw that your pet salon uses organic shampoos and other supplies. Are those products you buy, or do you make your own? Have you trademarked them and looked into distribution across your vertical?"

"What did I literally just say about acting like normal humans?" I sighed and waited for Chloe to catch up. "I apologize for all of that MBA talk."

"It's fine," she said. "Have you not figured out that Phoebe is doing the same to me all of the time? And anyway, I have an MBA too."

"Wait, you do?" I asked, and then tried to pretend that I was kidding because it felt bad to not know the state of your girlfriend's level of business degree.

"I wanted to run my own business," she said with a shrug. "My dad *strongly suggested* it."

"Did he know what kind of business?" I asked, and Chloe cracked up. "Sorry, was that mean?"

"No—well, maybe! And *of course* he didn't. That degree definitely gave me two extra years of parental approval though, worth every penny."

I laughed, but then noticed that Fiona's eyes were narrowed. "You didn't know your girlfriend had an MBA?" she asked.

"It's not hanging on my wall or anything," Chloe said.

Fiona frowned. "It's not on your LinkedIn profile?"

Chloe and I burst into laughter and followed Fiona into Casita Del Campo. The Mexican restaurant was painted hot pink outside, and a variety of bright colors, from room to room, indoors. It was a solid choice for giant platters of classic Mexican fare, but considering it was also the kind of place that hosted drag nights and flew pride flags, I had a feeling my friends suggested it for dinner tonight by typing *LGBTQ+ restaurants* into Google and texting me the nearest result.

I found that both deeply cringeworthy and endearing.

The host guided us to a table right away, and as Chloe and I sat down across from an intense Fiona, I felt like we were in some kind of bizarro job interview situation.

"Should I hand over my résumé?" I asked, even if I was the only one who knew what I was even talking about.

"Very funny," Fiona said. "By now my assistant would have already given it to me. And I wouldn't hire you, you look too nervous."

"Wow, she barely had a chance at this fake job," Chloe said, nudging me.

"What's that about?" Fiona asked, a sharp nod in the direction of Chloe's elbow. "Did Clementine tell you something about the so-called evils of capitalism and my involvement therewithin?"

"Oh, no, we're already on to capitalism?" Hailey squeezed into the booth next to Fiona. "Can we save the economic systems talk for dessert? Or never? Hi, you must be Chloe, I'm Hailey. I'm so sorry, the sitter was five minutes late, and even though I was going against traffic—anyway! What else did I miss?"

"Fiona would never hire me because I look quote-unquote too nervous," I said.

"Who wouldn't look nervous in front of Fiona!" Hailey laughed and leaned in to side-hug Fiona, a person who probably had never initiated a side-hug herself. "Wait, are you interviewing for a job? What did I miss? What's even happening? Chloe, I'm sorry, I should be getting to know you better but first I want to clear my confusion."

"No, I'm not worth getting to know," Chloe said. "Clear up your confusion instead, it's the better call."

I glanced over at Chloe while Fiona began reviewing her fifteen-point (!) interviewing system with Hailey. "Obviously Fiona's methods of taking over the world via finance or whatever are the most important thing we have going on, but—I don't know. Don't say you're not worth knowing."

"OK, Mom," she said with a grin.

"Must be nice! My mom never says things like that."

"Oh, mine either! *Sit up straight* or *get a real job*, those are things I'm used to."

"Getting a real job is a big focus of my mom's, too," I said.

"Wait, you *have* a real job," Chloe said. "You use Power-Point and Excel."

"Those are the main markers, yes," Fiona said in a serious tone that made all of us burst into laughter. "Though of course you do have a real job, Clementine."

A server stopped by to get our drink orders, and I noted that Fiona ordered a margarita. I also tried not to feel any sense of relief at that; my friends could have all the babies they wanted and our relationships would still be intact. Their happiness was top priority for them, and I knew it. Making wishes about the contents of my friends' uteri was not cool behavior.

"Is this still about your side hustle?" Hailey asked me after the server had left.

"Yeah, at least partially." I glanced at Chloe. "I guess it's time you know this about me."

"Wait, how does she not know?" Hailey asked.

"Well, I don't *lead* with it," I said, because that much was true. Even if Chloe and I had been real-dating, I'd absolutely wait longer to drop that I devoted as much time as I did to crafting horoscopic toys for cats. There was nothing suspicious about Chloe's ignorance on this specific matter.

I hoped.

"Clementine, you have to tell me," Chloe said. "Immediately."

"I don't understand you," Hailey said, shoving her phone at Chloe. "If I did anything this cute, it would totally be what I led with. It might be the only thing I told people about."

I watched Chloe's face intently as she scrolled my Etsy page. Sure, Chloe had an adorable dog and a business grooming other people's dogs, and she might be a fairly small person, but there was nothing *cutesy* about her. Despite that I still thought this whole thing was a terribly misguided and regrettable decision, I guessed I hoped that Chloe didn't feel that way, too.

"Clementine, do you mean to tell me you're responsible for the cutest fucking cat toys I've ever seen in my life? Man, you were making cat toys back when you couldn't even have a cat because of your boyfriend's whole thing—"

"—allergy," I corrected.

"Still. It must have been hard pining for a cat and thinking you'd never have one," she said. "I'm glad you do now. And I'm glad Small Jesse Pinkman has these to bat around. What's his sign, anyway?"

"He's an Aries, thanks for asking," I said. "What about Fernando?"

"Since he's literally a street dog, your guess is as good as mine. Based on personality, Gemini seems the safest bet."

Chloe glanced up at Hailey. "Someone named Michael just texted you, **poop emoji looks normal again.**"

Hailey frowned. "Did he type *poop emoji* or did he use the poop emoji?"

"Is the meaning vastly different depending?" Fiona asked in a horrified tone.

"You can sound like that all you want," Hailey said, smiling widely. "Once you have a baby, you have no idea just how many times you can text and talk about poop."

I felt a streak of something that felt like disappointment, but couldn't be, only a terrible person would be disappointed that soon all of her best friends would have babies and text about poop. "Wait, you just ordered a drink, are you—"

"No," Fiona interrupted me. "Hailey jumps the gun, as you know."

"It was more of a general poop-emoji-related warning," Hailey says. "But Michael's bad at using Siri—how can a person be bad at using Siri, you ask, I know, it's strange and adorable—so instead of the poop emoji, often it just says, you know. Poop emoji."

I glanced at Chloe to see what she thought about all this poop and poop emoji talk, but she was still scrolling through my Etsy shop.

"Let's talk less about poop," Fiona said, wrinkling her nose.

"Less about emojis too, maybe," I said, which cut whatever tension had sneaked in. Or maybe that was just in my head. Lately when it came to my best friends and babies and all the conversations that no longer involved me, it was hard to tell what was actually happening and what was an invented conflict that made me feel on the outs nonetheless. (Well, of course, and an actual text chain I was not part of.) I'd never at all felt conflicted about knowing I never wanted kids of my own, but I hadn't at all been prepared for how it would feel to be in a group where I was the only one who felt that way.

Maybe, if Will had wanted the same things I'd wanted, this part of adulthood wouldn't feel so lonely.

The server was back with our drinks and to take our orders, and I tried to feel—well, not *normal*, exactly. Less shot through with potential conflict and tension.

"How do you guys feel about clowns?" Hailey asked.

"Not positively," I said, as Fiona asked, "*Why?*" and Chloe barked out a "No."

"I'm planning Ellie's birthday party," Hailey said. "It needs to be perfect."

"Then I'd suggest a hard *no clowns* rule," Fiona said.

"Clowns do balloon animals," Hailey said with the tone of a lawyer landing a key piece of evidence in a trial. "Sometimes face-painting."

"Surely," Fiona said with a grimace, "there are other ways to achieve those two activities without bringing a clown into the mix."

"Does anyone even remember their first birthday?" I asked, which was apparently, from Hailey's and Fiona's and even Chloe's faces, the wrong thing to say. "You know what I mean. Only that it doesn't have to be perfect, and will Ellie care about a clown *or* balloon animals *or* face-painting?"

"People form memories around photographs," Hailey said. "When she's older, I want her to see pictures from this party and see how loved she was, always, by so many people. So every detail needs to be right."

I flashed back, high school study hall, me skimming the material before tests and Hailey reviewing handmade notecards and murmuring nervously about her GPA.

"It'll be fine," I said, but because I'd already said the not-remembering thing, I could tell that it didn't read as comforting. It was just a brush-off.

"As long as there are no clowns! So, Chloe, how did you two meet?" Fiona asked, back in interview mode again.

"I already told you this," I said quickly, because as grateful as I was for a topic change, not necessarily *this topic*. Was she suspicious? Out to poke holes in my story? The story was true, though. What was I worried about?

"It's cute hearing it from both people's perspectives," Hailey said, leaning forward like she was an eager child at story time and Chloe was the best librarian in the world. Was that all Fiona wanted, too? I couldn't tell if I was catching a whiff of suspicion off my friend or if that was just the stench of my own guilt.

"I'm a friend of Clementine's company," Chloe said. "So we'd met at one of the Big Marketing Energy holiday parties."

"I thought she rescued you from street harassment," Hailey said, as Fiona frowned.

"She did," I said, as Chloe said, "*Rescue* is a strong word."

Fiona's frown was still directed at us.

"Technically we'd met before," I said.

"But she had that boring boyfriend then," Chloe said.

Now Hailey was frowning too. "Will? He's such a sweet guy."

"I didn't say he was boring," I said. "Chloe just—"

"Picked it up from context clues," Chloe said with a laugh.

Fiona and Haley exchanged nervous looks. They were, I was certain, already planning the texts they'd send to each other later.

"What's the cutest dog you've ever groomed?" I asked Chloe, not only because I did genuinely want to know, but it also seemed the kind of subject that might unite the booth again. "Or can you not say?"

"Why couldn't I say?" Chloe asked, furrowing her eyebrows, an action I did emphatically not find extremely cute.

"Groomer/client confidentiality is I believe what Clementine is doing her best to respect," Fiona said. "Which I have a hard time believing exists."

"Correct, I can talk all I want about the cutest dogs, though you're all warned that now that I've started I may spend at least thirty minutes just on the Pekinese mix named Cappuccino."

All of us, even Fiona, squealed at that, and Chloe scrolled through photos of freshly groomed dogs as well as some impressive before-and-after shots, and before long our food was there and then it was much easier to pretend the whole meal had been more like the dog photos show-and-tell and way less like Fiona and Hailey's faces when Chloe had said the word *boring*.

After the check had come and we'd walked outside, I did my best to casually hug my friends good night and wait calmly while Chloe shook their hands. I knew that if Fiona was still in interview mode that Chloe in no way had landed the job, and I was eager to get home and away from this entire interaction.

Hailey cleared her throat right as I was about to head toward my car, after Chloe had already taken a couple of steps away. "I should . . . say something."

"Oh?" I asked in what I hoped was a very casual tone.

"Well, you know that Michael and Will are friends," she said with a slight shrug. "And they still are. So I just wanted you to know he's still sort of in my life."

"Oh," I said in what I hoped was a similarly casual tone. "Has he—"

"He hasn't said anything, as far as I know," she said quickly, reaching out and touching my arm. "But I hated the thought of you—I don't know. Things can be complicated, which is tough, but I feel like as long as we're all honest, it'll work itself out."

"Okay," I said. What else was there to say? Will was allowed to be friends with whoever he wanted, and so was Michael. No matter how hard I sort of wished that Will just sort of didn't exist as far as my own personal life went these days.

"Hay, where'd you park?" Fiona asked.

"Oh my god, *so* far away!"

"I'll walk you," Fiona said, looping her arm through Hailey's and barely waving goodbye again to Chloe and me before taking off down the sidewalk in what I pretended was not *great enthusiasm.*

Back in the car, we buckled our seat belts and I tried not to dread what Chloe would say.

"This might sound crazy," Chloe said as I started the car and pulled out onto Hyperion, "but I have an idea."

"I assume it's *never see my friends again.*"

She snorted. "What? No. Your friends are fine, even if they're on your ex's side, which is fine in theory but they could at least fake it around you. I was going to say you should let me sell your cat toys at my shop."

"Wait, what?"

"I know that it probably sounds like Phoebe and your capitalist friend are getting to me, but it just makes sense. Tons of my customers also have cats, and as cute as your shit looks on Etsy, I bet it's even cuter in person."

I shrugged, doing my best to seem modest. "It's pretty cute."

"Perfect. So you're in?"

"You don't want to . . . discuss any of that?"

"Your friends wanted to meet me because they had to satisfy their curiosity about this special woman who made their friend gay, as far as they see it, right? They've met me, I'm nothing special, they'll lose interest. By the time we break up, they'll be less weird with the first real girl."

I pulled up to a red light and shot her a look. "You're a real girl. And also you're not *not special*, remember?"

"Oh please, Clementine, you know what I mean."

I tried to imagine it, the next time, a woman beside me who was for real, who I'd confessed feelings to, who I'd kissed, who I'd had sex with, who I'd spent nights next to. A woman I hoped would be around longer than a couple of months. Would it go better then?

"I know it sounds dumb," I admitted, "but I just wanted all of you to like each other. The opposite feels symbolically bad."

"Your friends don't like your fake girlfriend? I don't think that's symbolic of anything," Chloe said. "Also, to be honest, I didn't try very hard to like them because of the whole temporary thing. A real girlfriend would try so much harder."

We were silent the rest of the drive to her apartment, but once I pulled the car over on her block, Chloe hopped out as if the mood hadn't seemed dire at all.

"See you Sunday for brunch," she said. "I'll drive since parking near Lady Byrd can be terrible and I'm not sure you're up for the task."

I smiled faintly and watched her let herself inside. My phone buzzed with a text, so I kept the car in park and checked my screen. I was hoping for a *Chloe's great!* or even just a *That was fun!*, even though Chloe had already called it and obviously I could feel that they just wished I was still with Will. Somehow I knew that a lie would make me feel better, like at least my friends were ready to support me. And, of course, not that they knew, but considering that I was also lying, it would even things out.

The text was just from the site I ordered my bras from, letting me know there was a sale on sexy robes.

knock knock

I jumped in my seat and held back a scream, only to see Chloe standing outside my car with Fernando on his leash. He barked three times in high-pitched succession.

"Shit, sorry," she said as I rolled down the window. "I was taking Fernando out and saw that you were still here and just wanted to make sure everything was OK."

"Sure, just having a minor heart attack is all," I said, trying my best to speak normally even though there was at least a split second I thought I was about to be murdered.

"Look, I know you're sad that no one wanted to split dessert with you," Chloe said, leaning into the car, just a little. "But the truth is, Clementine, that no one likes flan. It's disgusting."

I laughed, even as I kind of wanted to cry. "It's like a bunch of dairy products and caramel. What's not to love?"

"Come on, there's a parking spot open around the corner that even you can maneuver into. I'll make you dessert upstairs."

It was, even for a fake girlfriend, a romantic gesture, but that was because I pictured her baking a sheetful of cookies or even whipping up a batch of brownies from a box.

"I can't believe this is safe. In fact, I'm sure it's not."

Chloe rolled her eyes at me and pointed to my right hand, which was holding a marshmallow and a couple squares of fancy dark chocolate between two graham crackers. "I've been doing this my whole life."

"I'm pretty sure you're lying," I said, and she grabbed the uncooked s'more from me and held it by one end as she torched the other with an ancient-looking Bic lighter.

"This would be easier if you stopped shrieking," she said, which was news to me, but given that Fernando was regarding me with wide eyes and a cocked head, I couldn't deny that I'd apparently been, unawares, screeching as the flames neared Chloe's fingers.

We both burst into laughter as Chloe presented me the, somehow, perfectly burnt square. "I can't believe this worked."

"People never trust me," she said, putting together a second s'more. "Isn't this better than flan?"

"No!" I said, but then I took a bite. Somehow this dangerously built construction was *perfect*: gooey, sweet, just a little salty.

"You're lying," Chloe said, calmly torching her own s'more like she did this every day. Did she?!

"Hey," I said, as she shoved the whole s'more into her mouth.

"What?" she asked, or at least she asked something that sounded a bit like *what* while her mouth was full of s'more.

I had been *this close* to telling her how I'd needed this, how friendship in my thirties felt so much harder than it had in the decades before, and how my very fake relationship now seemed to be one of the last dominos primed to knock over my very real friendships. But as I watched Chloe stack up another pair of s'mores, I realized that she already knew.

"These are better than flan."

A grin overtook her face. "Clementine, I told you so."

Chapter 9

Baked Potato Curious

I'd hoped to get through the rest of the week as easily as possible, even though I still hadn't received the messages I'd wanted to from my friends. Yes, of course the group chat had resumed, but we were back to the standard conversations like Hailey asking for recommendations if she did something wild like switch up her nightly moisturizer, and Fiona sending us an article about investing for retirement that Hailey and I both promised to look at later. It was like the night at Casita Del Campo had never happened.

I wanted to be offended on Chloe's behalf, but I couldn't stop picturing Hailey's fast defense of Will or imagining the conversations that he might be having with Michael at any given moment. And I knew that no matter who I'd shown up with that it would have gone the same way. After all, Chloe was beautiful and funny and had an iCloud storage account ninety percent full of dog photos. She should have been enough for them.

I did my best to keep all of that from swirling nonstop in my head—though I couldn't say I was doing an amazing job at

it—throughout our kickoff meeting with the leads from Celebration Pictures about their upcoming gay romantic comedy,
Silly in Love. I often didn't have a whole lot to do in client
meetings; BME's exciting creative strategies were generally
what got people in the door. My role was full of logistics, requirements, limitations, and early on in projects I knew I could
come off as a killjoy instead of someone who just wanted to set
realistic expectations. After this many years on the job, I knew
to smile and feign enthusiasm early on, and worry about the
details later.

Unfortunately, that gave my brain plenty of spare energy
to worry that breaking up with Will hadn't only ended the
thing I'd wanted to end but also things I'd wanted to keep
intact, like the only two close friendships I had. I knew that
Hailey's baby and Fiona's future babies made our friendships
more work to schedule, but I was willing to do that work. I'd
schedule around babies, current *and* future! Now, though, it
felt less like we had different commitments and responsibilities, and more like my path was leading me far away from the
one my best friends were on together. Being single hadn't felt
as scary when I imagined having Fiona and Hailey's support.
After my breakup with Will, though, after watching Fiona and
Hailey walk arm in arm away from me, I didn't know what I
still had.

". . . media planning?"

I jolted out of my worst-case-scenario-ing and made an expression that I hoped would look exactly like I had been paying
attention this entire time.

"Yes," Phoebe said to Jeremy, who was a VP at Celebration
Pictures and our main contact at the indie film studio. "Clementine runs our media planning division, and she and her team
can place the entire campaign."

"Yeah, maybe," he said, leaning back in his chair like this
was the most casual part of his whole day. "We used to work

with a separate agency, but it just seems so old-fashioned now, you know? Thanks to dashboard automation, we can just do so much of it in-house these days."

"Sure," Phoebe said evenly, though not without sharing a brief look with me. I loved how polite she was with clients without ever seeming like she'd forgotten to be a person, too. "I know that Clementine would probably say that some nuance is lost in automation, but we're here to work with whatever solution you'd like."

The rest of the BME team stayed in the conference room as Phoebe walked the Celebration Pictures team to the parking lot. I got out my phone to check my email, but was stopped in my tracks by the sight of new messages from both Greg and Chloe.

"I wouldn't worry too much," Aubrey, who managed research and analytics—and shared Tamarah as an assistant—said with a polite smile. "Just because a client suggests Phoebe shutter part of the agency doesn't mean she's going to. Not right away, at least."

"I'm not worried," I said as calmly as I was capable of, considering I'd actually asked for the opposite of getting laid off, and—well, it was very much like Aubrey, who once forwarded me a WebMD article about lung cancer after she heard me coughing in my office, to plant a seed of terror in my gut.

Still, I'd very well known that cough had been due to a sinus infection. I didn't have as easy an explanation for a changing media landscape.

Phoebe leaned back into the room. One of my favorite parts of this job was the post-meeting talks, after the client had gone, and it was just us. Agency life had lots of playing nice, even in an ideally run company like this one. Being led by a smart and progressively minded woman did not negate the need to kiss client ass more than occasionally. It was great when they left and we could be ourselves again. Like, for example, it would have been an excellent time for Phoebe and the rest of the team, sans Aubrey, to laugh off Jeremy's suggestion that my entire role was outdated.

"Anything time-sensitive to discuss?" Phoebe asked casually instead. "If not, I say we reconvene tomorrow afternoon after everyone's hashed out their details. Clementine, feels like we're set for now, but we'll pull you back in if we need you. Sound good?"

It didn't, absolutely not at all, a client had just suggested I didn't even need to exist, but I smiled and nodded anyway. The day only got more annoying when I got back to my office and checked the five (!!) messages from Greg.

They started normally enough:

Me and Marisol think we should all get together soon to discuss more about Mom and Dad's party.

But progressed quickly to:

I have a lot of appointments this week so should probably be tonight.
Red alert: Marisol made reservations at Sammie's for 6:30, be on time!!!
Since Will broke up w u can you still handle the beverage situation or are we gonna have to figure it out

And, finally:

Come with beverage solutions!!!!

Normally the best thing that happened when my brother sent ridiculous texts was to screenshot them and immediately shoot them off to the group text. It wasn't only that last night's awkward dinner was still fresh in my mind; there was obviously more than a small chance that Fiona and Hailey would *actually agree with Greg.*

I didn't know how I could ever be a functioning person again if that happened, so I kept the messages to myself. And I remembered that the bright red *1* in the top lefthand corner of my phone was due to an unread message from Chloe, so I tapped back to find it.

How are you today?

Even though it was sent alongside a Dana Scully gif, I was still surprised at Chloe's thoughtfulness. Not that she'd been thoughtless, not exactly, but the entire *one of her best friends is my boss* thing didn't feel entirely considerate, and *considerate* sure felt like at least a neighbor of *thoughtful.*

Still, I felt weak between the meeting's end and Greg's wall of annoyingness, so I screenshot it after all and sent it to Chloe in lieu of an actual answer. I supposed it was my actual answer.

WTF is this Sammie's place we're going to tonight?

I sat up with a start at Chloe's message. **"We"?**

Wasn't that part of the deal? I'm your girlfriend until this party's over? The literal party, not being metaphorical or some poetic shit.

I couldn't ask you to do that, I typed. **Two nights in a row with my weird people? Greg's beyond weird. He's like a cartoon villain except his evildoings just consist of trying to make me feel shitty about my life.**

The scariest kind! Obviously I'm in, as long as you answer my question about Sammie's. I tried to look it up on Yelp and

please tell me it's the place with a cartoon baked potato on its sign.

That is indeed the place. Are you sure?

Yeah, it was asking an incredible amount of Chloe; Greg was not for the weak of heart. Not that Chloe was weak of— well, anything, as far as I'd seen. Still, it wasn't just that he and I couldn't stand each other, it was also that I didn't love who I was around him. Somehow the brattiest parts of my teen self found ways to weasel back in there, even if I was a full-on adult otherwise.

But it was also the bigger thing, the bi thing, the coming out thing. I couldn't believe how much coming out there was! I wished I could just check some box and have it announced to the world with a no-questions-asked policy. Talking about my personal life was already something I didn't love, but this felt even bigger because it was laced with *my sexuality* as well, definitely not something I brought up much if at all. Especially *not to my family*. When people perceived you as straight and everything seemed to be set at default, there was a simplicity in that, I now realized. Except it had never been my actual truth, and now the actual truth was on its way out there.

But Chloe texted back that she was sure, so I supposed I had to be too. I guessed somewhere deep down maybe I wanted to be? I tapped back to the thread with Greg and took a deep breath. There was, I knew, no going back from here.

Just so you know, I'm dating someone else, and she's joining me tonight.

Unfussy and succinct, an update of plans and a coming out, all in one go. All those skills I learned once upon a time to write marketing copy, coming in handy after all!

112 / Amy Spalding

It hit me with no shortage of force that this was exactly the favor Chloe had offered me with this ridiculous charade. If I were newly dating someone for real, I would have *in no way* felt comfortable enough sending that person a screenshot of my brother's latest nonsense. Family nonsense would be for later, when I was certain someone had strong enough feelings that it would take more than an annoying brother and my potentially even-more-annoying responses to him to make them run for the hills.

I picked her up right after work, and shot her a smile I hoped was more *grateful* and less *panicked*, though those two emotions were really duking it out for top honors at that moment. She was wearing what I'd already come to think of as her usual, a casual but bold-printed jumpsuit with bright Crocs, and I was already accustomed to her scent of what seemed like very high-end hair products. I wondered—I could actually barely get through the thought in my own head without laughing aloud.

"What?" Chloe asked, snapping her seat belt while I'd already pulled out back into traffic.

"I was just thinking how you always smell like fancy hair stuff, and it hit me that maybe it's fancy *dog* hair stuff, sorry, why am I even admitting this!"

Chloe cracked up. "Clementine, *of course* it's fancy dog hair stuff, does it look like I spend that much effort on my own hair?"

"What do you mean?" I asked. "Your hair looks good all the time, I assume a lot of product goes into it. Isn't that the thing with short hair?"

Chloe shrugged, running her hand through her hair. "I guess. I dunno, I buy all my hair stuff at Target. Which horrifies my mom."

"Oh, mine's the opposite. Once I was running errands with her and pointed out this moisturizer I use, and she was like, you spend *how much* on face cream? I didn't have it in me to tell her about the serums and toners too."

"Your face looks great, though," Chloe said, and I knew it was meant as a *so there* to my mother, but it still felt nice to hear.

"Thanks. Yours too. Pass along the compliment to Target."

She laughed again. "So what do I need to know about your brother other than that his texting style is a nightmare?"

"Before I even get into Greg, I guess I should tell you that him and his wife only know that Will and I broke up, and they—like my friends did initially—assume Will dumped me, and so I just sent a text that I was seeing someone new and she was coming tonight and—honestly I'm nervous to check my texts. I have no idea what he'll say or how he'll react. I know it's what year it is and it's Southern California and whatever else you're thinking, but—"

"Hey," Chloe said in a gentle tone I hadn't heard from her before. "Clementine, you don't have to explain homophobia to me."

"Sorry, I'm just—"

"No, I didn't mean it that way." She laughed, though her tone was still gentle. "Just that I get it. I'm on your side here. We can talk about it or you can also just tell me about the baked potato options at Sammie's."

"There are twelve kinds. But I always get the same one. Classic loaded baked potato. Why mess with perfection?" I sighed and looked out onto the sea of red lights, evening rush hour traffic back to the suburbs. "Greg and I never got along. We were just always so different. I guess I was always just kind of a dreamy kid who looked forward to going to college and growing up somewhere bigger than where I was, whereas I guess he was having fun in the moment, you know, friends he made in places that weren't extracurriculars or Gifted and Talented class. This is me telling you I was a nerd, I guess."

"I'd expect nothing else!" she said. "Same here, despite how I turned out."

"Yeah, exactly," I said. "My parents definitely expected more from me, career-wise, than this part of marketing no one even understands. They didn't go to college, so it was this big deal for them that my test scores were so good and I could get some financial support from these colleges that were interested in me. I mean, I still have student loan debt, but it felt really cool to be wanted. It *was* cool to be wanted, I hate that this has all worked on me, retelling my own life story like it's shameful now."

"My younger sister's one of the top three neurologists in the Bay Area," Chloe said. "Which, I'm sure you can understand, would put me at an accepted lower ranking within my family regardless, but in a Korean family . . ."

"I don't want to stereotype," I said quickly. "But, yeah."

"So what does your brother do?" she asked.

"He's a home inspector," I said. "Which is a great job, it sounds like, at least. But I literally have *no idea* why my family's now all, *Greg is a great success and Clementine is our disappointing failure.* Lost potential and all. In high school I didn't date anyone and went to prom with a big group from the yearbook staff, so I should have really succeeded at something, I guess. Greg fucked around in high school but then a few years later he met Marisol and got his job in his field, and it was like he decided to become a cartoon grown-up. It's like he associates having a good time with youthful nonsense or whatever, so it's all gone. He's humorless and obsessed with responsibility and hard work. Which makes no sense to me, because I think being an adult is mostly so much better—and way more fun."

"Hear, hear," Chloe said. "I like being old enough to truly appreciate youthful nonsense."

"Also, he's still up there," I said. "He's the one who runs errands for Mom and Dad and brings the kids over every Sunday night for dinner. I'm the one down here with my own life, even though, you know, say the word and I'd help out too. I'd come for dinner! But it's like I chose something else for my life, so they don't include me and that's just . . ." *Fine* was on the tip of my tongue, but even if not fully delving into my feelings was exactly how I wanted to proceed with this, abject lying didn't seem right.

"Anyway, it's just this thing within our family where Greg surpassed expectations so he's the winner now, and I didn't, so I'm the—I don't know. It doesn't make sense when I say it aloud. I like my life and I know it's good. And there shouldn't be winners and losers in families anyway! I know all of this. When I'm around them, though . . ."

I glanced over at Chloe, who had somehow unlocked my phone and was browsing Spotify.

"Sorry, I'm probably saying too much about this. Also, you could ask next time. I have some pretty personal playlists."

Chloe cracked up. "I would never browse someone's personal playlists. Just figured we'd both rather something else on instead of Kai Ryssdal. And you don't have to apologize for your family. That's the whole point of this, right?"

I wasn't sure; it felt a little above and beyond. But Chloe started laughing and hit *play* on *Abba Gold* and traffic lightened up, and before long we were pulling into the Sammie's parking lot, right on time.

Greg had texted that he and Marisol were already there, and it was then, while we were walking inside—well, while we'd started walking inside and Chloe stopped to take a selfie with the baked potato sign—that I saw his response to my earlier message.

???

It was, honestly, a better response to my coming out than I'd expected.

"Where is he?" Chloe asked as we walked in, turning her

head around every nook and cranny in the main dining area. Sammie's was like if a restaurant was also a grandmother's attic. Growing up I'd thought of it as a fancy meal out for my family, and somehow it still triggered the same feeling for me.

"The table in the back corner," I said. "Near the painting of fancy hats. The guy who looks like—well, not like me, exactly. Me if I were tall and in shape."

"And a man."

"Well, that too."

"Is that his wife?" Chloe asked, peering at Marisol, who was talking too intently to Greg to notice us. "She's hot."

Something tiny twinged in my gut. "Yeah, I guess so. I mean, pretty, I've always thought that, sure. Is she like your type?"

Chloe elbowed me. "Is she like *your* type?"

"My sister-in-law? No."

We both burst into laughter, and we were close enough that I guess Greg sensed that I was having fun and some kind of alarm went off in his head. He turned from Marisol and looked right at me, then at Chloe.

"You're late," he said.

"Oh my god, Greg, you know I have a farther drive, could we just start one conversation normally?" I asked.

"Also, it's seven sharp," Chloe said, looking at her phone.

"Mine says seven-oh-one," he said.

"Great, you win." I sighed and sat down next to Marisol, and I could tell as soon as my butt hit the chair that I'd flopped down like a petulant teen and not at all like an adult woman bringing her new girlfriend to meet her family. "Sorry, let's start over. Greg and Marisol, it's great to see you both. This is Chloe Lee."

Greg and Marisol exchanged looks, but Marisol only needed about a half second to spring back into being a regular human.

"It's great to meet you, Chloe," she said, hopping up to shake Chloe's hand. "I love your haircut, it's so daring."

Chloe poked me on the leg as she sat down, and I knew it was only so we could laugh later about *daring*, but a sudden rush of heat accompanied that brief contact, and even though no one—not even Chloe—would know, I felt a follow-up rush of embarrassment. Why was my body responding like a hot girl had her hand on my leg for more than family mockery purposes?

"I'm sorry," Greg said, then nodded at Chloe. "I'm probably too hard on Clementine. In my line of work, we take timeliness seriously. When lives are on the line—"

"Wait, aren't you a home inspector?" Chloe asked, and I choked down a laugh at her incredulous tone.

"I am," he said, with the gravitas of James Earl Jones narrating a documentary. "Imagine if I didn't do my job correctly. Someone could fall right through the floor of an attic."

"Sure," Chloe said, and her hand was back on my leg, squeezing this time. *Fuck.* "I'd never thought about it that way before."

"What about carbon monoxide?" he asked. "Silent killer."

Chloe squeezed tighter. "Can't be a minute late for that one."

"Black mold," he said, gesturing as if the mold was right in front of us, perhaps encroaching on the nearest wall art of an old Victorian shoe. A laugh burst out of me, and Chloe joined in almost instantaneously, and we were practically crying by the time the server approached.

"Should I . . . come back?" she asked with a wary tone.

"I doubt these two know what they want," Greg said, using the same black mold gesture toward Chloe and me, which only set us off again.

"Nope, we're ready, we both want classic baked potatoes," Chloe said. "And do you want to split a wedge salad?"

"Oh my god, *yes*," I said.

"You two are cute together," Marisol said as Greg went through a series of directions for a build-your-own baked potato. "Greg and I always order the same things too."

Greg narrowed his eyes as he finished ordering and shifted his attention to us. "So what's going on here, anyway? You never mentioned you were . . . whatever you apparently are."

"Bi," I said, as Chloe said, "Baked potato curious," and then we were both laughing again. It was maybe the most I'd ever laughed around my brother.

Will, of course, hadn't had much use for Greg either. His method for getting through any interactions had been a sort of disconnected quiet vibe, like he could either rock the boat or disengage. I'd understood—who wanted to get into it with anyone else's annoying brother?—but it had never made me feel particularly supported.

"Being bisexual had just never come up before," I said, in as serious a tone as I could muster, once our server had taken everyone's orders and headed off. "I was with Will for so long, but now . . ."

"Hey, I didn't ask," Greg said, holding out his hands like I'd just described going down on a woman in exquisite detail.

"You literally just said, *so what's going on here anyway*," Chloe said. "It's a big deal to come out, you know. It's a vulnerable act. You could give your sister a little grace and gentleness."

"Thank you for sharing with us," Marisol said, with a side-eye to Greg. "Both of you."

"Don't mention this to Mom and Dad," I said. "It's just that . . ."

I wished I had a way to end the sentence instead of just trailing off. Instead of just, as I was trying very hard not to do, shouting *It's just that the worst way I can imagine coming out to them is via you, Greg!!*

"You want to tell them in person," Marisol said. "Of course! And with Chloe, of course. At the party!"

"Of course," I said, though I supposed I hadn't really thought about this aspect yet, only the thought of not rolling into the party as a single person. Instead I'd really upped the list of everything entailed in a *surprise party*.

"So should we get through all of the agenda items for the party so by the time our food comes we can just relax and have a good time? I really want to get to know you, Chloe, but I do have OCD—the real kind, not the kind that people say to explain making lists—and will have a better time if we can cover these details first."

"ADHD here." Chloe raised a first in solidarity, as Greg stared at me. "Am I missing something?"

"I have ADHD too," I said. "It's kind of weird that hasn't come up yet."

"It's because you won't add me on Instagram where I post only the most obnoxious and basic memes," she said, as Marisol gasped.

"You won't add your own girlfriend on Instagram?" she asked.

"No, I just haven't even opened it much since—you know, a bunch of my photos are—" I thought about the woman in the photos, my old life, the different happy ending I thought had already been foretold. "Sorry, I know I'm taking social media way too seriously. I'll add you right now."

"Right after Marisol's list," Chloe said, but Marisol shook her head.

"This is way more important!"

Chloe swiped my phone from me and tapped for a few moments before handing it back to me. "Done. Marisol, proceed."

We got through the whole list fairly easily by the time our meals arrived, and I felt like Chloe was at least partially to thank for the swiftness. It wasn't that she participated much, but her no-bullshit vibe had clearly made its presence known, and Greg barely said a word that wasn't constructive.

It was, perhaps, the best family outing I'd ever had.

"It feels like we're in good shape," I said, swiping out of my Notes app and wondering if I should tempt fate and order dessert while this had mostly been so pleasant.

"There's still beverages," Greg said. "If you can't ask—"

"Let's not put Clementine in that position," Marisol said, a wise statement I don't know why she couldn't have made sooner in this whole process.

"What's the beverage situation?" Chloe asked, leaning back casually in her chair.

"Last time we had a family thing, Will had this friend who has a brewery come and serve beers, and everyone loved it," I said.

"Let's just ask Sadie," Chloe said.

"I don't know who that is."

"Pffff," she said, rolling her eyes. "The owner of Johnny's who you're always flirting with."

"I am *not* flirting with anyone!" I said. "Just finding community."

Chloe nearly spit out her Diet Coke at that. "Uh-huh, that's what they all call it."

Greg and Marisol exchanged looks.

"Long story short, I know someone who owns a bar, and I bet she can hook us up with a good deal," Chloe said. "I'll talk to her and let Clementine know the details. Good?"

"Thank you," I told her.

"It's nothing."

It wasn't, though. I almost couldn't believe how, suddenly, Chloe was the complete opposite of *nothing*.

After dinner we walked outside together, and Greg jumped into his Chevy Suburban while muttering something about relieving the babysitter. I waved goodnight and unlocked the Prius, but as Chloe was sitting down, Marisol turned in my direction and reached out to pull me aside.

"I have to admit," she said, "I was surprised too. But it's wonderful! Chloe's great. The two of you seem so well matched."

"Oh," I said, glancing over to my car where Chloe was scrolling on her phone. "Yeah. She's . . . she is great. Yeah."

"It's a relief," Marisol continued. "I was so worried for

you, being alone. I hear these nightmares from my single girl-friends!"

"I was . . ." I searched for the word to describe what I'd been in those weeks after breaking up with Will, to describe *technically* what I still was now, sans fake-girlfriend. "I was fine."

"No, of course, but, you know. None of us are getting any younger, it's good to have someone. Drive safely, text me when you're home, OK?"

I promised I would and got into the car.

"You OK?" Chloe asked.

"Simultaneously yes and no."

Chloe laughed. "Sounds like the human condition in a nut-shell."

I stared at her for only a hard moment before catching my-self and starting the car.

"What?" she asked as I pulled out of the parking lot onto the road that led straight to the 5 Freeway to take us back.

"Nothing," I said, instead of *How am I going to pay for my condo alone if robots take over my part of the industry and I get laid off* and *If this party goes off without a hitch will my family see me as a capable and successful adult even if these parameters seem odd* and *This thing here between us might be really nice if it were actually real* and *I hate that no one could be happy for me as my life actually is right now* and, also, unavoidably, *I'm still thinking of your hand on my thigh.*

Chapter 10

Thirty-Three Percent Fondue

I only, very lightly, dipped in and out of the group chat that had come to dominate my phone's messages. It wasn't that I didn't enjoy it—Chloe's friends were sharp and funny and interesting and thoughtful. They were the kind of friend group I wished I still had; somehow their relationships and parenthood and jobs hadn't pulled them all apart from each other, the way I could feel my own friendships ebbing. Post-dinner with Chloe, it seemed that perhaps they'd already ebbed.

I had still barely talked to Fiona and Hailey. That wasn't actually that unusual for us; we were all busy and didn't attend to our ongoing messages the way Chloe's friends did. The group chat had been lightening up for a while now. Still, I was too aware of it this time, hating the way it slipped down when I opened my messages app, how between Greg, Chloe, her friends' group chat, and the all-but-unbelievable times that brands texted me these days, my friends weren't even on my main screen right now.

So maybe it wasn't *unusual* but it still felt *significant.* I'd decided not to worry about it, so it was annoying that it was still circling my brain so much, like when you had a tiny cut in your mouth and told yourself sternly to leave it alone and yet the tip of your tongue kept finding it anyway.

If Chloe and I were real, I had a feeling I'd go in hard with her group. I'd forcefully friend all of them, maybe even Phoebe. We'd at least come to some sort of respectable work-life-vs.-personal-life friendship balance that made us both comfortable! It would be so easy because everyone made it easy. Chloe and my relationship had only existed for a few weeks as far as they knew, and yet I was included in everything like I was one of them. A conversation about the best snacks had turned into an impromptu Saturday afternoon snacks-potluck, and it was clearly assumed that I'd be coming too.

I couldn't remember the last time Hailey and Fiona and I had managed an impromptu *anything*.

Chloe told me she'd handle food as well as driving—not that it was far from my condo to Phoebe and Bianca's house—and I decided to let her, even though it wasn't really my speed. I had too many snacks and hors d'oeuvres recipes bookmarked to let an opportunity to make a creamy cheese or fresh vegetable option pass me by, but I was only a guest in this world. I'd leave it to Chloe.

She texted that she was outside, and I walked out to see Fernando bouncing up and down in the back seat of the Bronco. I climbed into the front seat and took a chance on leaning back and petting the hyperactive terrier. He rewarded my forwardness by leaning right into me as I scratched between his wiggling fuzzy ears.

"It's nice to see you too," Chloe said, and I laughed and fastened my seat belt.

"Sorry, I knew you'd be here. He was a surprise."

She shrugged and pulled back onto Rowena Avenue. "I'm getting sick of leaving him at home all the time. Big deal, the perfect dog can be perfect and he can be a maniac."

"That's the spirit," I said, and she turned to grin at me as she pulled up to a stoplight. It had been, I realized, so long since I'd had new people in my life. I'd been at my job for half a decade, and I'd had my friends in my life for even longer. No, Chloe wasn't technically *new*, if I counted the chat we'd had at my work party, but she also managed to be brand-new as a person in my everyday life. A year ago I think I would have said that I liked that I'd locked it all up, found a person for every role in my life, had it all set up by my mid-thirties. And now here I was, everything unlocked, and—well, sure, there was a surprising ease to it. But of course that was because it was fake; the real thing would never have fallen into place quite so simply.

At Phoebe and Bianca's, Chloe wrapped Fernando's leash around her wrist before unlatching the Bronco's trunk and lifting out a stack of Tupperware containers. She slid them to one side and—quite valiantly—tried to close the trunk with—well, it was hard to say. Her elbow? It wasn't a one-person job.

"Let me," I said, leaning past her and pulling the tailgate down. "You only have two arms, you know."

"Whatever," she said, as if that might not be true, and I cracked up.

"Come on, let me help."

She waved me off, and so instead I trailed her as we walked up to Phoebe and Bianca's. At least if one of the Tupperware containers fell, I'd be there to pick it up.

"Hey, y'all," Ari greeted us, swinging open the door. "Chlo, can I help you with these?"

"She's apparently fine," I said, which made Ari laugh. Maybe someday I'd get used to making a gorgeous Oscar winner laugh, but today was not that day.

"Good to see you, Clementine," she said, hugging me and then somehow swiping Chloe's stack away from her. "Hey, Fernando, good to see you, buddy. Chloe, I only found out when we took this private dog training class, but if the leash is around your wrist like that and Fernando bolts, you could break your wrist."

"I'm not sure he has the strength to bolt that hard," Chloe said, "but thank you."

I stayed close at her side as we walked into the large, sunny kitchen, and nudged her as soon as Ari's attention turned to Phoebe and CJ, who were discussing something about the shiny stainless steel espresso maker that took up nearly half of one counter. It was less a specific nudge and more of an *I see you* nudge, and we both burst into laughter when we met each other's eyes.

Nina appeared seemingly out of nowhere, dressed in a sheer black dress edged in shiny gold. "Clementine, I'm so glad you're here."

"Wait, am I underdressed? What's happening?"

She laughed and pulled me out of the kitchen and into the living room. It was a cozier space than the vast kitchen and dining space, though still just as stylish and current in a non-hipster and non-mid-century-modern way. It hit me that I was deep within *my boss's house* and I'd let myself get way too carried away by the current of the group chat and not thought about this detail enough. When one was up for a promotion, did one hang out near one's boss's coffee table?

Bianca sat on the sofa, smiling up at us like she'd just cured cancer. "Am I right or what?"

"About what?" I asked, suddenly nervous she'd figured something out about Chloe and me and our whole situation. Though *how*, I wondered. And who else knew?

"That's the dress," Bianca said, gesturing at Nina. "For the rehearsal dinner."

I looked Nina over. The dress was *gorgeous*, delicate fabric that hugged Nina's curves and shining luxe details that made it feel special. "Oh, wait, I recognize this."

"Bianca wore it to the Oscars the other year," Nina said.

"That's right," I said, because this was indeed the kind of LA crowd where multiple people had attended the Oscars. Ari, an actual winner. Nina, the significant other of an actual winner. Phoebe, a marketing mastermind invited by flush-with-award-noms studios. Bianca, the wife of a marketing mastermind. "Phoebe and Bianca went for *Back Home*. She has a photo on her desk of the two of you on the red carpet."

"I just don't think that it's me," Nina said in a very polite tone aimed at Bianca. "Not that it isn't beautiful."

"You hate anything with too much cleavage!" Bianca said in a frustrated tone.

"Not anything! And I didn't say I hated it."

They both looked to me, and I felt certain I was in no way ensconced enough in this friend group to actually make this call.

"I love the dress, and you do look amazing, but I'll just say that I never wear low-cut dresses so I understand."

"Oh my god, not two of you prudes," Bianca said.

"I'm not a prude! I wear very sexy underwear all of the time!" Nina said. "It's not even comfortable!"

"No, mine's very comfortable," I said, and all three of us laughed. "But I'm really sex-positive. I just love the necklines and hemlines of a modesty influencer, I don't know."

"Oh, god, I feel that. Anyway, Bianca, I appreciate the offer," Nina said, with a smile that seemed both familiar and practiced, the way you could still be careful with your closest friends' feelings. "But I think I'm still on the hunt for the perfect rehearsal dinner dress."

Bianca flashed a smile back at her. "Yeah, honestly, I figured. Go change before you get fondue on that."

"Ooh, is there fondue?" I asked.

"I think there's everything," Bianca said, waving her arm in the direction of the kitchen, as Phoebe and CJ walked into the room.

"The femmes are literally over here talking about dresses," CJ said, and everyone but me laughed at this because the truth was I felt an overwhelming glow of—well, the feeling was too big to be contained by a single emotion. I'd been worried when I'd thought of all of it ahead of me. It had been one thing to navigate the life I'd already had with this new layer—this queer layer. It had been scarier to wonder about the parts of life I *didn't* already know, the queer bars and the queer hangouts and the queer in-jokes. I saw the talk online, the insinuations that bisexual women who'd only had boyfriends weren't really queer, or at least *queer enough* to count. I'd seen tiny avatars of people with complicated haircuts explain who did and didn't get to be included.

But now that I was here, in the midst of this in the real world, not a social media platform on my phone, it didn't feel like that at all. No one was policing the perimeters or questioning who was here. I'd just been wrapped right up like I was one of this group. Maybe we were being lightly mocked, but I didn't care because I loved that being a woman who loved to talk about dresses not only didn't knock me out of this world but maybe even made me a stereotype within it. I couldn't believe how welcoming that felt.

"You OK?" Nina asked me, and I wondered what on earth expression my face had pulled while I'd had perhaps a too-strong reaction to being referred to as one of the femmes.

Bianca raised an eyebrow. Again, she seemed to know something. Eyebrows could question so much. "Just thinking about fondue?"

"Yep, exactly." I ended up following them back to the kitchen, and instead of dwelling on potentially weird vibes, took in the immense array of food lining the counter. Yes, there was a tiny Crock-Pot serving as a fondue pot, but there were also at least four hummuses, sliced fresh fruit and veggies that were less *generic supermarket crudités* and more *thinly sliced*

Honeycrisp apples and imported soppressata and flights of locally sourced honey. Chloe, meanwhile, was carefully prying the lids off of all the Tupperware containers.

"What did you make?" I asked her.

Bianca raised an eyebrow. "You don't know what your girlfriend brought?"

Having a fake relationship was so easy until suddenly it wasn't.

"I don't like help in the kitchen," Chloe said breezily.

"She didn't even let me help carry in the Tupperware," I pointed out as if to cite our sources thoroughly. "And she had Fernando's leash. Wait, where's Fernando?"

Chloe nodded to the window. I looked into the back patio area, where Fernando was attempting to win a round of tug-of-war with Nina and Ari's dog, who was about three times his size.

"He's very determined," I said.

"Should it concern me that our dog can't win against a very small dog?" Ari asked, and the crease between her brows made me think she was serious, even though Nina burst into laughter and shoved Ari out of the way of the feast spread out over the counter.

The contents of Chloe's Tupperware ended up being four different styles of kimbap rolls, from super traditional with beef over pickled radish to super hipster with ham, Gruyère, and cornichons. I was surprised to see this level of precision, with these perfectly cut rolls stuffed with rice surrounding diced, julienned, shredded goodies; it was tough imagining Chloe devoting the time and attention to each rice roll.

"Are these your mom's recipe?" Bianca asked her.

"The traditional ones. You should have seen her face when I told her about the ham and Gruyère ones," Chloe said with a laugh. "I legit thought my FaceTime froze, but it was just her judgmental face staring back at me for the length of time equal to her disappointment in my choices."

"Been there," it seemed like half of the room said at once, and it was much better laughing about our horrified mothers' horrified faces than dwelling on it much longer, and somehow that broke the seal and suddenly the eight of us were loading up our plates—which were a matching purple Fiesta dinnerware set, which I loved. Occasionally Will and I had been invited to dinners at his rich boss's Brentwood house, and it was a stiff level of wealth devoid of fun that didn't feel aspirational at all. Phoebe and Bianca's house was full of color and light touches, and if I ever had the budget to level up from my condo I'd love a home just like this one, though I had always worried Will appreciated those minimally fancy homes like his boss's too much for that.

As we began making our way to the back patio, Phoebe and Bianca excused themselves to get their toddler, Olivia, up from her nap. When she ran outside ahead of them, I felt the same sense of surprise I had over the precisely executed kimbap when Olivia ran right toward Chloe's outstretched arms. It felt more than silly to feel like one didn't know one's fake girlfriend at all, especially after only a couple of weeks, but Chloe Lee couldn't be pinned down at all.

"Liv, my favorite person," Chloe said warmly, and then shot me a look. "Cool your judgy eyes, Clem. Whatever you're thinking, kids love me."

I tried to give Olivia a kind smile. Why did I feel so awkward around children? I had so much more experience being a person than they did, but it always seemed like they were nailing it in ways I wasn't.

And if that didn't make me feel inept enough, I noticed Bianca's gaze on mine when she took a seat near me on the patio sofa, watching me for just a moment too long, even when it was clear that I was looking back at her. She, I was certain, had caught us. How, I wasn't sure, but she somehow knew. I mentioned it to Chloe on our drive to my condo later, but she shrugged it off.

"Why would anyone suspect that? If anything she's just still weirded out that I have a girlfriend, something I have consistently not had in like a decade."

"This *is* suspicious, then," I said.

"No, everyone assumed I'd break," Chloe said with a hand wave. "If they're all coupled up for eternity why wouldn't everyone else want that?"

"The thought isn't *that* terrible, is it?" I asked.

"Clementine, you don't need me to justify your dreams of locking it down in some cool and modern way with some babe with a strong jawline," Chloe said. "Also occasionally things are awkward with Bianca when one of us remembers that we dated a thousand years ago, but it always clears up."

"Wait, *what*?"

Chloe's mouth opened to respond, and it was almost as if I could read her mind, so I held up my hand to stop her.

"Yes, I spend enough time on Queer Instagram to know that it's all but a cliché to stay friends with your ex, I just didn't see that coming. All right?"

"Fair," she said. "You're a very good baby gay."

"Don't," I said, but I laughed because being teased by Chloe always felt a little warm and fuzzy. "Maybe it does make it more suspicious, though. Bianca's, like, va-va-voom hot, and I'm—"

"Twee woodland creatures and nerd glasses hot? Clementine, there's room for all sorts of hot here."

I pretended to ignore this instead of feeling even warmer and fuzzier due to that *hot*.

"Could you believe Ari told me how to hold my freaking dog's leash?" Chloe grumbled. "I've had a dog for nearly a decade longer than she has."

"That said." I spoke as gently as I could. "If you could break your wrist, really, you should probably rethink that."

"Fuck you, Clementine," she said, though with a grin. "OK, should I drop you off, or do you want to come with me while

I put away leftovers and then take Fernando on a walk? At this point I'm like thirty-three-percent fondue and I'm thinking your percentage might be similar. A walk sounds not only good but, you know. Necessary so it doesn't all congeal."

"Sure, I'll come with," I said. "Maybe I should interview you or something. I keep learning new things about you in front of other people."

"I hate to break it to you," she said, "but I think that's just what it's like in a new relationship. You just haven't had one since you were twelve or whatever."

"Eighteen," I corrected, though I knew what she meant. I'd be in a group hang with Will, or sitting next to him in class, and he'd drop some tidbit I'd never heard of before, *I played the trumpet in my middle school marching band*, and suddenly my world would get a little bigger than it had been before. Why did it feel the opposite with Chloe, things closing in on me?

Well, it was the dishonesty. It wasn't really that big of a mystery.

"Do you worry sometimes that lying to everyone we know wasn't the best idea after all?" I asked her as she crossed under Silver Lake Boulevard and turned toward her little side street. I knew that people from other places thought of LA as a giant city, but I loved how, instead, it was a thousand small towns shoved together. I guessed that I also loved that Chloe and I had ended up basically at opposite ends of the exact same small town, but what did it really matter? In a couple months' time our proximity would mean nothing.

"What?" Chloe scrunched her nose like I'd said something absolutely bananas. "No! Except for the dog leash stuff I'm basically getting treated like an adult by my friends, and you're going to have so many great ex-girlfriend stories when you start dating for real. Everything's going exactly like we planned."

Considering that I hadn't planned any of it, I didn't exactly think that was true.

* * *

A few nights later, Small Jesse Pinkman pounced ferociously onto my feet at what felt like the absolute middle of the night, though it was possible I hadn't been sleeping incredibly soundly. Sleeping with a kitten wasn't technically *sleeping alone* but I was still getting used to how big the bed felt, how quiet the room was without Will's breathing, how no one ever slung an arm over me and made me feel cozy and safe. If Will were here, I probably wouldn't have told him now nervous I was that my job could go up in smoke and my presentation would make me look like a fool, since feelings like those were more for inside of my brain than out, but from the very first night we spent together on, I was calmer with him than without. The without now, of course, was on purpose, but it was like my body hadn't fully caught up with that knowledge yet. My body still wanted less space in the bed, that slow steady breathing, an arm casually holding me in place.

I picked up my phone instead of dwelling on the fact that it was possible no one would ever make me feel particularly calm again. There was a notification from Chloe on my screen, which meant she'd texted since I'd gone to bed, and the pang in my stomach that this wasn't normal for her turned into an entire percussion section when I saw the words *emergency room*. Hopefully, I thought, I was only jumping to conclusions without my glasses on, but once they were on my face it was only clearer.

In the emergency room with a minor medical thing. Don't freak out, Clementine. I'm only telling you because 1) I may not be able to keep it from the group chat and so it'd be weird if you didn't already know and 2) do you think you can come get my keys from me and pick up Fernando in the morning and take him to doggie daycare because I'm in here for another day or two apparently?

Small Jesse Pinkman, apparently thrilled at the witching hour activity but unaware of the dramatic nature of our situation, bounded back and forth across the room as I bolted up and got dressed. Chloe's situation, that was, we were no *our*. The only *our* I had was with this kitten.

What hospital are you at? I'll come right now.

She responded right away. **Why are you awake? Tomorrow is fine. I'm at the Kaiser on Sunset. For tomorrow morning, the very earliest you will leave your home to come help me. And I will owe you so big. I'll pay you cash for this.**

We only argued about six more times before I kissed Small Jesse Pinkman goodbye and triumphantly headed out. Without traffic, the drive to the hospital was fast, and I nabbed a decent spot in the garage and managed to navigate to Chloe's floor. By the time I reached the reception desk, I realized I'd spent the entirety of the time in my car feeling victorious for wearing Chloe down and not appropriately concerned about whatever was big enough to get Chloe Lee into a hospital. And then I didn't know what to think because if everything I learned about Chloe made me feel like I didn't know her at all, why did I also feel so certain that it would take a lot to get her to the ER?

A frowning woman looked up from the central desk, just barely, and then back to the computer in front of her. "No visitors past eight thirty."

"Oh, it's my—" Chloe had told me to say it to gain late-night entry, but it felt like even more of a lie as it hit my tongue. Well, because it was. "My partner?"

She looked up again and nodded. "Name?"

"Mine? Hers?"

Her gaze softened. "Hers. I know it can be stressful being here. Take a moment."

134 / Amy Spalding

I wanted to fess up, that this was about the logistics of a long con of a shenanigan and not concern for my loved one. Except—well, it wasn't *not* that, too. Not my *loved one*. But my *liked one*, at least.

I got directions to Chloe's room and thanked the receptionist several times before heading down the corridor. I almost ran smack into a nurse as I approached the doorway, and he luckily laughed instead of looking as annoyed as maybe he should.

"You the girlfriend? She's waiting on you, worried about her dog," he said with a smile. "Here's what I tell everyone, even if it's awkward, exchange keys earlier than you think. It doesn't have to be a big thing. But if someone's your emergency contact, they should already have your key."

"OK," I said, nodding as if I was taking this all in for real. It had felt like a big deal the first time I'd listed Will as my emergency contact and not my parents, I remembered. Not that I'd ever been called; Will was like an anti-emergency kind of a person. "Noted."

"I know you'd be here anyway," he said. "But you could have already checked in on that dog and she'd be so thrilled to hear it. What's his name? Some Abba song."

"There's only one Abba song that's a name," I said.

"'Chiquitita'?" he asked, and I laughed.

"OK, maybe two." I thanked him and walked inside, where Chloe was in a hospital gown and sitting up in bed, looking pretty much normal despite the setting. "Hey, how are you? Obviously *not great*, I know, or you wouldn't be here, but—"

"Sit down," she said. "Keep me company."

I sat down in the armchair near the bed, glancing around the room. In addition to Will's lack of emergencies, my family had been low-medical-drama, too; the only time I'd ever been in a hospital room was after Hailey's daughter was born and Fiona and I had swung by the hospital both to meet Ellie and deliver a huge Sugarfish takeout box to Hailey. Those kinds of hospital visits were celebrations, though, nothing like this dim room in the middle of the night.

"What if I told you I'd been harboring a terrible secret?" Chloe asked, and as my heart dropped she burst into laughter. "I'm joking, Clementine, imagine. The only secret my body was harboring was apparently a collection of gallstones, so I'm gonna be down one organ as of tomorrow."

"Oh my god, what happens then? I don't even know what it does. I feel like all the organs are important, though. Sorry, I suddenly feel really stupid."

"No, don't," she said, still grinning. "It's something gross to do with digestion. You're better off not knowing. Why should you know? You're like a marketing person, not a doctor. Anyway, I should be home in a day or two. Fernando's all set up at this place already, it's where he stays whenever I'm out of town, so—"

"Would it be better if I just took him?" I asked, even though I'd never taken care of a dog and had no idea why I was offering. I just hated the thought of him alone in Chloe's apartment wondering where she was.

"You would do that?" she asked, and I didn't miss a streak of hope in her tone. "You know he's partly from hell, right?"

"I don't know why you always say things like that. He just seems like a dog to me. Just tell me what he eats and how much and when."

"OK, if you're sure," she said.

"Are you scared?" I asked.

"Of you dog sitting? No, you're trustworthy, Clementine," she said, and I caught a softness to her words that felt new.

"I meant of surgery," I said, smiling. "And, also, are you on drugs?"

Chloe gestured to the IV stand next to her. "So many drugs. It's like a party in here. Do I sound high?"

"You sound a little high."

"Man," she said, covering her face with her hands. "I don't want to seem high, I want to seem cool."

I managed not to exclaim that she was adorable this way, but only barely. "Do you want me to call or text anyone for you?"

"I can handle it. I can't believe you're here," she said. "I only texted you because it would have been suspicious or whatever to text anyone else. They'd be like, why isn't Clementine handling it?"

"Yeah, it's fine, I'm glad you did," I said as it hit me. Who on earth would show up for me in the middle of the night once this shenanigan was over? Sure, we hadn't been emergency people, but I still liked knowing if something terrifying happened that Will would be there, solid and dependable and radiating calming vibes. Did I have to list Greg and Marisol? That felt too sad for words. "I guess those kinds of emergency contacts go away when everyone's all partnered or whatever."

Chloe stared at me like I was the one on drugs. "Like people can only emergency contact the person they're fucking? You're only here because of keeping this thing going. If not for that I would have just sent a message to the group chat and someone would have jumped in. Probably CJ because they still keep those weird coder hacker shit hours from when they were in college and drinking Mountain Dew Code Red or whatever and never fully got back to normal."

"Wait, CJ was a hacker? I know they do back-end web stuff, is that how people get started in that? No, sorry, that's not important right now. CJ just seems so upstanding is all." It wasn't that I knew CJ well; they were quieter than most of Chloe's other friends, but there was a calm steadiness to them that radiated—well, not *that*.

"If it helps your understanding of them, it was like all social justice stuff, trying to clear debts for people and helping people delete their deadnames and whatever," Chloe said. "I mean, that's the stuff they admit to. One time they got us a really good package of Taylor Swift floor seats and I still wonder.

Anyway, I had an emergency the other year when I didn't have a fake girlfriend—"

"Excuse me," I said, laughing, "I believe I was just upgraded to fake partner."

She watched me for a few moments.

"What?" I asked, worried I'd misstepped somehow. What did I still have left to learn about queer relationships? How much was possible for me to get wrong?

"You're just really cute," she said, her eyes still on me.

A decent amount of blood rushed to my face, and suddenly Chloe's expression had shifted into something more familiar.

"Oh my god, why are you *blushing*?" She cracked up. "Anyway, I'm sorry if you've been brainwashed by straight society that your friends can't be your emergency contacts if they're married or whatever, but it doesn't have to be that way."

"No, you're right," I said, nodding even though it felt like of another era when I could have asked Fiona or Hailey for that.

"The other year I broke my arm and sent out the situation to the group chat," Chloe continued. "Those idiots didn't even check with each other, they just all showed up."

"That's pretty amazing," I said. "What happened to your arm? Was it from an unruly dog at work?"

"Look, this isn't going to sound good for me, Clementine," Chloe said, "but a woman I was trying to impress dared me to jump from one parked car to another, and let's just say she was *not* impressed."

"Chloe," I said, and we both cracked up. "May I ask if this was before you stopped drinking?"

"I wish I could tell you *yes*," she said, and we laughed so hard and for so long that the nurse leaned into the room.

"Sounds like you two are having too good of a time in here," he said.

"Sorry," I said, standing up. "I should probably go get Fernando. Text me his instructions?"

"Chloe, your procedure's scheduled for noon tomorrow,"

the nurse said, and then glanced at me. "If you wanted to be here, we'll get you set up in the waiting room. It usually takes a couple of hours, and then as soon as she's in recovery you can sit with her. And if her numbers are good they'll probably send her home then."

"No, don't skip work," Chloe said. "Phoebe's a hard-ass."

"I'm not afraid of Phoebe," I said, and we both laughed at the lie. "Phoebe will expect me to be here, I think, with you."

I stood up to go, and the nurse laughed as I headed toward the door.

"No, I'll get out of here, you can kiss your girlfriend good-bye in private."

I felt my cheeks pulse again with heat, and I tried not to make eye contact with Chloe as I waved. "I'll text you once I'm home."

"OK," she said. "I'm only telling you this because I'm high, but—I know it's minor surgery but I'm kind of freaked out."

I nodded. "Yeah. I'd be freaked out too. Can I do anything?"

"No, I'm just being a baby," she said, looking away from me.

I took a deep breath and then moved without thinking too much about it, squeezing in next to Chloe in her bed and wrapping an arm around her. I was prepared for a reaction that would humiliate me, but instead she leaned her head on my shoulder. This close to her, the smells of the hospital disappeared and all I could smell was *her*. We sat this way, silently, for so long that I caught myself nodding off.

"Go get my dog," she told me, poking me with her elbow. "And only come tomorrow if you really want to."

"*Really want to* is a weird thing to say about a hospital, but I'll be here." I disentangled myself from her and waved before grabbing her keys and finding my way back to my car. I wondered if after this whole thing was over we could spin another story as good as this one, the amicable breakup so good that Chloe didn't want me out of her life. If she and Bianca were such good friends now, surely it must be doable! Chloe single again, just how she wanted it, and me with someone who wanted me back, and all of this new world that had opened up and felt possible now.

And then I imagined being summoned to help Chloe through another injury caused by impressing another woman, and my gut twisted so hard with something that felt strangely close to jealousy that I knew I must be even more tired than I thought.

Chapter 11
Chicken Reputations

There was a buzz of noise when I showed up to the hospital midmorning, and I found Chloe's room already packed with her friends.

"I want to be clear that I told no one to come," Chloe said.

"It must be terrible that everyone loves you so much," I said, deeply regretting that *loves* as soon as it was out of my mouth.

"Shut up," she said with a smile. "Sit with me again. You're like a weighted blanket."

"That's not very flattering," I said, though I did cross the small room and sit down next to her in her bed, despite that we as a couple had made no physical moves in front of anyone so far. The truth was that I was comfortable like that, even if this were something else. Will and I hadn't dabbled much in PDA; it was hardly a secret that I liked keeping things to myself. Sitting next to someone in bed, of course, wasn't PDA, but there was a note of intimacy it conveyed, a familiarity with someone else's body in certain locations.

"CJ, I told Clementine about your hacker past," Chloe said, leaning into me like it was still last night and we were still alone.

"No, Clementine, you know Chloe," CJ said, their normally staid tone shot through with what I could tell qualified for them as *panic*. "It was more minor than it sounds."

"Hey, be gay and do crime, right?" I said, which made everyone laugh and me feel like I'd just leveled up in my public queerness. Maybe all that mattered was private queerness, that I was queer and knew it. I didn't need someone else's OK. Still, approval from this particular group was exactly the kind of thing that made me feel like this really was my world too.

I was also operating on practically zero sleep, and I knew that in this state I felt big emotions at extremely small things. Maybe saying memes out loud wasn't actually a big cultural step forward.

"How's Fernando?" Chloe asked me. "And Small Jesse Pinkman?"

"Wait," Ari said. "Who's Small Jesse Pinkman?"

"My kitten," I said. "A long story."

"Weird foster name?" Ari asked.

I shrugged. "I guess it wasn't that long."

"It took us so long to find our dog," Nina said. "Months! We saw a lot of weird names in that time."

"And then you named your dog Cristina," Bianca said, "as if that's normal."

"Excuse me, show some respect," Nina said. "She is Doctor Cristina Yang."

"I love that they both have TV names," I said. "So she came with that name too?"

"I want to lie and tell you that she came with that name," Nina said. "But I just really love *Grey's Anatomy*."

"You should have heard her walking in here," Ari said, beaming at Nina. "She thinks watching that show for twenty years has given her medical insight."

"Oh come on, you know it must at least *a little*. I know exactly what a lap chole is," Nina said.

"Do you think medical board exams are just the lingo?" Bianca asked her.

"Pretty sure that's most of it," Nina said, and we were all laughing again as a nurse walked into the room.

"I'm going to have to ask you all to clear out so we can take Ms. Lee to prep for surgery," she told us. "I can point you to the waiting room."

Chloe cheerfully bid everyone a goodbye, like it was the end of a party, but when I made a move to stand up, she grabbed my hand.

"You didn't tell me how Fernando is."

"Sorry, your friends are distracting."

"Tell me about it."

"He's fine," I said, which was true, though I didn't want to mention the sharp barks at any unknown-to-him sound he heard, from the moment we walked in from the parking lot to—well, I heard him as I walked to my car to head to the hospital just now. "I think he's worried I murdered you or something; he keeps giving me these suspicious looks, and he won't touch his food as if I've poisoned it. He did steal Small Jesse's breakfast, though, so he won't starve. And Small Jesse Pinkman keeps staring at Fernando with the widest eyes like he's the most incredible creature he's ever seen. This morning at around five a.m. they ran loops from my bedroom down the hallway to the kitchen and back, and it seemed like they were both having fun."

"If anything happens to me—"

"Nothing is going to happen to you," I said quickly. "I did a bunch of googling, and this is such minor surgery. No one needs a gallbladder, definitely not you."

"If anything happens to me," she repeated in a firmer voice, "will you make sure he's taken care of?"

"You're going to be fine," I told her. "So is Fernando. I promise."

"Don't tell my friends I'm freaked out," she said. "It's so embarrassing."

"Feelings are the worst," I said. "I'll never tell."

She pressed a kiss onto my cheek, as the nurse walked back in, and I realized I was still holding my hand to the spot when I joined Chloe's friends in the waiting room.

"You OK?" Phoebe asked me, as I dropped into the open seat across from her.

"Of course," I said, and then worried that sounded too casual for the situation. "I think I'm just the normal level of concerned."

Oh, god, as if calling out your emotions as normal had ever convinced anyone.

"You can take off as much work as you need to," Phoebe said. "Let me know if there's anything you need me to take off your plate in the meantime."

"No, I'm—" I caught myself because I didn't want to admit I wasn't having a particular busy week at work. Especially when I was asking for a bigger department. "I can manage."

"You don't have to manage," Phoebe said. "If Bianca or Olivia were in the hospital—"

"Well, it's not the same," I said, right as Bianca's gaze snapped over to us. "And hopefully she can come home today."

"I would have been a wreck from day one," Phoebe said, and Bianca grinned at her like she was the only person in the entire waiting room.

"I'm OK," I said, perhaps unwisely, as I felt Bianca study me again. Maybe she hadn't stopped. "I spent at least half of the night googling. Even WebMD couldn't scare me much. She'll be fine, I'm sure."

What did scare me, I realized, was the scenario I *hadn't* planned for today, which was spending already-stressful hours surrounded by Chloe's friends *but without Chloe*. Not that I could let any of them know that. So I focused on staying current on my email and responding to some messages from Greg and Marisol about Mom and Dad's party. I could feel that I had been too—well, not *busy*, but *preoccupied* to actually pull my fair share in planning, but I vowed to get my ass in gear. It had been so recently that I'd managed a job and a relationship and family responsibilities on top of that.

Ari and Nina took a walk to get us all drinks from Starbucks, and then Bianca, who worked in event photography, called in a favor to a restaurant her team had worked with recently and got a bag of salads and sandwiches dropped off. I hadn't eaten anything all day, but it was like the mood kept my hunger and me at an unknowable distance from one another. Plus I could feel how the group was sort of interacting around me; they were used to being a unit with Chloe and without me. It would have been a terrible time to let go of our whole scheme, but obviously had either of us foreseen a medical emergency, we would never have gone down this path to begin with.

Sofia sat down next to me and unwrapped a chicken sandwich. "Split this with me? CJ says chicken's overrated."

"I didn't realize chicken had a reputation," I said, and then CJ sat on my other side and explained their exhaustion with the chicken sandwich craze from a few years back. So far, of Chloe's friends, I'd interacted the least with CJ and Sofia, but I could still feel how they were both making an effort to take care of me, even if Chloe had been in their lives far longer than mine. It was the nicest that a dig at a food trend had ever sounded, and somehow all of us were still caught up in this conversation a bit later (for the record, Sofia and I still thought the Popeyes chicken sandwich was close to perfection) when a doctor approached our group. My heart sped up, but the doctor's expression was on the positive side of neutral and I was more than pretty certain you didn't give bad news with a face like that.

"Chloe Lee's family?" she asked, and I opened my mouth to say *friends* but noticed everyone else was nodding. "The surgery went well, and she's in the post-op bay right now. As soon as we take her up to recovery, probably in the next hour, we'll let you know and one of you can join her."

We thanked her and I could tell that, despite that maybe we hadn't been *worried* worried, any tension we'd still held fell away. I ate two more sandwich halves and decided I could stop refreshing my inbox for a little while.

"I'm really glad you're here," Phoebe said, and I realized she was talking to me. "Chloe's been alone for so long."

Everyone else nodded emphatically in my direction. Well, everyone but Bianca, whose nod was a bit more perfunctory.

"It's weird to think of her as alone," I said. "She has all of you."

Phoebe opened her mouth to respond, but then a staff member popped up to let us know that Chloe's one visitor was allowed to join her. And even though I'd known her the least amount of time, it was obviously decided I'd be the one to go. It hit me how quickly people slotted friendship into a lower category, as if these six people who'd given up their days to support their friend couldn't possibly compare to the woman who'd shown up only weeks ago and—

Well, I was sure I would feel differently if Chloe and I were actually together.

In the recovery area, Chloe was sitting up on a hospital bed and hardly looking like a person who'd just lost an organ.

"You look great," I said. "I mean normal."

"Thanks a lot, Clementine," she said with a snort. "Sorry I was so loopy earlier. I think the good stuff's all cycled out of my system."

"I feel guilty for being here," I told her. "Your friends know you better and—"

"I think I get to feel guiltier in this scenario," she said. "I just needed a date to a wedding and now you're taking care of my dog and my medical emergencies. Maybe we should . . ."

"No, I don't mind," I said, feeling a wave of panic despite that of course it would be easier without this. Wouldn't it? I hurried to make it make sense. "It would look bad if we broke up now. And there's no way I can handle Greg at the party without you."

"I feel like an idiot," she said. "You were right, this shit does go sideways."

"It's not sideways," I said. "I'm glad I could help. I know I'm not actually your partner or even your girlfriend but I hope we're at least—"

"Maybe we should just stick to the requirements," Chloe said. "Brunch so no one's suspicious, the wedding trip and everything involved with that, and your parents' party. If there's another emergency—"

"It'll look terrible if there's another emergency and I'm not there," I said, instead of dwelling on the fact that maybe Chloe didn't even see me as a friend.

"Fine," she said. "You can have all the other emergencies too."

I only had to argue a little with Chloe to let me bring her back to my condo once she was released—not due to anything I'd done, I knew, purely because Fernando was there.

He practically flew through the apartment when we walked in, and I felt weirdly like an intruder standing there for their reunion, so I headed to my office to catch up on work emails and, since I had this rare late afternoon at home, think about getting some crafting done as well. Small Jesse Pinkman joined me, and batted at my iMac's screen while I answered emails, and then pounced all over my carefully stacked felt pieces as I cut out crabs, scales, and twin cats. I kept the designer-grade catnip sealed up until I was ready to sew the pieces together, but his activated whiskers and wide eyes made me pretty certain that this whole area of my condo was basically a drug den for kitties. It had been easier, so much easier, making cat toys before I had my own cat, though it was much more fun now.

After I was caught up on my inventory—and Small Jesse Pinkman was sufficiently high—I scooped him up and headed out to the living room. Chloe was asleep on my sofa with Fernando curled at her feet, and I restrained from saying *awwwww* audibly.

Chloe stirred and glanced up at me. "I should call a Lyft."

"You can stay here tonight," I said. "Shouldn't someone keep an eye on you? And take out Fernando?"

She sat up and gently rested her hand on Fernando to wake him. He leapt up and barked several times while racing laps around the living room and kitchen. "You've done more than enough."

"Are you mad at me? Did I fuck something up?"

"Do I seem mad?" she asked in a sharp tone.

"I mean, kind of?"

"I'm mad at myself for thinking this would be easy," she said. "Normally my instincts are a lot better than this."

"Are you sure about that? Bear in mind you told me last night about the arm you broke impressing a girl."

The corners of her lips tugged upward. "*Attempting* to impress a girl, get the story right. Anyway, sorry, no, everything's just coming out shitty. You've done more than any fake girlfriend should have to do in the history of fake girlfriends. Until the official wedding shit kicks in, I won't drag you into anything else."

"You had an emergency," I said. "I didn't feel dragged."

"You know what I mean," she said, and the thing was, I did know what she meant. Chloe didn't want me around anymore. Not unless it was absolutely necessary.

"I promise I'll be fine at home," she said. "I just want my own bed."

Considering I'd been there when she'd gotten her incredibly simple aftercare instructions, I knew that I couldn't actually argue with her on that front. And, of course, why would I push for her to stay when all she wanted was to leave? So I said goodbye to Small Jesse Pinkman and drove Chloe and Fernando home.

"Promise me something," Chloe said, unbuckling her seat belt as I pulled up to her apartment building. "Like swear on your life, Clementine."

"I want to hear what the promise is before I—"

Chloe leaned over the console and pulled me into a tight hug. Her chin tucked over my shoulder, and her breath was hot on my neck.

"Thank you for everything," she whispered into my ear. "And if you tell anyone how fucking soft I am, I will absolutely murder you and raise your cat as my own."

Chapter 12
Fancy Cute

Even though Chloe wanted space from me, post-emergency, with a weekly brunch on the calendar and a group chat that rarely went silent, I wasn't sure how I could fully give her what she wanted. My previous habit of participating just enough on the text thread to let people know I was alive and definitely Chloe's girlfriend and not someone involved in a long con of a shenanigan was tougher to manage now that people addressed me directly and asked me specific questions about brunch ideas and wanted my opinion on the latest season of *Selling Sunset*, for example. I managed to skip out on a brunch, citing nonexistent preexisting plans with friends, and did my best to reduce my number of responses on the thread in general. If I couldn't fully disappear from Chloe's life until the wedding events began, I could at least make myself as invisible as possible.

Since I knew that Greg and Marisol had definitely been managing the lion's share of party planning, I offered to fully handle the invitations. The custom order conveniently arrived on a Friday night when the group chat had turned to talk of a last-minute drinks-and-dinner hangout, and even though I'd been eyeing the stack of cards and envelopes next to the long list of invitees, feeling like my guilt might have made me bite off more than my poor penmanship could chew, this *was* a convenient get-out-of-plans card to play. Now I had no reason not to order in a bunch of garbage food that no one else could watch me consume, crank up my favorite Broadway playlist, and get this task accomplished.

But the group chat was more powerful than I'd realized. **Do you need help, Clementine?** Nina texted.

From CJ: **Yeah, if you don't need to write personalized notes or anything, my penmanship is really good.**

My penmanship (are we calling it "penmanship" now?) isn't great but I'll find a way to help, Ari texted.

I wasn't sure there was a way to tell an Oscar winner—or anyone else in this group—not to come over. So I found myself holding off texting my address while hoping Chloe, desperate not to spend any extra time with me these days, would jump in to steer this world back to normal. **I am dealing with a collie who got skunked, but will come by afterward if I'm fit for human consumption. For the record, my penmanship is also great. I'll have a Penmanship-Off with you, CJ!**

I wondered if there was an actual skunked collie or if this was Chloe's way of getting out of it. The only good news in this whole situation was that Phoebe and Bianca had already declared their intentions to stay home with Olivia for a family night in, and so while my condo was about to be invaded by most of my fake girlfriend's best friends—at least my boss currently evaluating my merit for a semi-major promotion plus her definitely suspicious wife would not be in tow. The smallest of victories.

CJ and Sofia arrived first. I'd run a broom around, doing

my best to get up the cat fur that seemed to cover more sur-faces than Small Jesse Pinkman's size would make possible, as well as the catnip that I kept only in my crafting room and yet somehow trickled out like drug-laced glitter. Initially I'd also lit a candle because I worried my condo had its own scent that I'd become nose-blind to, but the Boy Smells candle had a shockingly sexy aroma for a friend hangout, so I'd blown it out almost immediately.

"Hey, Clementine." CJ greeted me with a warm smile, so warm in fact I almost felt at ease. Even after the hospital, CJ and Sofia were the least familiar to me; it might have been awkward hanging around my boss, but at least I knew Phoebe well, and by extension Bianca a little. Nina had similarly at least once been a coworker, and Ari's outward confidence and strong eye contact made it easy to forget that we didn't actually know each other very well. CJ and Sofia, though, were all but strang-ers, and their quieter demeanors didn't help matters. I doubted that great conversation about chicken sandwiches was going to come into play again tonight. I'd googled Sofia once I'd found out that she was apparently the same Sofia Hernández whose paintings I saw all over Instagram, bright and bold portraits and still lifes, and while I supposed that helped me get to know her—or *of* her, at least—better, the knowledge hardly put me at ease.

Especially now that she was in my home. Why couldn't Chloe have had a less intimidating friend group? Some queer folks with less expensive haircuts and more regular jobs. Ac-countants. Paralegals. Project managers. No, here it was all Os-car winners and TV writers and award-winning artists. And tonight they were all going to be *in my home.*

"Hi," I said, suddenly panicked that some of my wall art was from Etsy but the greater majority was from Target, and would Sofia think I had bad taste or was a poor supporter of the arts? Also how queer did queer people's apartments have to look? And I'd forgotten about the show tunes playlist blasting from my speakers, as well as my own appearance, which was just Sweatpants City. How had I managed to light and unlight a sexy candle and yet not even look in a mirror?

"Your place is great," CJ said, glancing around, as Sofia leaned in to look at a print hanging over my bookcase.

"Sorry, that's just from Target," I said, and she burst into laughter.

"Everyone does this to me," she said, turning to smile warmly at me. "Artists like Target too. Where else would I buy tampons?"

"Oh, god, I was afraid everyone else was like a Diva Cup person," I said, and then we were all laughing so hard I barely heard the doorbell ring. I let Nina and Ari in and watched as they too explored my front room and attached kitchen, all the while feeling weirdly relieved about the tampons thing, even as an Academy Award–winner was peering at my bookshelves. I knew it was connected to this feeling that my place some-how wasn't queer enough, as if being queer was something be-yond who you were attracted to and loved and had sex with and everything in those buckets. Like did my art and my tables look heterosexual? Except my queerness wasn't the scam here, just my relationship, so what was I so afraid of? Besides every-thing, really.

Though, also, regardless of any of that, it was super weird that a famous person was here, and weirder yet that polite soci-ety deemed it impolite to comment on that fact.

"Oh my god," Ari said in a tone that made me worry I should have indeed been worried about having everyone over, but then I realized she'd just noticed that Small Jesse Pinkman was curled up on the top level of his cat tree. Everyone crowded around her and for at least the moment I felt settled about these near-strangers in my home. Maybe there was some lying going on, but not about who I was or how I lived.

I tried to figuratively exhale.

CJ organized a big Taiwanese delivery order from Pine & Crane while I did my best to get everyone beverages even though all I had was some cheap wine and, of course, Diet Coke.

"Why are you apologizing?" Nina asked me, helping me carry drinks over to the coffee table. "Two-Buck Chuck and Diet Coke are the two main drinks categories, as far as I'm concerned."

"And you weren't expecting us," Ari pointed out, grabbing the wine bottle and pulling a multitool out of her pocket to flip open a corkscrew.

"Yeah, but you're here to help me," I said.

"We can forgive you for not also having a bunch of La Croix," CJ said.

"This time," Ari said with a wink, and then triumphantly uncorked the bottle. I could tell from the rustle in the room that we all found it fairly hot.

"I know you're probably wondering why I'm not just doing evites," I said, as we settled in and everyone divvied up envelopes and carefully tore the invite list into sections.

"Well, it's old people, right?" CJ asked.

"There was a lot of drama around the evites my aunt sent out last year for my uncle's sixtieth," Sofia said with a knowing nod.

"Oh, god," Ari said, as she and Nina burst into laughter. "There was basically an entire Evitegate at my parents' country club. It was all I heard about every time I called home."

"Bear in mind," Nina managed to get out through laughter, "this was in the middle of Oscar season. Ari's doing nonstop publicity and screening appearances, just up to her ears in FYC stuff, and then she'd call her parents and they'd be all, *Can you believe Gladys says she never got the evite but Bitsy sent it from her account and she can clearly tell it was opened!*"

"Her name is not Bitsy," Ari said. "Get the story right, babe. It's Mittsy."

"What's Mittsy even short for?" CJ asked in an astonished tone.

"Mittens?" I offered, which set us all off again, but we managed to break down the tasks and actually start working. CJ, Sofia, and I addressed envelopes, Nina carefully tucked cards into them and sealed them. Ari had originally agreed to help her, but was instead dragging a feather wand around the living room for Small Jesse Pinkman to pounce upon. We seemed like a good team, though I wondered how this whole weird night would feel different if Chloe was here. I felt even more like I was getting away with something without her around. Still, by the time the doorbell rang and the delivery driver handed me a very large takeout bag, the vibes were still comfortable, and we were all but finished with the task—except Ari, who seemed to have limitless energy for Small Jesse Pinkman.

"Are you two getting stressed about wedding stuff?" CJ asked Nina and Ari as the entire group worked quickly to safely move the invites aside while we set up all the takeout containers on my coffee table. In a flash I remembered my triumph at finding the overpriced West Elm piece in barely used condition on Facebook Marketplace, and driving to the outer valley with Will to pick it up. The table and I had had no idea just what we were in for.

"I don't mean stressed about getting married," CJ clarified. "Just the logistics."

"Yeah, the logistics are a lot," Nina said. "But my therapist is really excited for me to stay calm about things and I really like making her proud of me. Is that healthy?"

"I will say," Ari said, deftly grabbing a wonton with a pair of chopsticks. It probably went without saying but we all clearly thought this, too, was hot. "Compared to last year, this is a lot less stressful. And marrying the love of my life is a much bigger prize than any award."

"Even an Oscar?" Nina asked in a mock serious tone, and Ari laughed before leaning over and kissing her. "Look, we know you guys are all cool and not into the whole old-fashioned marriage and babies thing, and we probably seem like crazy people for doing all of this—"

"No one here thinks that," Sofia said. "Well, Clementine, we haven't known each other long, but I still feel like I can speak for you there."

"You can speak for me there," I said, while wondering about the world I'd somehow wandered into, where maybe the future I wanted wasn't considered the least popular choice, where I didn't feel immediately put on the defensive to want to find my own path.

"You look serious," Nina said to me, though kindly. I wondered what it would have been like if I'd tried to befriend her sooner, back when we worked together. This new part of my life might have felt less trepidatious if I'd already had a queer friend, especially a queer friend who also wore plus-size dresses and was just as femme as I was, if this world hadn't felt so separate from my own back then. Right now I couldn't fully understand why I'd fought connection so hard and for so long.

"No, I just feel like everyone's really happy for you two," I said, though I wasn't sure I had any right to be part of this conversation. What did two of the happiest and most successful people I knew personally need to hear from me? Nina was still looking at me, though, so I kept talking. "And whatever people want for themselves doesn't usually have anything to do with what they want for other people, as long as other people are happy. I don't know, sorry, I hate talking about feelings, is this coming out weird? I've had more wine than usual at this point in the night."

The four of them exchanged a look.

"What?" I asked, even though I maybe didn't want to know.

"Hates feelings, not into getting married, accidentally says really nice things?" CJ laughed. "Am I talking about you or your girlfriend? Hard to say."

"We are . . . not that alike," I said, though between the idea of Chloe and the wine, I flushed with—well, not *pleasure*, exactly. A little warmth.

"It's just really cute," Nina said. "Can I say that much? Or is that too many feelings and now you might die?"

"I get your cat if you die," Ari said quickly.

"Chloe's already claimed him in that event," I said. "Though I'm glad there's a backup plan."

"How nervous does it make you that your death's been discussed to this extent?" Sofia asked, and then we all laughed together again and I felt that I was part of something bigger than myself. It was the very last thing I'd tried for, and I felt a little guilty at how happy I was to have gotten it anyway. Why was I thinking about connections when I wasn't even *real*?

"Do you want to see pictures of my cat when he was a baby?" Ari asked, moving over to sit next to me. "I won't make you talk about your feelings and I think Nina's sick of looking at these."

Despite it all, I couldn't think of something I wanted to do more. CJ crowded in so they could also show off photos of their cat, and before I knew it, the food was consumed, the envelopes were all sealed and addressed, and Chloe's friends were heading out. I realized I hadn't looked at my phone in a while, and I unlocked it in a mild panic and not-so-mild surprise when I saw a pile of notifications from Chloe on my lockscreen.

Sorry, there's no controlling them. I'll do my best with this collie.

Deskunking still going on here. I'm not going to be able to make it. SORRY! I owe you one. I guess. I'm the one up to my elbows in skunked dog fur. Now I have to do YOU a favor?

That was, I'm sure you know, just a joke, but it didn't re-read great, so there you go. Are you ignoring me?

OK I'm home and going to shower at least seven times. Everything OK over there?

Out of the shower, let me know you're alive and that my friends didn't somehow accidentally kill you in a case of helping-too-hard.

I smiled at my phone, then felt ridiculous and tried to neutralize my face. *Then* I reminded myself that only Small Jesse Pinkman could see me and thus far he'd only been supportive of my face.

I'm alive. Sorry, I didn't mean to ignore you. Your friends were here and it was a lot (complimentary). I'm glad you survived the skunk situation. Does that happen a lot?

I shook my head. Someone who wanted space from me definitely didn't need follow-up questions.

Never mind, ignore me. I'm alive, your friends are great, and you definitely don't owe me an apology.

Though I supposed that someone who wanted space from me might not have texted so many times. I'd definitely assumed that dating a woman would be easier than dating a man; surely at least the communication part would be more intuitive from the beginning. Chloe, though, had only confused me so far.

And also, I reminded myself, we weren't actually dating.

Chloe sent a Dana Scully gif, her first in a while, Scully saying *Sure, fine, whatever.* I tapped a heart on it and wished things felt like they had before, which didn't make any sense because we weren't any less together than we were before her surgery. We were not together at all, and that was fine. More than fine! Chloe didn't want me, didn't want a girlfriend at all, and it didn't make sense that I'd have actual feelings for her. I, a queer woman, could like another queer woman without it being romantic or sexual. We were *friends*. Chloe, I realized, was my first new friend in a very long time. I'd hardly meant for that to happen, but now that it had I realized I'd miss her when this was all said and done.

Right now, I felt like I missed her already.

As the wedding trip to Santa Barbara grew closer, I did my best to train Tamarah more and more on the ins and outs of my job so that she could cover as much as possible. It was true that I'd only be gone for three days, but I knew that if any requests came in she was smart enough to handle them, and I wanted to empower her to actually do that. I'd gotten thrown into the deep end of the business at my first job when my boss would toss off to me tasks she didn't want to do, stuff way above my pay grade. It wasn't great management, but I'd been so nervous about doing everything right that somehow I did, and felt myself leveling up on my own. My goal was to do that for Tamarah, without that whole sink-or-swim thing. I imagined how much better I could have done right away if I'd felt supported and also not terrified.

Of course I hoped that if my pitch to Phoebe went well I'd get to promote Tamarah full-time to my new department, but right now I was afraid to even share a hint of that with Tamarah. Phoebe had sent an Outlook meeting request to me, for a little over a week after the wedding, and if it didn't go well, no one would have to know except me. Well, and Phoebe, but I assumed she'd witnessed hundreds, if not thousands of unsuccessful business pitches throughout her career. Before long, mine would have to blend in with the others.

It hit me at some point way past the point of walking back

this meeting or at least pushing it down the road that I'd never imagined myself as someone putting together business pitches or proposing leading an entire team. When I'd started at BME, I'd been just a little cog turning in a medium-size wheel, but when the wheel grew, the cog grew with the wheel. I knew that people like my brother loved to lead—I couldn't even tell if he was in charge of all his home inspections, but he never missed an opportunity to paint that picture. It wasn't all bombastic weird stuff, though, I knew. People like Phoebe loved to lead, too, I could see it in her eyes and hear in her tone when she addressed us in meetings. Phoebe was built for a job like this.

Sometimes I wondered if I'd gotten to my mid-thirties and was *just* figuring out what on earth I was built for. I'd never seen myself as ambitious, but I did like the idea of emulating someone like Phoebe, who not only had found success in this nontoxic environment, but still had time for her wife and her daughter and her friends. If I was going to go after this other life I wanted, enough to—well, blow up my previous life—I needed a career that had enough space in it for all those things I was still looking for, in a person I was still looking for.

Sometimes in quiet moments lately—or in this one when I was trying to focus on updating the cover tab in an Excel worksheet detailing an integrated media plan—I thought about how impossible it seemed to come by that balance, but how guaranteed it would be here. If my presentation didn't go well, if eventually Phoebe trimmed me back entirely and replaced me with a series of robots, I wasn't sure where I'd end up and still be happy.

"Clementine?"

I looked up to see Tamarah standing in my doorway, and from her tone I had a feeling this wasn't the first time she'd said my name. "Sorry, way too focused on this *Gravity of Honor* plan. Which I'm about to send you to proof. We should also spend some time talking about potential revisions based on—

yes, hypothetical client feedback, but also, since I'm going to be out part of next week, I want to make sure you're overprepared."

"Going all in is my favorite," she said, walking in and taking a seat across from me. I loved how comfortable she was; it had taken me far longer at my first assistant gig to do anything but hover uncomfortably near the doorway of my boss's office. "Have you thought any more about expanding the department? If I'm allowed to ask. I also might have seen something in your Outlook, so I'll admit I know it must be at least a possibility."

"Yes," I said, because she had full access to my work calendar and it made sense she'd seen the meeting in my upcoming schedule. There was no actual reason to hide from the truth, even if I didn't want to get her hopes up. Expanding the department would be such a good opportunity for Tamarah to really shine—if it happened. And I liked the thought of her seeing me going after something I wanted. In the future I wanted her to do the same for herself. "And—I mean, we'll see. I'm sure you can understand it's not really up to me."

She nodded thoughtfully in a way that made me realize she probably *did* think it was mostly up to me.

"The industry's in a weird place right now," I said, a little disclaimer so if instead of expanding we imploded, she'd feel warned. "So we'll see."

"OK," she said, a faint line creasing her flawless forehead. I bit back saying anything. Men telling women to smile was terrible, and so probably it wasn't great to tell your youthful assistant that you semi-regretted some of the brow-furrowing you'd done in your twenties that led to some permanent lines now. Young women should get to frown as much as they wanted; it was annoying your skin held on to the memories. "Yeah, Aubrey said something like that."

I did my best to look as if my interest had been lightly piqued, instead of on red-alert panic. "Oh?"

"Yeah, I mentioned that I hoped we could expand back here—"

There I really had to hold my expression in check.

"—and she gave me a whole lecture about AI and algorithms and changing technology and for a moment I thought, oh, my mom was right, I should have just become a nurse like my sister. People are going to keep getting sick, and if for some reason they didn't, it would at least be cause for celebration."

"Oh, god, does everyone have a sibling with the job their parents respect?" I laughed, and realized it was more than I'd ever said to Tamarah about my personal life. Too much? Sometimes I really did have no idea how to lead.

"Yep, you either have that sibling, or you *are* that sibling. Not that I'd know about that side of the coin."

"Nope," I said, smiling at her, imagining if my first bosses had seemed like actual humans to me. It wouldn't have been bad at all, I decided. "Not at all. But I don't think it's time to become a nurse just yet."

"Yeah, that's good." She laughed. "Considering my aversion to most bodily fluids, I don't think I'm cut out for it."

"Trust me, me either." I shrugged, doing my best not to look like Aubrey's comments hadn't gotten to me *yet again*. "Look, my honest answer is that I have concerns, too, but right now we're both needed members of this team, and we should focus on that and not gloom-and-doom reports."

"You're absolutely right." She beamed like I'd said exactly the right thing, which would have felt better if I could hang on to the sentiment more for myself, too.

"Thank you," she continued. "Not to be corny or anything, but I really do feel like I learn so much from you, so, seriously, *thank you*."

"Oh," I said, actually looking around as if she might have said this to someone else. "Sorry, you're welcome. I learn from you too."

She raised an eyebrow. "If you mean asking me what social media 'the youth' uses, sure."

"I'm not sure you understand how useful that information is," I said, and we both laughed. "OK, so we'll make sure over the next week that you can cover most of what might come up while I'm out of town."

"I won't let you down," she said, heading out of the room and leaving me to wonder if me and my plans would actually let her down, and soon.

The long wedding weekend started even earlier than the trip to Santa Barbara, kicking off with a private party at Johnny's the night before we were all heading up the coast. It was all friends, no family or colleagues, in lieu of two separate bachelorette parties, and the mood was somehow both noisy and cozy as I walked in, straight from work. (I'd changed in the bathroom before I'd headed over, a pink and cream-colored dress that was a little shiny and luxe, and tall strappy heels I knew I'd regret but made me feel my absolute cutest.)

I wasn't a complete stranger to Hollywood parties; occasionally clients would invite us to premieres, and I'd drag Will along so we could scoop up free drinks and apps within spitting range of sometimes-very-famous but usually just kind-of-famous actors. Will and I perfected holding the most neutral expressions while standing near celebrities, it was a challenge to see which one of us could act more indifferent. There was no guarantee that this double bachelorette party would be the same, but I did glance quickly from face to face as I approached the bar, more than a little curious about who might be here tonight other than the standard friends group, and with my face safely locked into nonchalance.

Since I saw none of the standard friends—nor any celebrities—I made my way to the bar and squeezed into an open spot. I hadn't been to Johnny's since the whole shenanigan with Chloe began, but the hot bartender—Sadie?—still smiled at me as if I was a regular.

"Hey," she greeted me with a grin. "The new usual? There are also custom drinks for the brides."

"I can't believe you remember that," I said.

She shrugged in a manner that was disarming, not dismissive. "Part of the gig."

"I do kind of want my new usual. Or is that not being appropriately celebratory? How are the custom drinks?"

She slid me a thick piece of paper listing drinks named for Nina and Ari. "They're good, how about you pick one and I'll make your usual as well."

"I haven't even found my friends yet," I said. "And I'm just going to roll in double-fisting? Sure."

"What are you saying about double-fisting?" Chloe popped up next to me. "Sorry I'm late. Am I late? Great Dane."

"Aren't those bigger than you?" Sadie asked, pouring my first drink and setting it in front of me. "Oh, sorry, we can discuss details later—it's a little crazy tonight, if you haven't noticed—but Chloe told me about your parents' party, and I can help you figure something out for drinks. Stop by next week to discuss? I can definitely cut you a deal."

"Yes, thank you," I said, and turned to Chloe. "Thank you, too."

She shrugged in a manner that definitely felt dismissive. "Sure. I said I'd help."

Great. We had basically arrived at the biggest part of our whole scheme, the initial event this whole thing had rested on, and I wasn't even sure if she wanted me around. I'd skipped out of this past week's brunch, too, claiming too much family party planning, when in truth I was just trying to give Chloe what she wanted. Or maybe I was hoping she'd protest, that I'd get a series of texts including Scully gifs. But she only sent a thumbs-up emoji, and that had been that.

"I meant to tell you," Chloe said, and a spark of something that felt like hope lit within me. "I'm all sold out of your cat toys. Every sign. I'll Venmo you but also can you bring me more?"

"Sure," I said, fighting my pride over this sales success story with my *whatever* about Chloe's vibe. "I have a few on hand, but I can crank out a bunch next week, post-wedding."

"Perfect. Everyone's out on the back patio," Chloe told me, as if we weren't on the same group chat, as Sadie poured my second drink. "Do you dance? I feel like my friends are not always a dancing crowd. CJ and Sofia, maybe."

"How's the music? Have your friends said?" Sadie asked. "Some minor DJ drama this week. Apparently the one we initially booked is actually—"

"Ari's ex?" Chloe laughed. "How do you book anything in this town without accidentally getting someone's ex though?"

"My thoughts exactly." Sadie pushed both drinks toward me and handed Chloe a La Croix. "Enjoy. The drinks, the music—"

"The double-fisting," Chloe said with a laugh. "C'mon, Clementine."

I followed her through the crowded bar to the patio, which glittered with twinkle lights. A small DJ booth and dance floor were at the edge, with chairs and small tables filling the rest of the space. When our friends waved us over to a few tables they'd shoved together, for a brief moment I forgot about everything except how lucky I was to be in this beautiful place surrounded by these beautiful people.

"Congratulations," I said to Nina and Ari, who despite the entire establishmentful of people here to celebrate them, looked fairly camped out at this table. Ari was wearing an incredibly cut navy suit over a low V-neck T-shirt, while Nina wore a boldly patterned dress in pinks and oranges, threaded through with a sparkly gold thread. On their own they were beautiful, but together they were somehow even more spectacular. "You both look amazing."

"You too," Nina said. "Where did you get this dress? No, we can talk about shopping later, and we will, but I feel like Ari and I should circulate, right? Now that everyone's here, you two can take our spots and we'll be back?"

"Yeah, we gotta make the rounds," Ari said, standing up and offering her arm to Nina as she did the same. "I feel like this is us until we're back from our trip in a couple of weeks, leaving y'all to it while we mingle. So this is my blanket apology if we don't spend enough quality time together until then."

"It was the same at our wedding," Phoebe said with a wave of her hand, and Bianca snorted.

"Well, not exactly. Those of you who were there will remember it was not exactly this elaborate an affair," she said, though she smiled at Phoebe like she wouldn't have had it any other way. I wondered with a pang if it was hypocritical to not want the whole thing—not the ceremony, not the piece of paper, not the babies and not the backyard—and still want someone to look at me just like that for the rest of my life.

"I mainly remember that I rented a tux and thought I looked dapper as fuck," Chloe said, "and then one of Phoebe's aunts thought I was the ring bearer."

"To be fair," Nina said, laughing as hard as the rest of us were, "didn't you rent a tuxedo from the little boys' section?"

"It's not my fault that tuxedo shops don't have small lesbian sections!" Chloe said, and hugged Nina and then Ari before taking a seat.

I did my best to convey some kind of warm greeting with my expression, but Ari pulled me into a hug, and then Nina did the same. And I couldn't help it; I loved this, the big messy group of people who welcomed me, sometimes with literal open arms. I squeezed into the spot next to Chloe, and laughed as CJ gestured to my two drinks.

"Sadie kind of made me."

"Wait, I just noticed," Nina said, instead of actually leaving. "You have *two drinks* and one is the custom Ari drink, and then one is just something else random?"

"Again, Sadie made me, I didn't say, *please, not the Nina cocktail*," I said.

"Really?" Ari asked with a grin. "You sounded very comfortable saying *please, not the Nina cocktail* just now."

"I was standing there, that's *exactly* what she said," Chloe said.

"This is character assassination," I said, as Nina and Ari finally managed to head off, at least as far as the next table. "Do you feel like you're sharing them with the whole world?" I asked, then worried it was way too strange of a question.

"Only nights like tonight," CJ said. "And the other Oscar season."

"Yeah," Chloe said, and chugged a bit of her seltzer. "Normally it's the way it always is. One of our friends is just kind of famous. It doesn't really affect much."

"It's so LA," I said, and everyone nodded in agreement and held out their glasses or cans to clink together. To LA indeed.

The substitute DJ was good, we all agreed, and once I'd had one and a half drinks, I followed CJ, Sofia, and Chloe to the dance floor. Part of me felt as off-kilter and on the defense as I had early on with Chloe, when it felt like all the knowledge and power was in her hands and I'd unwittingly tied myself to a potentially disastrous situation. Bosses and celebrities and other shocks lurking behind corners. No, I still had no idea what Chloe was thinking, but the truth was that it didn't feel as nerve-wracking this time around. Under the twinkle lights, moving to the music in a crowd of people that included CJ and Sofia, I didn't feel like I was flailing on my own. At the very worst, I was flailing alongside others.

Still, though, maybe it was the drink-and-a-half or maybe

it was the mood of the charged dance floor, I turned a bit from my newish friends and made it clear with my eyes, with a sway of my hips that I was dancing with Chloe. I was never on a dance floor purely to dance in a group. Saddle me, I thought, with a fake girlfriend, and I at least deserved to dance with said fake girlfriend.

Chloe, to her credit, pulled me in closer, her hand on my hip, her movements mirroring mine. Even though I'd asked for this, beckoned her even, in a flash of heat I realized that I'd never danced with another woman, not like this. I hadn't danced with *anyone* in over a decade besides Will, not like this. There were so many new firsts again.

How long, I wondered, Chloe's touch sending warmth through my body, would it be until I had something like this for real? Our lips inches away from each other's, our hands pulling our bodies closer. Why couldn't I have gotten rescued all those weeks ago by someone who actually wanted me? How would I feel at this moment, if it wasn't just for show?

"You're very good," Chloe said, pulling me closer still. "Promise me that we're going to burn down that dance floor at the actual wedding reception."

I moved with her, felt the press of her body against mine, wondered if it had just been a very long time since anyone had touched me or if I wanted to know how it would feel for specifically Chloe to touch me more.

"Hey," I said sharply, mostly to distract myself from the disastrous possibility that it was the second of those two options. "I feel like I have no idea what's going on."

She furrowed her eyebrows, though still managed to keep dancing. "About what?"

"After your surgery I felt like you didn't want me around anymore. And tonight you're all—"

"Well, Clementine, we've gotta put on a good show," she said, throwing back her head and swaying close to me. She smelled like her fancy products and sweat. Unfortunately that was an upsettingly hot combination. "Also when did I say I didn't want you around? You're the one bailing on brunch to deal with your family party errands. Which I could have just helped you with afterward instead."

"You could have just said that," I said, annoyed that she hadn't and also at how sexy I found her neck suddenly.

"So could've you," she said, looking back at me and grinning. "You look cute tonight. I mean, you always do. Fancy cute, though."

"You're really—" I stopped myself, because what was there to say? Annoying? Frustrating? *Hot?* "Fancy cute, too."

Chloe laughed. It was true, though, she was in a floral-patterned jumpsuit that was a little fancier than her standard ones, and she was wearing hot pink suede oxfords I'd never seen before. "Thanks. I don't think anyone would mistake me for a ring bearer tonight."

"No chance," I said.

"Are you still mad at me?" she asked.

"I wasn't mad," I said. And I couldn't think of anything else reasonable to say, and so I left it at that, right as the DJ played a Chappell Roan track that made the entire dance floor cheer. Chloe and I pushed in closer again to CJ and Sofia, and before long it was like we'd become friends with everyone around us.

By the time we took a break, I'd kicked off my shoes like a carefree person I really wasn't, and Chloe went scrambling through the crowd to find them while CJ and Sofia headed in to get the biggest glasses of water the bar would give us.

"We have to head out," Phoebe told me as I made it back to our tables. "But we'll see you tomorrow in Santa Barbara. I know Nina and Ari'll be busy with a million things, but Bianca and I were thinking the rest of us should meet for lunch at the Julia Child place on our way in. Sound good? We can finish coordinating on the group chat."

"Sounds good," I said. Back in the 1990s, Julia Child had proclaimed her love for a taco stand in Santa Barbara, and decades later people still waited in a cartoonishly long line to order. In LA I was thrilled that almost every restaurant I loved took reservations, but vacation was always another story, especially in beachy Santa Barbara where the pace of life was so dialed back to begin with. Standing in line felt like a luxury, not an everyday inconvenience.

Chloe was back almost as soon as Phoebe and Bianca said good night, triumphantly wielding my heels.

"My hero," I said as she sat down next to me. The sound of the crowd around us created a little pocket of privacy, and I did my best to give her my most serious look. "Remember at the beginning, or the almost-beginning of all of this? You didn't tell me about Phoebe, and I said I didn't want to be left in the dark anymore?"

"Is someone else your boss too?" Chloe asked with a laugh.

"You *have* been making me feel like you don't want me around," I said. "And I don't believe that you don't know that. Remember this was all *your* idea. So keep me in the loop with whatever is going on, OK? You made me feel like you didn't want me around, that it was better if I gave you space. So I did, and now you're acting like that was a choice I made, and not something you contributed to in any way. This whole thing when I don't know what you want, I thought you agreed to be open with me."

Chloe got up and then dropped down right in front of me, and I realized she was helping me step into my heels. "Please don't laugh. I was trying to be nice, and now I just feel like a shoe salesguy."

I laughed too and let her buckle the ankle straps gently. "Thank you."

"Please don't make me fake break up with you," she said, taking a seat even closer to me so that no one even in a quieter crowd could have heard her. "Do you want me to admit I'm shit at all of this? I obviously didn't think my body would reject an actual organ while we were in the middle of this. You've had to do way more than I asked and—I don't know. I wanted to give you a break."

"Well, yeah, I know." I nudged her with my elbow. "You said that back when it happened. And I told you I didn't mind, remember?"

She waved her hand. "I wanted to give you an out. People say they don't mind all the time."

"Not me. I've been really honest with you, haven't I?"

She agreed with that while my stomach panged with a reminder that maybe my honesty hadn't been as all-consuming as I claimed. Chloe couldn't have suspected how I'd felt dancing with her, how the touch of her hand on my hip seemed to connect directly with every nerve pathway in my body, racing directly toward my center. That wasn't a lie, I reasoned. That was just my body, and how my body reacted was out of my hands. My brain still knew exactly the terms of our deal, and soon the wedding would be past us and our time would be even more numbered, and I could start my actual new life for actual real.

Chapter 13
Take Back Some Danger

"I can't believe you agreed to that taco stand," Chloe said when she rolled up to my place the next morning. "Julia fucking Child says it's good and now I'm doomed to eat overrated plates of peppers for the rest of my life. Thanks, old white lady."

"Uh, you're welcome," I said, and Chloe burst into laughter.

"I meant Julia Child, not you, you idiot," she said, though she hopped out to help me with my bags. "Who's taking care of Small Jesse Pinkman? Is this the first time you're leaving him? Are you OK?"

"I'm very uncomfortable with this, but my assistant's handling it," I said with a grimace. "You know I hate overlapping worlds, but I remembered she'd said something about cat sitting for one of her neighbors, and honestly she's one of the people I trust most to handle things, so."

"I'm proud of you," Chloe said, as we got into the Bronco and buckled up. "Small Jesse Pinkman deserves the best care, even if now your assistant will know what kind of toilet paper you like best."

"Oh, *god*, I didn't even think about that," I said, as she laughed at my expense. "No, you're right, it's worth it."

"He'll be fine," she said in a kinder voice than I was used to from her. "It's so hard leaving them, I know. I wish Fernando could text me to let me know how he was doing."

"It would be so cute if they *could* text," I said. "Even if it was just emojis."

"Why would it be *just emojis*?" Chloe shrieked. "So in this world, they have the power to use phones but *only emojis*?"

"Why is that so weird? I feel like the power of the English language might be beyond them. Emojis are so straightforward."

"Oh my god," Chloe said, but she grinned at me. "Are you ready?"

"For what? A whole weekend devoted to a couple's eternal love while we're there scamming the system?"

"Uh, no, and what system?" She gestured to her iPhone in its dashboard mount. "Are you ready for the amazing playlist I made for us to get there and back?"

"That," I said, "I'm absolutely ready for."

She tapped *play* and the opening notes of "Ya Got Trouble" from *The Music Man* rang out. "That's right. It's wall-to-wall musicals."

"Hell *yeah*," I said. "Did your friends tell you when they came over to help me the other week that I had a Broadway playlist blasting? They all acted really nice about it but I definitely did not feel very cool about the whole thing."

"Oh, please," she said. "They're all nerds in their own ways. No one said anything to me about that night except that your condo's great and your cat's amazing."

I imagined being discussed in my absence, in a group that contained both my fake girlfriend and my actual boss, with only compliments. A rush of warmth was too intense for me to worry about other possibilities that the fears of being talked about behind your back usually brought up. The stuff I worried Fiona and Hailey talked about these days in the texts they sent directly back and forth, our group chat quieter than ever.

"You know, I was so nervous about hanging out with some queer friend group," I said, leaning back against the headrest and letting the morning sunlight warm my face. "But I haven't felt like I was, you know, entering some new culture or something. It's been easy."

"Yeah, you nerd, it's because you're super queer," Chloe said with a laugh. "What new culture? It's *your* culture, remember?"

"No, I know, just—you know. Outside of Instagram meme accounts I followed, my life just felt really straight before. Straight friends, straight boyfriend. And when you're—you know, you look like me? I can tell people just read me as straight."

"Ah yes, the invisible femmes," Chloe said. "I mean, not to me. I always knew about you."

I turned to look out the window because I didn't want her to see how much that made me smile. "Wait, you did?"

"Yeah, you've got bi written all over you," she said.

"That's so funny," I said. "Growing up, I would have *never* thought that. I felt like in movies or TV shows or whatever, bi people were always, you know. Like wearing black leather and having sex outside of some hot club at three a.m. or whatever. All mysterious and dangerous and *provocative*. Not, you know, wearing some twee dress with glasses and sensible shoes and listening to show tunes while home by an appropriate hour."

"Uh, Clementine, I've hooked up with a lot of bi girls," Chloe said. "Some twee dress with glasses and sensible shoes basically *is* a bisexual stereotype."

Chloe passed up the entrance to the 5 Freeway and pulled into a McDonald's drive-thru. "I assume we want giant Diet Cokes for the road."

"Great assumption, yes."

"Stereotypes are hard to shake," she said, glancing at me. "So don't let me come across like I don't get it. The shit people say about Asian girls, it still gets to me sometimes."

I bit back a *does it really?* because even though Chloe had told me she hated it when people acted like her emotions didn't run deep, I guessed that it still surprised me more than a little. Despite her literally making me promise not to speak of her secret softness, I still saw her as tough.

"I'm being quiet," I said, "because on this subject I am just a white lady who hasn't experienced any of that."

"Good girl," she said with a smile, and pulled forward to order our Diet Cokes. "You know, all that quiet and submissive bullshit. It doesn't help that I'm like the size of a large doll."

"You're such a badass, though," I said.

"Yeah, well, I think it's because I feel like I have to be," she said. "Like, I can feel that, you know? People expect me to be sweet and quiet, so I'm like this instead."

"Again, white lady disclaimer," I said, and she laughed as she pulled up to the first window and paid for our sodas. "I know all the societal stuff is racist and bullshit and terrible. But I also think you *are* a badass. Two things can be true at once."

"Yeah, yeah," she said, but she threw me another smile. "I dunno, I have this reputation, you know. My friends still refer to me as their friend who punches people or the one who got thrown in jail. That shit all happened in my twenties."

"Wait," I said, as Chloe pulled up to get our drinks. It was the most anticipation I'd ever felt in a McDonald's drive-thru. "You were *in jail*?"

"They, like, use that story as an example of how feral I am," she said, pulling back onto the street in the direction of the freeway. "Chloe can't control her temper, punches a guy right in the face. And I *did* punch a guy, right in the face, that much is true. But that asshole who then *pressed charges* called me and the girl I was with a fucking slur. But he was a white guy with a fancy car and a law degree, so obviously it was me, the queer woman of color, who paid for it."

"Wait," I said again. "Do your friends know that? I know you know them a million times better than I do, but it doesn't seem like something they'd talk about that way. Also not to doubt your version of the story."

"Nah," she said. "They bailed me out, and Phoebe has an ex who's a fancy lawyer who does pro bono work, so she handled it. I didn't feel like getting into it. And I think they do know that if I punched a guy that he deserved it."

"Truth," I said.

"But also . . ." She sighed and stared straight ahead, in a way that seemed beyond paying attention to the road. "I'm angry all of the time, and I don't know how other women, queer people, people of color, considering the state of the world and all, how we're not all just punching assholes whenever they give us an excuse, you know?"

Greg's face flashed into my mind and, even though I knew it wasn't what Chloe meant, I laughed in recognition anyway. "Yeah. I'm not usually in punching mode but I hear you."

"Ooh," she said, perking up in her seat. "I forgot I put this on the playlist. There are honestly a lot of bangers in *Annie*."

I laughed and leaned over to crank up the volume of "Easy Street." "Making a playlist is an important part of a road trip, so I'm glad you remembered. I used to be so good at stuff like that, back before I broke up with Will."

"Good at playlists?"

"No, just . . . making things nice. Remembering to do shit. Getting up every morning and doing yoga. Dinners with leftovers for lunches the next day. It's like he left and I went feral."

"Yeah, he was boring, you needed to take back some danger," Chloe said, pulling onto the 5 Freeway. "OK, trip's officially begun. I feel like it doesn't count when you're still on surface streets."

"Oh my god, believe it or not, I think that too," I said. "Also, Will wasn't boring. I know you'll never believe me, but he wasn't. He just had an idea of our life together that didn't actually take *me* into account, you know? Just this idea of a wife and a mom and this whole future together that made me feel like he'd never actually seen me."

I realized I'd never quite realized I thought that until the words left my mouth, and the awareness rattled through me. This hardly felt like the best place for a bunch of post-relationship processing, though, so I leaned forward to crank up the music—"La Vie Bohème" from *Rent* had just come on—instead.

Driving to Santa Barbara always started as a slog, heavy traffic up the 101 through some of the most boring parts of the regular Valley and then the way-out Valley. The sites were strip malls and little else, until suddenly you rounded a corner, and there it was, the crashing wet blue of the Pacific Ocean. Paradise had been creeping up on you all along.

"Is there a reason Ari and Nina wanted to get married here?" I asked, as Chloe swung the Bronco off on the exit that would lead us to our lunch plans. "Like did they meet here, or one of them grew up here?"

"Nah, Nina said they wanted an easy destination wedding, and since they own a place in Palm Springs that apparently didn't feel destination-y enough for them. It feels random but I've seen photos of the venue, it's going to be beautiful, blah blah."

I laughed. "I've never had, like, the greatest attitude about weddings, but, I don't know. The thing that's given me pause is how generic so much of it feels, you know? Taking these steps everyone takes in a way that feels like you're legally required to. But it hasn't felt like that? Even last night felt really special. Is it embarrassing to admit that?"

"No, the embarrassing thing is having such wonderful

friends who are so happy and *good*," Chloe said. "Trust me. Bianca and Phoebe's wedding was so great and poked all these holes in my feelings about big weddings, you know?"

"Yeah, annoying."

Chloe found a parking spot, and we walked up to the restaurant, where everyone else was already in the long line. We'd all literally seen each other mere hours ago, but the truth was that it was always a little exciting seeing your friends when you were out of town together. Or even your fake girlfriend's friends.

As we waited, I chatted with CJ about work—they actually worked on the back end of digital ads at a fairly large entertainment site network so in some ways we did the same job from different angles—and with Phoebe about our favorite restaurants around work, for some reason, and even with Bianca, because as much as she still made me nervous, I wouldn't survive if I didn't find out where she'd gotten the bright patterned maxidress she was wearing. And I felt like most plus-size people who loved clothes were usually pretty excited to share intel with each other.

I got so wrapped up in that conversation that it felt like we barely waited in line at all, and by the time we were all seated with our food—and Chloe was elbowing me so I'd notice how many of our friends had ordered what amounted to plates of peppers—I decided that whatever suspicion Bianca once had seemed to have cooled off. Though of course I knew I could have just been overestimating the value of a conversation about shopping on Instagram.

We caravanned to the hotel after lunch, and it was in the hotel lobby, as I was standing next to Chloe, behind Phoebe and Bianca, and in front of CJ and Sofia, that it hit me. Chloe had told me that Nina and Ari were handling the accommodations for everyone, and I'd had far too many other things on my mind to think of it any further. Task managed, fantastic.

But now I was standing here, waiting to check into Chloe's and my *room*, singular. There was, it hit me, only one bed.

How had I gotten this far in this fake girlfriend scenario without predicting this exact situation? They built entire romance novels around them, for god's sake! I had somehow agreed to this weekend, packed my bags, cheerfully sipped Diet Coke and sang show tunes for two hours up the coast, and yet it hadn't occurred to me at all.

I tugged on Chloe's arm, though I hadn't yet decided how I'd ask her if she was prepared for what was about to happen while surrounded by her friends who would hardly expect us to be surprised by the situation. But then Phoebe and Bianca stepped away, and Chloe gave me a look before walking up to the front desk. "Room for Lee. Or maybe it's under Hayes. Maybe both."

I stared at her so intently she must have felt it.

"What?" she asked.

I gestured with my arms out to my sides.

"Did you lose the power of speech?" she asked, before turning back to the front-desk clerk to get our key cards. For the room we were sharing together. That only housed one bed.

I all but dragged Chloe away from her friends, down the corridor just a short distance to room 107. "Just one room."

"Clementine," she said with a heavy sigh, and turned away from me to tap the key card against the sensor. "What did you think the setup would be?"

We walked into the room and I stared at the bed. It was large—larger than mine at home, at least—but it was still just the one bed.

"You're being weird," she said, tossing her suitcase on the bed with surprising ease and unlatching it. "At what point did it hit you we'd be in the same room?"

"Somehow literally just now," I said. "I don't know. This whole thing's been a weird blur at times. Somehow I've overthought the wrong parts."

"Come on," she said. "Hang up your nice stuff so we don't look like dirtbags."

"Speak for yourself," I said, but I followed her example and got my nice dresses into the closet next to Chloe's array of suits and jumpsuits. "You'll be the best-dressed ring bearer here."

She grinned at me. "To be fair, that suit is from the boys' side of J.Crew."

"When's dinner tonight?" I asked. "Is that the next thing on our agenda?"

"Well, I think CJ and Sofia want to go look at some old religious boring thing, right?" she asked with a roll of her eyes. Santa Barbara was as full of historic monuments, like the Old Mission that I'd been to on multiple field trips, as it was full of wine and beaches and other ways to relax. "I'd rather get in the pool. But go see some old building if you want."

"Thanks, you make both sound really great," I said. "I didn't bring a suit, so maybe I'll go with them, if you don't think that's weird."

"Uh, I think it's weird you didn't bring a suit," she said.

I shrugged, trying to look casual. Thin people reminded me of myself as a little kid, complete confusion over why anyone wouldn't be one hundred percent pro-pools. "Public-ish pools can be weird for me. I just don't always feel like being the fattest person there."

Her head whipped around, and she stared at me. "Clementine. That makes me really fucking sad. Especially because you probably have some old-timey retro swimsuit and you look superhot in it."

"It *is* pretty old-timey," I said with a laugh to disguise the fact that Chloe's words actually made me choke up a little. "No, it's fine, sorry, it's not about me, it's just about how other people can be weird sometimes and I don't always want to deal with it."

"Ugh," she said loudly. "Fine. Let's both go see an old building."

"It wasn't completely boring on my last field trip," I said, flooded with gratitude that she'd change plans for me, and we both laughed. And it actually turned out that California state history was way less boring when you were with a few friends in the bright sunshine on a weekday off from work. Everything seemed less impossible by the time we got back to our room—post a quick stop at a nearby restaurant for some wine for three of us and a cheese plate for all of us—and I managed to calmly unpack into the hotel bathroom all the various creams and gels it took for my face and hair to look presentable, without dwelling too much on the accommodations. Despite the terrifyingly ridiculous scenario I'd found myself in, it was increasingly tough to worry about anything in this sun-drenched beach town where everything seemed to be designed around drinking wine, glimpsing the ocean, and doing very little else.

My phone buzzed while Chloe was exploring our little private patio (this was definitely the nicest I'd traveled) and I'd been thinking about joining her. Our room did back up to the Metro train, but the little outdoor space was still inviting as hell. But *yikes*. The only message worse than a work emergency. Well, or than a frantic weird passive-aggressive text from Greg. OK, far down in the terrible category, but still concerning.

Hey Clementine, could you stop by our hotel room? Thanks, from Bianca.

"Do you know what this is about?" I called out to Chloe. She pointed at her earbuds and waved me away, and I didn't know what else to do besides make my way to my boss's and her wife's hotel room. Surely if it was some kind of work emergency or if Phoebe had made the decision not only to not expand my department but to shutter it altogether, Bianca wouldn't have been the one to summon me.

"Hey," Bianca greeted me, opening the door and stepping

aside. She looked perfectly vacation-y in a hot pink caftan. "Chloe told me you forgot a swimsuit and assumed I over-packed, which was accurate."

"Oh, I—" I shook my head. "I'm good. Sorry she texted—"

"She also said you don't always love public pools in a casual way that small people say things like that," Bianca said with a little smirk. "Anyway. I was going to head down anyway, so let's all go together."

I studied Bianca in her hot pink caftan, the tied strings of a bikini visible, and wondered just what swimsuit I'd be agree-ing to.

"Here," she said, apparently reading my thoughts, pointing me toward the dresser where three two-pieces were laid out. One was solid black, not usually my vibe, but with a modest cut that was pretty retro. I didn't hate it.

"I forgot the other option," she said, and I wondered if some magically perfect suit would appear. "The other option is we tell your girlfriend she's being a meddling pain in our asses and we sit poolside in whatever you want to wear and order cock-tails while we talk about online shopping some more."

"You can do whatever you want," I said. "Don't feel like you have to babysit me. I'm really fine. I mean, I know you're really confident and cool and whatever and—I don't know. I have no more complaints with my body than I guess anyone does about theirs, but I just feel like sometimes people can be shitty to fat women in swimsuits so I keep myself out of those situations."

"I'm genuinely flattered you think you have to explain any of this to me," Bianca said with a grin. "Girl, I get it. I work out at this awesome all-sizes gym because I love a dance class but I grew weary of thin women telling me I was so brave to be there. Yeah, I know I seem confident, but it's more that I fight back against all of that bullshit because I love pools and also because I think I look great in a bikini. And I'm sure you do too. So come or don't come, but between me and Chloe, trust me, no one's going to bat an eye at you without some serious consequences."

I shrugged, feeling myself wanting to give in, to feel like a kid again when the excitement of getting into a big fancy hotel pool outweighed literally any other possibility. "Is Phoebe coming?"

"God, no, Clementine, I'm not making you put on one of my bikinis in front of *your boss*," she said with a shriek, and then we were both laughing and I somehow felt the most comfortable I'd been in—well, ages, really. How did these people keep doing that, just upping that comfort level constantly?

The borrowed swimsuit was still a little sexier than I would have ideally picked for myself, but—no surprise—Bianca also had extra caftans and coverups to offer me, and I felt almost comfortable as I headed down to the pool with her and Chloe. And maybe I imagined it, but the way Chloe's eyes dragged along my body when I tried to casually slip out of my caftan at the pool's edge made every uncomfortable part of the afternoon worth it.

Chapter 14

Two Liars at a Wedding

It was late when we—our new grouping, the whole group minus the two brides who were busy with in-town family—got back to the hotel from our dinner at Bibi Ji, and we were all so stuffed with saag and curry and uni biryani and more garlic naan than I'd ever had in my life that only Chloe offered up a tepid suggestion to hit the hotel pool or bar, and instead we all headed off in pairs to our rooms. The realization that I'd somehow managed to tuck away for most of the day hit me with a red-hot flash of panic as Chloe let us in and I stared at the bed, which looked smaller than it had in the daylight.

"Do you want the bathroom first or last?" Chloe asked me in a casual tone, riffling through her suitcase.

I played out the two scenarios, lying down in bed first and waiting for Chloe to join me, or getting into the bed with her already there. I hated both of these!

"Should I sleep on the floor?" I asked, like an idiot. It wasn't even close to a normal offer and I knew it! "I don't know, sorry, is that easier somehow?"

"No, it's weird," Chloe said. "I'll take that as a *sure, Chloe, you can have the bathroom first.*"

She walked off, closing the door behind her, while I pawed through my own bags. I'd brought a faded T-shirt I usually slept in, swag from an action movie I worked the marketing for a million years ago at Paramount, and sweatpants for lounging, so I'd have to sleep in the whole stretchwear look. At home I slept in the T-shirt and underwear only, but that felt more than mildly risqué in this current scenario. By the time I was in the bathroom and in my formal sleepwear attire, I frowned at my reflection and slipped out of my shirt to put my bra back on. Everything was just perkier that way.

The truth was that I hated that I wasn't more confident with my body when it came to other people. I liked my body, and Will had never made me feel anything less than attractive the entire time we were together, even though I was bigger at the end of our relationship than I'd been at the beginning. He complimented my style when we went out, and in bed he made it known with his eyes and hands and mouth that my body was exactly the body he wanted.

I knew it was something I'd have to confront when I dated again, of course, but there were all the other parts too, like swimsuits in public and thin people not understanding how any of it actually felt.

Not that I had any room to complain around Chloe and her friends. Not in that department, and not about anything else, either. And I knew I wasn't always that comfortable with Fiona and Hailey, my thin friends who never quite seemed to get it, but I hated how often I thought of them poorly lately, when nothing had changed except the addition of some people who wouldn't even be in my life after a few more weeks. If Fiona and Hailey understood me better, I knew, things would be easier. But I didn't know how to bridge that gap. Right now it felt easier to let it keep widening instead.

I opened the bathroom door and tiptoed to the bed, where Chloe was sitting up, calmly scrolling her phone. "The doggie daycare sent me six perfect photos of Fernando plus a video. I am tipping them so well."

"Oh yeah, Tamarah sent me some good ones of Small Jesse Pinkman earlier," I said, grabbing my phone to show her. "I can't believe how much I miss him. Is that weird?"

"You think everything is weird," Chloe said, but grinned at me. "Missing pets is normal. Will you turn the lights off before you get in bed?"

I tried to flip the switches casually, but somehow *missed* and looked like I was just swiping randomly at the wall. And since the lights were still on, Chloe absolutely saw it happening.

"Everything OK over there?" she asked with a laugh. "You seem to be still wearing your glasses."

"I'm good," I said, successfully flipping the switches and waiting as darkness descended over the room before approaching the bed. It was a big hotel-size king, but still seemed impossibly small to get into. Of course there was the fact that for months now I'd been in my own king-size bed with no one else but Small Jesse Pinkman. And then of course there was the fact that it was *a bed* and Chloe was *not my girlfriend* and *seriously why had I not considered this horrible possibility* but also *how horrible is the possibility really when Chloe held me the way she did on the dance floor only one night ago even if clearly nothing would ever happen between us.*

"You OK?" Chloe asked.

"No, yeah, of course," I said, doing my best to slip into the bed like some kind of weightless magical creature. "This is just weird, right? Can we say it's weird?"

"I don't know what you're talking about, Clementine," she replied in that infuriatingly chill tone of hers. "I share beds with randos all the time."

A laugh burst out of me. "Oh, I'm a rando now? Cool."

"Sorry, are you one of those people who loves to share beds with people? Every night since your boring boyfriend left has been the emptiest and the loneliest ever?"

"Oh, god, no," I said, maybe not fully having realized it until saying it. "I love having the bed to myself, actually. I mean, besides Small Jesse Pinkman of course. Will could be good at helping me stay calm, but a purring kitten is maybe even better equipped for the job."

"Don't worry, I'd never forget Small Jesse Pinkman, and his myriad of talents." Chloe snorted. "I dated this girl who always tried to touch my feet with hers in the middle of the night. She thought it was romantic. Sorry, I don't think anything with feet is romantic."

"Not your kink," I said, "got it."

Chloe snorted harder. It might have been an actual laugh. "People treat me like I'm a freak for being happy being alone. But I love sleeping through the night not worrying if my feet are going to be randomly touched."

"You understand that it's not a binary thing, right?" I asked. "It's not *be single or have your feet touched against your will*, you know."

"That has not been my experience," she said, but I could tell from her tone that perhaps I'd won this round.

"I never had to worry about that with Will," I said. "Unexpected foot-touching."

"Yeah, and you still left him," she said.

"That makes it sound easy," I said, even though ultimately in so many ways, it had been. "I did have to blow up my life to—I don't know. Go after what I'm actually looking for. I lost my guaranteed future. My friends, I'm sure, think I made a huge mistake and maybe I'm realizing they didn't know me very well either."

"Tell me, Clementine," Chloe said, "what *is* this thing you're looking for? Besides that it's gayer?"

"I don't know," I admitted, even though when I talked to

Will it had been so clear. "There's this whole expected life, I guess, the things society says you're supposed to do to be a valid person, and so much of that just isn't on my list. I want to find someone outside of that."

"Even though you admit it's good to have a whole bed to yourself."

"Well, sure," I said. "Right now it's very easy to want that."

"Oh, *fuck you*," Chloe said, but her words were tinged with such sweetness.

"In my head," I said softly, "it doesn't feel like an either-or. This thing I want. I want to fall in love and have it be forever. And just because I want it on my own terms—I don't know. It's like everyone else is doing this one thing because that's what people do. I guess this is the part I have a hard time spelling out. Why didn't I want everything Will wanted if I was in all-the-way for him?"

"Well, it's been, what, eleven weeks or something and you're already getting ready for the girl you're going to fall in love with next?" Chloe's smirk was apparent even through the darkness. "How 'in all-the-way' were you actually?"

I thought about digging in and finding the words to describe what sometimes felt like the indescribable: how I'd pick up clues of the life Will thought we'd have together and feel this heart-jabbing stab that it wasn't only that we didn't want the same things but that maybe somehow after all these years we didn't even know each other well enough to realize it. What had all those years been built on? And if what my heart sought out felt so natural to me, why did the relationships other people had so often make me chafe when envisioning myself in them? Why did all of this feel like an ill-fitting garment?

"I'm going to sleep," Chloe said. "I'm getting tired and I like picking on you when I have more mental energy."

"OK," I said, hoping it sounded *breezy* and not *wait is this yet another existential crisis?*

"Don't touch my feet during the night," she said.

188 / *Amy Spalding*

I cracked up more than I probably normally would, so relieved to have anywhere to put my thoughts other than the steaming stew of worry bubbling over in my brain. "No problem. Enthusiastic foot consent only."

We spent the next day in Santa Barbara almost identically to the first. The friend group minus Nina and Ari met for brunch at a beachside restaurant, and afterward roamed the nearby beach while cartoonishly beautiful things happened like trios of dolphins turning flips in the air right before our eyes.

"It's like a Lisa Frank Trapper Keeper," CJ said in a reverent tone, which struck me as the funniest thing I'd heard in ages. It did not escape my notice that, around these people, there were so many new funniest things ever.

"It's so gorgeous here," Phoebe said, and we all concurred. It was so gorgeous in fact that I was barely thinking of the fact that Phoebe held my future's fate in her hands and I'd ended up on a destination wedding vacation with her.

"My family assumes I must see the ocean all the time," Sofia said. "But I don't know about the rest of you, I never make it out to the beach."

"You never make it past Western," CJ said, and we all laughed for a second and then were silent, each of us clearly doing the geographical math. I couldn't remember the last time, this trip excluded, I'd left my little pocket of Eastside Los Angeles either.

"Santa Barbara sounded so random when Nina and Ari told us," Chloe said. "But I get it now that we're here."

"You've been here before," I said. "Or you wouldn't have such big thoughts about the peppers, probably."

Chloe elbowed me. "Yeah, back in my dirtbag younger years. One time we got here to stay with my friend Jenn's friend and her girlfriend, but the friend had left the girlfriend like two nights before we got here, the girlfriend forgot we were coming, and she just kept weeping and trying to drag the futon back in from the yard."

Phoebe raised her eyebrows. "Why was the futon in the yard?"

"I guess when she got dumped she put all her stuff on the lawn to be dramatic, I don't know. Jenn got the lawn futon. All they could find for me to sleep on was some leftover child's mattress. Whenever people are like, oh wow, Santa Barbara, what a beautiful part of the state, I'm like, yeah, for me to sleep on a four-foot-long mattress while a woman I don't know weeps."

"You have a lot of very specific experiences you nonetheless hold to be universal," I said as the group of us reached the shoreline and walked in, just up to our ankles.

"Is this about foot girl?" Chloe asked.

"Well, it's not *not* about foot girl."

"Who's *foot girl?*" CJ asked.

"I'm never telling you anything again," Chloe said with a sigh, which was funny given she was the one who'd first uttered the phrase *foot girl* and I let her know that. "You sound like a lawyer."

I noticed that CJ, Sofia, Bianca, and Phoebe were exchanging looks, the universal *is this couple being normal snippy or are we already somehow in the middle of someone else's fight* expressions.

"I bet my parents would be super proud if I were a lawyer," I said, hoping my tone would let everyone know everything was fine and dandy. It was, wasn't it? "Though could that outdo Greg?"

"He is *saving lives*, Clementine," Chloe said, and pulled me further into the cool water. "Sometimes I feel like I'm having a normal conversation and everyone thinks I'm about to attack."

"You even *sometimes* think you're having a normal conversation?" I asked with mock innocence, and we both laughed.

Standing in the sunshine in the Pacific Ocean with a person I kind of *adored*, I realized, life felt really good.

Adored like a friend, of course. I mean, a friend whose laugh filled me with joy and whose jawline stirred feelings somewhere lower than my gut, but that was all just being bisexual and having a hot friend. That much had to be true.

The wedding party had an afternoon spa appointment, and I'd planned to spend that time in the borrowed caftan reading a book on our hotel room's tiny private patio, but a text from Ari to the group chat showed up while the six of us were hanging around the hotel bar, around the time I'd planned to wander off. **Clementine, I know you're technically not part of the wedding party but I wanted to make sure you were still going to show up. See y'all soon.** Then a follow-up text from Nina: **Gender-affirming manicures only!**

"What does that even mean?" I asked without thinking, and then felt very much like a baby gay for asking what was probably an exceedingly obvious question in front of all of these very-much-not-baby gays.

Chloe laughed, though. "I think that's because before Phoebe and Bianca's wedding, we went to like this super heterosexual nail salon, and they couldn't make sense of the idea of two brides."

"You're forgetting that Phoebe kept commanding, *just do me like a man*, which didn't help to clear up any confusion," Bianca said.

We headed out of the hotel, down the block to the spa. As much as I would have liked a moment or two alone with a book, I couldn't deny it was nice being included in this part too. It was like, if I squinted a little, I was an actual part of these people's lives. I wondered if this was how the Talented Mr. Ripley felt. Minus the fake name and the murder and the fact that he was in it alone and I had Chloe. So, probably different. And *better.* I had it better than the Talented Mr. Ripley! That was something, maybe.

"I love the thought of Nina and Ari prepping the employees at this place," Phoebe said with a laugh.

"If someone says 'do me like a man,' they just mean they don't want any nail polish but their cuticles should still be attended to!" Chloe intoned like an overzealous coach, and we were still cracking up as we walked into the serene and understated spa. Nina and Ari were already there, hanging out in robes on a fancy chaise and drinking champagne, like a cartoon of affluent people having a spa day. There was also another group of friends—a slightly younger set of four people who had the complicated haircuts and intentionally mismatched patterns of people who were of both LA's Eastside as well as the Internet.

Ari ran through introductions, even though it sounded like her group of friends and this one had already met at a few various occasions. It was a relief, I thought, that I'd been pulled into a group like this one, people my own age and older, with haircuts that didn't make my long bob look too boring. When I was dating for real, I wondered if there would be a way I could suss out someone's friend group ahead of time—though that seemed slightly inappropriate somehow, and also it was weird to realize how soon that time was coming. In a couple weeks, it'd all be behind us.

Considering that I wasn't a real part of the wedding party, I'd planned to take advantage of a free mani and pedi, but Ari talked me into a bunch of treatments she swore by. Since the skin of celebrities was—apparently, if Ari was any example—blemish-free and gleaming with some kind of inner light, I found it physically impossible to say no. Was it bad form to be here under such false circumstances and then have a team of experts buffing and scrubbing and moisturizing my every pore? I genuinely didn't want to find out; I'd never glowed before.

Our groups had spread out a bit—Nina and Ari had rented

out the entire spa, and we were taking advantage of the luxuri-
ous space. So I found myself completely alone, waiting my turn
for a pre-facial scrub, when Nina and Ari dropped onto the
sofa on either side of me.

"We're really glad you came today," Nina said, beaming
at me.

"So glad," Ari echoed, shoving her hair back from her face.

"It was really nice to invite me," I said, undeserving of this
special attention from the brides. "And completely unneces-
sary! Way above and beyond."

"If you and Chlo had started dating any sooner . . ." Nina
said, and Ari nodded emphatically.

"We feel weird that you're not more included," she said,
and my stomach lurched a little. There was only one person
who should feel weird about the entire scenario, and it was me.
Well, two people, but I was pretty sure Chloe didn't feel weird
about any of this. Was Chloe capable of feeling any weirdness?
Though of course she would have been included no matter
what. Here I was, though, an imposter both figuratively and
literally soaking up expensive spa treatments.

"It hasn't been very long," I said as casually as my conscience
could manage, as casually as I could cut myself off without
tossing in a *and it's complete bullshit!*

"In earth time, no," Nina said. "In sapphic time, it's been
ages. So, anyway, this is just our cheesy way of saying we're really happy that you're here, and that you're a part of today, and
that if you'd literally started dating any sooner you'd officially
be part of the wedding party, too."

Before I knew what was happening, they crowded in from
both sides, and I wondered if this was the guiltiest anyone had
ever felt while buried in a group hug.

The afternoon went on much longer than I think any of us
had anticipated, and we had to rush back to the hotel so we'd
have enough time to get ready for the rehearsal dinner. I was a

little buzzed on champagne and conversation, which helped a little to dampen the way that group hug had exacerbated my existing guilt.

A little.

"I'm starting to feel really weird about all of this," I said as I pulled together my outfit from various sections of my suitcase and the closet. "Like we went into this whole thing, like, power to the single people. But now we're just two liars at a wedding."

"Oh my god, two liars at a wedding, great theme, I love it," Chloe said, cackling as she disappeared into the bathroom, returning only moments later in a perfectly cut black and gold jumpsuit. The gold threads were metallic in the light, and I'd never seen her look so glamorous. "What?"

"You just—you look amazing. Should we have coordinated outfits?"

"No, that's weird, of course not. Did you think that was some secret part of gay culture?"

I stepped into the bathroom and pulled the door closed behind me. "No, sometimes you just see those perfectly coordinated couples, you know?" I called.

"Yeah, gross. I hope you and boring man weren't like that."

"His name was Will—no, it's *still* Will, he's not dead. And, no. Will worked in tech—oh my *god*, Will *works in tech*, again, he's not dead, anyway. He's a hoodie and jeans guy."

"Oh yeah, I do vaguely remember him. Didn't he wear a hoodie to one of the holiday parties?"

"Yeah, he said that was his formal hoodie," I said. "I didn't know you met him at the party. It's . . . I don't know. I'm surprised you never mentioned it."

"I didn't meet him," she said. "But you and I talked for a long time, and later on I saw you with him. Not a big deal."

I guessed that it wasn't, though something about the memory felt dangerous in retrospect. A domino poised to knock over everything I'd set up. But we were tight on time, so instead of playing back that night or the greatest hits of getting up the nerve to end my relationship, I shimmied into my dress. It wasn't metallic, but it was a dark floral pattern that looked a little nighttime and, I hoped, a little sophisticated. Normally I felt way too twee to even strive for elegance, but the occasion seemed to call for it.

My skin glowed all over from the spa—now that I knew that celebrities got treatments like full-body facials, I understood a little more why we appeared like mere mortals next to them— but I still applied my basic makeup, and then finished up with my fancy-occasion-only LoveSeen lashes and my boldest berry-colored lipstick. Chloe's face when I stepped out of the bathroom was enough confirmation for me that I'd nailed the look.

"You're such a good fake girlfriend," Chloe said. "You look amazing."

"Seriously, Chloe," I said. "Right now I don't feel like I'm righteously pulling one over on mainstream society or what-ever. I just feel like we're lying to your best friends."

Chloe flashed a grin at me. "That's because we *are* lying to my best friends. And it's for everyone's own good!"

"That," I said, "cannot possibly be true."

Chapter 15
Last Call

There was something about coming back to a hotel room on the second night there that felt a little like coming home. Chloe and I had hardly developed the routine of a couple who spent every night together, but we seemed to at least have found a rhythm carrying our things into the bathroom to complete our nightly rituals.

I still wore a bra under my nightshirt and sweatpants over my underwear to bed, though.

"That was actually nice," Chloe said, walking in from the bathroom in her faded Boygenius T-shirt and pajama shorts. "I've gotten used to all the wedding shit from boring people I went to college and grad school with, I forget some of it isn't terrible. Like when you actually think the couple involved should stay together forever."

"No, totally," I said, my guilt a bit abated thanks to the dinner, one of those events where I was too caught up in the night to dwell much on anything outside of the moment. "The toasts tonight were nothing like that. People are so specifically happy for Ari and Nina to have found each other, not just that people are getting married because marriage is the one true way to happiness or whatever. I mean, I don't want to die alone or anything, but I want it to be about the person and not checking off some box. Anyway, I guess I'm also not *that* surprised by tonight. Your friends are pretty amazing, and nothing's felt like one of those paint-by-the-numbers, cookie-cutter weddings."

"Annoying but true," Chloe said with a laugh. "OK, last call, I'm turning out the lights."

"Last call?" I asked, and we both laughed as she flipped the switch and got into the other side of the bed. We did the thing of purposefully being extra quiet to let each other know it was time to get some sleep, or at least try. Except—

"What *is* that?" Chloe asked, sitting up.

I tried to parse the clanging sound. "A trolley? The whole *clang clang clang* thing? A train?"

"Yeah," she said. "I think it's a train crossing."

I'd heard the clanging occasionally since we'd gotten here, briefly in the background here and there. "Trains don't cross for long."

"Listen to you talk like some kind of train expert," Chloe said, lying down again. "Though, sure, that's true."

The clanging didn't stop, though. After a few minutes, Chloe got up and peered out the window.

"There's no train, but the crossing things are stuck down or something."

I sat up in bed, aware that we had to be up in several hours for a not *not* important event. "Should we call someone?"

Chloe waved a hand and climbed back into bed. "Like the train police?"

"I don't know, I guess not 911." I closed my eyes and tried to forget about the constant noise, but even at the late hour I wasn't someone who could just sleep through an ongoing *clang clang clang.*

"This sucks," Chloe muttered. "Sorry, did you manage to fall asleep? Did I wake you?"

"No, of course you didn't, can normal people sleep through something like this?"

"It's cute you think you're normal," Chloe said. "But also, no. I'm sure it'll get fixed soon."

I sighed and stared at the ceiling. "I hope you're right."

"We'll have to figure out something to do until it stops," Chloe said, and I was certain a note of something different laced itself into her tone. That, though, couldn't be. Whatever that *something different* was had never actually existed between us. It was a curiosity in my head only.

Still, I wanted to make sure. Not that I wanted it to be true, I was only curious if it was. I was merely solving a mystery! So it—curiosity—was the only reason that I turned my head and shifted my weight to my side. How could I accurately weigh Chloe's intentions if I couldn't see her? In the dark room in the middle of the night, though, her eyes still kept everything guarded anyway.

To be fair, no matter how well I could see her, Chloe was great at keeping everything guarded.

I felt her shift before I saw that she was turning toward me, too. Her knee bumped against mine and her elbow grazed my hip. It reminded me of a couple nights ago, dancing together on Johnny's back patio, the creamy expanse of her neck and the feel of her hip brushing against my thigh. Her hand on my waist with purpose. That night's air had throbbed with music, but this room was so silent that all I could hear was the *clang* and Chloe's breath—or was it mine?

Even in the dark I could feel her studying me. "What do you think, Clementine?"

Normally, I knew, I would have worried it was a tease. Chloe seeing how far she could take it, a joke somehow meant for both of us yet firmly within her own control. But I could hear her breath louder now, could feel the heat from her body only inches away. It wasn't, I was certain, a tease, but maybe it was a dare. And since she'd been the one to ask, I answered back with my hand on her waist. It wasn't the hottest of moves, but I knew that it made my intentions clear. I knew that it was exactly enough.

Chloe leaned in and pressed her lips to mine. *Oh.* I'd forgotten about kissing, I realized, because kissing was something that could become so casual and lived-in. Kissing could be a greeting and a goodnight, or an I'll see you when you get back from the hardware store and before we clean the kitchen. But not when kissing started, when kissing was new, when kissing was standing near a fire as the flames licked in your direction, threatening to burn you and everything else down in the process.

I wanted very much for this to go on, to escalate, to throw open the door even though before I'd been too nervous to even think about this door existing. A hum buzzed within me, though, that I wanted it to come from Chloe. I'd stay right here at the doorway until she pulled me in. She had to feel the buzz too, had to recognize my specific want calling from within. She had to know me well enough for that.

Chloe inched closer still and kissed me again, more pressure from her soft warm lips this time. I opened up to her and ran my fingers through the short hairs at the nape of her neck as her lips parted and the kiss deepened. Her tongue was gentle but insistent, and a shiver rocked through me as I wondered where else she might taste me tonight.

The kiss ended only to pick up again, as if we'd gotten it so perfect we couldn't believe it and wanted to do it again, exactly the same way. This time I'd barely waited for her, though; this time I tried to let her know that I was insistent too.

"Chloe," I murmured when the kiss ended, leaving my thoughts there, just her name on my tongue, instead of *can you believe how good this is* and *whatever you want to do next is exactly what I want too.*

"We can stop if you want to," she said quickly.

"Wait, do I seem like I want to stop?" I shook my head. "Sorry. Maybe you do and you're trying to be polite about it."

"Excuse me," she said, sliding her hand down my side and grabbing my hip. Her force, even through the layers of my sweatpants and underpants, sent a bolt between my legs. "Have you ever seen me be polite?"

"No, that's one of my favorite things about you," I said, letting her pull me closer so that we were pressed up, overlapping in places, under the covers. "Maybe I should say something."

Chloe kissed my neck, sucked hard for a brief moment that elicited a gasp of surprise from me. "Clementine, I'm well aware you've never been with a woman before. That's one of the starting points of this whole thing. Are you freaked out now that it's finally happening?"

Finally? I wanted to ask, but didn't. For me, in general? Or did she mean with each other?

"No," I said, and I realized she was watching me seriously. "Thanks for asking, actually."

"I know I give you shit about your baby gay ways," Chloe said with a low rumbly laugh I'd never heard from her before. I wanted to press my face into her throat to feel it. "But I actually do want to make sure you're OK for whatever we're doing tonight."

"Sure," I said, nodding instead of shouting *I'm very OK with this!* "It's less that you're a woman and more that—I mean, Will's the only person I've been with. If I was in bed with a man who wasn't Will, I'd be—well, I don't like the term 'freaked out,' but, you know."

"Not *not* that," Chloe said.

"Right. Maybe I'm bad in bed. The only person who'd know is Will, and I'm also the only person he'd been with, so how would he know."

"I guess we'll have to find out," Chloe said, smirking and drawing closer still. Our legs bumped against each other's and it only made sense to rest my knee atop her leg to fit together better. The small shift in my position wasn't so small to my body though; awareness and need radiated from my center as my thighs parted. I was awakened.

Chloe and I kissed again, messier now, as much about teeth and tongues as our lips. She shifted her weight so she was leaning over me, but hooked her arm around my leg to keep it where it was, wrapped around hers. In this new position, her thigh rocked against me as we kissed, and even though we were fully clothed and were only *kissing*, my hips sought her out, ready for action we hadn't yet started.

"Hang on," I said, catching my breath. "It's just been a while and—"

"We can stop whenever you want," Chloe said.

"No, I don't want to, but it just feels embarrassing I was about to—I mean, we're just kissing."

"Clementine," she said in that low throaty voice again. I wondered if I could come from a voice. "I was absolutely fucking you with my leg. Was that not apparent?"

I laughed. "I thought it was just lucky positioning for me."

"I guess I'll have to make it more obvious." She held my gaze, sliding her thigh up and then down, up and down, up and down. This time I let my body go. My hips raised to find her, to grind against her, to make my search for pleasure and release abundantly obvious.

Chloe clutched one of my breasts, her thumb finding my nipple achingly hard even through my many layers. "Wait, Clementine, did you wear a bra to bed?"

"I'm not very good at this there's-only-one-bed part of the shenanigan," I said, panting, needing more to climb over the edge. Not that I planned to stop my ascent. "My boobs are—I don't know. I worry about how they look without a bra on. Gravity and my mid-thirties and all."

"Fuck, do you not know how—" Chloe laughed again, and

this time I did it, leaned in and pressed my face to her neck to feel it, feel her. She was thunder on a sweltering summer night. "Remember when you asked me my type and I wouldn't tell you?"

I nodded as her thumb circled me, her thigh rocked against me, the pressure swelled. The train tracks clanged in the background, and I didn't care. Let it become the soundtrack to all of this. "I remember."

"That's because there was no way I could tell you how I lose my mind over girls like you," she murmured right into my ear. "These goddamn hips, thighs I want to bury myself in. Your tits you've got hidden away under a million layers. You would have known—"

"Known what?" I asked, feeling braver now, flicking my tongue into the hollow at the base of her neck and her low groan, lapping into the crevice, tasting her skin.

"Known I've thought of doing this since I met you," she said, and shoved up my T-shirt. The dress I'd worn earlier showed glimpses of my bra straps from certain angles, so I'd worn one meant to be seen, black lace with sheer panels. From the look on Chloe's face, it had been the right one for tonight in more ways than one. And maybe, something deep inside me had worn it for right now, too.

She brought her face low to me and sucked my nipple through the thin material of my bra, while her leg moved faster. I clutched her ass while my hips bucked, and the heat and tension imploded as I came with a guttural moan. It sounded like a stranger's voice, and in that moment that much felt accurate. I'd never imagined myself getting off with someone who wasn't Will like *this*, this frantic fast desperate way. Right now I felt brand-new.

"Let's get these off you," Chloe said, tugging down my sweatpants just as I was about to worry that my orgasm meant we were done for the night. "Fuck, Clementine, these matching panties."

"What about you?" I asked, feeling bold as I slipped off her T-shirt. Underneath, her breasts were small and round, tan nipples already hard, and I asked her permission with a look before dipping down to take one nipple into my mouth and then the other. Chloe made small sounds of satisfaction as I licked, sucked, explored, but I wanted more; I wanted an ugly uncontrollable guttural force to overtake her, too. I wanted for her what she'd given me.

"Tell me what to do," I said, pushing myself forward so that I was leaning over her.

"Don't worry about me," she said, grabbing my ass with both hands and shifting further so my thighs were on either side of hers. "Come here."

"How much closer do you want me to come?" I asked innocently, but I spread my thighs wider across hers, arched my back so my breasts were close to her face.

Chloe grasped my waist with her hands, though one hand skimmed lower, her thumb dipping just under the edge of my underwear, then lower, between my legs, stroking lightly over my underwear. "You're so wet."

"You know it's been a while for me," I said.

She raised an eyebrow, gave me a little grin. "It was hardly a complaint, Clementine."

"I'll take these off," I told her, hooking my thumbs into my underwear on each side.

"Don't you dare," she said, instead pulling them gently aside and finding me with her fingertips. I gasped at the skin-to-skin contact, but her movements were gentle at first, small strokes that made me moan with pleasure. Chloe seemed to know when I was ready for more pressure, more direct contact, and I was so relieved this experience was with her, someone who knew me so well by now. Someone who could watch me as she touched me to know exactly what I wanted.

Chloe took her hand away, and just as I was about to argue

in protest, she rested two fingertips on my lips. We watched each other as I opened my mouth, sucked my own taste from her fingers, took in her full length. After a moment, she pulled her fingers out and found me again, sliding up into me in one swift motion.

"How's that?" she asked, moving slowly.

I rolled my hips as we worked out a rhythm together. "You feel so good. I'm—it's OK I'm on top?"

Chloe looked up at me, her lips apart, a look I couldn't quite read on her face. Disbelief? "It's, to say the very least, Clementine, more than OK that a woman with the body of a goddamn goddess is on top of me while I fuck her."

She somehow managed to unclasp my bra with her other hand. I made hard eye contact with her as I slipped out of it, switching up my rhythm as I rode her hand. I was no longer worried about gravity's effects, now that I was giving Chloe what I knew she wanted. I couldn't believe I'd thought I might get into bed with a woman and not know what to do. Had anything ever come more naturally to me than this?

Chloe grabbed my shoulder to pull me closer, burying her face between my breasts as she thrust harder. I slipped my hand between my legs, impatient for another explosion, to feel maybe even newer again. Sometimes Will would stop me when I touched myself. *Hey, give me a chance first*, he'd say, even though the way I saw it was that I was getting off *with* him. When Chloe touched my arm, I worried for a split second that she'd say the same thing.

"My turn," she said, and this time it was my fingertips on her lips, my taste on her tongue. The thought was almost too much, and while I was still in her mouth, I let my weight settle on Chloe and slipped my other hand between my legs. It was an overload, her tongue licking between my fingers, her fingers moving hard and fast, my hand at my own throbbing center, and only another few moments flashed by before another orgasm hit me like a bolt of lightning and I cried out in agonizingly blissful release.

"Clementine," she said as I collapsed next to her. "Jesus, that was hot."

I laughed, though a blush of nerves hit my face now that it was over and my want wasn't guiding me. "For a first-timer?"

"Oh shut the fuck up," she said. "You know that was good."

"I honestly didn't expect it would go like that," I admitted. "I worried—well, it can feel . . . I don't know, embarrassing? Will was used to me, and I didn't know how it would be with someone else. I feel so needy about it, my body's just like . . . in search of getting off."

"I love how needy your body is," she said. "There's nothing embarrassing about that. I feel like women are taught to be selfless even when we're getting fucked. And for what?"

"What about you?" I asked again.

"I'm fine," she said with a flick of her hand.

"Do you not want me to—"

"No, of course that's not it," she said quickly. "But I'm feeling great. I had a really good time fucking you. I'm just—it takes me a while? And people don't expect me to be—you know, people talk about how wild I am. It doesn't go with that kind of reputation to be like, it's fine, it's gonna take me forty-five minutes to get there, and any of the methods you're considering should actually be pretty vanilla."

"I've got forty-five minutes," I said. "And I'm pretty vanilla too."

"I was being facetious," she said.

"I want to get you there," I said. "No matter the timing."

"Fine," she grumbled.

"Just what I wanted to hear the first time I try to make a woman come," I said, kidding but also really not kidding at all. I'd thought we were both having a good time; did I misjudge her that badly? But then Chloe laughed her low throaty laugh, and then it was easy letting go of my nerves and my fears she didn't want me in the same ways I wanted her, because, god, how that laugh undid me.

"What do you like?" I asked, turning to kiss her. We kissed for a while longer, but it felt different now, with the knowledge we had of each other. Dirtier, full of secret meanings and codes.

"I like this a lot," she said, kissing me sweetly.

"Well, me too," I said. "But I want to make you come."

"Your mouth on me," Chloe whispered in my ear. "I can't stop thinking about it. If you're good with that?"

I was—very much so—and even more so, if that was even possible, I was undone by the knowledge of her fantasizing about me. Even so I shivered as we rearranged ourselves on the bed and I slid Chloe's boy shorts down and off. I'd—though not exactly like this—been fucked before, after all. It had been different with Chloe—but it would have been different with anyone who wasn't Will.

No matter how many instructional *Autostraddle* articles I'd read, though, no matter how much porn I'd watched, going down on a woman felt entirely new for me.

Still, I ached to give Chloe what she'd given me. If the off-hand way she'd initially shrugged away getting off tonight had more to do with her than me, I wanted to prove to her just how much I wanted this too. It was hardly that I was just making good on orgasm promises; right then the thing I wanted to do most in bed was make Chloe Lee come. And, anyway, it was tough finding anything *not entirely positive* about the experience of sliding down her body, gently pushing apart her legs, finding her with my mouth. I was tentative to start, I knew it, gentle as I found my bearings. Chloe made soft, encouraging sounds I knew were for my benefit. I hadn't pushed her past the point of control yet, but I liked having a goal. She tasted musky, salty, and also somehow just like her.

"You taste so good," I told her, and the room was so quiet I heard her breath hitch.

Wait, the room was quiet.

"The railroad crossing's fixed," I told her.

"Yeah, yeah. I was promised an orgasm," Chloe said, and even though *obviously* I knew we didn't actually have sex tonight to kill time while we couldn't sleep, her words and that hitch in her breath were all I needed to move past *tentative*.

"Oh, god, Clementine," Chloe said, running her fingers through my hair and tugging. It was like I could feel her everywhere and impossibly still wanted more of her.

"How's it going?" I asked, immediately regretting my phrasing, like a waitress stopping by a table to check on refills and not the person with her face buried only moments ago between Chloe's thighs. "I mean—"

"You're so fucking cute," Chloe said, and I couldn't help it, couldn't help pulling myself up to be level with her, kissing her for not only her words but the adoring tone she'd said them in. I wasn't sure I was skilled enough at any of this to give her what she wanted, but then she kissed me back, rough, her hips rocking against mine.

I slipped my hand between her legs and watched her eyes clench as I stroked her wet heat. "I'm doing OK?"

"You're doing more than OK," she said, nodding, her eyes still closed, her hips working faster. "I told you I'd take a while. That's not about you."

"I just want to make sure I'm giving you what you want," I said, and she opened her eyes and held my gaze as I kissed my way back to her center. Her sounds grew from *encouraging* to *enthusiastic* as I licked, sucked, traced lines with my tongue that felt like delirious fantasies, only emboldening me more. I didn't feel particularly slick at any of it, but between the roll of Chloe's hips against my face and the sound of her moans blurring out the rest of the world, she seemed transformed into a pulsing force of desire. I knew my inexperience didn't matter.

"Do you want me to . . ." I watched her face as I nudged a finger at her entrance, and as she nodded I slid into her. I was overwhelmed again, shocked I could be enough for her, amazed to find myself here. But it washed over me that we were in this together; it might have been about pushing Chloe over the edge but I was the lucky one, after all, helping her push past that point of pleasure. When she let out a ragged groan and tightened around me, I felt like we'd both won some kind of prize.

"*Fuck*," Chloe murmured. "That was *good*. Thanks, Clementine."

"You're very welcome," I said, trying not to feel too good about myself as I settled back in next to her. People gave hot women orgasms all the time. It had just never been me before.

"You look very smug," she said, and I laughed.

"I feel kind of smug. Not at you, just at—I don't know. The world? We're just two random people in this hotel room but it's been fucking magic in here tonight."

"Like magic fucking?" she asked with a laugh, and I was glad she was joking instead of calling me out on how potentially weird I was being. Was everyone this full of joyful power after having queer sex for the first time? "You're allowed to be a little smug."

"Good," I said, glancing at her in this quiet moment we were in. "Thanks for making this—I don't know"—I couldn't conjure up the word that said how I felt, relieved and grateful and exquisitely wrung out but also not *too much*, Chloe Lee and I did not do *too much*—"Perfect."

Yeah. That was definitely *too much*.

Chloe, though, smiled and took my face in her hands, pulled me close for a kiss. "Thank *you*, Clementine. You made it pretty perfect for me, too."

I leaned in more, eager for more of her, but I saw Chloe's gaze slip to something behind me.

"*Shit*, we've got to be up in way fewer hours than I thought."

I followed her gaze to see the clock radio, and grimaced at the late—well, *early* hour. Why would the universe give me all of this exciting queer power without any extra time to enjoy it?

Chloe, though, reached down to pull the blankets back up

over us in a move that felt less like *let's do this some more* and more like *good night*. "Let's get as much sleep as we can."

"Does this—" I cut myself off because I wasn't sure how I wanted to end the question. Does this mean things have changed? Does this mean you just wanted to make sure I got this experience while I'm fake-dating you? Does this mean actually you meant that thing about your type and my body and maybe this entire time we've both thought about what this would be like? Does this mean it surpassed both of our expectations?

Does this mean maybe we could try doing this for real?

"Does this what?" she asked, somehow sounding half asleep already.

"Does this hotel have a breakfast bar?" I finally asked instead.

"Hell *yeah* it does, Clementine," she said. "Sleep tight."

Chapter 16
The Wedding

As I'd drifted off to sleep, I'd had hopes of waking up early. Chloe and I would have a conversation about the night before—or, at worst, a lot of hot morning sex. But I must have hit *snooze* without realizing it, and so we were basically both running late before even getting started. There was absolutely no time for thoughtful conversations about what was happening here between us—and no time for orgasms, either, though I knew we could get that accomplished more easily and quickly than that conversation about what was next for us.

I genuinely wasn't sure which one I craved most.

The wedding party was meeting at the venue for professional hair and makeup, and—in another fit of generosity—Ari and Nina had invited me to partake in this as well. It was incredible to watch a team get this particular wedding party ready; I'd been in Fiona and Hailey's weddings, and those had both been pretty standard affairs. I'd worn traditional bridesmaid dresses—neither of which had been super flattering for me—and gotten the same blowout that every woman got, making us look vaguely related or cult-y or both.

Today it was like everyone's individuality was celebrated. The wedding party was wearing shades of pinks, reds, and oranges, solid-color garments from long dresses to perfectly tailored suits to jumpsuits that were both dashing and heart-throbbingly tough. Or maybe it was just easy to think that because of how Chloe looked in hers, luxe swagger and glamour rolled into one.

I did my best to treat her neutrally, though I could hardly think of anything but our night together. The rest of the group, of course, would assume we'd been sleeping together for months now; my jumpy giddiness at the sight of her and of the sensation of her sitting close to me wouldn't make sense to anyone else. From Chloe's standard demeanor I wasn't sure it would make sense to her either. Maybe for her it hadn't been the night it had been for me. Maybe for her this was standard hotel hookup behavior.

My phone buzzed while I watched a makeup artist apply a subtle eye makeup look to Chloe, and since I was probably staring in practically a creepy manner, I was relieved for the interruption.

Until I saw the screen. **RED ALERT!** Greg had texted to Marisol and me. **We should have a meeting this weekend to discuss the party! We are down to the wire!**

I sighed deeply.

"Everything OK there?" Sofia asked me. She'd also opted for a jumpsuit like Chloe, but unlike Chloe's red fabric, Sofia's was a vibrant orange that popped against her tan skin. Everyone truly looked their most beautiful, and I was a little overwhelmed by all of them.

Sex had really rattled my brain.

"Yeah, just my brother and this party, which I don't think necessitates a *red alert*," I said, tapping out a reply that we could talk about the party once I was home from my friends' wedding. I thought back to Greg and Marisol's wedding, which was also fairly cookie-cutter, and to add insult to injury I hadn't even been asked to be part of it in any way.

"It's soon, though, yeah?" CJ asked. They were in a Barbie-pink suit and looked incredibly cool and joyful all at once. "Then the whole thing's done and no more red alerts until—I don't know, Christmas, I bet."

"Christmas for sure," I said. "But you're right. It's just a couple weeks away."

I tried to make eye contact with Chloe to gauge her reaction to that. Did that timeline still hold significance to us? Had that all fallen away now that we were—well, also, what *were* we? I knew I was naïve to assume things had automatically changed because of sex. It wasn't the sex, though—despite that it had been good enough to have changed just about whatever it wanted. Things had felt so open between us, no pretending or holding back, just the two of us and everything we actually wanted. At least physically. We hadn't gotten around to the rest of it, but I had to hope that soon we would.

Not that I knew what I wanted! But the truth was that I was starting to feel like it was *this, exactly.* Chloe, in bed and on road trips and nudging me about stupid inside jokes about peppers. This group of friends who'd already come to support me and make space for me and make sure I was taken care of. If this fake thing worked so well, didn't it make sense to do it for real?

Last night, after all, we'd really done it for real. Not the sex, either. Last night we'd said what we wanted. Last night we hadn't held back.

"You're making a weird face," Chloe said, sitting down next to me. The makeup artist had applied liquid liner so precisely, and Chloe looked even tougher and hotter than usual. I stared down at her thigh next to mine and willed my hand to stay in place in my lap. We weren't a squishy couple, after all, in Chloe's words. It'd be strange if suddenly I couldn't keep my hands off of her.

"Just my regular face," I said. "Well, my regular face with better makeup."

"Hi, Clementine?" A person with a clipboard walked up to us, their face in a polite but clenched expression. "I'm so sorry, but I think it's a good time to take you down to the venue while the wedding party attends to a few pre-ceremony duties."

There was some mild pushback from CJ, Sofia, even Bianca and Phoebe, but I let the polite person lead me out. And not just because Chloe hadn't made even the mildest effort to keep me there longer. She wasn't squishy, I reminded myself. And, despite their politeness, the clipboard person was fairly intimidating. There was no reason for me to stick around anyway. I'd only be in the way, and there'd be plenty of time at the reception to—

I caught myself and laughed. To *what*? To stare at Chloe and hope she gave me a sign as to what she was thinking? To gaze at her lips, her hands, her neck, and think about the worlds I felt we'd opened up last night? To lean in close to her, as if a brush against her skin would be enough to quell the desire that still pulsed hot in me now?

The venue was at the tasting room of a local vineyard in downtown Santa Barbara, with a courtyard full of sunshine and greenery within the property that felt open and private all at once. The space had been decorated with flowers to match the vivid reds, pinks, and oranges of the wedding party, and I genuinely felt a little stunned at the beauty.

I'd assumed I'd have to fill a lot of time before the ceremony began, but cater-waiters were already circling with trays of wine and hors d'oeuvres, and a small group of people I vaguely recognized from the rehearsal dinner gestured for me to join them. There were a couple of other *significant-others-not-significant-or-long-term-enough* to be included in the wedding party, as well as friends of theirs, and even though no one had met me for longer than five minutes previously, I felt that I'd been made a part of this sort of ragtag group of others.

It was no day, I knew, to be maudlin; we were literally here to celebrate the love of people we cared about. I had fancy cheese and a beautiful rosé coursing through my veins—on top of the heap of good endorphins buzzing through me from my night with Chloe. Still, it was hard for me not to think about the life I'd all but stumbled into, this fake and temporary thing that felt so solid and real, and how many years I'd spent thinking I had everything I already needed and not trying for more. The time I spent knowing Will and I wanted different things but hoping somehow the situation fixed itself. Going to so many weddings together where the choices felt like ones I'd never make, all the while holding Will's hand and trying to ignore the look on his face. Watching my best friendships slip into a lower priority and having no idea how to fix it.

And yet here I was, feeling pretty fulfilled, all things considered. I had no idea it was possible to get everything you wanted—well, most of what I wanted, the whole job thing was at best still up in the air—and feel to some degree like I shouldn't enjoy it at all. Not if it wasn't actually real.

Then I thought of how Chloe had looked at me last night, how Chloe had pulled me in for a kiss, and I wondered if maybe I could enjoy every last bit of it after all.

The venue filled with guests, and I stayed with my new group as we guessed who belonged to whose family and whose first time it was attending a lesbian wedding. (To be fair, it was my first time, but it was like being queer canceled that out somehow.) A couple folks figured out the path taken by the cater-waiters from the kitchen, and we positioned ourselves to get first selection off the trays each round.

A live band began a set of instrumental love songs, old and new, cheesy and perceptive, sweeping epics and bangers. We were urged to our seats by the clipboard person and team, and

I sort of marveled at the way the space had been filled with chairs in rows at slightly different angles. It wasn't a giant outdoor area but it felt full in the best way, a big group circled up to celebrate two people.

I watched as the wedding party walked down the center aisle, circling around so no one had to crane their necks to see. Chloe's friends looked *gorgeous*, special-occasion-dressy like a wedding called for but so *like themselves* in a way that felt rare. And Chloe—I couldn't stop staring at her. The figure she cut in that red jumpsuit. The strong jut of her chin as she walked through the crowd. The way her eyes sought out mine and we held each other's gazes for a moment long enough others noticed.

A thrill tangibly shook through the room as Nina and Ari walked out together, arm in arm. Nina's dress was a vision of creamy organza and chiffon, and her brown waves cascaded elegantly around her bare shoulders. Ari was in a tuxedo in the same shade of creamy white, perfectly cut slacks and blazer, matching shirt unbuttoned almost to her waist. I genuinely felt overwhelmed at their beauty, both separately but especially together, and a little hitch pulled in my chest that—

Well, I still didn't want the life Will had wanted for us. But there was nothing about the event happening here that felt like it was for other people. It wasn't about fulfilling certain roles or doing what society wanted. As Ari and Nina read the vows they'd each written themselves, I was relieved that I heard others sniffling before I admitted I was tearing up more than a little myself. It felt exactly like the celebration of these two women and the love they'd found together.

". . . The truth is that when I met you, I didn't know you were someone I could wish for," Nina said, looking right at Ari as if no one else was there. "And it didn't matter because of course I couldn't help but wish for you anyway. So it wasn't just that you felt like a wish granted, though you did. It was that when you came into my life, you made it so much bigger. You made all my dreams feel like they were possible. If you were there, loving me, what couldn't we have together? And I can't wait to spend the rest of my life finding out."

It wasn't, I knew, that suddenly I wanted to get married or change the life I'd been searching for. That much I knew; I could long to find someone to spend forever with and still do it in a way that felt like it was just for me. But something felt opened up, shaken loose in me, that everyone's possibilities were bigger and more unique than I'd realized.

"... I had a lot of ideas for how my life would go," Ari said to Nina, a laugh pulling at the edges of her words. "The people in my life were mostly nice enough not to use the actual phrase *control freak* but I could read between the lines. But when I met you it hit me how my plans and lists and demands didn't matter the way I thought they did, not when someone this unexpected could make me rethink all of it. And it's so special to share my life with someone who shakes everything up and challenges me and makes me see how much bigger this world is than the little narrow view I had. I love that you said something about spending our life together finding things out, because that's exactly how I feel too—sorry, I'm going off-script here, I'm just so in love with you and this life we already have and all the future lives we're going to share together."

There were so many people, I could feel, not just Nina and Ari but *so many people*, who were like me in that they wanted exactly the life they saw for themselves. Maybe it was just the rush of love at this perfect fucking wedding but I'd never felt less of a distance from others. Nina and Ari clearly hadn't planned any of this with the world's expectations in mind; they'd done it for themselves and the people they loved. They'd done it for *each other*. And I couldn't believe it had taken me this long to realize how many people were finding the specific lives they wanted too, no matter how they looked to other people, no matter other people's expectations.

Whatever it was that I wanted, I'd never felt so sure it felt OK to find it. Though as the music swelled, and Chloe followed the rest of the party through the venue to the receiving line, we locked eyes again and I hoped we might be able to find whatever it was together.

Chapter 17
Figurative Bingo Card

The wedding party had more photos to take, so I followed my new group inside where the venue had been magically transformed during the ceremony with round tables, a bar, and a dance floor. My table assignment sat me, currently, alone, but I temporarily moved to another table with the others waiting for their dates until the wedding party minus the brides appeared.

"Were you too bored?" Sofia asked as they crowded around me, then laughed as everyone realized they weren't at the right table. I waved goodbye to the new group and navigated my friends over to the right spot.

"No need to be bored when in the company of the hot young people," Chloe said with a wave of her hand toward the other group.

"No one's that much younger than us," CJ said, and their obvious eschewing of *hot* made us, minus Chloe, laugh.

I glanced at her and her furrowed brow, and leaned in close. My lips were close to her ear in a way we never were in public. It was genuinely hard not to brush my lips against her, scrape my teeth against her earlobe. "If I wanted a young fake date I'm sure I would have nicely mentioned this when I turned your offer down."

She snorted and a warm rush of gratefulness hit me that maybe she'd been a little insecure or—well, jealousy wasn't an attractive trait, but I felt certain that there wouldn't have been brow-furrowing if she wasn't also considering the possibility that this was real. "You'd have to learn TikTok like a youth."

"I'm in charge of media planning, buying, and execution for my job," I said with a laugh. "I already know TikTok like a youth. Or at least an approaching-middle-age person who knows how to market to youths."

"Clementine is very good at thinking like a youth, yes," Phoebe said, and I tried to take that as a hopeful sign that all my work aspirations weren't already dead in the water. Maybe I shouldn't have emphasized my approaching-middle-age-ness in front of Phoebe, though obviously Phoebe knew how old I was.

Chloe was still leaned in closer to me than usual, and even though it wasn't good for that pulsing beat of need within me, I counted it as a positive sign overall. I wanted something about last night to be tangible, and the lack of space between us felt like proof it had happened.

"Also I hear TikTok is very gay," Phoebe continued.

"*Very*," I said.

"Or at least your algorithm is," CJ said with a laugh. "Which is basically your soul."

"I hope that isn't true," Phoebe said with a frown. "The soul thing, not the gay thing."

CJ shrugged, and soon we were all laughing again. It hit me that today had the feeling of the last day of camp, the new friends you made in record time about to disperse back into the world. Except in this case, they'd still have each other, and I'd be dispersed alone.

Unless, of course—

I couldn't decide how unhinged it was to think it was possible. Could I really put so much faith in a furrowed brow and a couple of shared glances? The look in Chloe's eyes last night when she kissed me? The gaze we held earlier today, the gaze we held last night?

Luckily, saving me from dwelling on any of it any longer, the brides arrived to raucous applause, and they sat at a table of honor, just the two of them. Servers streamed in with salads and small plates, and I let myself lose track of my concerns for at least the meal. The meal, though, went on for a while, course after course, and by the time we were taking the last bites of our steaks and salmon and vegetarian risotto, the DJ was playing and the mood felt full of just about anything but *concern*. My only concern, I realized, was wondering just how long it would be until Chloe and I were alone together again.

And not for conversation.

Still, it was *a party*. I danced in a group with most of our table, and joined my new-ish kind-of-friends as well. It felt like we were all constantly moving, to the dance floor, to wait for custom cocktails at the bar, back to the table to chat, rest, recharge.

Chloe's arm brushed mine as she sat down next to me at the table, where I'd been chugging Diet Coke and chatting with CJ about digital media. Chloe and I hadn't touched on the dance floor—I couldn't be sure of her reasoning, but I knew that I didn't fully trust myself to touch her only a little when what I wanted was absolutely my hands over absolutely all of her—and I nearly jumped out of my seat. My skin seemed to have gained a new ability, some kind of doubled sensation of contact. I felt like an open gasoline line dangerously ready to blow at the sign of any spark.

"You OK there?" Chloe asked with a raised eyebrow.

"I'm fine," I said, wondering how much I should admit to her. Though that much I felt she could probably feel on my skin, smell from my pores. My hunger suddenly felt tangible. "Just . . . you know, *impatient*."

"Oh, sure," she said with a curt nod. "I'm feeling impatient too."

"Wait, you are?" I asked, because no matter the magic of last night, no matter that Chloe had also said *perfect*, I knew that it must have been more special to me than to Chloe. For me, a series of firsts. For her—well, it hopefully was more than getting head from a newbie. Still, she'd had nights like that before, I had to assume. Maybe—hopefully?—she had feelings for me, but I'd still been pretty sure I had been the only one aching to get back to that room and that bed.

I'd definitely been sure I had been the only one who was willing to admit it.

"Come with me," she said, standing up and reaching out for my hand. I laced my fingers through hers as we walked through the reception room and realized it was the first time we'd held hands like this, a couple for the whole world to see. A little squishy.

Chloe led me down a hallway and nudged an unmarked door open. "Come on."

"What is that?" I asked.

"It's an old storage closet for business paperwork and shit."

"Why do you know this?" I asked. "Why are you showing me this?"

"You know that I'm very nosy," she said. "So while you and CJ were having whatever conversation about robots and digital media, I gave myself a little tour, and thought, if I'm going to get to fuck Clementine in that dress before late tonight, I'd better find a good place for it."

"*Chloe*," I said, as heat flooded into my face—and parts further south.

She tugged me into the room and locked the door behind us. It felt unreal, a dirty dream or the loose plot of a porn, but here we were in a dusty room with sunshine flooding in from a high window, and Chloe kissed me as if she'd been as ready as I was.

"Have you done this before?" I asked her, watching as she stood there with the warm light illuminating the sharp lines of her jawline and the softness of her cheeks as she smiled in my direction. I felt like the luckiest person in the whole world right then. "Sex in a broom closet?"

"Storage closet," she corrected, grabbing me around the waist and pulling me close again. "Do you see any brooms in here?"

I pointed to the corner. "There's literally one right there."

"Stop looking for brooms," Chloe said, covering my mouth with hers. I gave in to the kiss because I couldn't control myself, but was ready to pull away and head out from this room. Tonight would come soon enough.

Chloe, though, knew exactly what she was doing, and deepened the kiss as one hand let go of my waist and found my breast, and soon we were making out frantically against a stack of file boxes, like teenagers who'd just heard about second base.

"We can't do this," I said, trying to get back both my breath and my self-control. "People are walking past this room."

"I'll be very quiet," Chloe said in a soft voice that still, somehow, sounded only like sex. Chloe Lee, begging for me with her tone. "And it's at least a little hot, isn't it? Knowing people are innocently walking by us while . . ."

She grabbed the hem of my dress, pushed up the skirt, and hooked her thumb through my underpants right over my hip. I gasped at both the surprise and the impropriety of the action. Last night had been like a dream, slowly finding something together in the quiet dark. This was boldness in the fading last light of sunset.

"I won't actually do this if you don't want me to," Chloe said, soft and low. I wondered if she already realized what her voice could do to me. I felt embarrassingly transparent. "Just say the word . . ."

"You know I want you to," I murmured, leaning back against the wall and wrapping a leg around Chloe's hip. "It's all I can think about and I think you know it."

"Did you wear these panties for me?" she asked in a husky voice, tugging them aside and then back, playing with the fabric between my legs as she watched me. "I guess you know all of my weaknesses now."

I'd managed to mostly keep Will out of my head since last night, but watching Chloe restrain herself at just the sight of me made me realize just how long it had been since I'd felt this desired. Will and I had been two horny teenagers when we first slept together; I'd marveled at sharing my body with someone else, and the intimacy of getting off with this guy I'd been crazy about. Afterwards I'd felt both new and full of wise secrets, even when I was away from Will. And when I was away from Will, most of what I thought of back then was getting back to Will, back to his bed and his body and the new places we found together. Still, had I ever felt this singularly appreciated? Had he ever drawn so sharp a breath as he gazed at my body?

"What are you thinking about?" Chloe asked.

"How nice this feels," I said. "The way you look at me."

For a moment it felt like her lustful gaze clouded over with something else, but then she leaned me back harder into the wall and pressed into me. When I'd dreamed of this new life I'd had, having sex in a storage closet right outside of a queer wedding reception had not been on my figurative bingo card.

And it was perfect.

After another earthquaking orgasm, I eagerly unbuttoned Chloe's jumpsuit and slid my hand into her boy shorts.

"You don't have to," Chloe said.

"I *want* to," I said, turned on by her slick heat, all that wetness because of *me.* "I love how you feel. Let me at least try. I feel like I've at least proven myself by now."

"It has nothing to do with you," she said quickly. "Look, yeah, I'm very good at what we just did. I'm aware. No one's into me for the other part."

"Chloe," I said, and slipped my hand back into her jumpsuit, lightly, gently. "I'm very in to you for this part."

She laughed and wrapped an arm around my neck, pulling my face close to hers as I touched her. "You know I didn't mean that. Girls get bored, you know. Coaxing me toward orgasm for another half hour for good karma or whatever."

"Do I seem bored?" I asked, switching up my rhythm and marveling at the surprised pleasure registering on cool, badass Chloe Lee's face.

"OK, not at this second, no," she said, covering her face with her hands.

"I could give a shit about karma," I said. "It's the hottest thing I can think of right now, touching you like this. Chloe, *look at me.*"

She dropped her hands, made eye contact again.

"I love how you look when I—" I stroked with more pressure, the way I liked touching myself. Chloe's breath told me she liked it too. "Watching you get there was one of my favorite things about last night. I want to keep doing it. Even if I'm new and awkward and ready to take direction."

Chloe grabbed my wrist, and I worried she would pull me away. Instead, she moved my hand for me, a little faster and rougher, until I kept the pace on my own.

"Nice work," she said with a smirk, her eyes meeting mine. "You're a fast learner."

"Can I admit how many articles and how-to guides I read?" I asked, and she laughed. "I wanted to be ready."

She smiled, all traces of the smirk gone. "For me?"

It had never been her, of course, when I'd studied up. It had only been the idea of someone, not a real person at all. But now the only person it had mattered for, after all of this, was nothing but real.

"I'm sorry if someone ever made you feel bad about this," I murmured, as I continued touching her, as her breath grew more ragged and her gaze sharper. "I want to know what people thought was better to do with their time than exactly this."

"Oh, *fuck*," she muttered, pressing her face into my shoulder and letting out a groan against my bare skin. I sucked gently on her neck, light pressure so it wouldn't show later, then lowered my lips to suck softly at one of her nipples, then the other.

"Take your time," I told her, realizing I felt confident now, holding Chloe's pleasure in the—well, literally the palm of my hand. "This is the only place I want to be right now."

"You make it—" Chloe cut herself off with a soft moan. "You make this part so easy, Clementine. You're so fucking easy to believe in."

This was it, I knew, exactly what I'd been looking for when I'd walked away from the life I could have had. Someone new who maybe needed someone like me, someone who didn't see this as time and patience but an earth-shatteringly hot way to spend an afternoon. When, a few minutes later, Chloe came with a growl, I felt nearly undone, and it did not escape her notice.

"Let me get you there again," she said, and I laughed and shook my head.

"You've done plenty already," I said, though I didn't fight it, didn't fight her, didn't fight the waves of pleasure that shook through me shortly thereafter. It was nearly another ten minutes later when we finally emerged from the storage closet— Chloe first, then me moments later as not to arouse suspicion.

I stopped by the restroom on my way back to the reception, and laughed at my reflection. Hair disheveled, dress and bra straps somehow twisted together over one shoulder, a smudge of dust on my bicep that was cartoonishly *yes-I-just-got-fucked-in-a-broom-closet.*

Bianca stepped out of one of the stalls and walked up to the sink next to mine as I dabbed at my arm.

"I ran into something," I said quickly, and she laughed.

"Like someone's vagina?" she asked, and I choked on the shock of it, and then we were both cracking up. "Get yourself cleaned up, girl, the professional photographers are doing an intense candids round now. I'm extremely sex-positive but it'd probably be nice if you didn't look so JBF in Nina and Ari's wedding album they show their future kids."

Bianca helped me tame down my hair and fix my dress, and when we strolled back to our table I felt the picture of poise and dignity.

"There's more photos," Chloe said as I sat down next to her, in a tone that very much indicated we had not just spent our time down the hallway doing exactly what we'd done.

"Yeah, I heard. Bianca helped me get myself back together."

She frowned and glanced in Bianca's direction. "What did you say to her? Did you tell her what just happened between us?"

"Chloe, I looked like a cartoon of someone who'd just had sex in a closet. I didn't really have to say anything."

Chloe frowned.

"Is it so bad someone knows?" I asked. "It's something couples do."

Not that it had been a thing Will and I had ever done. The most adventurous location we'd ever managed in all of our time together had been the back seat of his car a few times, and he was always too nervous for it to be anything more than a quick way to get off when it was our only option.

"You know I don't do PDA," she snapped.

"I'm pretty sure you were the one who yanked me into a broom closet and fucked me up against a stack of boxes, so I don't know why this is on me now?" I tried to say it quietly, and like a joke, but I felt asea again. I felt like I'd lost my ability to know anything.

Chloe leaned forward, clearly scanning the room for something. "Maybe you can go join your youth table for a while."

I poked her arm, hoping it translated as *why are you being like this?*

"It's not official wedding party photos," CJ said, in a helpful tone. "I'm sure it's fine if you're sitting with us, Clementine. Though if you want to hang out with the hot youths again, we'd all understand."

Chloe flashed me a look. "Well, Ari and Nina apparently gave a heads-up about the photographer while I'd stepped away, so I didn't get a chance to ask any follow-up questions. So maybe it would make sense to just . . . you know. Err on the side of whatever."

"Okay," I said, but more like a question, like despite whatever had just gone sideways, she'd break into laughter and tell me she was kidding, kiss me on camera like the squishy people we weren't really but maybe might be someday.

"Wedding party only," she clarified instead. "Not plus-ones."

CJ, Sofia, Bianca, and even *my boss* exchanged grimaces, and I didn't wait for Chloe to say another thing I hated. I got up and left.

Chapter 18
Your Most Annoying Friend

I pushed my way through the crowded room and back toward the outdoor area, which glowed pink under the late afternoon sunlight. As soon as I'd run through the last set of doors, I ran into someone with a solid *thud* and wondered just how much further my day could fall, from the heights of pleasure less than an hour ago to knocked literally down to the ground.

"Oh, god, Clementine, I'm so sorry." The person extended a hand to pull me up, and I realized it was the Johnny's bartender, Sadie. She was dressed in an indigo suit over a patterned knit top, casual and formal all rolled into one.

"No, it was me," I said, back on my feet but not feeling much better for it. "I didn't see you earlier at the bar. But to be fair, we did get lazy and mainly just drink the wine at the table."

"Oh, no, I'm not working the wedding, my partner's friends with the brides," she said, and I felt my face burn.

"Sorry, of course, I didn't mean to imply—"

"No apology needed," she said. "It's good to see you. Beautiful wedding, right?"

"The most beautiful," I said. "I'm not usually a wedding person, but—"

"Oh, I know. This thing put all my notions of doing the thing at city hall someday way out of my head. Though I think I'd have to become a lot richer magically, so there's that."

"Yeah, there's definitely that."

She smiled right at me, that magic bartender connection energy. "You OK? Besides getting knocked down?"

"Just . . . I don't know. You know that drink you're working on that you gave me to help with my previous man trouble? And my . . ."

Sadie grinned. "Future-slash-current girl trouble?"

"Anyway. I could use one of those right now."

"Hold that thought," she said, slipping away, and I wondered if, despite the seemingly bonhomie vibe of that interaction, I'd also just somehow made it too weird. Bartenders were people, too. In their off-hours they probably didn't want to hear too much about one's future-slash-current girl trouble.

Except, no, Sadie returned a couple minutes later, her hands holding out two tumblers.

"I thought you weren't bartending," I said, recognizing that shimmering pink drink.

"Eh, I played the bartender card, they let me back behind the bar," she said, handing me one of the tumblers. "Cheers to girl troubles. Even when they suck—well, I guess it's often fun getting there. Tell me to shut up if this has been one of those unfun exceptions."

I clinked my glass against hers. "No. It's been pretty fun."

She gave me an understanding nod, and we finished our drinks in silence as the DJ's music filled the air around us.

"Thanks," I told her, after I'd tipped my glass back for the very last sip. "I can't believe I was rude enough to assume you were working the wedding, and then you still made me a drink."

"To be fair, I did work that party just the other night," she said with a kind smile. "But you're really welcome. Come by next week and I'll do an even better version of this one, OK? I should go, my girl loves this MUNA song so I think I'm needed on the dance floor. Join us?"

"Maybe later," I said, and waved as she headed inside. My phone's home screen was empty of the messages I guessed I'd hoped I would have by now, so going in didn't sound great.

Outside all the way now, I spotted an empty bench at the edge of the property, a little corner tucked away. But as I was about to take a seat, I spotted a fuchsia dress doing the exact same thing.

"Oh, sorry," I said, jumping back when I saw that it was Bianca.

"Sorry why?" she asked coolly, sitting down but looking up at me with one eyebrow cocked.

"I thought I was alone," I said. "I assume you did, too."

She shrugged. "Just wanted a quieter spot to read texts from our nanny and stare at photos of my kid like a codependent and anxious person. Two things I'm trying really hard not to be."

"Oh," I said, and sat down next to her. "If it makes you feel better, you don't seem like one." It was the understatement, I thought, of the year. Bianca was cool and collected, period.

"It does make me feel better, thanks." She scrolled through her phone for a few silent moments before glancing at me. "You OK?"

"Maybe I'm being stupid," I said, knowing that the adult thing to do was probably exactly what Chloe suggested, time with other people. I could be inside right now, at the other table or dancing to "I Know a Place" with Sadie and her partner. All of it sounded wiser than pouting alone.

"I didn't ask if you were being stupid," she said, a smile tugging at the corner of her lips. "It was a little rough in there."

I couldn't believe how *good* it felt hearing that, her words landing in an empty spot in my chest. "I knew what I was in for, but . . ."

Bianca nodded. "I've known her a long time, and I know

what it looks like when she's panicking, even if how it looks to others is—" She cut herself off with a laugh. "You know, just general asshole behavior."

"Yeah," I said. "I do know."

"You shouldn't take it the way it seems," Bianca said. "No, sorry. You have every right to take it the way it seems. You seem like someone who has healthy boundaries."

I actually snorted I laughed so hard. "Sorry, no. I'm not sure that I do."

"When Chloe told us you two were dating, you know, I was worried. She'd had a crush on you for so long. And you didn't seem . . ."

"I didn't seem *what*?" I asked, waiting for it. Queer? Real? Worthy of her?

And also—what? *A crush? For so long?*

"As invested. You play your cards close to your chest, you know," she said with a raised eyebrow.

"To be fair," I said, not sure why it felt safe saying it to one of the most intimidating people I knew—hell, *my boss's wife*, "so do you."

"Well, sure," she said with a laugh. "But I know myself. You, less so. I thought, Chloe's been saying for years that relationships aren't for her, that all she needs is Fernando, and then suddenly you're here and she's making heart eyes at you and you're at a distance."

Sometimes there was no stranger sensation than hearing how someone else saw you.

"And then I thought—well, jesus, Bianca." She let out what could only be described as a cackle. "Our group is *so much*. And you just got thrown in with all of us. And *then* I thought, oh, *god*, and *her boss is here!*"

"Yep," I said, validated that finally—finally!—someone else pointed out the awkwardness in that. "Which of course Chloe hadn't mentioned to me."

"No, of course she hadn't." Bianca laughed to herself for a while longer, and even in this mood I couldn't help but join in. "Anyway. I really was sure she was bound to get her heart broken."

I rolled my eyes. "Yeah. That was never going to happen."

"Because you're in way more than you seem," Bianca said lightly, but I knew it was an acceptance. She thought she saw me as I was, my intentions laid bare. And I didn't know why that was what did it, but I couldn't keep going a moment longer.

"No," I said. "Because I was never in it to begin with. And neither was Chloe. This was all some terrible—it feels so fucking stupid saying it out loud."

Bianca watched me quietly, but instead of the suspicious gaze I expected, her expression was open, waiting.

"She needed a date for all of this," I said, waving my finger in a circle to indicate the wedding and assorted events. "I guess I needed one, too. The way my brother and sister-in-law were talking about me behind my back, I couldn't show up at my parents' anniversary party alone. And the way my friends— well, and being a baby gay, apparently. Girl experience so the first real girl isn't scared off. So whatever you thought you saw in me, that's all it was. A fake girlfriend."

"Uh-huh," Bianca said. "I'm sure that's all it was."

I wasn't sure *exactly* what I'd expected would happen when I finally, maybe inevitably, let someone in on this whole charade, but it definitely wasn't *bold nonchalance.* "What do you mean?"

"Well, I can tell that you and Chloe constructed this little story where you were putting on some show for us," Bianca said. "But all I saw were two people falling for each other."

"We were good at the scam," I said, and Bianca laughed.

"No, you aren't. Really, *you*? Who thought earlier I wouldn't be able to tell you and Chloe had just hooked up and tried to make casual bathroom conversation with me?"

I cracked up. "Sorry, is that not proper bathroom conversation protocol?"

"It's *adorable* you two thought it was something fake," Bianca said. "But I don't even really know what that means when the two of you are so—hell, Clementine, I don't know. I know she's acting like an asshole right now. But you've probably blown up her whole world. If you've got the patience to see it through, I think it's going to be really good on the other side of things."

I hugged my arms around myself. "I'm not sure that's true. But I guess it's nice to hear."

"You know your most annoying friend who's always right about everything?" She gestured to herself. "That's now me."

"We're only friends until this thing is over," I said. "And that contract runs out in two weeks, after the family party."

"First of all, that seems pretty unlikely to me. But second of all, even if you and Chloe do have some weird arrangement, the rest of us aren't in on that. I'll continue to be your most annoying friend who's the most correct about everything. Can you imagine trying to stop me?"

"To be fair, no." I smiled faintly. "Can I ask you something? Feel free to tell me to mind my own business—"

"Oh, I will."

"I expect nothing less," I said, my smile feeling a little less faint already. "I've had the same couple of best friends basically since I moved back to LA after college. And it's *hard.* They mean so much to me but I feel like to them especially that friendship is like the lowest priority. And one has a baby and the other wants to, and if it's already—you know, a dinner every other month at best, which is like advanced mathematics levels of difficulty to get scheduled, I feel like it's just going to get less than that. But with all of you, it's just not like that. So what am I doing wrong?"

"Being friends with straight people?" she asked, and then laughed. "I'm kidding. But I do feel like queer people can prioritize friendship differently, chosen family and all. People used to get kicked out of their families of origin and even though that's not the situation for any of us, I think we still feel that, the way we can be more to each other than people we see only when we've got time, and also that sometimes friendship means making time, even when it's—your words—advanced mathematics level of difficulty."

I nodded, feeling guilty for being a little surprised that intimidating-as-hell Bianca was saying something that resonated with me somewhere deep in my gut. To be honest, I hadn't thought a lot about the feelings of this group of friends; I just felt that they were getting something right that I hadn't managed to.

"Not to sound a million years old," she continued, "but I see all the memes people post about brunch, which—sure, I have definitely spent fifty bucks on what amounts to a couple of scrambled eggs, haven't we all. But then I think about all the queer people and anyone else who didn't feel welcome or didn't want to go to church on Sunday mornings and so they carved out their own thing instead. Not to say I'm always honoring my queer elders, trust me. Sometimes I just want mimosas and overpriced eggs."

"Sometimes that's all that I want, too," I said, and we grinned at each other.

"You're not doing anything wrong," Bianca said. "Friendship is just a lot of work and life is busy. Phoebe and I know we've got it easier than most people; we can pay for a babysitter every week so we can have brunch without worrying about diapers and tantrums. It might not be as easy for your friends. Plus you feel guilt constantly anyway! Guilt if you're with your friends and not with your child, and guilt if you're with your child and not with all these people who love you. Every time we skip out on something I feel a little shitty. And I feel shitty when we *don't* skip out. As someone who likes being good at everything, parenthood is a real challenge."

234 / *Amy Spalding*

I thought of Hailey, how much she wanted everything to be perfect, how easy it had been for me to write that off because her current goals involved things like clowns and face painting. It wasn't even because I couldn't take those things seriously—though to be fair I supposed I did not take them very seriously—but because I could only see what they symbolized for me, just more items on the list of how much Hailey's life had nothing to do with mine anymore.

"I meant to cheer you up, but you somehow look even more serious now," Bianca said with a laugh.

"I'm not sure I know how to be a very good friend now," I said with a shrug. "I've been so worried about myself. And my friends don't need me and I—god, I don't know. It's all harder than I want it to be."

"I don't know your friends, obviously," Bianca said. "But I know Chloe very well, and I feel like I know you well enough by now to say this. Sometimes the scariest thing is the idea of actually getting what you're after. Things end up hard because it can be easier to make them that way than just—"

She cut herself off with a knowing smile, and I followed her line of sight to see Phoebe and Chloe walking toward us. It would have been a nice moment for some clarity, but Chloe's expression gave nothing away.

"It's time for cake," Phoebe said. "And I've heard it's going to be a good one."

Bianca grinned and stood up to join Phoebe. "Ari was off shooting something when the cake decision was locked in, so Nina took me along on her final tasting. Y'all, it's *great*."

"I'll join you in a minute," I said, and watched them walk back inside.

"You're OK?" Chloe asked.

"Sure," I said. "You warned me I wouldn't be in photos, so I wasn't in photos."

Chloe shifted her weight from one foot to another, shoved

her hands into her pockets. "I didn't mean that you had to leave."

I shrugged, suddenly lonely out here without Bianca, without anyone who seemed like they might be on my side. "Erring on the side of whatever."

"You'll come in for cake, though, right?" she asked.

"Sure. I trust Bianca's review."

I followed Chloe in, still feeling hollowed out from the inside, alone in a way I'd been too busy to process. If this was all pretend, then no matter what Bianca said, maybe soon I wouldn't have anything left at all. There was just my parents' party and we were through.

The cake was light and airy, notes of vanilla and citrus and the hint of cardamom. I laughed along with jokes and danced with the whole group and had seconds and then thirds of dessert. Despite every single count against it, I'd still never had so much fun at a wedding before.

We were some of the last to leave, outstaying the younger crowd of friends—which felt like something of an ego boost we all needed. Back at the hotel we said goodbye, because we were all headed back to LA sometime in the earlier half of the day and had decided that just for once we could skip brunch.

I didn't know what would happen in our room, but ultimately it was that we each got ready for bed (I decided I could cede the bra and sweatpants) and quietly got under the covers in the darkness, facing away from each other.

"I set an early alarm so I could hit up the hotel breakfast," Chloe said, and I waited for the invitation and the softening in the tension pressing against us. "So feel free to ignore it when you hear it."

"Yep," I said, instead of any of the things I wanted to say to her. "I will."

Chapter 19
Consider Yourself

I knew what I hoped for on our drive home, but I didn't actually know what to expect. What I got was "Hello, Dolly!" blasting through the stereo, an ice-cold can of Diet Coke waiting for me in the cupholder, and very little conversation as Chloe followed the 101 down the coastline, through the Valley, and back to Silver Lake.

"Where are you going?" I asked, when Chloe passed up the 5.

"My place," she said as if that had always been the plan. I decided not to ask questions because, honestly, the order of drop-offs was a very small concern to me compared to everything else that had happened over the course of the last two days.

She parked behind her building and gestured toward her apartment. "You're coming up?"

"Am I?" I asked, but I followed because I couldn't think of a better thing to do that didn't involve a heartfelt conversation I didn't have the nerve to start. Inside it was quiet without the sound of Fernando dashing around and barking seemingly indiscriminately out the window, but Chloe turned the show tunes playlist back on and that meant that it was "Consider

Yourself" from *Oliver!* playing when she walked up behind me and swept my hair aside before kissing the back of my neck.

I knew what I should have done, as a person who'd had some therapy and also followed a lot of therapy meme accounts. Two steps forward from Chloe's lips and then a real conversation to clear up what, exactly, this was. But what I did was lean back into it, fitting my ass against her hips. Her kisses grew sharper and her teeth scraped the nape of my neck while she gripped my hips. We ground against each other as her teeth sank into my tender skin, and I'd never felt so grateful for not starting a conversation.

"I've been dying to get you in my room," Chloe said, guiding me with her hand urgently at the small of my back, through her apartment to her bedroom. "I kept thinking about fucking you in my bed."

I felt myself pause, sorting out what this meant after—well, there were so many *afters*.

"What?" Chloe asked.

"I've been thinking about it too," I said instead of what I should have said. Though of course these particular thoughts had been mixed between the other ones, of wondering if it was all already over before it had really even started for real. Unless Bianca was right and it had been real the whole time. Wouldn't I have known?

Now, though, that all seemed far away. Nothing seemed bigger than the knowledge that Chloe had been thinking about me, thinking about me here, thinking about me in her bed.

Chloe slipped her brightly striped crop top off over her head before pulling off my dress in one slick move. "Fuck, look at you."

"Look at *you*," I said, unbuttoning her jeans, feeling a million miles away from anything that wasn't this. "Is this how you pictured it? When you thought about me here?"

"It's a good start."

She walked me toward her bed, but I pushed back against her. "I'm always first," I said, though I wished I hadn't said *always*, this was only our third hookup after all. "I want you first this time."

"Clementine, you don't have to—"

"I want you first this time," I repeated.

Her eyes flashed with what I knew was hunger, but since I knew she'd want to try to talk me out of it anyway, I kept going. Chloe back against the wall with her jeans and boy shorts down and my face between her legs.

Even at this new angle, I felt more confident this time, like Chloe was all I needed to consume in order to survive. It was the first chance that we'd truly been this alone together, no fellow hotel room guests one room away, no one outside a closet door; Chloe's enthusiastic sounds told me she was as aware of our privacy as I was.

"This isn't sustainable," Chloe said, her hands in my hair. "Let's move into the bed, yeah? You're gonna need physical therapy if you stay like that until I come."

"It'd be worth it," I murmured into her inner thigh, but dutifully waited for Chloe to pull back her comforter and sheets and climb into bed. I sat at her feet but she pulled me toward her, and in a flash turned over me to grab the headboard with both hands.

"Oh," I said, throbbing at the thought of what I realized was about to happen. "Are you going to—"

"Sit on your face?" she asked with a grin. "Only if you want me to, Clementine."

"Did you picture this?" I asked before she settled herself on top of me. My entire body shook at the overwhelming heat of it all; it was tough to remember anything I'd ever experienced that was as hot as Chloe on top of me right then.

"I pictured a lot of things," she said, moving her hips slowly at first. I wondered if one could pass out from someone else's pleasure. "Mainly you, though, not me. How'd you talk me into this, Clementine?"

I paused just a moment to make my point. "I don't feel like I had to do much convincing."

"No, I was an easy sell today—*fuck*, just like that. *Yes*."

It felt like the rest of the world had been blotted out. There was nothing left except for Chloe's pleasure. I could tell she was trying to hurry up for my sake, so I slowed things down, doing what I could to make her feel safe enough to take the time she needed. The time she wanted. By now I knew exactly how her breath hitched, how taut tension filled her body, how she cried out when her release was close, and so I knew just the right moment to push her all the way over the edge and feel her explode above me.

"That was some real queer 201 shit," she said in a ragged voice, lying beside me. "You're leveling up—don't look so smug."

"I'm not *smug*," I said, even though I was, again, a little. More than a little. I felt like the luckiest girl in the world. What couldn't the two of us do together?

Chloe leaned over to her nightstand and riffled through the drawer. "I pictured this too. You into it? No pressure, genuinely."

I nodded at the harness, glittery purple strap-on, and lube, though hopefully not so eagerly I looked deranged. "I'm into it—I mean, the thought of it. You know it's all firsts for me."

"But you've been researching," Chloe said with a laugh as she turned away from me to get ready. "How-to guides. Porn?"

"Oh, yeah, plenty of porn," I said. "I didn't want to seem like an idiot when I got into this situation."

"Well," Chloe said, kneeling in front of me and nudging my thighs open, "mission accomplished, Clementine."

I let out a sharp gasp as she entered me, and we watched each other as we moved together, rough almost from the beginning.

I'd been so ready for her that I only made it a few moments before crying out in almost shocked bliss. We kept going, of course, because we were just getting started. We switched positions, me on top, her behind me, up against the wall again. Finally, back in her bed, she held my gaze with hers as she moved in an agonizingly slow rhythm. Every nerve in my body trembled for her, but this time I waited. This time I wanted it to go on as long as possible.

"I pictured it," she said soft and low, and I felt it start, the rumble through my entire system, "just like this."

I cried out as I let go of everything, arching into her as waves of pleasure quaked through me. Had I ever felt like this? It seemed impossible.

"You're very good at that," I told Chloe when I could breathe again. "Look as smug as you want."

She grinned at me. "Yeah, yeah. It was a team effort."

I laughed at that, pressing my face into her shoulder. I wasn't into cuddling, per se, but I also found her very hard to resist. "If we keep playing like this, we'll definitely win the playoffs."

"All the way to nationals," she said. "Man, sports metaphors aside, we should have started the lessons way sooner."

I didn't like the way she said *lessons* but my brain was still a swirly mess of post-orgasm chemicals so I decided not to push it.

"Think how good you'll be for the first real girl," Chloe continued, and that snapped my brain right out of it.

"Why would you say that?" I asked softly. "I thought we—"

"Oh," Chloe said, raising her eyebrows. "Man, I did know better than to get into this with a baby gay, but here we are—"

"*No*," I said, sharper than I realized I would. "Don't say that like an asshole. Because you're not an asshole, and also because you must know I'm not that naïve, and I don't think something changed just because we had sex. The way we've been talking—the things we've said—"

"We have the whole arrangement between us," she said. "And we're also attracted to each other, sure. It doesn't have to be more than that."

"But . . . but it could be," I said gently. "I mean, I *like* this. I like you. And not because of the way you just made me scream—well, not *just* that. And I think that you—maybe you also . . . I think we're good together, and—I don't know. We're already kind of doing this. Maybe we just don't put an end date on it?"

"I told you that I don't date," she said.

"Yeah, and you also told me people don't want you for who you really are, and that you're not worth waiting on, and also that some girl did weird stuff with her feet to you—"

"I mean, they were cold, it was fine," she said.

"You know what I'm saying, Chloe. That maybe it didn't work out before for you, but I'm not them."

"I'm great alone," she said.

"I never said you weren't."

"No, but you're like them," she said, jabbing her finger into the air to indicate *them*. "You think you can't really be happy unless you have someone, and even if you're qualifying that as a partner and not a wife or husband, it's all the same thing. You alone is incomplete. And I think that's *bullshit*, Clementine, because I'm doing great, and you were too. We don't *need* this."

I couldn't believe this was the conversation we'd found our way into, only moments after what we'd just done together. I knew that, even though it had yet to happen to me, that I was capable of having emotion-free sex, physical pleasure only. I was also practically positive that it hadn't been that with Chloe at all.

"No, I didn't say we did, just—"

"You're the one talking about how you don't want to die alone," Chloe said, and I almost felt like I was imagining things because it felt like such a terrible thing to say, much less at a time like this. "I've got news for you, though. Unless just the most tragic shit happens, we're all gonna die alone."

"OK, fine," I said, getting up and pulling on my bra before slipping back into my dress. Having this conversation mostly naked couldn't be making anything better. "I think you understand it's a turn of phrase, but, fine."

"This doesn't even have anything to do with me," she said. "You're so afraid to be by yourself that you're trying to make this work, when I told you from the start it never would. Time's about up and you're panicking."

"That's not true," I said. "Just because I want to find someone and fall in love forever doesn't make me an idiot. It doesn't mean I can't tell how I feel about you."

"You know, I actually thought that doing this would make me feel better around my friends," Chloe said. "Finally equal in their eyes or whatever. But instead I had to hear all this shit, like everyone at the wedding being all, *oh it's so great you have Clementine.* Like I'm so much better off, you know. Me alone can't cut it."

"Your friends know you can cut it," I said. "You cut it great."

"You barely know them," she said. "Maybe they don't think that at all."

"They're just happy for you," I said, hoping she wasn't right about that, at the very least. Of everything she'd said so far, somehow it cut the deepest.

"I've done so many things since I've known them," she said. "Gotten my MBA. Started my own business. I ran a half-marathon once! And when are they over-the-moon happy for me? When I've got a girlfriend."

"I don't think it's like that," I said softly.

"After I had surgery, it was all the same shit, *thank god you had Clementine.* But the thing was that I thought I had *them* already. I didn't *need* you."

"I'm not saying you do." I shook my head. "You know

what, I don't know what I'm doing. There's probably not a lot of things more humiliating than trying to convince someone she likes me while she's saying that she doesn't. I'm going to get a Lyft."

"Don't get a Lyft," she said, frantically getting dressed. "I'll take you home."

"Fine." I walked out of her bedroom and waited at the door for her. On the ride home I thought about how I'd known better when we got back to her place today than to let her kiss me instead of having a conversation, but I'd still done it anyway. I'd led myself right to my own heartbreak.

In my condo I tried not to cry as I lavished attention on Small Jesse Pinkman. Maybe Chloe was right and nothing had actually changed. Maybe I was a naïve baby gay who'd let some orgasms convince me something bigger had happened. Maybe after some sleep in my own bed I'd see it all more clearly.

But when my alarm went off Monday morning, nothing felt clear at all, and the only person I wanted to hear from hadn't reached out. However real or fake it was, the one thing I was certain of was that now it was over.

Chapter 20

Other People's Happy Endings

I could not believe after the weekend I'd had and whatever *conversation* or *fight* or *situation* that capped it all off that I had to get up on Monday morning and go to work, but that was being an adult. It felt like you rarely just got to sit home and weep along to sad show tunes, even when the situation called for it.

At work I chugged my iced espresso while getting through the emails from when I was out as well as everything that had come in from the East Coast since the day started. Working on Pacific time was beginning each day running a little late.

Phoebe leaned in, looking bright and well rested. "I'm sure you have plenty to get through too but I just wanted to say hi."

I tried to gauge from her tone what she knew. "Hi. I feel like I need another full day of sleep, and you're all . . . well, not looking half dead."

"Oh, it's because we have a kid and on nights we're not doing anything, we all go to bed at like eight o'clock," Phoebe said. "Last night I think it was closer to seven thirty. When I was young and considered myself cool, I used to roll my eyes when I heard people talking about kids and early bedtimes."

"'Early bedtimes? That's for the straights!'"

I couldn't believe I was making a joke like that to, even after the last couple months, my boss, but Phoebe cracked up.

"Exactly. Turns out early bedtimes come for us all. Anyway, I'll see you in a bit in the weekly meeting. We might push it a few since I came in to the news that Celebration definitely wants to use us for *Silly in Love*, and I'd like to get a few initial tasks crossed off my list if possible."

"Oh, great," I said, opening my planner and jotting it down. "When's the release date again? Early December?"

"Oh, don't worry about it," Phoebe said casually, heading out of my office. "They decided not to use us for media planning. So you don't need to worry about it. See you in a bit."

Fuck. Her casual tone couldn't actually match reality, could it? I was trying to make a case for expansion, and before I could even fully plead my case I was somehow losing business. Would it be a smarter move to just cancel that upcoming meeting, hang on to this gig as it was as long as I could, and think about what was next? My guidance counselor—who, sure, hadn't been great at his job—had looked at my stellar math scores and told me to become an accountant. Was that the right move now?

"Hey, boss," Tamarah said, stepping into my office with her hands hugging her mug of green tea. "How happy was Small Jesse Pinkman to see you? Or is he like my mom's cat and had to snub you for a while first?"

"No snubbing, pure happiness," I said. "Thanks again for helping out. Is it inappropriate I asked? Is it weird you know what my condo looks like? Or where it is? Or what kind of toilet paper I use?"

She gave me a look to suggest it was indeed very weird I'd asked that, so I laughed as if I'd been kidding about all of it.

"How was the wedding?" she asked.

"It was good," I said.

"That's very convincing," she said with a laugh, and I shook my head.

"No, it was really lovely. Weddings aren't always my thing,

but it was a good one. It was just one of those long weekends and I guess the arrival back to reality's hitting me a little harder than usual."

"I feel that. My therapist says whenever you feel that way to try to take what you can from your vacation into your real life."

I pictured Chloe singing at the top of her lungs in her car, holding me close as we danced, rolling her eyes about peppers, pushing me toward pleasure and then far past. All of that gone from my real life.

"But I'm also like, yeah, not sure if I can carry in all my favorite things from vacation to my real life," Tamarah said. "If I got to lie on a beach every day and hang out nonstop with all my favorite people, I'd probably be great to begin with."

"Seriously," I said, feeling glad that even though I never would have breathed a word about therapy to a boss of mine— even now!—I liked that Tamarah knew that she could. Even if I was only half her boss, really, I liked what we'd forged here. If I had to ship off to become an accountant, I knew Tamarah would do well in whatever was next for her.

OK, I'd gone quickly from having some light concerns that expanding my department wasn't the best idea directly to getting CPA-certified and finding a non-sinking ship for my brilliant assistant. There had to be a few steps in between. Right?

I glanced down at my phone to see that the group chat was as alive as usual—well, the modified one that CJ had created the other week so we wouldn't bother Nina and Ari the week of their wedding and now their honeymoon. I wasn't sure what I'd expected; I guessed maybe that it would have been so simple as Chloe texting the rest of the group without me, and it would be just one more group chat that others were fine seeing me fall off of. I went back to how it had been, though, before I'd felt like maybe they weren't just Chloe's friends, but mine too. I didn't weigh in, I didn't add anything unless I was explicitly asked, and I tried not to watch for Chloe's messages too closely.

The only person who was participating less than I was, though, was Chloe.

Because life apparently had not given up disappointing me today, I got a couple of red alerts from Greg and decided it would be less annoying to just drive up after work than to face his responses if I tried to bail now.

Since it was quiet at work for a Monday—and I tried desperately not to see that as some further proof of my imminent failure—I slipped out a bit early and headed up the 5, parking myself at a Chili's a little ahead of schedule. On Instagram I saw that I'd been tagged in at least a half dozen posts from the weekend, and because I apparently liked rubbing salt into wounds, I tapped through the posts from Bianca, Sofia, CJ, and even from a few people I'd only met over the weekend. In photos I looked like that new person I'd felt like when I was alone with Chloe, brimming over with laughter and conversation, a smile that reached my eyes and beyond.

And maybe I was a little out of my head with—well, whatever one feels when one has ended things with one's fake girlfriend, but I couldn't ignore Chloe in the photos too, especially Chloe in photos with me. Her eyes on me like I was the most interesting thing in the room, maybe in the world.

That part hadn't been fake too, right? We hadn't actually been that good at faking. I wanted to be sure of that, surer than I was.

My phone buzzed with a notification from Slack, and instead of some agency meme someone was sharing on the #general thread, it was killjoy Aubrey sharing a link to an article about how ad agencies were adjusting to changing landscapes. There was no way there would be anything in there that was going to make me feel better, so I managed to head right back to Instagram. There weren't any additional tagged photos when I refreshed, but the picture at the top of my feed was of Fiona and Hailey at Club Tee Gee, our old regular bar when the three of us had low-level gigs and only frequented spots with decent happy hours. *So happy this bar and the two of us are still standing after all these years!*

I knew that I hadn't exactly tried with the two of them lately—not since Chloe and her friends entered the picture, really, but back before that to my breakup and maybe even a little once the breakup became that thing in the back of my mind that I couldn't let go of. Back before talk of babies and futures that felt radically different from mine. Still, if plans were so hard to make these days—and I genuinely knew that they were, and that maybe I should have tried a little harder to be accommodating—they'd managed to do it. Just not with me.

Greg walked in and sat down across from me. "Where's your girlfriend?"

"She's not—honestly, she's not my girlfriend anymore."

I watched him for his reaction, but he only picked up his menu.

"Hi, Greg, it's nice to see you too."

He grunted out some kind of greeting. "I always get the Crispy Chicken Crispers. Glad they're still making them."

I laughed, deciding I might as well live and let live. "That's a bizarrely redundant name."

He gave me a look, so I turned to my menu as well, even though I knew I was getting Baby Back Ribs. When in Rome and all.

"She was gonna bring those Korean things," Greg said. "For the potluck buffet. Can you get those somewhere else?"

"Really?" Maybe living and letting live wasn't going to work for me after all. "You find out we broke up and that's what you're asking me? Sure, Greg. I will fill the kimbap void."

"They just sounded really good," he mumbled.

"Yeah," I said. "They would have been. What else do we need to discuss?"

"Hang on, Marisol gave me a list." He leaned back and reached into his pocket. "She wanted to come but Lulu's got a cold and we can't ask Mom and Dad or Marisol's parents to keep an eye on them."

"Is Lulu OK?" I asked.

"It's a cold," he said. "It's not like when you feel sick. If you had kids you'd understand they just get sick all the time. Walking germ machines. No big deal."

"Yeah, I know people with kids," I said. "I understand kids get sick, I just wanted to make sure my niece was OK. You don't need to use everything I say as an excuse to make some kind of dig, you know. I'm having a shitty day and this has real this-could-have-been-an-email-not-a-meeting vibes."

Greg handed me the list, written in Marisol's perfect cursive. "I hate email."

"I wasn't being literal," I said. "Well—not entirely. Does it always have to be like this?"

"Like what?" he asked, as a server showed up to get our drink order. As good as a giant chain restaurant cocktail actually sounded, between my energy level and the drive back, I went with a Diet Coke.

"What were you talking about?" Greg asked. "Emails or something?"

"Yep, that's it. Anyway, let's sort out everything remaining. It sounds like almost everyone RSVP'd and Dad's weird former coworker won't end up spoiling the surprise?"

Greg actually laughed at that. "Yeah, Jerry's wife texted me, *don't worry, Jerry's not going to say anything!* Like three days in a row."

"Honestly, that makes me feel like he's going to even more," I said with a sigh, and Greg laughed even harder.

"He means well."

"I guess," I said. "This is why I try not to make friends at work, honestly. Keeping the Jerrys out of my life."

I thought of Phoebe, kind of my friend despite how hard I'd fought it. Tamarah, who I'd trusted enough with my home and my kitten. Chloe, who would have never entered my life without a work party. Were they my Jerrys?

"Who knows," Greg said. "Dad loves golfing with Jerry."

Maybe I'd just had a rough few days, but somehow that was the most insightful thing I'd ever heard my brother say.

Something had clearly happened by the time I got home from Chili's, because the regular-minus-the-brides group chat had quieted, and a new one had popped up. Regular, minus the brides, minus Chloe.

Clementine, I just wanted to touch base and make sure you're OK. Or not OK! I guess I just wanted to touch base, and I'm sorry I didn't know at work today or I would have been slightly more useful than telling you about early bedtimes. Or at least I like to think I would have been.

If you're free tonight and want something to do, Sofia and I could make you dinner or meet you wherever.

I'm still your most annoying friend, just a reminder.

Sofia says I should mention that it doesn't have to be tonight, just text one of us and we'll make plans this week. Or later on. No expiration date.

In lieu of responding, I burst into tears and took to my bed with my kitten and a queer romance novel. What had Chloe told them? She clearly hadn't made me a villain or I wouldn't have that flood of very sweet messages. Still, I couldn't imagine what she'd said about our breakup, how she'd made it look from her point of view.

I did my best not to think about any of that and opened the book instead. I knew that in a universe where things made sense, reading about adorable couples who got happy endings should probably make me feel even worse. They'd just never worked like that for me, though. Even during those sleepless nights next to Will, wondering how I could get what I wanted without throwing a grenade right into the center of my life, preordained happily-ever-afters made me feel hopeful. If fictional people could get everything they wanted, surely I could manage at least a little, right?

It was weird to look back on that time now, though, because Will had literally *moved out*. I had to put all the utility bills in my name only, and I had to remember all the stuff I apparently only did because another human was there as a reminder. My rolled-up yoga mat was still next to my bed, like nothing had changed, except the fine layer of dust it had gathered in its time off from its actual purpose. I couldn't imagine doing yoga, or eating a dinner that didn't arrive thanks to Grubhub or Caviar or Uber Eats. In fact, Will would have gently urged me to pick the delivery app I used the most and to stop paying for the others. Will definitely hadn't seen the full person I was, I knew, and I didn't wish him back into my life, but he'd been a good roommate. In so many ways he'd helped me be the person I wanted to be. That grenade I'd thrown, I knew, had blown a Will-sized hole out of my world.

But somehow the removal of Chloe Lee from my life, not even my real girlfriend, barely even five feet tall, had blasted a crater-size chunk out of *everything*. It was the kind of thing I knew I couldn't confess to anyone. I felt like Taylor Swift, singing more songs about that dirtbag she'd spent a few months with than the guy everyone thought she'd end up marrying. Will and I had nearly two decades, a real relationship. And Chloe had ended things terribly! She'd been mean and unfair and—I hoped, desperately—dishonest.

Still, what I thought about was the way her eyes crinkled up when she laughed, the way she sang off-key at the top of her lungs, the way she'd always been ready to come to my defense.

I buried my face in Small Jesse Pinkman's fur and breathed

along with his purrs. Before long he got distracted by a piece of lint on the floor and sprang away into action, and I went back to the book. Maybe I was destined to only read about other people's happy endings, but for now that sounded better than a world without them at all.

Chapter 21
Don't Bother, They're Here

What I wanted to do with my spare time was dive into stereotypical breakup activities: singing along to breakup songs, eating expensive ice cream straight from the container, refreshing their ex's pet grooming business's Instagram. Instead, my downtime was going toward building a presentation deck, even though I wasn't sure if I believed in my own cause anymore. I still owed it to everyone else to get the job done.

My phone vibrated with a message while I was reformatting some year-over-year data— post-Chloe, my weekends had truly changed for the more boring—and I glanced at it with more desperation than I was comfortable with. I'd been avoiding almost everyone. There was nothing that felt right to say to Chloe's friends. My friends probably weren't missing me—plus I knew how pathetic they thought I'd been as a single person! I couldn't bear getting those Laura Linney looks again. Greg, somehow, was the only person I was successfully texting these days. Since he hated email, I'd experimented with sending a voice memo, and he'd sent one right back. It had taken over thirty years, but my brother and I had finally figured out a communication method neither of us hated.

The message on my phone, though, was from Fiona. Since there was no way she could know about my breakup, I hoped it couldn't be too bad.

I'm sure you're already on your way up, but if it's possible, could you pick up a few cartons of soda? Hay forgot and we are going to reach Cold War worst-case scenario levels of nuclear meltdowns soon if this problem isn't solved in a matter of seconds.

Something sounded in my brain like an alarm, or one of those clichéd dreams where it was the morning of the final exam and you'd never remembered to go to class until today. A brightly colored Paperless Post danced in my mind's eye.

Today, I knew in a flash, was Ellie's first birthday.

"Shit, shit, shit," I yelped, slamming my laptop shut and leaping over Small Jesse Pinkman in a move that startled both of us. In my full-length mirror, I saw exactly what I was—a desperate and unkempt woman who had barely left her bed over the last few hours.

Summoning every bit of magic in the universe—plus my tried-and-true makeup routine and an atmosphere's worth of dry shampoo—I was out the door and pulling into the nearby 7-Eleven's parking lot only eight minutes later. I bought nine kinds of nonalcoholic carbonated beverages, as if volume could replace thoughtfulness, and texted Fiona a photo of my trunk chockful of my haul.

Drive fast, she texted before I could even back out of the parking space. **If you get pulled over, tell them one of your friends is about to die. Because if these sodas don't get here soon, we're not all making it out of here alive.**

I glanced at Waze and grimaced.

You should know that despite our warnings, there is a clown on the premises. Not metaphorically speaking.

I closed my eyes, breathed deeply, and told myself this would all be fine.

My phone buzzed yet again. **Oh and I assume Hay told you Will is here, but I'm telling you too.**

The very worst part about how mad I was is that I had no right to be at all, and I knew it. I was the one who'd dumped Will. I was the one who'd completely forgotten about this party. I was not the only one who could have advocated harder against clowns, but I still bore some brunt of that responsibility. I was clown complicit.

Traffic was lighter than usual, though I wasn't sure if that was a favor or a fuck-you from the universe, considering what I was racing toward. Parking in the suburbs was easy, so I was able to pull up right outside of Hailey and Michael's home and start yanking cartons out of the trunk.

Fiona strode down the walkway toward me. "What the hell took you so long?"

"It's a long story," I said, even though *I forgot* was only two words long.

"You look terrible," she said, grabbing two cases of Diet Coke. "But you've saved the party. However much a clown party can be saved."

I followed her around the house to the backyard, where a shockingly large group of people were gathered. Maybe no one had noticed I was just arriving now. Except that I caught Hailey's eyes, and she looked back for only a long moment before rushing away to help Michael set out a large sub sandwich.

"Hay's going to self-destruct," Fiona said. "And Michael's too nice to do anything about it. We're going to have to snap her out of it."

I shrugged. "I'm not sure she wants that from the person who was over a half hour late."

Fiona eyed me before heading over to deposit the soda into coolers between the snack table and the—*shit*—table piled high with presents. All of this was exactly the kind of stuff Will wouldn't have let me forget, and I didn't understand how I could be flailing so much when it had been right to end it. Could you buy a baby a gift card on your phone while the party was going on? How did babies get gift cards anyway? Did they have email addresses? Was there any way out of this where I didn't look like a thoughtless asshole?

"Fiona said you brought twelve dozen cases of soda," Hailey said, appearing in front of me, practically vibrating with the same kind of nervous energy she used to bring to school during midterms and finals and the PSATs. "You're my hero. I can't believe I forgot non-juice beverages! Today was supposed to be perfect."

Her extremely unwarranted gratitude was so surprising that at first I forgot to speak.

"I knew it," Hailey said. "It's bad, right? You can tell no one's having fun?"

"No, everyone's having fun," I said, gesturing around the crowded yard with an expertise I did not actually have. "Look how many people came! The weather's good—not too hot, not weird and overcast. There are *a lot* of kids here, but I don't hear any crying."

"That's because there's a clown!" Hailey said, in the exact opposite tone I would have used.

"See? Perfect. You nailed it!"

"OK," she said, nodding quickly. "When Ellie's older and asks about this party, you'll tell her all of that?"

"Sure, of course," I said, heartened that Hailey thought I'd still be in her life then. "I should say—"

"Sorry to interrupt," a woman said, cutting in between us. "Hailey, would you remind us where your bathroom is? I know you haven't dealt with potty training yet, but it adds a whole extra urgency to the whole thing."

"Of course, I'll show you," Hailey said, dashing off.

I glanced around the yard, not sure if I was looking for people to talk to or people to avoid. Mainly I wanted to blend in, be invisible amongst the married couples, the families, the happy suburban people who I knew would only see me and my life as failures. I wanted to time travel, even as little as twenty-four hours ago, when I could have loaded up my car with sodas ahead of time, bought too many presents from one of the adorable toy boutiques on the Eastside, set out my most flattering dress, *not forgotten*.

"You look terrible," Fiona said, popping up next to me.

"You said that already."

"I mean it double. Where's the girlfriend?"

"Work," I lied. "Schnauzers."

She nudged me, and I glanced over to see a sleek matte blue flask in her hand, like a Prohibition-era Stanley Cup.

"Are you drinking at a child's birthday party?" I asked.

"It's the only way I'm getting through this."

I laughed and took the flask from her, tipped back a swig. "Did the clown already leave? I don't see him anywhere."

"No, and don't let him hear you," she said, tucking the flask back into the pocket of her jeans. "He lurks where you least expect him."

I grimaced. "Is that normal for a clown?"

"There is no *normal* for a clown," Fiona said. "OK, I have to rescue Alex from Hay's neighbor who keeps asking him for free legal advice. Come with?"

"No, go save your man, I'm fine," I said, and walked over to the snack table for some organic cookies and a Diet Coke. And then when I turned around to locate a shady spot to hang out, he was right there.

"Hey," Will said.

"Oh," I said, "hi."

He looked the same, and he didn't. Instead of his usual T-shirt and jeans, he was wearing—well, still a T-shirt and jeans, but the shirt had nary a tech company logo on it, and the jeans looked like they'd cost money this decade and not a previous one. His brown hair still flopped down over his left eye, but his smile was tentative. It wasn't at all how he'd spent nearly two decades looking at me.

"You look nice," I said.

"You too," he said, and I laughed.

"I definitely don't, I got ready in like three minutes and it shows."

Will shook his head. "You always look great, Clementine."

We were both silent, and then we both opened our mouths at the exact same moment. I'd been dreading this moment, but I'd never thought about the fact that he would just feel like Will, that maybe he would always just feel like Will.

"I heard you're seeing someone," he said, looking away from me.

"Kind of," I said, which was almost the truth. "What about you?"

He shrugged. "Kind of here too. My therapist says I shouldn't jump into anything, and I think that makes sense."

"You're in therapy?" I was so surprised that I practically shouted it, and the look of horror on Will's face made me feel like I was an even bigger asshole than the day had already established.

Until I noticed the clown-shaped shadow cast over both of us.

Until I felt a poke in my side. From, horrifically, a balloon sword.

The clown gestured for me to take the sword, which *for no good reason* I did. He pulled a second sword out of god-knows-where, honked his own nose, and assumed a dueling stance. Getting trapped in clown warfare felt like unnecessarily harsh karma for forgetting about this party.

"En garde!" he cried, as his pants fell down, revealing giant red-polka-dot clown boxers. Were there lingerie stores for clowns? Was it Bozo's Secret?

"I'm a . . . peaceful person," I said, stepping back from him, as children shrieked with laughter in the background.

"Sure!" the clown said, undeterred by my combination fear and disinterest. "Any balloon animals for you two?"

I waited for Will to acquiesce.

"I think we're good," Will said. "But thank you for your service."

The clown ambled off to his next unsuspecting victims, and I burst into relieved laughter. "'Thank you for your service'?"

"I panicked!" Will grimaced. "I didn't want him to squirt me in the face with that flower."

"No, truly, I'm honestly impressed you sent him on his way. I guess therapy's teaching you some things."

I regretted it as soon as it was out of my mouth. Coming from someone's ex, that kind of thing just sounded mean and petty. But Will was *nodding*.

"Yeah, you know, it's a long time coming."

"Will? I don't think I handled anything very well," I said, the words tumbling out of my mouth faster than I could think through them.

"No, you didn't," he said. "But I probably didn't either. We can call it a draw."

"That's really generous of you," I said. "Thank you . . . for your service."

Will cracked up. "It was good to see you, Clem. I'm gonna check if Michael needs any help with the grill."

I waved to him and watched him roll up to Michael like the grill expert he most assuredly was not. Still, I could see how he was someone newer, someone better now. It wasn't only seeing him in a T-shirt that hadn't started off as swag; he was sending away clowns and talking to a therapist. Meanwhile, I was lying about the status of my not-even-real relationship and providing beverages in lieu of having anything to actually offer in friendship to Fiona or Hailey these days.

I'd been willing to blow up my whole life for a chance at what I actually wanted, but right now the only one blown to bits was me—standing here, alone, somehow still holding a balloon sword.

Chapter 22
Tell Me a Story

Staring at countless search results showing me exactly what I didn't want to be true about the future of my career hadn't exactly been my favorite hobby when I wasn't—was it fair to call it heartbroken? Tracking what I felt and if it made sense that I did or did not feel it was exhausting. *Everything* these days was exhausting—and I still had a huge, potentially career-making or -wrecking presentation *and* a family party with similar stakes to get through. Was that just what adult life was like? Always having at least a figurative presentation and family party to get through?

The appointment with Phoebe had seemed so far away when I'd gotten that Outlook meeting request, but now it seemed to be racing toward me, full throttle, while I metaphorically flailed. My flailing, I know, looked very calm to a third party, just quiet googling while my heart sunk further with each new article read, but inside I looked like one of those flappy guys outside of a used-car dealership.

Finally, absolutely out of all other ideas, I picked up my phone and texted. **You're probably too busy for this, but I**

have a work presentation later this week and could use some professional advice.

I had no idea if it was the right thing to do, if I should have worked up some preamble first, but I barely got the chance to get the thoughts out when my phone buzzed. Fiona had never texted back so quickly on a weekday; it was as if she'd been typing before I'd even sent the request. **Yes of course! How's tonight?**

I was more than surprised in about a thousand ways, from the speed of the offer to the possibility that she could make time that quickly and of course that we hadn't actually made plans or seen each other outside of Ellie's party in practically months—nor had we even tried. Still, I agreed immediately, and Fiona promised she'd head out from her office as early as possible. After work I swung by Whole Foods, despite the hellscape of their parking lot, and took my time selecting fancy cheeses and a wine I picked out by googling *best cheap wine at whole foods*, knowing that Fiona's *as early as possible* had a vastly different definition than my own. But I was still assembling everything and giving Small Jesse Pinkman samples of cheese when my doorbell rang.

"Your consultant has arrived," Fiona said, brandishing a greasy paper bag from Tommy's and a drink carrier I was certain held two fountain Diet Cokes. Her bob was freshly sharp since I'd last seen her, edges that could cut a man, and she was in a beautifully tailored blue button-down with black pants I was fairly certain cost about as much as my entire wardrobe did. Perfect classic Fiona.

"You're earlier and . . . fast food-ier than I expected," I said.

"Number one business tip," she said, walking past me and unloading her things onto my coffee table, right next to the cheese tray and wine bottle. "Surprise them with the unexpected."

"Hang on, should I start taking notes?"

She laughed and grabbed a loose French fry from the bag. "I'm joking. Remember when I lived across the street from a Tommy's and we'd start out our pre-gaming with chili cheese-burgers?"

"That feels so long ago," I said. "As well as poorly advised."

Fiona stepped out of her pointy-toed five-inch heels and sat down at the coffee table. Small Jesse Pinkman approached her hopefully. "I forgot you have this cat now."

"His name is Small Jesse Pinkman, and he's like at least half of my Instagram grid now, so I don't know how you could forget." I didn't want to feel prickly about my kitten, but it was weird that this tiny being I loved more than I could have ever expected seemed proof to some of my singlehood, my loneliness, my propensity to end up dying alone.

"I apologize to you and to Small Jesse Pinkman," Fiona said. "May his tiny meth empire reign. Sit down, these things are only good while they're hot."

"We're adults now, you know," I said. "We could sit in chairs. Even at my kitchen table."

Fiona waved her hand. "Much cozier this way."

I eyed her shirt, the luxe material conveying all the expected wealth-and-power signals someone in her position, I supposed, should be conveying. "What if you get chili on that?"

"The dry cleaner's gotten out worse, trust me," she said. "Alex got himself an Instant Pot and some book about soups."

I laughed at her tone. "Do you mean a cookbook?"

"Come on, sit. Why are you hovering like an untrained waitress?"

At that I felt whatever was tight in my chest loosen, at least a little, and I sat down across from her. What sounded like dozens of my bones and joints seemed to pop at once, and I couldn't shrug it off when Fiona's eyebrows lifted up high.

"You sound like someone just poured milk on a bowl of Rice Krispies," she said, which was true and cruel and so funny

I burst into laughter at my own expense. "What happened to your whole yoga thing? That used to be about a third of your personality. Work, cat toys, yoga."

"Ha, ha," I said, fighting an actual smile. "I don't know. When Will moved out, I kind of fell apart—"

Fiona's expression migrated into that *oh poor you* look, that Laura Linney look again. "Clementine. I'm so sorry you had to see him at—"

"No, don't," I said. "I fell apart *schedule-wise*. I stayed up too late and I hit *snooze* too many times, and I took seventeen photos of Small Jesse Pinkman instead of getting into the shower when I was supposed to. The cat toys were easy to keep making; people kept ordering them and I don't flake on customers. Yoga? It's so easy to ignore. Feel sad all you want for my core, which undoubtedly has suffered, but—well, no, at the moment, I wouldn't say I'm *fine*, but—no, I'm fine. As far as the face you're making goes, I'm fine."

Fiona held up her hands. "Sorry, I won't say another word."

"No, don't, I'm not saying to shut up. I'm saying that you don't understand and no matter what I said, you and Hailey kept treating me like breaking up with Will, a thing I did very intentionally, was the worst tragedy that could befall a person."

Fiona watched me silently and then plowed into her chili cheeseburger, so I decided to do the same.

"You're right," she said, finally, when we were on the other side of the burgers. "But it's been months and we don't actually understand what happened, you know. You seemed so happy, and then, wham, it's over, and we're suddenly expected to take your side against Will."

"There's no *sides*," I said, and glanced over at the cheeseboard. "Will you be horrified if I have cheese as dessert?"

"Cheese as dessert is an underrated choice," Fiona said. "No judgment here."

"Ha," I said, and then focused intently on slicing a chunk of brie to sandwich between two apple slices. "You're full of judgment. That's one of your main things."

Fiona laughed. "Sure. Not about this, though. In fact, I'm joining you in your cheese dessert."

I watched her survey her options as I weighed exactly how to word it. "I honestly didn't know how to talk about my feelings about Will to you and Hailey because not wanting marriage and kids and all of that, these sort of expected so-called adult life goalposts, I never wanted to seem like I disapproved of your lives and your goals. It just wasn't for me. And for a long time I thought Will and I were on the same path—and I *loved* that path, I loved being on it with him. But when he started bringing up kids and weddings and, you know, maybe moving to someplace with better school districts, gearing up to talk to my dad for permission, I knew that we had to let go of each other so we could get what we wanted with people who wanted it."

"That makes sense," Fiona said, and I waited for the *but*. "I'm glad you told me."

I smiled and ate another slice of cheese. "I'm glad I told you too."

"So," Fiona said, drawing the word out. "What is it that you want anyway?"

"You know, just a little more freedom than that. Living where I want, like exactly right here. Having a cat be the biggest of my responsibilities as far as keeping someone else alive. And, you know, who knows how this presentation at work will go, but even if I'm not expanding my team at work I think my role's stable enough for now that maybe I can travel a little, have some adventures. Have hobbies that aren't my Etsy thing or—well, work. Someone to do all of that with. I think that's everything I thought of before, you know, *bye, Will, and now I'd better lock down someone else fast or I'll die alone.*"

"Ha!" Fiona literally covered her mouth. "Sorry. I hate it

when I sound so clearly triumphant. I just knew that your whole deal with the dog groomer was a rebound thing."

"Her name is Chloe, and she wasn't a rebound," I said. "To be honest, she wasn't anything. *We* weren't anything. You and Hay seemed so fucking *sad* for me, no matter how many times I tried to explain. And Chloe needed a date to her friends' wedding, so—"

"Wait a minute." Fiona set down her cheese. "Are you telling me, Clementine Hayes, that you hatched a motherfucking fake dating plot?"

"Now *you* wait a minute, Fiona Stockton. *You* know about fake dating?"

"I read at least two romance novels a week," Fiona said. "Obviously I know about fake dating."

"You're running the entire finance team at Pantheon and you have time for two romance novels a week?"

"I read on the elliptical," she said. "Sometimes audiobooks in the car. Holy shit. I don't know whether to be highly offended at all of the lying you've been doing, or extremely impressed."

"Don't be impressed," I said, leaning back from the coffee table. "I did the most clichéd thing I could have done."

Fiona nodded knowingly. "You caught feelings."

"Yep. I fell for a person who went out of her way to tell me repeatedly she didn't want a relationship with anyone."

We laughed, together, even harder. Somehow it felt like the hardest we'd laughed in a very long time. It barely made sense to me that I'd told her basically *everything* and yet I hadn't felt this safe with her in longer than I could remember.

"Bold question," Fiona began, and I steeled myself for—well, with Fiona, it could be anything. "Did you try telling her how you felt?"

"Well, sure, I *tried*," I said. "I told her I thought what we had was good. It's not easy saying, *Oh, hey, I know this was supposed to be fake when it started but I find you very funny and kind of a swoony hero and it probably shouldn't have taken sleeping together for me to realize how I felt but—"*

"I mean, Clem, you could have literally just said *that,*" Fiona said. "You could have also literally just told Hay and me about wanting something different than Will did. Just because Hailey and I are old married women and, yes, Hay did literally move back to the outer suburbs for the school districts, none of that means we wouldn't have understood that you wanted something different. All three of us want something different. There are a lot of ways to do this whole life thing."

I shrugged. "You two have all your chats without me these days, like just because I'm not planning on my own babies that you can't discuss any of that in front of me. Just because I don't want that for myself doesn't mean I'm not interested. You're my best friends, and I love that two of the coolest and smartest women I know are going to raise very cool and smart kids. But the way Chloe's friends are with each other—I don't know. I shouldn't be thinking about Chloe or her friends. But they're all doing different things with their lives and yet it's like they're all in it together."

Fiona arched one of her eyebrows, a power move I was certain she launched in powerful meetings in front of powerful executives. "Clem, I wish I had videos of your face any time Hailey or I discuss anything to do with children. Even on a generous day, I'd hardly call you *interested.*"

"I'm just . . ." I stared down at my lap. Why did it feel so gross and messy saying feelings aloud? "I'm worried. We used to see each other multiple times a week, and then once a week, and now it feels like if we manage every other month it's a miracle. We don't even text every day anymore. And that was before all of this, so don't blame it on how I kind of disappeared into my fake relationship. Once you both have kids, maybe we'll never see each other again. Definitely not me, the one who has nothing to contribute about babysitters or whatever toys are in style or pediatricians or whatever else."

"First, I will always have a lot more going on than baby-sitters and toys and pediatricians—and so does Hailey." Fiona shot me a look. "Also, wow, Clementine admits aloud to a fear? I never thought I'd live to see the day."

"What are you talking about?" I asked, even though it struck a resonant chord somewhere way down in my gut. "I mean, you're a badass bigwig. You know being vulnerable is the worst."

"Sure, sometimes. This isn't business, though. This is one of my longest-running friendships, and I didn't think the same rules applied.

"Let me ask you something," she continued. "Did you ever tell Will about this path you thought you were on together? When he started bringing up all the babies he wanted and school districts he had his eye on, did you say, *Hey, Will, this isn't in my cards and maybe we should discuss what we're both looking for since we're hardly getting any younger?*"

"Excuse me, I am only eleven months older than you," I said.

"Yeah, and your skin's still dewier and I resent you deeply for it," she said. "Seriously, though. I love you very much but you're shit at letting people in. Hay and I are *your people*, and yet look at everything you'd never bothered to tell us."

"I thought you were coming over to give me business advice," I said, trying to wipe my eyes in a way where it wasn't at all obvious I'd teared up a little.

"This *is* business advice!" She let out her brusque laugh. "I'm joking. Only a little. Let's get to it. And uncork that bottle of wine, dammit, I'm not sure camembert is supposed to be paired with *Diet Coke*."

I grabbed the corkscrew while thinking of Chloe and her friends, the somehow incredible conversations that had centered around Diet Coke and other beverages. Of course I'd always known they were temporary, a fake girlfriend and a fake new friend group, but I missed them and their presence almost as much as I missed Chloe. I wondered if it would be OK to reply to that very sweet group chat, acceptable to iron out some new dynamics even if Chloe never talked to me again.

"You know," I said, carefully uncorking the wine as if it wasn't the first search result in that *cheapest wines* list, "one thing I loved about fake-dating Chloe or whatever was the way her friends really prioritize each other in a way that—I don't know. I know the three of us are busy and it's not always easy for Hailey to drive down, but maybe we could try harder. I talked to Chloe's friend Bianca about it—her daughter is around the same age as Hailey's, and she said it's easier for her because she has the money for a lot of childcare. I get that Hailey doesn't, so maybe we could make it easier for her."

"Clem, are you suggesting we actually make a habit of driving up to the land of box stores and chain restaurants?" Fiona asked, holding out an empty wineglass to me. "Pour heavier if we're discussing future dinners at a Red Lobster."

"First, do not besmirch the good name of Cheddar Bay Biscuits, and, second, yeah, I am suggesting we make it easier on her, if that's how we get to see more of each other," I said. "And in return I will try to *occasionally* tell you one of my feelings."

"Great opening offer," Fiona said, nodding. "I look forward to negotiating the terms of the deal with you. OK, let's get into your work thing while we're still completely sober."

I explained my initial idea, my light pitch to Phoebe, and barreled past the little voice in my head telling me not to be so revealing about business to Fiona, a person who knew so much more than me, and told her the rest, too. The client saying he'd automate it all if it were up to him. Aubrey's doom-and-gloom prophecies. The campaign I wasn't even working on. Every article I'd found suggesting the exact same thing. I hated how naïve Fiona must have thought I was, how weak and small this attempt of mine must have seemed to her.

"Well, obviously, that's all terrible," Fiona said, refilling her wineglass. "But on some level, I'm sure, none of this is exactly news to you, right? So tell me, despite all of this, why you're making this presentation."

I gulped down a mouthful of wine, then another. Opening up about my business instincts *to Fiona* was exactly the kind of scary exercise that had made me hold off asking for help for this long to begin with. She was a shark and I was like a well-meaning fish who helped Finding Nemo along his way. "I could look at last quarter's numbers against the numbers from the same time last year—"

"No, don't worry about last year's numbers right now. You're very smart and obviously you pitched this idea because you believed in it, so if it's bad on paper why did you say it in the first place? Everyone thinks business decisions are only made on data, but there's this other element no one wants to talk about, the draw most of us have for hope and new ideas and the story of how we're getting there. So tell me a story."

So I did. I tried to forget that she was my most intimidating friend, and that my research had only led to warning signs, and that talking about my deep feelings—even about entertainment marketing—was hardly my strong suit. I just spoke. And even though Fiona had some feedback for me, I could tell she connected with my words and saw almost precisely where I was coming from. To see that recognition from your toughest critic of a friend felt more validating than I realized possible, and I tried to hold on tight to that feeling.

Chapter 23
Girl Trouble

After a sizeable portion of both the cheeseboard and the bottle of wine had been consumed, Fiona hugged me goodnight and headed out. My phone buzzed a whole bunch while I was cleaning up, but I—ignoring both my ADHD and irrational hope that it could be Chloe—forced myself to get everything into the dishwasher before checking. It was actually more texts from the latest formation of the group chat.

There were only about a million reasons I hadn't responded to anyone so far. Navigating my life post-Will had been tricky enough, but the truth was that no matter how much that Fiona and Hailey hadn't understood my actions or maybe even had been on Will's so-called side in their heads, they'd been my friends first. There was never any doubt that I could go to them. But even with all these texts sitting there, on a thread created just for me, it didn't feel straightforward to me. Sure, I followed enough sapphic meme accounts to know the stereotypes about staying friends with your ex, but did it extend to your ex's friends if your—well, it felt deeply disingenuous to refer to Chloe as my ex anyway. We hadn't been real, and also we hadn't even broken up. We'd each made our feelings known to each other, and what was there left to say about that?

But it couldn't have been clearer that they were making an effort, so I decided to at least respond. **Thanks, everyone. Sorry I've been MIA. I'm OK—for proof of life you can check with Phoebe who's seen me every day.**

I thought about Fiona's big push for vulnerability and started typing a second message. **I honestly don't know the politics of this so it feels awkward. But I do miss everyone and if dinner offers are real I would love that. I haven't eaten anything since Santa Barbara that wasn't attained through Grubhub, a drive-thru, or a Chili's.**

Then I took a deep breath as if texting was a cardio workout and started a new text just to CJ. **If you have time/headspace for this, I'm pitching a department expansion to Phoebe this week, and I know you mainly just work on the back end of digital advertising stuff, but I'd still love your POV from your side of things.**

CJ responded as quickly as Fiona had earlier. **Clementine, all I like to do is sit around and talk about media nerd stuff and normally no one wants that from me. Want to grab a drink at Johnny's tomorrow?**

I realized that I did, and so we made plans for the next evening. Walking down the block from work, I thought back to the night that random terrible men shouted random terrible things about my ass right before Chloe came to my rescue. Back when I'd truly been a baby gay, with no idea what to expect from this new world. What would have happened, I wondered, if there'd been no terrible men, no heroic Chloe, just me and a bar I was a little afraid of?

Despite everything, I was glad there had been all those things that night.

I was the first to arrive at Johnny's, so I grabbed an open spot at the bar and waved hi to Sadie, who made her way over.

"I'm glad you're here," she said, which was a nicer greeting than I expected from a bar I wasn't sure was my territory after the—could I call the end of a fake relationship a breakup? A fakeup?

"I just got in new menus and wanted to show you," Sadie said, leaning over to grab a thick sheet of paper from a box behind the bar. "Before you ask, yes, they're still in Comic Sans."

"Is that like a thing the youths like?" I ask. "Bad fonts?"

She laughed. "Clementine, I'm in my thirties and I have no idea what fonts the youths like. It was my uncle's favorite font, so here we are."

"Oh," I said. "The titular Johnny? Amazing of you to honor his font then."

"I try," she said with a grin, placing a new menu in front of me. "Check out the exclusive cocktails section."

I scanned the menu, landing on it with a start. Girl Trouble. "Oh my god."

"I hope that's a good *oh my god*," she said with a laugh.

"I'm honored," I said, legitimately overwhelmed at having even inadvertently left a tangible mark on this place, only months after walking in for the first time. "And I'm ordering one, of course."

"Yeah, obviously, and this one's on the house," she said. "Also we should finalize everything on your family party. It's coming up soon."

"Ugh, yeah," I said, and she laughed.

"It'll be good. The part with drinks, at least. The rest I can't help you with."

CJ walked in and sat down next to me, and I couldn't believe how happy I was to see them and their perfect buzz cut and button-down and jeans. Sadie poured a second Girl Trouble for them, and we clinked glasses and got right into talking about my presentation without dwelling on anything awkward at all. I attempted to order tacos for us, but CJ said if I'd been subsisting only on delivery and Baby Back Ribs that I deserved a well-balanced meal. We ended up wandering down to Bulan, where Sofia met us for vegan Thai food, before the three of us headed to CJ and Sofia's apartment, where the conversation turned from the digital media landscape to the latest episodes of *Selling Sunset* and *And Just Like That*, two shows we all hated and watched vigilantly.

It was all less awkward than I expected, because we really had all become friends since that first brunch, but walking back to my car later without Chloe, I felt so alone I actually shivered.

One of the last things she'd said to me flashed back, probably just a paraphrase now, a game of telephone I'd played with myself as I'd passed it back and forth in my head since that confusing and then glorious and then even more confusing Sunday. *You're so afraid to be by yourself that you're trying to make this work.* It was the kind of thing, I knew, that had hurt because there was truth buried in it, at least a little. How much truth? Was it all because it felt lonely walking from a vibrant warm apartment toward an empty car, no one to share those little post-hang-out bits with, like how stunning Sofia's artwork looked but also especially in comparison to the second bedroom—next to a tech-nightmare array of CJ's gaming stuff? How their cat watched me from a high cabinet while I ate, like a sniper ready to handle things if I made one false move?

They were real people, too, which was a thought I almost immediately dismissed for being ridiculous—what else would they be?—but at first, Chloe's group had felt practically like this starter pack of queer friends or something, a queer Pantheon Cinematic Universe group of superheroes. It was the kind of thing I wanted to confess to someone—*Can you believe at first they were like the Queers of the Cosmos or something?*—so maybe I did hate being alone, wanted it to be someone else, anyone else, more than I wanted to admit.

Except that it was Chloe's laugh I heard, imagining if I'd confessed that to her, whispered *Queers of the Cosmos*, somehow just lightly mocking enough to let me in on the joke too. That, I knew, was why I was lonely now, driving back home. I didn't miss being part of a couple. I missed being a part of a couple with Chloe.

"How embarrassing is that?" I asked Small Jesse Pinkman when I arrived home. "We weren't even an actual couple."

He mewed at me and I decided to read it as *but weren't you, kind of, at least?*

"You're very wise, Small Jesse Pinkman." I kissed the top of his head and had gotten more than halfway through my nightly skincare routine before it hit me that D-Day was tomorrow; I had an appointment with Phoebe in which my fate was up in the air. And I was as ready as I could be—well, I thought, *almost.* Since Fiona had brought up vulnerability, I could admit to myself—at least a little—how much I pushed back on so I didn't have to deal with it. Before my appointment tomorrow afternoon, I'd need to do the scary thing and walk in to talk to her.

I Slacked first, because I could read people well enough to know who actually appreciated an office drop-by and who would say *sure, come in now* while silently resenting the intrusion.

"Is this still a good time?" I asked, leaning into Aubrey's office. She looked up from her computer and nodded curtly, so I made myself step in.

Our office vibes were actually very similar—despite the years worked here, minimalist and impersonal. Like most people, I'd read that piece of advice that you should never keep more in your office than you could carry out in a bank box if you were let go. That wasn't my reasoning; of course it was just that I wanted to keep my personal life far away from this building. I'd always wondered if Aubrey felt the same, though of course to find out would be to violate that very belief system.

"So this may surprise you," I said, hoping that covered *you will likely think this is an extremely stupid plan,* "but I'm actually interested in expanding my department."

Aubrey nodded. "Sure. Makes sense."

"Wait, what?" I asked.

She lifted an eyebrow in what looked like confusion. "You're the one interested in expanding your department but you don't think it makes sense?"

"No, I do," I said. "I just didn't think that you would."

Aubrey shrugged. "All right."

I sat down across from her, even though the vibes were less than *pull up a chair*. "You've said plenty about the future of media planning and buying. And I guess about advertising in general."

"I lead the analytics team," she said. "I realize that's only me and half an assistant, but I still take it seriously."

"Well, you know, same."

"Of course. Anyway, staying on top of industry trends is an important part of why I'm here."

"Sure," I said, wondering now why I'd thought this was going to be such a great idea. "OK, so the thing is that I'm curious to hear what your concerns would be. I think there's still a lot I can bring to BME, but ignoring potential threats isn't going to help me get there."

"No, why would it?" Aubrey asked in such a genuinely confused voice that I laughed. "Why do you think it's so important to me to survey the landscape?"

"Well, let's just say that if we were defending a piece of property, you'd be the one checking the perimeter and I'd be hiding inside pretending there isn't a perimeter, maybe," I said.

"Do I have a gun in this scenario?" she asked, frowning. "This is troubling."

"Sorry, I made it weird. Anyway, tell me your concerns. What should I be ready for? If you want to, of course. I get that I'm using you for free business advice."

"We're on the same team," Aubrey said. "Also I'm on the clock so this isn't free."

"I'll buy you a latte, or whatever coffee thing you like," I said.

"Again, I said we're on the same team," she said, though she smiled faintly. "I'm sure we've read all the same materials. But I'm happy to just tell you a few things top of mind for me. And the coffee thing I like is just hot water with lemon."

I made a face without meaning to. "Sorry, that's just—"

"It's very invigorating," Aubrey said. "People underestimate it. My wife once told me that she thought it sounded terrible, but since then she's come around to my side."

"OK, I'll take you out for hot waters and lemons to thank you, sound good?"

"Very, thank you," she said, and smiled more widely. "Let's dive in."

It wasn't a talk I expected to leave feeling *good*—and, to be fair, it wasn't—but I felt neutral at worst, slightly empowered at best, and by the time Phoebe and I sat down together in the conference room later, I felt as ready as I could be.

"I'm excited to dig into all of this with you," Phoebe said, leaning back in her chair. Since it was Friday, she was as casual as she got at the office, a floral-print button-down and expensive jeans over AF1s, and I realized I missed seeing her on weekends when this was more her norm.

"Thanks for taking the time," I said. "I could of course give you a PowerPoint presentation—and, to be honest, originally I'd planned to—of my budgets this year versus last, versus the year before. But I'm sure you already know all those numbers."

"Well, not by heart," Phoebe said with a laugh. "But, sure. I know the general trend and that it's been going upward."

"So I'd rather just talk." I wouldn't, of course, *rather* at all! But I trusted Fiona as well as that gnawing pit of recognition in my stomach that perhaps my feelings shouldn't be under the strictest of lockdowns. "I thought a lot about what Jeremy from Celebration said, as well as Aubrey's thoughts on the matter."

"I like having people like Aubrey on the team," Phoebe said with a nod. "I have this level of pie-in-the-sky, dream-big ir-rationality in me. I couldn't have left the studio and started this place when I did without that part of me. And that's exactly why I need people who are nervous about everything, so that this whole place isn't constructed atop pies in the sky."

"Unstable, maybe, but delicious," I said, and smiled. "I'm glad you feel that way, and I'm so glad you did. This is my favorite place I've ever worked, and I admire you so much for founding this place with a sense of creativity and fun. I genuinely like coming here to work every day. And I think our clients love working with us too; I know we do incredible campaigns with strong results, but I think a lot of boutique agencies do as well. But not with our attitude or our sense of creativity or the way we approach solving problems. And I'm sure that's why people come back here, even with other options."

"I think you're right," Phoebe said. "We're not the cheapest and we're not the youngest and coolest, and yet our clients keep showing up."

"Exactly. And that's why I think expanding my team makes sense. We're already not building our business on automated, standardized approaches. We work closely with our clients, and with each other. So, yes, media planning and buying is changing, and I'd definitely like to investigate how those changes can help us work smarter or faster when it makes sense. But I also think our individualized and personal approach is what we're great at, it's why clients seek us out, and it's why they stick around. I don't think it's old-fashioned to focus on what sets us apart, and I also stubbornly don't think a robot can do my job better than I can."

"For the record," Phoebe said with a smile, "I don't think a robot can either."

"The other day I was talking to a friend who's a high-up at a huge entertainment company, and she said that for all the focus business has on data, people like stories, and hope for something exciting. It's the whole thing where we can show clients exactly what their target audience is watching, and those shows just *feel wrong* and so we buy ads on other shows anyway. That part doesn't come from knowing data or fine-tuning an algorithm, you know? It comes from knowing people and knowing this job."

Phoebe nodded, but stayed silent, so I kept going.

"I'm not asking for a huge new allocation of budget and resources," I said. "I think we actually could benefit from some research subscriptions to help us level up and let our clients feel that we're looking out for them in that arena. And I'd love to have someone like Tamarah full-time. Tamarah specifically, if she's interested. And I'd ideally promote her, and then a coordinator could work under the two of us. I know that would take away half an assistant from Aubrey, but I'm sure there's some kind of solution there, maybe even working together more so we can let the data that matters guide some of our decision-making. And basically that's where I'd love to start, and if our growth stays consistent, I'd look at adding some individual media specialists in the future."

I slid a packet toward her. Tamarah had designed the layout, and Fiona had sent me notes on it this morning that were only slightly terrifying. A victory already.

"Here's all the numbers you basically already know, as well as some forecasts, my budget requests, and all the words I just said aloud, but, you know. In print and therefore a bit more eloquent."

"You're plenty eloquent," Phoebe said. "But thank you. I'll review all of this, but I have to tell you now how much everything you said means to me. When I thought about the kind of company I wanted to run, I wanted it to be people's favorite job. Working studio gigs there was so much *Game of Thrones* shit, so many politics and so much fear. And I never thought that was how people did their best work. So to hear all of that from you is really validating."

"Honestly, I should have said some of that sooner." I shrugged and tried to look more casual about all of it than I was. "I'm not very good with saying how I feel but I've decided to work on it."

"Well, this world can really do a number on us," Phoebe said. "As queer women we're used to guarding ourselves in a culture that's still not always amazing for us, even in this industry—sometimes especially in this industry—and it's no wonder it bleeds into the rest of life. Before you think, *wow, Phoebe, that's so perceptive*, that is straight from the lips of my therapist."

I laughed. "That *is* perceptive, to be fair. My compliments to your therapist."

"She'll love it. Seriously, though, at least as far as I'm concerned, don't worry about any of that bullshit, OK? I'm around for real conversations about the company and the industry and how you're feeling about any or all of it." Phoebe leaned forward in her chair, resting her chin in her hand. "And—I don't know. Should we say something about the current elephant in the room?"

"I think this is a necessary evil of dating your boss's friend," I said. "Or—well, I'm sure Bianca's told you. Of *not* dating your boss's friend."

"Bianca did tell me, yes." She raised her eyebrows. "We both think the fake-dating thing is absolute bullshit, though."

My stomach clenched. Why did I continue this conversation after the business side of this had just clearly gone *so well*? Vulnerability was one thing, but I felt like I just threw a grenade and then chased after it. "I'm sorry. Like I've said, I really had no idea that Chloe's group of friends included you, and if I'd known going in—it was definitely not on my list of good ideas to spend months lying to my boss."

Phoebe cracked up. "Oh, stop it, Clementine. The bullshit part is that you two thought it was *fake*. OK, maybe you had some weird array of rules and—sorry, let's pretend we're not at work right now—maybe you weren't sleeping together—"

I tried to keep my face neutral but obviously something slipped, and now Phoebe was laughing even harder. And, against every fiber of my being, I was, too.

"You two idiots—sorry, don't tell HR I called you an idiot—were just *dating*. You can call it whatever you want, but I wouldn't say that either one of you is particularly good at faking anything. We're a pretty honest group in general."

"We weren't, though," I said.

Phoebe adjusted her glasses. "Spending all your time together, helping each other with your various projects—"

"I mean, it was arranged. And that also sounds like friendship. Or at least the way your group does it."

"Sure," Phoebe said. "I was also going to say hooking up, which I know some friends do, but I also am aware those aren't the kind of friendships you or Chloe tend to have."

I didn't know how to respond to that.

"I know this is hard," she said. "And complicated. I'm your boss, and I'm also your friend, and I only want to make you uncomfortable in a way that's fun, and not actually do harm to you. So I'll let you get back to your office, but I hope you do know that I still do consider you a friend, and I hope that if you need anything or want to talk that my door is figuratively—and usually literally—open."

"Thanks," I said, standing up but still trying not to look too desperate to escape to the safety of my office. "I genuinely appreciate it. I'm just bad at—well, maybe all of it."

"Only some of it, I think," she said with a laugh, hopping to her feet and following me out of the conference room. "Let's circle back on this sometime next week, OK?"

"Oh, god, the stuff I'm bad at?" I asked, and she laughed

so loudly that our office coordinator Aiko gave us a look of judgment mixed with concern that only a Gen Z youth could manage.

"No, the media planning proposal," Phoebe said, holding up the printouts I'd given her. "Sound good?"

I met her gaze and nodded, feeling—well, accomplished, maybe? I'd said exactly what I'd wanted to say, and I could tell it had landed with Phoebe. Maybe it wasn't enough to make all of my work dreams come true, but it still felt like I'd done exactly what I'd set out to do.

Fiona, who'd known my meeting time, had already texted on the group thread—its first new message in weeks—to see how it had gone. When I responded with the truth, that was, positive-with-a-side-of-maybe-nothing-actually-changes, she and Hailey still sent the kinds of emojis and gifs befitting a victory (champagne bottles, Oprah shouting *YOU DID IT!*, etc.) and asked if I wanted to celebrate after work.

I started messaging that we should wait until I had an actual victory to celebrate, but then two things hit me at once. First, I'd just thought to myself how much like a victory this felt no matter what, and it was OK if other people—my very best friends, at that—knew that. And also my very best friends, notoriously harder and harder to schedule with, were making time for me in a few hours, the exact thing I'd wanted from them. Why on earth would I say no to any of it?

We met up at L & E Oyster Bar, and Hailey pulled me into a tight hug like one of us had been off at war.

"I should say that I don't hate hearing about your kid," I said. "Sorry my insecurities made it seem that way."

"Oh my god, don't put Fiona's words in my mouth," she said with a laugh. "I'm sorry I don't always know how to be a person who makes and keeps plans anymore. I'm sorry I barely talked to you at Ellie's party except for shrieking about soda. I'm sorry it seems like sometimes I'm just saying *poop emoji* over and over. If you can try harder with me now, I promise

I'll make it up to you once Ellie's in kindergarten. Or middle school. Maybe college. But eventually."

"Deal," I said.

"OK, I ordered us two rounds of drinks like we used to do at the ends of happy hours," Fiona said, sitting down with us. "A lot of oysters too."

"You know, we aren't young and broke anymore," I said. "I can drink cocktails at normal speed at whatever price they normally cost."

"Please, I love a bargain," Fiona said. "Oh, Clem, I thought of the solution to your whole not-being-able-to-function-alone problem."

"What are you talking about, and also, could we not call it that?"

"I heard your creaking joints the other night. If you need other people involved to keep you accountable to yoga, can't you just take a class?"

I made a face. "No offense to you two thin blond people, but I don't feel like taking an LA yoga class with a bunch of thin blond people. And don't say I look great in yoga pants, I'm aware, but the world is not always such an open-minded place about butts like mine in yoga pants."

"They can't *all* be like that," Hailey said. "The classes, at least. I know we can't speak for all the thin blond people."

"I think it's sweet you still consider Hailey blond when her roots look like that," Fiona said, and the three of us laughed so hard we were in tears.

"Actually," I said, something flashing in my memory. "Bianca said something about some all-sizes gym she goes to. I'll see if they have a yoga class."

Fiona gestured as if she was waiting, so I got out my phone and texted. Bianca's response was fast: **They do have yoga classes! I've never gone because I'm not really a zen person, but I'm willing to give it a shot if you are. I'll send you a link to the class schedule.**

284 / Amy Spalding

"OK, it's happening," I said, putting my phone back in my bag.

"Good girl," Fiona said. "Now tell me everything about your pitch meeting. Word for word, like I need to take minutes."

I glanced at Hailey. "I have a feeling it'll be extremely boring for anyone who isn't Fiona, so don't worry, I'm not going to do that."

"Everyone likes corporate intrigue!" Fiona said. "Think of all the movies!"

Hailey and I exchanged a look, and the three of us burst into laughter, and it felt so good and solid. We threw back our drinks like young people trying to score a deal, and caught up on each other's lives without any huge deal made about the last few months. No, we wouldn't have a weekly brunch, but we scheduled another night out in three weeks, per my recommendation, at the Chili's up in the suburbs. I really did love the Baby Back Ribs. Though not nearly as much as I loved my friends and was committed to finding whatever it was to keep us going. And if that was chain restaurant food up in the place I'd been desperate to move away from, that was more than fine with me.

At home later, tipsy more on the evening with my friends than the cocktails, I felt a warm glow pulse through me, and I decided not to extinguish it with—well, whatever I usually tamped down earnest feelings with. I picked up my phone while I sat on the couch with Small Jesse Pinkman and I scrolled through my texts.

I miss you.

And then, as if to prove I hadn't completely gotten good at being open with my feelings yet, I promptly turned off my phone and retreated to the coziness of my bed. Chloe's response either did or didn't exist—Schrödinger's text—but I knew that telling the truth was one of my best moves in a long time.

It flashed at me, brand-new, the next morning. No text, just a gif of Gillian Anderson as Dana Scully, and a warmth surged through my chest.

I wanted to believe.

Chapter 24
Red Alert

The morning of Mom and Dad's surprise party was bright and blue—the kind of thing people not from Los Angeles would have assumed you could take for granted, but I'd been readying myself for something gray and hazy and terrible, and also readying myself for Greg somehow blaming me for it.

I got to Greg and Marisol's five minutes early, and joined them in the backyard where they'd already set up a huge tent for shade.

"Old white people need to be protected from the sun," Marisol said cheerfully.

"Young white people too, look how pasty I am," I said. "OK, young-ish. Anyway, what do you need me on?"

"Greg needs someone else to get all the tables set up—though he won't admit it. Hmmm, maybe that's a better job for me. Tablecloths and chairs as we go? And dealing with everyone as they arrive?"

"Sure, I'm on it," I said.

"Also, I'm sorry, Greg told me about Chloe—"

"I'm really OK," I said. "It's fine. I mean, no, I have feelings, and I'm sad and I miss her but, you know, I'm OK. Thanks for checking in on me."

"Well, sure, of course you're OK," she said like a person who'd never sent a *poor lonely Clementine* email in her life.

"Anyway, I'll get to work. Let me know if you need anything else."

The truth was that I wanted to be snottier about all of it, but I liked Marisol so much—loved her, even—and there were so many worse ways to spend a morning than out in the sunshine. Thanks to my new yoga class, none of my joints were even making noise as I carried chairs around the yard and got tablecloths into place.

My phone buzzed with messages from my friends—the two group chats that ruled my life—and Sadie, all around the same time, and I ran to the front to lead them in. When Fiona and Hailey had heard that my other friends had offered to take charge of the potluck situation, they demanded to contribute as well. I wasn't sure Fiona had cooked anything in her life, so I wasn't surprised she rounded the corner hoisting a professional-looking container.

"It doesn't mean that you care less if you pay a caterer," she said with an eye roll.

"You were the one who offered," I said, "but thank you. Thank you, everyone."

My gut told me I should be genuinely shocked that these people were all here, including my boss and a couple of people who were so freshly back from their honeymoon that they were still tan. But rationally I wasn't surprised at all; these people had all formed actual friendships with me, and this is what actual friends did.

"What's going on?" Greg walked up and looked around at the group arranging the food next to the steam trays of tamales that Marisol had already set out. (It was extremely hard not just sitting down to consume several tamales.) "We told people to start arriving in a half hour. Also are all these people on the invite list?"

"These are my friends who're helping with the food," I said. "I told you that."

He eyed them suspiciously and walked off, which was rude but definitely for the best.

"Sorry about that," I said. "I don't know how to explain other than that's always my brother's vibe."

"That was so exciting," Fiona said. "I've heard about him for so long."

"We went to high school together!" Hailey said. "You'd think I'd at least get a greeting."

"Not really how he rolls," I said. "I'm going to make sure everything's good for Sadie to get the bar set up—y'all can introduce yourselves and figure out how to lay out the food?"

"On it," Ari and Phoebe said at the same time, and I felt like you couldn't leave anything in better hands than with two alpha lesbians running things, so I walked over to make sure Sadie had everything she needed. Per their web site, I knew that Johnny's did on-location events, but I was pretty certain that this was their first straight wedding anniversary in the suburbs. Sadie had even given me a deal, though I planned on tipping extremely well for—well, for all of it. Seeing her here, seeing all of my friends, I felt more taken-care-of than I could have imagined.

Mom and Dad's friends started arriving before long; when you were in your twenties and thirties, no one ever came until at least thirty minutes after the start time on the invite, but apparently sometime between then and your sixties you started showing up ten minutes before. It was fine, though, the drinks were flowing and the spread looked amazing and even Dad's weird friend Jerry was smiling.

"What did you end up telling Mom and Dad to get them to stop by?" I asked Greg, keeping an eye on the time. Any minute now.

"I just invited them to lunch," he said. "It wasn't some big complicated thing."

I sighed and headed back to my friends, who had fully claimed one table right in the center. "Y'all don't have to stay, you know. I'm sure you have way better things to do with your Saturday than this."

"We really don't," CJ said in their standard dead-serious tone.

"Yeah, I have a babysitter for three hours," Hailey said, "and I am getting every last minute out of those three hours."

"Us too," Bianca said.

"Clementine," Greg hissed at me, appearing out of nowhere like some kind of annoying magic trick. "Mom and Dad are pulling up."

"Should we all yell *surprise!*?" Marisol asked, walking up next to Greg.

"Maybe *Happy anniversary!* has more clarity," I said. "If we can get everyone onboard with that quickly."

"I got you," Ari said, jumping up and quickly making the rounds.

Mom and Dad peered into the backyard a few moments later, and magically everyone chorused *Happy anniversary!* almost in unison. Despite every irritating moment that led to this, I was grateful for all of it to see how happy they both looked.

"Was this the two of you?" Mom asked Greg and I, hugging him and then me.

"Me and Marisol, yep," Greg said. "And Clementine helped."

"It was the three of us," I said quickly instead of punching Greg, which is what I felt like doing. I knew, of course, that I hadn't done as much as the two of them, this being their house and all, but *come on.*

"Thanks so much, kiddo," Dad said, hugging me, and lowering his voice to a whisper. "Jerry accidentally told me last week at the club, but, don't worry, I didn't mention it to your mom."

"Oh, god, I knew that would happen," I said, cracking up. "He's a force of chaos. Thanks for keeping it still half a surprise."

"It made it fun knowing how excited she'd be," Dad said with a smile directed at Mom, who was talking to Marisol and the kids. I thought about the four decades they'd been together and the care they still took with each other, and I felt lucky to celebrate them today.

"I can't believe how many people showed up," Mom said. "It's going to take us an hour just to say hi to everyone."

"Longer if Jerry tries to tell stories from the club," Dad said. "We should get started then."

I saw that their gazes both snagged at exactly the same moment, obviously when they realized that a table full of queers—plus Fiona and Hailey—was right smack-dab in the middle of their friends.

"Clementine's friends are here," Greg said as if he was alerting them to a nest of rats on the premises. "It's like back in high school, remember, she couldn't do anything without everyone she hung out with."

"Pretty sure that was everyone in high school," I said.

"Well, some of us grew up," Greg said. "But I guess that's having a real job and real responsibilities for you."

"Dude, come *on*," I snapped. "I don't know if you're actually unaware of this or just conveniently forgetful, but I do have a real job besides making cat toys. I run an entire department for a company that I'm very proud of. Also, the cat toys are pretty profitable! And I know I don't have kids, and I absolutely understand they're a bigger responsibility than Small Jesse Pinkman or whatever—"

"Who is Small Jesse Pinkman?" Mom asked. "Is that the woman you've been dating? Greg said something about you being bisexual now."

Oh my god.

"I'm not bisexual *now*," I said. "I'm bisexual . . . in general.

And, thanks, Greg, for not letting me come out to Mom and Dad on my own time, even though I asked you for that."

Greg stared at me, as if he'd never expected to be called out for anything by anyone ever. "I was trying to help. I thought maybe it would be easier if I—"

"Well, you were wrong. And, no, Mom, Small Jesse Pinkman isn't a woman. He's a cat. *My* cat.

"And"—I turned back around to point at Greg—"before you say a word about cat ladies or spinsters or whatever, there is nothing wrong with living alone with a cat. Or bringing all of your friends along as your date instead of your spouse or partner. Those people have been there for me, and I know you and Marisol think I'm so sad and lonely, but it would be impossible for that to be true considering the people my life is full of."

"Clementine," Marisol said in a gentle voice, "I'm sorry if I ever—"

"Today is about Mom and Dad so I really want to keep it about them," I said. "But today is the last day I'm tolerating any of this, OK? You all made me feel so shitty about myself that I—"

I shook my head, cutting myself off. "I'm sorry. Happy anniversary, Mom and Dad. I love you both so much."

I walked off toward my friends, but Mom cut me off at the pass.

"I feel like an idiot," she said. "Jesse Pinkman was that little drug dealer on the show your dad used to watch."

I nodded, blinking back tears. "That's true."

"Clementine, I know it's always been tough between the two of you." Mom looked like me, short and curvy, and sometimes it was a little like seeing myself in the future—though with more sensible patterns and colors. "And we all know Greg likes to make himself the hero of every story."

"It's weird no one ever calls him out on it, though," I said, though the *no one* felt wrong, because one person had.

"Your father and I are so proud of you," she said. "You just always made it look so easy. You were so good at school, and you found this career doing whatever it is with ads and marketing, and we just never felt like we had to say anything. It was so obvious you were doing great. Greg struggled with so much of it, and we're so happy with how his life's turned out."

"No, completely," I said. "Me too. Marisol's amazing, and even if the kids hate me, they're amazing too."

Dad walked up to us and touched my shoulder. "I just want you to know that I watched all of the episodes of *Queer Eye*."

"And you know how much we love Ellen!" Mom said.

"I hope you know you could have told us sooner," Dad said. "We just didn't know because you and Will seemed so happy."

"For a long time we were," I said. "And this isn't about him at all. It's just about me. Not today, though! Today's about the two of you."

"Don't worry about us, we've had forty years of todays," Mom said. "When you find someone like your dad and I have, your love's big enough to hold everyone else, too."

She pulled me in for another hug. "Well, sweetie, we should go make the rounds before Jerry starts in on one of those stand-up comedy specials he's been watching on Netflix."

"*Hurry*," I said, and watched as people from throughout my parents' lives greeted them. I hoped that someday, even if I never had decades with anyone, there were enough people in my life to fill up this many tables.

It hit me, though, that something was missing. *Someone* was missing. And not because I was lonely, or because I didn't want to die alone, or because being at an anniversary party really did make you think about the beauty of spending your life with someone who loved you. Missing Chloe had nothing to do with any of that. I thought of Mom's words, a love big enough to hold everything. I *loved* Chloe, I realized with a shock. What I felt for her had room for all of it. For all of me.

"I—I have to go," I said, rushing over to my friends' table.

"Not to sound like I'm seventeen and sneaking out of a—can y'all cover me? There's something I need to—"

"I actually think you should stay," Ari said with a nod behind me.

I understood from her tone—and that practically every single other person I knew, coworkers and ex-boyfriend excluded, were already here—what was happening, but I still had to turn to see it. I had to turn around completely to see Chloe Lee walking toward me, clad in her brightest Nooworks jumpsuit, Fernando's leash in one hand and a stack of Tupperware in the other.

"Kimbap's here," she said, stopping right in front of me with a grin that threatened to melt my heart down into a pile of ashes. "Fernando, sit."

It was when he sat down that I realized his leash was looped safely around Chloe's thumb. And it didn't escape her notice that it hadn't escaped *my* notice.

"Here's the thing, Clementine," she said. "I hated how people used to treat Fernando. He's a *dog*. The worst thing I could imagine was holding back his awesome semi-feral-except-for-me energy, making him some robot dog who barks on command. For some reason—even though I work with dogs *for a living*—I couldn't see past this decision I'd made almost ten years ago when I slowed down my car and let him jump into it. But the older he was getting, the crankiness was dialing up, and I was like, what the fuck am I doing? And then my algorithms had me following all these queer dog trainers who specialized in force-free dog training, and—I mean, look at him!"

"He's sitting so properly," I said, feeling proud of him even if I had no right to. "He's a good dog, though. He always has been, even when he's running around like he's on dog cocaine. I totally get why you'd be scared to take away from that."

"The canine cocaine? Sure." She met my eyes again. "There's this thing they taught me in our first class, not to think of this stuff as commands, like I'm leading the dog military or something else terrible, but cues. I'm just cuing him up for stuff. Which I like, I guess. I mean, it's working, we're both still ourselves, so, yeah."

"I'm so glad, Chloe. Well, thanks for bringing the kimbap," I said, because I didn't know what else to say. Seeing Chloe in the backyard of a home in the suburbs was almost too much. A nonreligious miracle or something. "You were totally off the hook on that, though."

"No, I promised to bring you a bunch of white people Korean food, and I don't break promises." She laughed and shook her head. "I actually have broken a million promises over the years, but I'm working on that too."

"Oh," I said, smiling. Smiling more? Had I ever been so happy to be in someone's presence? "Are you in force-free training too?"

"Something like that. Bianca's got me going to her kickboxing class so I get to punch people, but with consent."

I laughed. "I'm not sure how any of that qualifies as *force-free*, but that sounds so good for you. Not to sound patronizing."

"Nah, it *is* good for me. Can you help me with these?"

I lifted the containers out of Chloe's arms while trying not to act like it was a huge deal she was letting me help her, and led her over to the shaded tables holding the feast.

"This is a good spread," Chloe said, surveying the offerings.

"Your friends helped a lot," I said.

"Yeah, I think you have to call them *our friends* now." She bit her lip and flashed me a look, and I felt untethered seeing the shock of the want and need in her eyes. "OK, so I was worried I'd do this part badly, so—hang on . . ."

Chloe dug into her pocket and pulled out a folded-up piece of paper. "Since I'm bad at saying things aloud, I wrote you a letter, which I'm going to read to you. No, fuck, this is already stupid."

"It's not," I said quickly. "Read me your letter."

Dad's friend Jerry walked past us briskly, grabbing a bunch of kimbap and three deviled eggs before walking off.

"This is," Chloe said, "the perfect setting for this. Just like I imagined."

"Come on," I said, taking her by the hand and leading her and Fernando away from the crowd, inside the house. "My brother's kitchen. More like you pictured."

"Yep, exactly this." She let go of my hand and unfolded the piece of paper. "Seriously, though, stop me if this is too cheesy."

"I want to hear your letter," I said.

"*Dear Clementine,*" she read. "I feel like I'm reading a book report."

"Is that part of the letter or just how you're feeling?" I asked, and she laughed.

"*Dear Clementine. I'm sorry I've acted like such a complete asshole and I said things to you like* I don't need you *instead of the truth which is that I had all these big feelings for you and had no clue what to do about it. I've never been good at relationships and so when someone incredible showed up in my path, instead of being real with her*"—Chloe glanced up at me—"*with* you, *I came up with this whole fucking plan instead of just asking you to dinner like an emotionally mature person would have done. Instead of walking you outside to your car and kissing you that very first night.*

"*The truth is that I'm the same as Fernando. I like who I am, even if maybe that's semi-feral. I like my friends and I like my life and I like my business and—well, I love this guy.*"

Fernando barked as if he knew, and we both laughed.

"*And I know how people saw me,*" she continued, "oh that Chloe, she's so crazy, she'll punch a man for looking at her the wrong way, *and even though that isn't actually me, it's not* not *me. I still thought there was this—god, this is so embarrassing to say aloud. Like this* untamed quality *in me. And I didn't want*

296 / *Amy Spalding*

to lose it. I didn't want to compromise for someone, especially someone who's just gonna end up disappointed by the actual reality of me anyway, just mainly a person who wants to hang out with her dog and listen to musicals, and so I had this whole no relationships *thing. Like compromise is only bad.*

"And then I met you and you had all of that figured out, this idea that you could put together the kind of life you wanted without having to follow any of the rules that didn't suit you and the truth is that you made me rethink everything, Clementine. You're so fucking worth compromising for.

"Also, my friends were right when they were all thank god you have Clementine. *I realized that they didn't mean* thank god you have someone like anyone at all, *but that was all I could hear. They meant what they said,* thank god you have Clementine, *specifically you and how much happier I am because you're part of my life.*

"I was such an incredible jerk to you at the wedding. All I could think of was you ending things two weeks later, finishing up at your parents' party and then you jumping on the apps to find someone actually deserving of you. The thought of seeing you in all the photos later was gonna break my heart, and instead of admitting that, it was like I couldn't stop finding new ways to treat you like shit.

"I know you might not want to forgive me and that'd be more than fair, but I do promise that I'll work on being less of a feral asshole. Sincerely, me."

She refolded the paper and started to tuck it back into her pocket, but I stopped her.

"Can I see it?" I asked, and she nodded. Her handwriting was even and cute, and it made the letter look like a note someone would have passed me once upon a time in school. My name, written by her hand, shook something deep inside of me. "Wait, what's this thing at the end?"

"Oh, no," she said, trying to grab it back from me. "I had this idea I would sing Abba's 'Take a Chance on Me' and then

I thought it was the dumbest thing I'd ever written down, so I tried to scratch it out but—"

"I'm sure you've written down way dumber things," I said, and she laughed.

"Thanks for that."

"Chloe," I said, realizing how I'd missed how her name felt in my mouth, knowing that, in and of itself, wasn't enough. Not yet. "There's really nothing I want more than—well, than *you*. But also it was kind of messy and bad sometimes, and I don't want to let all that stuff go again."

"No, you shouldn't, I was a real asshole to you and you deserve better than that." She leaned in close to me, looked up into my eyes. "But I'm working on being better than that. For you and for everyone else I care about. And I'm sorry I treated you the way I did."

"Yeah?" I asked, leaning in closer too. "I'm sorry, too. I definitely did want to find someone else to spend my life with after the thing with Will ended, and—well, I know how he made me feel, like it didn't matter what I wanted or who I was, just that there was a plan for life and he was going to do the plan. And if I made you feel like I was just doing that, you were part of my new gay plan—"

"Clementine," Chloe said with a laugh. "I loved being part of your new gay plan. Look, I didn't believe any of that baby gay shit I said. I'd just had such a stupid embarrassing teenage crush on you. And if I wasn't built for a real relationship, how else was I gonna have you all to myself?"

I laughed, my face flushed at the thought. "Really? All those times we hung out at company parties talking about bacon-wrapped dates?"

"Clementine," she said almost reverently, and I expected a diatribe about the wonder of canapes. "You're my dreamgirl."

I actually let out a little yelp of surprise, and she burst into laughter.

"Sorry, should I have just said, yeah, the bacon-wrapped

dates really got me going? Come on. You're interesting and so smart and your laugh's so—god, is there a word that's like infectious but doesn't sound so dire?—and in case you forgot, I would build a shrine to celebrate your body."

I yelped again at that, and now she laughed even harder.

"My friends all knew," she said. "I talked about the hot girl at Phoebe's office all the time. It was like our inside joke, my unrequited pining. I never thought I'd get so lucky to— anyway. Of course I ended up fucking it up. So I'm here now to tell you I want to figure this out together. And I know I should have told you sooner, and maybe if I were you I wouldn't forgive me, but—"

I covered her lips with mine, kissing her like we never had before, sweetness and openness and the future stretched out ahead. We were good at this too, I felt right away.

"I should have told you sooner, too," I said. "When I met you, I thought maybe you'd ask me out, and I was like, oh, maybe it could actually be this simple."

Chloe snorted. "God, imagine that, me just asking you out instead of all of this."

"You know what's funny," I said, sliding my arms around her waist. I hadn't actually ever held her like this, and I liked how it felt, close but casual, too. "I kind of liked all of that, actually."

"Oh, absolutely, me too, we're a couple of weirdos," she said, cracking up. "Bianca kept telling me, *you know that no matter what you called it, you two were just dating.*"

"She said the same thing to me." I leaned in to kiss her again. "Maybe it's true, and maybe we were just two people running away from having one real conversation. But I want to figure this out with you, too."

"I know I seem semi-good at all of this today," Chloe said, "but it's gonna be messy. I'm probably going to get weird again."

"Well, I'm still not very good at real conversations, so, yeah. I think messy and weird are assumed at this point."

We kissed again, and watched each other as the kiss ended.

"We're *together*," Chloe said. "I kind of can't believe it."

"Me either." I took a deep breath. "Just being honest, feelings and all, that I was falling extremely hard for you. You're so brave and so funny and you find so many little ways to take care of me when I need it. And now that this is something we're doing *on purpose*—well, I know this is going to sound a little like a threat, but I'm going to fall in love with you, Chloe Lee."

"*Fuck*," she said, and for a split second I worried I'd ruined it, gone and said too much or shared the wrong thing. But even before Chloe said another word, I felt that go. I knew her enough by now to trust her with my words. To trust her with my heart.

"That's the most romantic thing anyone's ever said." Chloe shook her head and grinned. "I try to write a whole letter for you and here you are just undoing me with your beautiful threats. I guess I'll have to threaten you right back, because I'm falling in love with you too, and the truth is that I've been doing that for maybe this whole time."

I kissed her again, and then she was kissing me, and we continued this back-and-forth until our lips ached and our breath was lost.

"Wait," Chloe said, stepping back. "I have an idea."

"Better than this?" I asked, tugging her to me again.

"No, check it out," she said, pulling her phone out of her pocket and tapping a few times before victoriously holding it in the air.

"What . . . is happening?" I asked. "Did you just change your Facebook status like it's 2006?"

"I was playing the Abba song for you!" she said, making a face and looking at her phone screen. "It was going to be super romantic."

"It's romantic enough without Abba," I said, grabbing her by the collar and kissing her again.

"Red alert!" Greg shouted from the next room, and we burst

into giggles and pulled away from each other like teenagers caught making out by a parent as he walked into the kitchen. "Some Abba song just started playing over my speakers."

"I feel like you should think about how often you employ your red alerts and what for," I said. "Chloe. Did you somehow connect to my brother's Bluetooth speaker system?"

"That doesn't seem possible," she said. "Normally I can't even do something like that on purpose."

"Could you," Greg said, sighing with all of the apparent effort in the world, "please do something about it?"

"What's to do?" she asked with a shrug. "People love Abba. Who am I to giveth and then taketh away?"

Greg frowned. "Didn't you two break up?"

"Yeah, red alert, queer women are really good at doing that and getting back together," Chloe said with a laugh.

"That's not how to use a red alert," Greg said, which made Chloe and I shriek with laughter.

We headed out of the kitchen and fit ourselves into an empty spot at the table of our friends. Chloe slipped her arm around me, and I looked at her in surprise.

"Not too squishy for you?"

She pulled me in tight. "Red alert: just squishy enough."

Epilogue

A Year Later

"OK, if you have everything handled, I'm going to head out."

Tamarah looked up at me from her computer, and I could tell how much she respected me by how hard she was fighting not to roll her eyes.

"You've taken time off before," she said. "For longer than six hours, at that."

"Oh, shut up," I said with a laugh. "I know we're about to get feedback on the Argon Films proposal, and given the tight timing, you may have to handle it. Though if you hit any snags—"

"I won't hit any snags," she said with a youthful confidence I wish I'd had. I loved seeing her grow into her new role as media planner here; I felt a little weird about taking too much credit for anything but it did thrill me to have built a little department and elevated people who were great at their jobs. At the end of the day, we weren't saving lives or anything altruistic; we were marketing movies and TV shows. That said, since Phoebe had built a better little world here, free of so much of the bullshit I'd seen coming up—and still heard gossiped about—I loved the extra responsibility I'd taken on in the last year, and the work I did to ensure this better version of the entertainment industry stayed that way, less toxic in as many ways as we could manage.

Obviously, the most important reason I'd pushed to expand my department was for BME; a bigger team could handle work better as well as take on more work. But I'd had a second benefit in mind, of course, no longer being two-thirds of a team of one-and-a-half so I could also take more than a day or two off at a time without checking my phone constantly. The whole future I'd wanted for myself had a lot more travel and adventure than just the occasional long weekend, but I was still getting there. For now I was still the type of executive who got nervous about leaving six hours early, even with a more-than-competent staff in place.

Speaking of adventure, though, Chloe's Bronco was idling outside the office, and I rushed to get into it. The show tunes playlist blasted out through her speakers, and she belted along with "Defying Gravity" in lieu of a greeting.

"Hi," I said. "Is this a hint for this so-called surprise?"

"No, this is pure musical theatre enjoyment," she said dismissively. "Also I just did a really stressful adult thing and I need—wait, why did you say *so-called*?"

I laughed and leaned over to kiss her. "Like a colonoscopy?"

"No, Clementine," she said in mock impatience, and we both cracked up. It had officially been one year for us—one year and some change if you counted from the night she rescued me from street-harassing assholes—and I still laughed more than I ever had in my life leading up to that night. Leading up to Chloe.

"Is that really the first thing you think of when you think *adult*?" she asked, turning up Hyperion like we were headed to my place, which I assumed we weren't. "Picture less butt stuff, more office stuff like paperwork and financial information."

"Also terrible," I said. "I mean, obviously, depends on the butt stuff."

"Obviously," she said. "I have a disclaimer."

I laughed. "About butt stuff?"

"No, I think we're good there," she said with a grin. "Anyway, I know that you know that I am like firmly *not* a person who plans cute anniversary events or—OK, has ever done this for one solid year with a person, period, so it's possible I've done this extremely weirdly. Let's just say I'm rethinking all of it."

"Extremely weirdly sounds perfect," I said.

"I made reservations at Saffy's tonight too," she said.

"That sounds like an extremely normal anniversary thing to do," I said, and she laughed.

"I'm never going to avoid a tradition that involves a meal out," she said. "Also, how anti-relationship-establishment are we, anyway? At any given moment there are dozens of Eastside queers in our vicinity practicing ethical non-monogamy and renting bigger apartments for their throuple situations, and we're just like . . . not interested in getting married. Unless someday it makes sense for health insurance or whatever, in which case you can totally wife me up for bureaucratic reasons."

"Totally, I know. I like feeling antiestablishment, though," I said. "Even if we're actually boring."

Chloe made the turn onto Rowena, and I gave her a look.

"Are we just going to my place? If my surprise is sex, we could have done that at your apartment, which was closer."

"Clementine," Chloe said with a sigh, which made me laugh. "No, we are not going to your place. And I hardly think sex counts as a surprise."

I managed to stay silent the rest of the short ride, even though Chloe literally made the familiar turn in front of my condo development and then parked right out front of my place.

"Just be patient," Chloe said, jumping out of the car and waiting for me to follow.

"I didn't say a word."

"Yeah, your thoughts are loud as hell," she said, taking my hand and tugging me to the main entrance. I waited for her to unlock the gate with the key I'd given her a few months back; even though we weren't living together, we spent more nights together than apart and so spare sets of keys had been exchanged fairly unceremoniously.

"What's . . ." I hurried to keep up with Chloe. "I don't think I'm good at patience."

She stopped across from my condo and grinned. The morning sun glowed behind her, and it struck me for maybe the millionth time how gorgeous she was. For all that our lives could be tied up with other people, between our friends and my job, I often never felt more like I'd gotten everything I'd ever wanted than in these moments when it was just Chloe smiling right at me.

"Your lack of patience isn't news to me," she said, pulling me in for a kiss. "OK, another disclaimer, I can still get out of this if you look horrified when I tell you."

I laughed. "I love surprises that come with this many warnings."

"I told you I'm bad at this," she said. "But here goes anyway. I know our friends think we should have already U-Hauled at some point last year, but I also know things have been working really well without that."

They had been. As hard as it had been for me to get used to living alone, I'd eventually figured it out. For a person with ADHD, getting a semi-functional routine had been tough for me at first, but just like work and my catnip side-hustle, I forced myself to figure out a system that actually worked for me. It turned out I hadn't needed a partner under the same roof to keep myself chugging along; I'd needed meal planning and an advanced yoga class.

And the truth was that there were just a lot of things I *liked* about living alone—even if calling it that was slightly disingenuous, considering how often Chloe and Fernando spent the night at my place. Still, I loved committing even harder to my own slightly ridiculous twee style throughout my place. I loved having time to decompress after work. I loved watching all the overly dramatic prestige TV shows Chloe hated, with only Small Jesse Pinkman for company. I wasn't sure he was a fan either, but unlike Chloe he didn't ask a thousand questions that could have been gleaned simply by paying more attention.

And I knew she liked her space, too, room to come home alone and spend time doing whatever was easier without me around.

"But also . . ." Chloe shrugged, holding out her arms, like a much cuter shrug emoji. "We know we're in this for the long run. It could probably be *easier*. So when your weird neighbor listed this place . . ."

It hit me with a bolt of lightning, a gust of wind, the earth shaking beneath my feet. For Chloe, I knew, these weren't small words. This was a force of nature.

"You bought the place next door," I said in awe.

"I'm officially preapproved to buy the place next door," Chloe clarified. "In case I'd gone off the deep end and you were like—"

I wrapped my arms around her and covered her lips with mine. She was still adding disclaimers, which was so funny to me that I also ruined the kiss by laughing.

"So you're happy?" Chloe asked. "I'm not about to do the weirdest and worst move possible?"

I felt it rear up, that old familiar gut reaction that said it was safest to hold back the full force of my emotions. Remembering to push past that had honestly been harder than getting up an hour earlier for yoga class or building out a meal planning list every week, but it turned out that it might have been just as good of a habit to develop. Honestly, better.

"I love that you did this," I said. "Or that you're preapproved to do this. I know our friends will probably think we *have* gone off the deep end, but I can't think of anything more romantic than this. I mean, for us, not in general."

Chloe blushed, and I laughed at that because it happened whenever I called her romantic or thoughtful or a good girlfriend, even after a year. I loved how tough she was; just last week she'd screamed at a guy who'd nearly blown through a crosswalk while we were out taking a walk with Fernando, and the guy had deserved it. But I loved, too, how tender she was, how she kept me stocked with NyQuil and tissues when I had a cold, how she cooked me dinner whenever she knew work was extra busy and my meal-planning was about to go out the window for the night, how she once spent an entire weekend installing cat shelves around my condo for Small Jesse Pinkman just because I mentioned I thought he'd like them.

"I do have bad—well, not ideal news about tonight," Chloe said, lacing her fingers through mine and pulling me toward my condo. The truth was that we'd gotten slightly squishier, at least when we were alone with each other. "I had to ask Ari for help getting the reservations—"

"You're only a mere mortal after all," I said.

"Yeah, exactly," Chloe said, beating me to opening my own door. "But there was some kind of misunderstanding I choose to blame her for and, anyway, she made a reservation for all eight of us, and when I tried to fix it, she somehow thought I wanted to make sure Fiona and Hailey could also come, so. That's our night out."

I laughed and hugged her tightly, burying my face on her shoulder and laughing some more. "Just us and literally eight of our closest friends for a romantic dinner. Honestly, that sounds about right."

Chloe slipped her arms around my waist, and I felt the shift in vibes. After all these months, her eyes still seemed to drink me in like it was the hottest day of the year and I was a glass of water, dripping with condensation.

"In the meantime," she said, "we have more than a few hours to ourselves."

"Yeah, I think we'll survive."

"I spent a long time thinking I didn't want this," she told me as we walked down the hall to my bedroom, and I nodded because of course I knew. "But I think somehow I just knew I didn't want it with anyone but you, Clementine."

"Oh my *god*, Chloe, you have to warn me when you're going to sweep me off my feet like that," I said, my head dizzy from her words and the sentiment behind them. And as we pulled each other into bed, I glanced out the window at the building next door and thought about the future, when Chloe would be right there, because of me. I wished I could tell my old self not to worry so much that she wasn't sure what she wanted. She was going to stumble right into it anyway.

Girl Trouble Cocktail

Makes one cocktail

2 ounces tequila or mezcal
1 ounce watermelon juice
.75 ounce lime juice
1 ounce Aperol
.5 ounce ginger syrup (substitute ginger ale if you don't want
    to make ginger syrup!)

Shake with ice and strain into a rocks glass over ice. (If you use
ginger ale instead of syrup, just add it at the very end.)

Enjoy!

Acknowledgments

A month before I was set to turn this book in, my beloved editor left. I was heartbroken! Then I loved my new editor, so I was thrilled to turn in the first draft to her. Before she could read it, she also left! "What signs do you think the universe is trying to give you?" a friend asked. Great question! Luckily, finally I ended up in the supportive, enthusiastic, and very savvy hands of Alex Sunshine, who brought so much to this manuscript and these characters, and who I feel incredibly grateful to in so many ways.

Thank you, as always, to my tirelessly optimistic agent Kate Testerman. So glad we've been working together for over a decade now! Your early eagerness about this manuscript definitely helped me get through the more stressful times—no small task!

Thank you to Jane Nutter, Michelle Addo, Jackie Dinas, Matt Johnson, and the entire team at Kensington Books. I appreciate every single thing you do for me and my books! Thanks so much to Kristin Dwyer and Molly Mitchell at LEO PR; y'all do so much for me, even when I ask you to investigate very silly things, and it is so appreciated.

Thanks to Suyoung Yo for your time and your thoughtful conversations and notes about the manuscript, plus, of course, thoughts on hipster kimbap. Thanks to Jessie Weinberg for your witty, wise, and encouraging feedback. Thanks to Jasmine Guillory for being an early reader in that terrifying between-editors time when hardly anyone had read it! Thanks to Adam Grosswirth for, as always, being my go-to for cocktails talk.

Thanks to all the group chats that keep me going, with a

special shoutout to Kayla Cagan and Allegra Ringo! That said, every single thread in my Messages means the world to me. Thank you to Jessica Hutchins; there are so many conversations we've had that were vital as I was writing this book.

Thanks to all of the writers, artists, creators in my life: you keep me so engaged and inspired, which in this day and age is more than a minor miracle. Thank you also to all of the writers, artists, creators *not* directly in my life; refilling the figurative well and feeling inspired as hell is the only way I can keep making the art I want to make.

Thanks to my mom, Pat Spalding, for your support.

Thank you to all of my readers from throughout my career. I love that I get to keep doing this!

Finally, to everyone who came out later in life or is thinking about it, this one truly is for you. Not long ago I saw a project pitched as a character coming out later in life; the character in question was seventeen! I thought, how far we've come, but also, excuse me, *what?* Cheers to coming out at any age, but especially in your thirties, forties, fifties, and later. Cheers to coming out when you want, on your own terms. I hope you get as much support as you need! There's no deadline for being yourself; the cool thing about being a person is, as long as we're still around, we get to just keep at it.